Critical Inquiry:
Some Winds on Works

Alexander C. H. Tung

Taipei : Showwe Co.

First published 2009 by
Showwe Co.
F1, 25, Lane 583, Rei-guang Road,
Taipei, Taiwan

ISBN 978-986-221-195-3

Preface

    This book contains a collection of sixteen papers which I have written and published during the past thirty-two years (1976-2008). The lengths of these papers vary greatly from seven to over forty pages. But these papers have a common interest: they are each a critical inquiry into a certain literary problem found in a particular author or a specific work. The authors concerned are mostly British (Milton, Blake, Wordsworth, Coleridge, Shelley, Keats, Arnold, and Graham Greene) and partly American (Emerson, Frost, O'Neill, and Hemingway). The genres involved are mostly poetry and partly fiction, drama, and prose. One can see that my studies tend mostly towards romantic authors or romantic works.

    But each paper collected in this book is far from a romantic piece of exposition, as it seeks to clarify or solve the literary problem concerned by analytical thinking rather than by wild imagination, although I must allege that I do have a sort of visionary imagination from time to time in approaching any problem to be clarified or solved and, indeed, I often have original insight into the problem. In fact, each of the papers is rendered in a clear, simple style often associated with classicism rather than romanticism.

    Classic or romantic, a literary scholar's paper is supposed to shed light on something in question. It therefore has to adopt an effective approach to the studied subject. As you read this book, you may find that I have adopted various approaches to the authors or works I am concerned with. But the most frequently-used approach is that of New Criticism, which emphasizes close reading of the text. In fact, all approaches—biographical, sociological, psychological or philosophical—must be aided by textual analysis.

    A literary work is both visible and invisible. It is visible when it appears in written or printed words which readers may read. But the value of a work does not lie in this visible aspect of the work.   It lies, rather, in the invisible content, i.e., the idea or ideas together with the feelings or attitudes the words stand for, or the thing or things which the author has once conceived and the reader may later catch in reading.   The visible verbal form, as we see in a book, may be marred or ruined by any of the four elements.   But the invisible verbal content is endurable so long as it has not yet faded out of one's memory or left a people's mind.

Yet, the content, along with the form, of a literary work is subject to criticism from the four winds.   Very often a piece of criticism is indeed like a gust of wind.   It may blow against the work and lessen its value by tearing away not just its pages but also its framework of ideas.   However, there are also times when the wind may bring some extra values to the work, some petals of flowers, for instance, to decorate the book or symbolize its flowery content.

Still, in my imagination, every piece of criticism is but a vain wind and every literary work is an endurable rock.   No matter whether the critical wind is good or ill, no matter whether it blows against the work or from it, over the work or under it, on the work or beneath it, the work remains ontologically all the same, essentially undamaged and unaffected in its time of existence.   Nevertheless, critics are forever vain enough to create critical winds for or against the rocky work.

With this imagination, I confess that the sixteen papers collected herein are for me but "some winds on works": they are the vain winds coming from my inner critical self to touch on some rocky surfaces, aiming more to arouse people's attention than to effect any change in the authors or works.   Meanwhile, however, I also understand that this book of mine will itself become a strong rock likewise, facing all vain, critical winds from everywhere.

Contents

"Beauty is Goodness, Goodness Beauty": Shelley's "Awful Shadow" and "Ethical Sublime"

I. Truth, Beauty, Goodness

Truth, beauty, and goodness are said to be "the great transcendents of the classical tradition" or "qualities of divinity" or "three great ideals ... representing the sublime nature and lofty goal of all human endeavor."[1] Whatever they are, they are indeed "an ancient and venerable triad of values," and, as Steve Mcintosh conceives them, they "actually serve as attractors of evolutionary development that pull evolution forward 'from the inside' through their influence on consciousness."[2] Western philosophers have from the very beginning been concerned with problems divisible into these three basic categories of ideals or values. Plato's metaphysical theory of Forms, for example, is primarily concerned with the epistemological category of Truth; his mimetic theory of art and his idea of the artist as divinely inspired have stepped into the aesthetic category of Beauty; and his consideration of justice and other virtues of state and soul deals all too obviously with the ethical category of Goodness. But what exactly are truth, beauty and goodness, respectively?

The word "truth" certainly can refer to a human being's quality or state of "being true": to loyalty, trustworthiness, sincerity, genuineness, honesty, etc. It can also refer to a statement's being in accordance with experience, facts, or reality.   And it can ultimately refer to reality itself.   A moralist may praise a person for his truthful speech or behavior.   A scientist may claim truth for a scientific fact or statement.   Yet, it takes a metaphysician to tell us that truth is not just what is verifiable and tangible before our eyes, but, rather, as Plato conceives it, the unchanging Form, the invisible Universal, or the immaterial, abstract Idea.

Besides referring narrowly to good looks or a very good-looking woman, the word "beauty" designates broadly the quality, or the thing having the quality, attributed to "whatever pleases or satisfies the senses or mind, as by line, color, form, texture, proportion, rhythmic motion, tone, etc., or by behavior, attitude, etc."[3]   What provides a perceptual experience of pleasure or satisfaction is sensual or outer beauty; what pleases or satisfies the mind is often such mental or inner beauty as kindness, sensitivity, tenderness, compassion, creativity, or intelligence.   But, for a metaphysician like Plato, the real beauty is the absolute form of Beauty, the one abstract Beauty that is distinct from each and all of the beautiful things and separate from them, which is "completely beautiful, purely beautiful, unchangingly beautiful" (Urmson 297).

As an abstract noun, "goodness" indicates the state or quality of being good.   But a vast variety of things can be good.   Goodness can come from being suitable to a purpose or from producing a favorable result.   We have good lamps, good eggs, good exercise, good excuse, good eyesight, good men, etc.   When used in conjunction with "truth" and "beauty," however, "goodness" is restricted to an ethical sense: it is synonymous with "virtue," meaning "moral excellence" and referring to such things as kindness, generosity, and benevolence.   Plato, it is said, recognizes four cardinal virtues: wisdom, courage, moderation, and justice.   But for

Plato Goodness or the Good is finally the highest idea and the source of all the rest of ideas.

Although truth, beauty, and goodness seemingly occupy three distinct and separate realms (call them epistemological, aesthetic, and ethical realms, or whatever), philosophers as well as ordinary people often fail to distinguish among them. Ordinary people, for instance, often refer to a loyal, honest person as either "good" or "true" and say that kindness is a person's "good virtue" or "inner beauty." This laxity of verbal usage is in effect like the ambiguity found in Plato's use of the word *kalon* to mean both "beautiful" and "noble" so that "exact translators prefer to render *kalon* as 'fine,' which while blander than 'beautiful' is suitable to both ethical and aesthetic contexts."[4] In fact, when Socrates says that beauty is *prepei* (appropriate), he has also mixed up an aesthetic idea with an ethical one. And when Plato ranks goodness as the supreme idea, he has subsumed the idea that "the truly real and the truly good are identical" (Thilly 81).

So far, in introducing the ideas of truth, beauty, and goodness, I have repeatedly referred to Plato on purpose. As many critics have pointed out, Shelley is heavily influenced by Plato: he read Plato and translated Plato's work, and, as James A. Notopoulos has suggested, his Platonism is a unity of all kinds of Platonism.[5] In relating Shelley and Plato to the topic of truth, beauty, and goodness, however, what I need to emphasize particularly are two points. First, in Plato's doctrine, truth, beauty, and goodness are all highly valuable ideas or forms, and all ideas or forms are for him "non-temporal, as well as non-spatial"; they are "eternal and immutable" entities that "subsist independently of any knowing mind" though they can be "apprehended by reason" (Thilly 82). Second, in Plato's doctrine, all ideas or forms "are logically interrelated and constitute a hierarchy, in which the higher forms 'communicate' with lower or subordinate forms," and "the supreme form in the hierarchy is the form of the Good" (Thilly 82).   Indeed, as Plato's cosmology is "an attempt to explain reality as a purposeful, well-ordered cosmos, and the world as an intelligence, guided by reason and directed toward an ethical goal" (Thilly 84), goodness is naturally singled out as "the *logos*, the cosmic purpose" (Thilly 81) to govern all other ideas including truth and beauty.

II. Shelly vs. Keats

It is well-known that in his "Ode on a Grecian Urn" Keats makes the urn say to man: "Beauty is truth, truth beauty."   As Cleanth Brooks has pointed out, "we ordinarily do not expect an urn to speak at all" (155).   So it is only in the poet's imagination that the urn is personified and claimed to be able to say anything to man. In fact, when the urn says "Beauty is truth, truth beauty," it is "telling," not so much in words as in what it shows, a generalization which is exemplified by the urn itself.   The urn, as described in the poem, represents the eternal, for "when old age shall this generation waste,/Thou shall remain" (46-47).   When it remains, it will continue to tell its "flowery tale" and "tease us out of thought/As doth eternity" (4, 44-45), and its "leaf-fringed legend" will forever haunt about its shape with boughs that cannot shed leaves, with figures "for ever piping songs for ever new," and with lovers "for ever panting, and for ever young" (5, 24, 27), while the streets of the little town in another picture on the urn "for evermore/Will silent be" (38-39).   If the urn with its pictures and figures represents the eternal, it is like truth or it is a truth.   But while the urn represents truth on the one hand, it nonetheless represents beauty on the other hand, for it is called not only "still unravished bride of quietness" and "foster-child of silence and slow time" but also "Attic shape" and "Fair attitude" with "brede/Of marble men and maidens overwrought,/With forest branches and the trodden weed" (1-2, 41-42).   The well-wrought urn, in other words, typifies both beauty and truth, and so it is qualified to tell man that "Beauty is truth, truth beauty": a beautiful piece of art like the urn will forever remain, as truth does, to show us its beauty as well as the truth it contains, though what it contains, just as the urn does, may be some plain, guessable facts along with some mysterious details beyond our surmise.

Keats's Grecian urn does contain for him truth and beauty (Brooks 21).   Truth and beauty are in fact the two values Keats lived for.   As we know, all romantics feel keenly the inevitability of change, the unreliability of phenomena, and the ephemerality of all things.   That is why Shelley says, "Naught may endure but Mutability" ("Mutability," 16).   But Keats felt even more keenly the romantic agony brought about by change.   His own anticipated short life naturally accounts largely for this agony.   And his poems, such as "On Seeing the Elgin Marbles," "When I Have Fears That I May Cease To Be," and "Why Did I Laugh Tonight? No Voice Will Tell," largely express that agony.   Facing the ephemeral, ever-changing world, romantics naturally aspire after what is eternal, unchangeable, and immortal.   This aspiration is uttered most impressively in Keats's "Bright Star, Would I Were Steadfast as Thou Art."   And the "still steadfast, still unchangeable" bright star is naturally linkable to the Platonic idea of Truth as the unchanging Form.

Keats, of course, did not actually reach for the bright star, nor did he seek blindly for the abstract and invisible Platonic truth.   For him, "what the imagination seizes as Beauty must be truth" and for him "the Imagination may be compared to Adam's dream—he awoke and found it truth."[6]   So, for Keats, beauty is indeed truth, and beauty is "seized" by imagination.   Now, what Keats's imagination seizes as beauty ("the truth of imagination" as he called it) is naturally the poet's vision, which can be rendered into poetry.   It follows, then, that poetry is Keats's lifelong goal; it is his embodiment of beauty and truth.   He tells us his goal in *Sleep and Poetry*:

> O for ten years, that I may overwhelm
> Myself in poesy; so I may do the deed
> That my own soul has to itself decreed. (96-98)

He even tells us that he has his regimen of poetic training: following Virgil, he will first "pass the realm of Flora and old Pan" and then deal with "the agonies, the strife/Of human hearts" (101, 124-5).

In Keats's poetic career, there were times of course when he felt that "death is intenser than verse, fame, and beauty" ("Why Did I Laugh Tonight?" 13-14), that poesy is not "so sweet as drowsy noons,/And evenings steeped in honied indolence" ("Ode on Indolence," 36-37), and that "the fancy (i.e., imagination or 'the viewless wings of Poesy') cannot cheat so well/As she is famed to do" ("Ode to a Nightingale," 33, 73-74).   Nevertheless, Keats is for sure the most purely devoted poet to poetry and the purest aesthete among the English romantic poets.   He seems to be the most wholly immersed in the duad of truth and beauty.

Compared with Keats, Shelley is not so pure an aesthete, for he never seems to be content with the duad of truth and beauty: he yearns more for goodness.   Keats, to be sure, also concerns himself with ethics, with the realm of goodness.   After claiming "A thing of beauty is a joy for ever" at the very beginning of *Endymion*, he does not merely profess that

> Its loveliness increases; it will never
> Pass into nothingness; but still will keep
> A bower quiet for us, and a sleep
> Full of sweet dreams, and health, and quiet breathing.
> (2-5)

Keats has in fact gone on to tell us a theory of the "pleasure thermometer," a theory on how immortal delight may derive from "a fellowship with essence," that is, from purging away mutability from the things of beauty by fusing ourselves "first sensuously, with the lovely objects of nature and art, then on a higher level, with other human beings through 'love and friendship' and, ultimately, sexual love."[7]   This content has indeed combined truth (immortality) with beauty and goodness (love and friendship).   However, Keats's chief concern here is with beauty, not with goodness: the poetic romance of Endymion is told for pleasure, not for morality.   That is why Keats says in the Preface, "I hope I have not in too late a day touched the beautiful mythology of Greece, and dulled its brightness."

When Keats touched Greek mythology again in *Hyperion* (1818) or *The Fall of Hyperion* (1819), he had at first meant to be ethical. He proposed to solve the problem of "*unde malum?*" (whence and why evil?) in *Hyperion*.   But the answer offered by Oceanus is: "... 'tis the eternal law/That first in beauty should be first in might" (*Hyperion*, II, 228-9).   In Oceanus' view, Saturn was dethroned not by blank unreason and injustice, but by a higher excellence in the natural progressing of things or the stage-by-stage development of time.   Oceanus' "first in beauty" (instead of "first in goodness") is a phrase picked by Keats, and it betrays Keats's propensity for replacing ethical terms with aesthetic ones.

In *The Fall of Hyperion*, the story has grown into a dream vision, and it contains an induction somewhat like Wordsworth's *The Prelude*, involving the theme of "the growth of a poet's mind."   In the induction, Moneta admonishes the poet to ascend steps and usurp the height of poetry by becoming one of "those to whom the miseries of the world/Are misery, and will not let them rest" (148-9), that is, by becoming "a sage;/A humanist, physician to all men" (189-90).   But this moral tone cannot be sustained by the story of how Hyperion fell in the course of time.   Keats's ethical concern (with the poet's social or moral function) somehow fails to go well with his beautiful mythology, which is primarily aesthetic rather than ethic in nature. This may be part of the reason why the epic stays unfinished.

Keats's preoccupation with beauty, rather than goodness, is repeatedly revealed in his letters.   We have mentioned that he told Benjamin Bailey (in a letter of November 22, 1817) that "what the imagination seizes as Beauty must be truth" (Bush 257).   We may recall, too, that to George and Thomas Keats (in a letter of December 21, 1817) he says, "... with a great poet the sense of Beauty overcomes every other consideration, or rather obliterates all consideration" (Bush 261).   It is his preoccupation with beauty, of course, that makes him "hate poetry that has a palpable design upon us" (letter to John Hamilton Reynolds, February 3, 1818, in Bush 263).   And it is his preoccupation with beauty, too, that makes him advise Shelley impolitely: "you might curb your magnanimity and be more of an artist, and 'load every rift' of your subject with ore" (letter to Shelley, August 16, 1820, in Bush 298).

Shelley showed his magnanimity not only in inviting Keats (who was ill) to come and stay with the Shelleys in Pisa for the winter, but also in his lifelong fighting for the benefit of mankind. Anyone who reads Shelley's biography is sure to have the impression that Shelley was indeed a revolutionary before a poet. Since his Eton days when from his own experience "he saw the petty tyranny of schoolmasters and schoolmates as representative of man's general inhumanity to man," he has "dedicated his life to a war against injustice and oppression" (Abrams et al, 661).   In 1812, he visited Ireland to engage in radical pamphleteering and was seen at several political rallies, in his support for freedom of the press and the extension of equal rights to Catholics and in his hostility to the coercions of church and state.   In other years, no matter whether he was in England or elsewhere on the Continent, Shelley never ceased to speak for the revolutionary ideals of liberty, equality, and fraternity. When he drowned in 1822, he was collaborating with Leigh Hunt and Byron on the journal *The Liberal*, which, needless to say, was a radical organ free from prosecution by the British authorities but good to publish their revolutionary ideas for the good of society.

Very little of Keats's work is manifestly linkable to his contemporary political or religious status quo.   In contrast, very much of Shelley's work is all too easily connected with his reactions to the contemporary affairs of church or state.   According to Kenneth Neill Cameron, Shelley has left us a picture of his social philosophy not in his poetry alone, but also in his prose.   In his *A Philosophical View of Reform*, Shelley has expressed his theory of historical evolution: "history is essentially a struggle between two sets of forces, the forces of liberty and the forces of despotism" (Cameron 512).   In regard to the continent of Europe Shelley "felt that the existing despotic governments could be overthrown only by revolution, and his letters and work show a constant attention to the development of such movements—in Spain, in Naples, in Paris, in Greece, as well as in Mexico, South America and Ireland" (Cameron 514). Shelley's poetry also plainly shows the same social philosophy:

> Shelley's analysis of the contemporary situation in England and its reform movement will be found in "The Mask of Anarchy" and "Swellfoot the Tyrant"; his views on the revolutionary movement on the continent, in the "Ode Written in October, 1819," the "Ode to Liberty"—on the Spanish revolution of 1820—the "Ode to Naples"—on the war of the Kingdom of Naples against Austrian domination—and "Hellas"—on the Greek struggle for liberation from the Turkish empire; his interpretation of the rise and fall of the French Revolution and the emergence of the tyranny of the Quadruple Alliance, in "The Revolt of Islam"; his general theory of historical evolution, in "Queen Mab" and "Prometheus Unbound." (Cameron 515)

Even Shelley's poetic theory is widely different from Keats's in that one tends more towards a pragmatic theory emphasizing the poetic function of doing good while the other tends more towards an objective theory stressing the function of creating beauty. While Keats asserts that "with a great poet the sense of Beauty overcomes every other consideration," Shelley believes that "to be a poet is to apprehend the true and the beautiful, in a word the good which exists in the relation," and that "poets are the unacknowledged legislators of the world" (*A Defense of Poetry*, in Ingpen, VII, 111-2 &140). So, for Shelley poetry is not just to delight but to instruct as well. Poetry is, furthermore, the best means for moral training:

A man, to be greatly good, must imagine intensely and comprehensively; he must put himself in the place of another and of many others; the pains and pleasures of his species must become his own.   The great instrument of moral good is the imagination; and poetry administers to the effect by acting upon the cause.   Poetry enlarges the circumference of the imagination by replenishing it with thoughts of ever new delight, which have the power of attracting and assimilating to their own nature all other thoughts, and which form new intervals and interstices whose void for ever craves fresh food. Poetry strengthens that faculty which is the organ of the moral nature of man, in the same manner as exercise strengthens a limb. (*A Defense of Poetry*, in Ingpen, VII, 118)

III. Beauty Is Goodness

Shelley never let an urn or anything else tell us directly that beauty is goodness.   However, as we have suggested above, he did go much further than Keats into the realm of goodness: his life was a struggle for mankind's moral reformation and social change, and his work was written primarily for the sake of goodness rather than beauty.   This is best illustrated in his habit of using ethical terms for an aesthetic object.   And his "Hymn to Intellectual Beauty" serves as an obvious example.

As "Beauty" is the subject (and object) of the hymn, we naturally expect to see a piling up of praises for the beauty of the subject or object.   But, as the poem proceeds, what we see is at first an emphasis on the Beauty's being "Intellectual," that is, nonmaterial, thus "unseen among us" (2).   Then we find this "Spirit of Beauty" is described as no other than the possessor of what we often call "inner beauty" or "goodness" since it does "consecrate ...," its light "gives grace and truth to life's unquiet dream," it is the "messenger of sympathies," it is expected to "free/This world from its dark slavery," and its spells did bind the poet to "fear himself and love all human kind" (13, 36, 42, 69-70, 83-84).

This "Intellectual Beauty" is best represented by the Being the Poet in *Alastor* images to himself as his ideal love.   The Poet "dreamed a veiled maid/Sate near him, talking in low solemn tones": "Her voice was like the voice of his own soul" and "Knowledge and truth and virtue were her theme" (*Alastor*, 151-3, 158).   In fact, the maid is "Herself a poet" and her theme includes "lofty hopes of divine liberty,/Thoughts the most dear to him [the Poet], and poesy" (*Alastor*, 159-61).   As Shelley explains in the Preface to this poem, the maid is "the vision in which he [the Poet] embodies his own imaginations" and the vision actually "unites all of wonderful, or wise, or beautiful, which the poet, the philosopher, or the lover could depicture" (Ingpen, I, 173).   In other words, the maid represents the Poet's ideal beauty and ideal goodness.

Now, we must know that *Alastor* is highly autobiographical.   If we cannot agree with N. I. White that "the over-idealistic poet as described in both the Preface and the poem is undoubtedly Shelley" (I, 419), we can at least agree with Evan K. Gibson that "the youth [i.e., the Poet] of the poem has a number of characteristics in common with his creator [i.e., Shelley]" (568).   If the poem is "the story of a youth who, after living a life of solitude, falls in love with a vision of his 'soul mate,' a creation of his own mind, and perishes of disappointment" (Gibson 548), this youth is so similar to Shelley himself that we may safely assert that the maid is indeed the embodiment of Shelley's "intellectual beauty," which is but another name for the idealist's idea or form of Goodness.

The maid in *Alastor* is an unnamed person with "intellectual beauty" or virtuous goodness.   In *Epipsychidion*, another highly autobiographical poem of Shelley's, the "Sweet Spirit" or "Seraph of Heaven" (1, 21) has a name (Emily), and the maid is identified with Teresa Viviani, a 19-year-old daughter of the governor of Pisa in 1820.   Teresa was confined in the Convent of St. Anna, but she attracted Shelley's interest and became his ideal object of love.   No matter whether Emily can be identified with Teresa or not, and no matter what biographical facts scholars can gather about the symbols of the Sun, the Moon, the Comet, the Planet, etc., exploited in the poem, we are sure that Emily represents the Being whom Shelley's spirit often "met on its visioned wanderings" and whom Shelley once met but could not behold because she was "robed in such exceeding glory" (191, 199).   As she is "soft as an Incarnation of the Sun" and "her Spirit was the harmony of truth" (335, 216), she can be no other than the archetype of "intellectual beauty" or virtuous goodness. That is why she is said to be "a mortal shape indued/With love and life and light and deity,/And motion which may change but cannot die" (112-4).

In *Epipsychidion*, Shelley refers to Emily as "the Vision veiled from [him]/So many years" (343-4).   In Greek, "epi" is a preposition meaning "upon," and "psychidion" means "little soul." Thus, Emily is naturally the "little soul" that Shelley asks to mate with.   Psychoanalytical critics have interpreted the poem variously. While most critics take Emily as an imagined target for sexual completion (in the sense of physical coition, spiritual merging of souls, or returning to maternal plenitude), Ghislaine McDayter takes her as a case to explain the poet-speaker's trace of primary castration, a lack projected into the feminine Other. Each psychoanalytical interpretation may be plausible in its own right. Yet, I believe, we need not probe so deeply into the psyche. In the Advertisement, the poem is said to be like the *Vita Nuova* of Dante. In a letter of June 18, 1822 to John Gisborne, Shelley says, "It is an idealized history of my life and feelings" (Ingpen, X, 401). Indeed, the poem is as autobiographical as *La Vita Nuova.* But it is even more like Dante's work in that Emily has become a muse-like figure, an idealized soul mate and a spiritual inspiration for Shelley, just like Beatrice Portinari, who has become Dante's idealized, muse-like, soul mate and spiritual inspiration. As we know, Dante's conception of love is Platonic: for him true love is possible only for the innately good and the noble-hearted; the loved Beatrice is a glorious agent or symbol of the divine, real in body but ideal in soul. As Emily is Shelley's Beatrice, she is aptly called "A divine presence in a place divine" and apostrophized as "Spouse! Sister! Angel! Pilot of the Fate ..." (*Epipsychidion*, 135, 130).

Shelley's ideal beauty is indeed the possessor not only of physical or outer beauty but of intellectual or inner beauty. So Ianthe needs Queen Mab's teaching to become "sincere and good" and have virtue to keep her footsteps in the path she has trod (*Queen Mab*, IX, 200-6), although her soul can now stand "All beautiful in naked purity,/The perfect semblance of its bodily frame,/Instinct with inexpressible beauty and grace" (*Queen Mab*, I, 132-4).

Shelley, as we know, kept his revolutionary spirit all his life and, therefore, the valuable women in his work are often those who can sympathize with his struggle against tyranny and injustice. Cythna, thus, is not just Laon's sister or sweetheart; she is the hero's soul mate as well, whose struggle along with Loan is to leave us "All hope, or love, or truth, or liberty" (*Laon and Cythna*, IX, 3718).

Shelley calls the revolution of Laon and Cythna "the *beau ideal* as it were of the French Revolution" (letter to a publisher, October 13, 1817, in Ingpen, IX, 251).   According to Lori Molinari, "the revolution Shelley envisions is primarily moral and psychological rather than political or military" (99).   What makes the *beau ideal* in the revolution is the couple's gradualist approach of using the power of words to effect moral reformation.

In *Prometheus Unbound*, moral reformation is also most important, and Asia is also a revolutionary's soul mate although, unlike the confident, Amazonian Cythna, she is at first "submissive, diffident, eager to learn and quite passive until roused by an intuition of Prometheus's release" (King-Kele 184).   She asks Demogorgon the question of "who made terror, madness, crime, remorse" and reminds him that Prometheus gave mankind hopes, love, fire, speech, etc. (*Prometheus Unbound*, 2.4.19ff.). At the end, after overthrowing tyranny, her union with Prometheus through love brings the world "Gentleness, Virtue, Wisdom and Endurance" (4.562).

As a contrast to Cythna and Asia, Iona Taurina in *Swellfoot the Tyrant* is not the *beau ideal* for a revolutionary heroine.   She is not as chastely devoted and wise as Cythna and Asia.   Comparing the satirical drama with "Ode to Naples" and "Ode to Liberty," Thomas H. Schmid remarks: "Where both of the Odes can be seen to use conventional virginal and/or matronly female images to celebrate the possibilities for national independence latent in the 1820 constitutional declarations of Spain and Naples, *Swellfoot the Tyrant* employs a radically eroticized and sexually powerful representation of Caroline of Brunswick to question England's own readiness for constitutional reform" (76).   Iona's revengeful revolution is not in line with that of *Prometheus Unbound* or *Laon and Cythna*, nor is she depicted as a heroine of virtuous goodness.

Beatrice in *The Cenci*, however, can also be counted as one of those who fit Shelley's "favorite pattern of tyrant, slaves and resisting heroine" (King-Hele 133).   In the play's Dedication, Shelley mentions the "patient and irreconcilable enmity with domestic and political tyranny and imposture" which, Shelley says, Leigh Hunt's tenor of life has illustrated (Ingpen, II, 67).   In the play, in effect, Beatrice is Shelley's image of a holy girl ruined by a tyrannical father and a religious authority, who stand for domestic and political tyranny and imposture.   She is stained by her father's rape, coerced into parricide, and forced to become a determined liar, but she remains, in his own words, "the angel of [God's] wrath" (*The Cenci*, 5.3.114).   In other words, Beatrice is still a maid embodying intellectual beauty or virtuous goodness although, as Michael O'Neill has suggested, revenge is "a particularly dangerous form of 'loathsome sympathy' for Shelley" (87).

In contrast to the virtuous maids as mentioned above, the Witch of Atlas is a sort of "la belle dame sans merci."   "The all-beholding Sun," Shelley writes, "had ne'er beholden/In his wide voyage o'er continents and seas/So fair a creature": "her beauty made/The bright world dim, and every thing beside/Seemed like the fleeting image of a shade" (*The Witch of Atlas*, 58-60, 137-9).   Yet, she is in fact "a sexless thing" or "like a sexless bee/Tasting all blossoms and confined to none": she will "pass with an eye serene and heart unladen" among "mortal men" (329, 589-92).   She "played pranks among the cities/Of mortal men," but "little did [any] sight disturb her soul" (665-6, 545).   She is indeed a wizard-maiden lacking understanding sympathy with the problems of mortal creatures.   In other words, she has physical beauty only; she has no real substance of intellectual beauty or virtuous goodness.

For Shelley goodness is certainly the sublimated level of beauty. A woman's physical beauty has to be elevated to the level of intellectual beauty to become immortal and worthy of high esteem. The sublimation or elevation of beauty is a Platonic idea, of course. But Shelley has put this idea into practice not only in dealing with women but also in writing about a thing of beauty.   In "To a Sky-Lark," for instance, he elevates the bird to the level of a "blithe Spirit" and a "Scorner of the ground" (1 & 100).   What he emphasizes in the poem is not only the fact that the unseen, singing lark can be a symbol of "unbodied joy" (15), but also the fact that the high-in-the-sky lark can be a symbol of high nobility.   That is why it can be called "Scorner of the ground" and compared to a hidden poet, a high-born maiden, a golden glow-worm, an embowered rose, etc.   When the poet says, "Thou of death must deem/Things more true and deep/Than we mortals dream" (82-84), the sky-lark is indeed sublimated with divinity.

IV. The Awful Shadow

The word "shadow" occurs very frequently in Shelley's works. If we look closely into its contexts, we will find that the word is very ambiguous in connotation.   Shadow is of course a shade or a dark image in direct contrast to light.   When the Witch of Atlas is depicted as lying "enfolden in the warm shadow of her loveliness" (*The Witch of Atlas*, 61), the shadow may mean just a shade. However, when Shelley asks that "From the world's bitter wind/[the reader should] Seek shelter in the shadow of the tomb" (*Adonais*, 457-8), the shadow suggests safety in the dark besides its cool shade. When Julian says, "I met pale Pain/My shadow, which will leave me not again" (*Julian and Maddalo*, 324-5), the shadow suggests not only a dark shade but also something perpetually accompanying someone.   When in the Conclusion of *The Sensitive Plant* the narrator says, "Where nothing is—but all things seem,/And we the shadows of the dream" (9-12), the shadows suggest insubstantiality besides darkness.   And when in *The Mask of Anarchy* Hypocrisy is described as "Clothed with the Bible, as with light/And the shadows of the night,/Like Sidmouth" (22-240), the shadows connote evil secrecy in addition to any possible sense.

It is difficult and unnecessary to list all possible connotations that go with Shelley's usage of the word "shadow."   But it is feasible to point out the basic types of connotations existing in Shelley's mind for the word "shadow."   Shelley, as we have said above, is a Platonist.   As a Platonist, he must have been influenced by Plato's Allegory of the Cave, through which we are told that the things we perceive as real are actually unreal like shadows on a wall while reality is to be found in the ideas or forms which are intelligible only when we ascend into the light of reason or of the Good.   Hence, for Shelley the primary connotation of "shadow" is insubstantiality or being unreal.

Nevertheless, shadows as unreal or insubstantial entities are still powerful factors affecting our daily life.   Humans are forever under the sway of shadows.   According to Carl Jung, everyone carries a shadow, which is a part of the unconscious mind derived from repressed weaknesses, shortcomings, and instincts.   Although the shadow is not necessarily evil, it certainly represents "our darker side, the part of ourselves we would prefer not to confront, those aspects that we dislike" (Dobie 57).   Hence anybody or anything repugnant to our psyche is a shadow.   When to the sky-lark Shelley says, "Shadow of annoyance/Never came near thee" ("To the Sky-Lark," 78-79), the shadow does carry the repugnant force.

As a repugnant object, any shadow can be described as "awful," in the colloquial sense of "being very bad or unpleasant." But for Shelley a shadow is often not repugnant but "awful" in the sense of "awe-inspiring" and "fear-causing." In *Prometheus Unbound*, Asia sees a "Spirit with a dreadful countenance" (Act 2, 142). The Spirit says, "I am the shadow of a destiny/More dread than is my aspect" (Act 2, 146-7). Here, the Spirit is surely "awful" for his dreadful countenance and dread-causing potentiality. Likewise, when Shelley refers to "Intellectual Beauty" as the "awful shadow of some unseen power" ("Hymn to Intellectual Beauty," 1), he does regard it as an awe-inspiring presence that causes fear. That is why he further says, "Sudden, thy shadow fell on me;/I shrieked, and clasped my hands in extacy" (59-60). The awful shadow has indeed become "awful Loveliness" (71).

Now, we can assert that although shadows are Platonic nonentities, Shelley is obsessed with two types of shadows. On the one hand, Shelley is strongly opposed to but wholly obsessed with the Jungian type of shadows, which include the despots, devils, villains, tyrants, etc., who find their concrete examples in the poet's life (his father, the Eton or Oxford authorities, state ministers, kings, church leaders, etc.) and in his works (the Sultan Turnkey, Ozymandias, Jupiter, the Cenci, Anarchy, Mahmud, etc.). On the other hand, Shelley is strongly awed by but also wholly obsessed with what I would call the Shelleyan type of shadows, which are the embodiments of "Intellectual Beauty" or virtuous goodness or celestial divinity, such as exemplified by the idealized female idols in his works (the unnamed but pursued maid in *Alastor*, the initiated Ianthe in *Queen Mab*, the adored Emily in *Epipsychidion*, the ruined Beatrice in *The Cenci*, etc.), by the idealized, anti-despotic, revolutionary heroes and heroines (Zeinab and Kathema, Laon and

Cythna, Prometheus and Asia, etc.), and even by the idealized Demogorgon, the "mighty Darkness" which will "wrap in lasting night Heaven's kingless throne" (*Prometheus Unbound*, Act 2, 3& 149).   All such idealized figures are, as it were, so many Constantias, so many "thronging shadows fast and thick" falling on Shelley's eyes and striking in him a "deep and breathless awe, like the swift change/Of dreams unseen" till "the world's shadowy walls are past, and disappear" ("To Constantia," 7, 23-24, & 33).[8]

The characteristics of Shelley's "awful shadow" are fully, though sometimes paradoxically, enunciated or suggested in his "Hymn to Intellectual Beauty."   In the beginning of the poem, Shelley says:

> The awful shadow of some unseen Power
> Floats though unseen among us,—visiting
> This various world with as inconstant wing
> As summer winds that creep from flower to flower.   (1-4)

In these four beginning lines, we are informed that Intellectual beauty is an awful (awe-inspiring) shadow, the shadow belongs to or comes from "some unseen Power," it is still unseen, but it is there floating among us or visiting this various world inconstantly.   This shadow is awful probably because of its origin, its invisibility, and its inconstant visits.

In the second stanza, Intellectual Beauty is hailed as "Spirit of Beauty" and said to be able to consecrate with its own hues all that it shines upon.   Here one question arises: If Intellectual Beauty is an unseen shadow, does it have hues and can it shine?   If it does, it is certainly mysterious and therefore awful.   Anyway, the Spirit is now away from the world and gloom is "cast on the daylight of this earth" (22).   In such a gloomy state, the poet goes on to the third stanza and says, "Thy light alone ... Gives grace and truth to life's unquiet dream" (32-36).   Here it is certified that the awful shadow does have light, and it is further suggested that the shadow can give grace and truth to human life, which is like an unquiet dream.

In the fourth stanza, we find this statement first: "Man were immortal, and omnipotent,/Didst thou, unknown and awful as thou art,/Keep with thy glorious train firm state within his heart" (38-40). This is a belief uttered in the subjunctive mood.   The poet believes that Intellectual Beauty, though an awful shadow, has a glorious train; and if it along with the train could keep firm state in man's heart, man would become immortal and omnipotent.   In this stanza, then, Intellectual Beauty is hailed as "messenger of sympathies/That wax and wane in lovers' eyes" (42-43).   And then it is called nourishment to human thought, like darkness to a dying flame (44-45).   It is indeed paradoxical that darkness can nourish a dying flame.   But, as it is, a dying flame does look all the brighter if it is put in a darker place.   Here we see that Shelley is speaking for the awful shadow's dark, mysterious power to nourish human thought.   So, in the last three lines of this stanza, Shelley asks the messenger not to depart as its shadow came, lest the grave should be a dark reality.

Since Intellectual Beauty as the awful shadow is not an evil spirit but a good angel, so to speak, to mankind, it is not a ghost the poet as a boy sought for; it is not among the "poisonous names with which our youth is fed" (53).   So, in the fifth stanza Shelley says that the shadow fell on him and made him excited "at that sweet time when winds are wooing/All vital things" (56-57).   And, thus, in the sixth stanza, Shelley says that he then vowed to dedicate his powers to this awful Loveliness so that the world would be freed from its dark slavery.   And finally in the last stanza Shelley prays:

> Thus let thy power, which like the truth
> Of nature on my passive youth
> Descended, to my onward life supply
> Its calm—to one who worships thee,
> Whom, Spirit fair, thy spells did bind
> To fear himself, and love all human kind.　(78-94)

From the above analyzed enunciation with its suggestions we can conclude that Intellectual Beauty as the awful shadow is indeed not an evil power but a good, useful power to mankind. Its origin may be the Supreme Goodness. It is mysteriously dark and unseen as a shadow, but it is forever there ready to visit us when we need it. Awful as it is, it has a glorious train and it is therefore able to shine, to give us light, to bring grace and truth, to nourish human thought, to make us sympathetic, to supply calm, and to make us love all humankind. For Shelley, then, the awful shadow is in fact the "awful Loveliness": it can help him free the world from dark slavery and prevent the world from death, from getting into the grave of a dark reality. Shelley's good friends (Hogg, Byron, Leigh Hunt, etc.) and beloved women (Harriet, Mary, Claire, etc.) as well as all those heroes and heroines in his works may be counted as among "the glorious train" that have worked with Intellectual Beauty (the Shellyan awful shadow) to help the poet fight against the bad ghosts (the Jungian awful shadows) personified in the villains, despots, etc., in his life and works.

V. The Ethical Sublime

In "Hymn to Intellectual Beauty," Shelley has indeed turned intellectual beauty into spiritual goodness, thus exposing his ethical, rather than aesthetic, propensity.   In the poem, in actuality, he asks an ethical question that has, perhaps, puzzled him all his life: "Why man has such a scope/For love and hate, despondency and hope?" (23-24).   Regarding this question, he further avers: "No voice from some sublimer world hath ever/To sage or poet these responses given—/Therefore the name of God and ghosts and Heaven,/Remain the records of their vain endeavor" (23-28).   Shelley (especially the early Shelley), as we know, is an atheist.   He does not believe in the doctrines of the Orthodox Church.   But, as shown in this poem, Shelley believes in "some sublimer world," which provides no voice concerning human ethical problems and, yet, must be the abode of "some unseen power" which is the origin of the awful shadow called Intellectual Beauty.   Now, what is this unseen Power and what is this sublimer world?

The 18th century preceding Shelley's Romantic Age was an Age of Enlightenment, in which rational inquiries were made into all sorts of things.   Among the topics inquired into, the aesthetic ideas of the beautiful and the sublime were very popular.   In his "Philosophical Inquiry into the Origin of Our Ideas of the Sublime and Beautiful," Edmund Burke asserts that "whatever is fitted in any sort to excite the ideas of pain and danger, that is to say, whatever is in any sort terrible, or is conversant about terrible objects, or operates in a manner analogous to terror, is a source of the sublime" (310).   Burke also postulates that

> ... sublime objects are vast in their dimensions, beautiful ones comparatively small; beauty should be smooth, and polished; the great, rugged and negligent; beauty should shun the right line, yet deviate from it insensibly; the great in many cases loves the right line, and when it deviates, it often makes a

strong deviation; beauty should not be obscure; the great ought to be dark and gloomy; beauty should be light and delicate; the great ought to be solid, and even massive.   They are indeed ideas of a very different nature, one being founded on pain, the other on pleasure. (311)

Among other examples of the sublime, Burke gives the idea of "general privations" such as Vacuity, Darkness, Solitude and Silence, which, according to Angela Leighton, "cause terror because they are spaces which no longer simply proclaim the infinite spaciousness of God," but instead they "mark a kind of absence" (23).

Gathering and modifying the general ideas of the 18th-century sublime and beautiful, Kant in his *Critique of Judgment* has, among others, these pithy statements:

The beautiful in nature is connected with the form of the object, which consists in having definite boundaries.   The sublime, on the other hand, is to be found in a formless object, so far as in it or by occasion of it *boundlessness* is represented, and yet its totality is also present to thought.   Thus the beautiful seems to be regarded as the representation of an indefinite concept of understanding, the sublime as that of a like concept of reason. (390)

We call that *sublime* which is *absolutely great*. (392)

... the sublime is not to be sought in the things of nature, but only in our ideas.   ... the sublime is that in comparison with which everything else is small.   ... the sublime is that, the mere ability to think which shows a faculty of the mind surpassing every standard of sense. (393)

The feeling of the sublime is therefore a feeling of pain arising from the want of accordance between the aesthetic estimation of magnitude formed by the imagination and the estimation of the same formed by reason. (395)

Sublimity ... does not reside in anything of nature, but only in our mind, insofar as we can become conscious that we are superior to nature within, and therefore also to nature without (so far as it influences us). Everything that excites this feeling in us, e.g. the *might* of nature which calls forth our forces, is called then (although improperly) sublime. (396)

Based on such 18ᵗʰ-century aesthetic ideas of the sublime and the beautiful as Burke and Kant have expounded, we can see, Shelley's "some sublimer world" must be a "great, absolutely great" world, a world "dark and gloomy" to mankind, thus "awful" and "founded on pain." Besides, it is a boundless world "not to be sought in the things of nature" though we can imagine it as a totality. To approach this world is to feel pain probably because, as Kant supposes, there is "the want of accordance between the aesthetic estimation of magnitude formed by the imagination and estimation of the same formed by reason." But, I must add, it is even more probably because the world is no longer merely an aesthetic object of Beauty which gives pleasure, but has rather turned into an ethical ideal of Goodness which is ascetic by nature.

As to Shelley's "some unseen Power," it naturally refers to the Supreme Goodness that resides in his "some sublimer world."

According to Angela Leighton, the 18th-century sublime is an aesthetic

> which relies heavily on support from religious belief; which derives its vocabulary from the language of mystical transport; which transforms the large expanses of the universe into images of the Deity; which converts obscure sight into imaginative visionaries; which proclaims the written word inadequate by comparison to the godly imaging of the poet.   (23)

Although Shelley remains a radical and an atheist throughout his life, he "cannot subscribe but uneasily and anxiously to such an aesthetic" (Leighton 23).   In denying any "poisonous names" ("God and ghosts and Heaven," etc.) for the imagined Supreme Goodness, however, Shelley's Platonism had led him to transcend this "various world" of inconstancy into the "sublimer world" of immortality, the chief of which is the only real, omnipotent entity with full light to produce its ethically "awful shadow," which in turn with its lesser light has shadows coming to visit this "various world," which is full of unreal and bad shadows.

It becomes clear, then, that in Shelley's Platonic, ethics-oriented mind, there is an unnamed and unseen Power that stands supreme in the hierarchy of all eternal Forms or Ideas, among which Intellectual Beauty is but an "awful shadow" of the Supreme Power and, yet, it also has its own light to bring us truth, grace, love, hope, etc., so as to defeat and annihilate the Jungian shadows of villainy, tyranny, vice, evil, etc.   Thus, Shelley has combined the aesthetic category of the sublime and the beautiful with his ethical ideas into a doctrine-like system which we may call the "ethical sublime."

Shelley's idea of the "ethical sublime" is best expressed in "Mont Blanc." Mont Blanc, as we know, is the highest peak of the Alps. It is therefore most sublime in terms of landscape. In the poem, however, the sublime peak with its "subject mountains" (62) stands not only for "some sublimer world" with its ravine of Arve, its pines, crags, caverns, ice and rock, rainbows and storms, glaciers, etc., but also for "some sublimer world" in which the "everlasting universe of things/Flows through the mind" (1-2), a world which "has a mysterious tongue" to teach "awful doubt" and "repeal/Large codes of fraud and woe" (76, 80-81), where dwells "apart in its tranquility/Remote, serene, and inaccessible" the "still and solemn power of many sights,/And many sounds, and much of life and death" (96-97, 128-9). This still and solemn power may come down "in likeness of the Arve" from "the ice gulphs that gird his secret throne,/Bursting through these dark mountains like the flame/ Of lightning through the tempest" (16-19). The "awful scene" the power creates may launch the poet into "a trance sublime and strange" with "One legion of wild thoughts" seeking "among the shadows that pass by,/Ghosts of all things that are, some shade of thee [the power],/Some phantom, some faint image" (15, 35, 41, 45-47). Such a power may bring "a flood of ruin" (107). It may also become the "breath and blood of distant lands" (123). The voice of such a power is "not understood/By all," but a poet representing "the wise, and great, and good" may "interpret [it], or make [it] felt, or deeply feel [it]" (81-83).

In interpreting "Mont Blanc," Angela Leighton claims that "it is the purpose of the poem to address the landscape as a possible sign of some greater Power which the poet desires to realize as a voice" (61). Shelley, according to her, is a skeptic. As a skeptic, Shelley "denies the presence of a creative God behind the landscape"; he "yearns for license to imagine an alternative origin of things, which is the origin also of his own creativity" (62).   The desert has come to be "Shelley's characteristic landscape of the sublime, because it is the landscape of lost presences or absent Power" (Leighton 65).   The sublime landscape is then associated with the Power within it, which serves to energize the poet's imagination.   "Such a Power is one that the skeptic denies, but the poet fears to lose" (Leighton 72).

I agree that Mont Blanc typifies for Shelley the sublime aspects of silence and solitude, but I cannot agree that Shelley is so skeptic as to deny the presence of a creative Power behind the sublime landscape and seek instead to create with his own imagination an unnamed deity that is "neither the beneficent Creator, nor the tyrannical Ahrimanes, but an absolutely remote and unknown presence" (Leighton 69).   For me, the Power lurking behind Mont Blanc is also the Power pushing the West Wind: it is at once destroyer and preserver, and it is like the spirit of revolution, creative in the sense of ever-changing the imperfect present for the future perfection.   Thus, when in the end the poet asks the question— "And what were thou, and earth, and stars, and sea,/If to the human mind's imaginings/Silence and solitude were vacancy?"—it is not a negative question to deny the "thou" or the Power as nothing but vacancy, but a positive question to suggest that the "thou" or the Power, for all its silence and solitude, is actually not mere vacancy: it is rather a mysterious presence always exercising its influences for the Good.   In other words, the concluding question of this poem is like that of "Ode to the West Wind" ("O Wind,/If Winter comes, can Spring be far behind?"): it is a prophetic question aiming to ethically console us rather than discourage us.

What lurks behind Mont Blanc may be a "dormant revolutionary potential" which, as Cian Duffy has convincingly explicated, is connected with the Assassins depicted in Shelley's little-known and unfinished short story, *The Assassins* (1814). According to Duffy,

> by likening the sect's dormant revolutionary potential to "awful" natural phenomena (the "imprisoned earthquake" or charging "lightning-shafts") Shelley figures the Assassins—in the most explicit possible terms—as the *agents* of Necessity. Violent revolution is itself, these images imply, an awful, *natural* phenomenon—an instance of the *natural* sublime. (90)

Shelley's *Prometheus Unbound* is set mostly in a Ravine of Icy Rocks in the Indian Caucasus.   The locale is no less sublime than Mont Blanc.   It is in truth even more sublime for the moral highness displayed therein.   In the Preface to this lyrical drama, Shelley tells us that he has "a passion for reforming the world," that his purpose "has hitherto been simply to familiarize the highly refined imagination of the more select classes of poetical readers with beautiful idealisms of moral excellence," and that "Prometheus is, as it were, the type of the highest perfection of moral and intellectual nature, impelled by the purest and the truest motives to the best and noblest ends" (Ingpen, II, 174 & 172).

Now, outwardly we do see a revolution in the drama: the Car of the Hour arrives and Jupiter is dethroned, only to sink ever, forever, down.   But a prior and greater revolution occurs in Prometheus's heart.   He changes his hate for Jupiter into pity.   This radical, moral reform is part of the necessity to effect the marital reunion of Prometheus with Asia and to bring about another Golden Age celebrated at the end of the work.   Prometheus achieves his sublimity, indeed, less through being physically unbound at the Precipice than through being morally unbound by his hate.   His boundless pity for his enemy and his boundless love for mankind are what makes him especially sublime.   It is this sublimity that dispels the factor (namely, hate) causing his disintegration and makes possible his reunion with Asia, who is his soul mate and the symbol of love.[9]   And it is this sublimity, as Sandro Jung has suggested, that makes "the essential difference between Aeschylus and Shelley's *Prometheus Unbound*" (90).

In the drama, Demogorgon is an enigmatic character. Commentators have usually equated Demogorgon with necessity or thought of him as process.   Paul Foot reminds us that by etymology the name "Demogorgon" means "people-monster," and therefore Asia, who descends into his cave to question him, is an "agitator" to rouse people to action (194, 197).   This interpretation may be acceptable in a political way of consideration.   In an aesthetic and ethical way, however, the etymological sense of "people-monster" may just go to stress the idea of "the awful or sublime aspect to the people" rather than the idea of "the revolutionary people as a monster."   In the drama, Demogorgon is described as "a tremendous Gloom" (1.207), a "veiled form" sitting on an "ebon throne," and "a mighty Darkness" filling "the seat of power" (2.4.1 & 2-3).   Yet, contradictorily, he is also described as "Ungazed upon and shapeless; neither limb,/Nor form, nor outline; yet we feel it is/A living Spirit" (2.4.5-7).   He lives in a place where one must go down through "the grey, void Abysm" to reach (2.3.72).   He is, therefore, identifiable with the Genius of the Earth and the Sovereign Power of the Terrestrial Daemons.   But, according to Thomas Love Peacock's account, Demogorgon is the father of the Sky, the Earth, and the

Underworld as well as the Fates.[10]   And for Angela Leighton he is presented "like the Power of 'Mont Blanc,' as a bleak and non-sentient alternative to the God of Christianity" (90).

Anyway, when Jupiter calls him "Awful Shade" and asks him what he is, Demogorgon replies, "Eternity," and says, "I am thy child, as thou wert Saturn's child,/Mightier than thee; and we must dwell together/Henceforth in darkness" (3.1.51-56).   It is paradoxical that the child is said to be mightier than the father.   It is also paradoxical to say Demogorgon has "rays of gloom/Dart round, as light from the meridian Sun" (2.4.3-4).   And it is even more paradoxical to let a dark entity from the abyss soar high to heaven to dethrone Jupiter and bring him back down to everlasting darkness.   All these paradoxes can be understood, nevertheless, if we regard Demogorgon as the greatest Shelleyan shadow, a Form of the supreme and eternal Goodness, which is aesthetically dark and ethically awful but has real light like the Sun to dispel the Jungian shadow of Jupiter and bring hope to mankind by helping, through necessity or process, this world's another great Shelleyan shadow, i.e., the Prometheus unbound or Goodness reformed.

Shelley's last and unfinished poem, *The Triumph of Life*, is also fraught with his idea of the ethical sublime.   The poem, to be sure, is strongly influenced by Petrarch's *Trionfi* and Dante's *Divine Comedy*, as seen in its *terza rima* form, its content of procession and victory embedded in the word "triumph," its dream-vision as the framework of the story, and its moral purpose.   However, the native influence of Wordsworth's "Ode: Intimations of Immortality" is also there to be felt strongly, as both poems are focused on the same theme: the process of life.   And the theme is a sublime topic, especially when it involves reflection upon the purpose and the end of that process.

In Wordsworth's poem, we may recall, life is portrayed as a process of forgetting the preexisting Soul, of losing the "visionary gleam," which is comparable to the starlight's fading "into the light of common day" (54-76).   Now, Shelley's *The Triumph of Life* begins with a common day when "the Sun sprang forth/Rejoicing in his splendor, and the mask/Of darkness fell from the awakened Earth" (2-3).   On such a day when life goes on as usual, the poet has a somber vision of the human race: he sees a chariot moving with a captive multitude in a procession and then he finds a guide (identified as Rousseau) who helps him make sense of the pageant of life and tells his own life-story.   This visionary framework, I think, suggests that the poet has not forgot his soul; he still keeps his visionary gleam; his light has not yet faded into the light of common day.

The light/dark imagery is what brings sublimity into relief in the vision.   While some of the captive multitude walk mournfully within the gloom of their own shadow, some flee from it as it were a ghost (58-60).   The chariot comes on the silent storm of its own rushing splendor and a deformed Shape sits within it beneath a dusky hood and double cape, crouching within the shadow of a tomb, with a crape-like cloud overhead tempering the light (86-93).   The charioteer is a Janus-visaged Shadow and the Shapes drawing the chariot are lost in thick lightnings (94-97).   Moreover, the charioteer is blindfolded: he cannot see the chariot beams that quench the Sun.   According to Rousseau (who is likened to an old root growing to strange distortion out of the hillside), the shape within the car is "Life" (178-83).   Our life is full of shadows and phantoms (Napoleon's, Plato's, Bacon's, Caesar's, etc.), but Life conquers "all but the sacred few" (128).   Pontiffs like Gregory and John will just rise "like shadows between Man and god" till the eclipse of the true Sun (288-92).   When "a Shape all light" offers Rousseau a crystal glass, he only   touches it with "faint lips," but then a new vision bursts and the fair shape wanes in the coming light (352, 358, 411-2).

The light/dark imagery may seem to be confusing.   Yet, it is all clear that Shelley is here using the Platonic metaphors of the Sun with its light and shadows from the light, together with Wordsworth's idea of "true light fading into common light rather than into darkness."   In Shelley's vision, the true Sun is the Supreme Goodness: it produces the light of hope, of truth, beauty and goodness.   However, the ordinary sun is not the true Sun for ordinary people.   The ordinary sun just goes to make all sorts of unreal shadows or phantoms.   Our life is the process and outcome of a war, and the outcome is often a triumph, in which the victor is but a deformed Shape beneath a dusky hood, his charioteer but a blindfolded Shadow, and his horses but invisible beings lost in thick lightnings.   Victory as embodied in the chariot may have its glory, splendor or lightnings, which may eclipse the true Sun and fade its true light.   But, after all, the victor and his chariot, charioteer, horses, and captives are themselves but unreal phantoms or shadows. Only a truly good man can be better than Rousseau and the men divine, and can accept the "Shape all light" and drink from her crystal glass with true effect.

VI. Conclusion

In Shelley's *The Triumph of Life*, Plato is not among "the sacred few" that are not conquered by Life.   But Shelley is no doubt a Platonist.   Like Plato, he is an idealist, believing in the invisible, intellectual Forms or Ideas as the eternal universals and debasing the tangible, physical objects as unreal shadows or phantoms removed from the ultimate reality.   So, poetic imitation is for him not "reproduction as nearly as possible of external forms, but imitation of the ideal."[11]   Like Plato, too, he is ethics-oriented, ranking Goodness as the supreme Idea, seeing a purposeful cosmos directed towards the Good, preaching virtuous goodness or "intellectual beauty," and regarding the "ethical sublime" as higher than the "political sublime" and the "aesthetic sublime."   That is why he describes Julian (his vicarious self) as a man "for ever speculating how good may be made superior" (*Julian and Maddalo*, in Jungpen, III, 177).

In *The Triumph of Life*, military and political giants (Alexander, Caesar, Napoleon, etc.) are also not among "the sacred few" to free themselves from Life's triumphal chain.   In *Prometheus Unbound*, Shelley makes Fury lament that "The good want power, but to weep barren tears./The powerful goodness want: worse need for them" (1.625-6).   In real life, Shelley had seen tyrants and despots, villains and evils.   He was once an enthusiastic devotee to political revolutions and won his name as a radical.   But we know his radicalism was but the result of his will to struggle for human freedom, for the ethical ideals of liberty, equality, and fraternity.

The church men divine are likewise exempted from "the sacred few" that can detach themselves from the triumphal procession of Life.   Shelley describes Julian, i.e., himself as "a complete infidel, and a scoffer at all things reputed holy" (*Julian and Maddalo*, in Ingpen, III, 177).   In real life, Shelley was blamed and punished for being an atheist and skeptic.   But in the Advertisement to *The Necessity of Atheism*, Shelley claims that "a love of truth is the only motive which actuates the Author of this little tract" (Ingpen, V, 205).

In fact, Shelley is skeptical towards the religious idea of "God" because He is conceived as a revengeful tyrant sitting on a throne in heaven much like an earthly king (King-Hele 35).

Even Rousseau, the guide in *The Triumph of Life*, fails to become one of "the sacred few."   Rousseau has not actually drunk from the crystal glass offered by the "Shape all light."   He is a great thinker but he "feared, loved, hated, suffered, did, and died" (200). Nevertheless, his writings have sparks which kindled a thousand signal fires including the French Revolution and enlightened people with the educational idea of living righteously and close to nature. According to David V. Smith, "Shelley was fascinated by the aesthetic as well as the political genius of Rousseau's writing" (119), and both Rousseau and Shelley sought to "change [people's] traditional beliefs on morals and religion" (125).   Although Shelley was a revolutionary before a poet, he at last came to understand that Rousseau can be his guide and moral reformation is better than political revolution as a way of setting up the state of Goodness.

In his essay "On Life," Shelley says, "We live on, and in living we lose the apprehension of life" (Ingpen, VI, 194).   He also says that "man is a being of high aspirations ... there is a spirit within him at enmity with nothingness and dissolution" (Ingpen, VI, 194).   In *A Defense of Poetry*, Shelley says, "A poem is the very image of life expressed in its eternal truth" (Ingpen, VII, 115).   He believes that poetry can awaken and enlarge the mind "by rendering it the receptacle of a thousand unapprehended combinations of thought" and poetic imagination is the "great instrument of moral good" (Ingpen, VII, 117-8).   He even asserts that as a poet is "the author to others of the highest wisdom, pleasure, virtue and glory, so he ought personally to be the happiest, the best, the wisest, and the most illustrious of men" (Ingpen, VII, 138).   So, unlike Plato, who does not trust poetry in consideration of its ethical function, Shelley considers poetry as the best way of moral reformation.   In a time when "the wise want love, and those who love want wisdom" (*Prometheus Unbound*, 627), poetry is Shelley's only resort for sublimating the Soul.

Shelley's large quantity of poetry is subject to any new study or interpretation.   A lot of his poetry certainly has the defects of shoddy workmanship, unvisualizable descriptions, and incoherent imagery. Such defects are the result of neglecting the intrinsic beauty while striving for extrinsic goodness.   Occasionally, of course, as suggested by David Taylor in speaking of his *Prometheus Unbound*, Shelley may demonstrate his attention to the intrinsic form of the work as a means to express his ethical or political idea.   Yet, more often than not, his language is abandoned to emotional and sentimental treatment of his theme.   And this is where he differs most from Keats.   While Keats's primary concern is with Beauty, Shelley's is with Goodness. Keats is Adonais, the beautiful child of Urania; death makes him "a portion of the loveliness/Which once he made more lovely" (*Adonais*, 379-80).   Shelley is Alastor, the Spirit of Solitude; he died like the unnamed poet in the poem, in pursuit of his ideal shadow, a form of his intellectual beauty.   As an aesthete, Keats does not like Wordsworth's "egotistical sublime" (letter to Richard Woodhouse, October 27, 1818, in Bush 279); I think he does not like Shelley's "ethical sublime," either, for he wishes Shelley to curb his magnanimity (letter to Shelley, August 16, 1820, in Bush 298).

Shelley's magnanimity is seen in his definition of Love: "It is that powerful attraction towards all that we conceive or fear or hope beyond ourselves when we find within our own thoughts the chasm of an insufficient void and seek to awaken in all things that are, a community with what we experience within ourselves" ("On Love," in Ingpen, VI, 201).   This magnanimous Love is "the bond and the sanction which connects not only man with man, but with every thing which exists" ("On Love," in Ingpen, VI, 201).   And all of Shelley's poetry is the expression of this Love, including the works containing the Jungian shadows (awful for being repugnant) as well as those containing the Shelleyan shadows (awful for being dreadful and admirable) or both.

In "The Two Spirits: An Allegory," Shelley lets a spirit warn the other that the shadow of ruin and desolation is always tracking one's flight of fire like night coming over day.   In response to this warning, the other spirit says, "If I would cross the shade of night,/ Within my heart is the lamp of love,/And that is day!" (10-12). Harold Bloom takes the two spirits as the Blakean Specter and Emanation (323-5).   I think, however, they represent two poetic views of life: one somber, the other shiny.   The shiny view is based on the poet's hope for and faith in Love.   And I agree with Donald Reiman that Love and Hope are cornerstones of Shelley's ethical philosophy, "Love its motivating force, and Hope for the ultimate triumph of Good over Evil the sustainer of its energy" (542-3).

Shelley's private life may be not so admirable as his poetic career.   His irresponsible involvement with women, his tendency towards radicalism, atheism and skepticism, and even his impractical Platonism and idealism may be repugnant to a lot of his contemporary moralists and after.   But when we consider his entire poetic career in the light of "Intellectual Beauty" or virtuous goodness or the "ethical sublime," who would not repeat Byron's words written to John Murry at the time of Shelley's death: "You were all brutally mistaken about Shelley, who was, without exception, the *best* and least selfish man I ever knew.   I never knew one who was not a beast in comparison" (quoted in Abrams et al, 663).

Notes

1. Quoted, respectively, from online passages under the headings of "About Trinity," "A Philosophy of Living," and "Truth, Beauty, and Goodness" (a lecture by Rudolf Steiner). The websites are: (www.trinityschoolnc.org/at_mis_cmmnctng.html; www.personal.kent.edu/~jicattles/TBG.htm; wn.rsarchive.org/Lectures/TruGoo_index.html).

2. From the Introduction to his "The Natural Theology of Beauty, Truth, and Goodness" (www.integralworld.net/mcintosh4.html).

3. From the definition of "beauty" in *Webster's New World Dictionary*, 2nd College Edition, 1982.

4. See the entry of "Plato's Aesthetics" in the online *Stanford Encyclopedia of Philosophy* (plato.stasnford.edu/entries/plato-aesthetics).

5. Notopoulos differentiates and discusses three kinds of Platonism: natural, direct, and indirect Platonism. See his *The Platonism of Shelley*.

6. See Keats's letter to Benjamin Bailey (November 22, 1819).

7. See note 7 to *Endymion* in Abrams et al, eds., *The Norton Anthology of English Literature*, 5th Edition, Vol. 2, 801.

8. Constantia was one of the nicknames of Claire Clairmont. The poem was written obviously to celebrate Claire, but the name "Constantia" can refer to any constant image whose voice, "slow rising like a Spirit, lingers/Overshadowing [Shelley] with soft and lulling wings" ("To Constantia," 1-2).

9. M. H. Abrams holds that Prometheus is like Blake's Albion: he was once whole but has fallen into division, only to redeem his lost integrity through love. See his *Natural Supernaturalism*, 299-307.

10. See note 9 in Reiman & Powers, *Shelley's Poetry and Prose*, p. 141.

11. The point is made by Melvin Solve in his *Shelley: His Theory of Poetry*, p. 73, and quoted in Earl Schulze's *Shelley's Theory of Poetry*, p. 16.

Works Consulted

Abrams, M. H.   *Natural Supernaturalism: Tradition and Revolution in Romantic Literature.*   New York: Norton, 1971.

Abrams, M. H. et al, eds.   *The Norton Anthology of English Literature.* 5th Edition, Vol. 2.   New York: Norton, 1986.

Allott, Miriam.   *The Complete Poems of John Keats.*   London: Longman, 1986.

Bloom, Harold.   *The Visionary Company: A Reading of English Romantic Poetry.*   Revised and Enlarged Edition.   Ithaca & London: Cornell UP, 1971.

Brooks, Cleanth.   *The Well Wrought Urn.*   New York: Harcourt, Brace & Co., 1947.

Burke, Edmund.   *An Inquiry into the Origin of Our Ideas of the Sublime and Beautiful.*   Rpt. in part in Hazard Adams, ed.   *Critical Theory Since Plato.*   New York: Harcourt Brace Jovanovich, 1971. 303-312.

Bush, Douglas, ed.   *Selected Poems and Letters by John Keats.* Boston: Houghton Mifflin Co., 1959.

Cameron, Kenneth Neill.   "The Social Philosophy of Shelley."   *The Sewanese Review.* L,4 (Autumn 1942); rpt. in Reiman & Powers, 511-519.

Dobie, Ann B.   *Theory and Practice: An Introduction to Literary Criticism.*   New York: Heinle, 2002.

Duffy, Cian. "Revolution or Reaction? Shelley's *Assassins* and the Politics of Necessity." *Keats-Shelley Journal.* Vol. LII (2003), 77-93.

Foot, Paul. *Red Shelley.* London: Didgwick & Jackson, 1980.

Gibson, Evan K. *"Alastor:* A Reinterpretation." *PMLA.* LXII (1947), 1022-1042; rpt. in Reiman & Powers, 545-569.

Ingpen, Roger & Walter E. Peck. *The Complete Works of Percy Bysshe Shelley.* 10 Vols. New York: Gordian, 1965.

Jung, Sandro. "Overcoming Tyranny: Love, Truth and Meaning in Shelley's *Prometheus Unbound." The Keats-Shelley Review.* No. 20 (2006), 89-101.

Kant, Immanuel. *The Critique of Judgment.* Rpt. in part in Hazard Adams, ed. *Critical Theory Since Plato.* New York: Harcourt Brace Jovanovich, 1971. 379-399.

King-Hele, Desmond. *Shelley: His Thought and Work.* 3rd Edition. London: Macmillan, 1984.

Leighton, Angela. *Shelley and the Sublime.* Cambridge: Cambridge UP, 1984.

McDayter, Ghislaine. "O'er Leaping the Bounds: The Sexings of the Creative Soul in Shelley's *Epipsychidion." Keats-Shelley Journal.* Vol. LII (2003). 21-49.

Molinari, Lori. "Revising the Revolution: The Festival of Unity and Shelley's *Beau Ideal." Keats-Shelley Journal.* Vol. LIII (2004), 97-126.

Notopoulos, James A. *The Platonism of Shelley.* New York: Octagon Books, 1969.

O'Brien, Paul. *Shelley and Revolutionary Ireland.* London & Dublin: Redwords, 2002.

O'Neill, Michael. "The Gleam of Those Words: Coleridge and Shelley." *The Keats-Shelley Review.* No. 19 (2005), 76-96.

Reiman, Donnald H. "The Purpose and Method of Shelley's Poetry," in Reiman & Powers, 530-544.

Reiman, Donnald H. & Sharon B. Powers, eds. *Shelley's Poetry and Prose*. A Norton Critical Edition. New York: Norton, 1977.

Schmid, Thomas H. "'England Yet Sleeps': Intertextuality, Nationalism, and Risorgimento in P. B. Shelley's *Swellfoot the Tyrant."* *Keats-Shelley Journal*. Vol. LIII (2004), 61-85.

Schulze, Earl J. *Shelley's Theory of Poetry*. The Hague & Paris: Mouton & Co., 1966.

Smith, David V. "Der Dichter Spricht: Shelley, Rousseau and the Perfect Society." *The Keats-Shelley Review.* No. 19 (2005), 117-131.

Taylor, David. "'A Vacant Space, an Empty Stage': *Prometheus Unbound, The Last Man*, and the Problem of Dramatic (Re)Form." *The Keats-Shelley Review.* No. 20 (2006), 18-31.

Thilly, Frank. *A History of Philosophy*. Revised by Ledger Wood. New York: Henry Holt & Co., 1951.

Urmson, J. O., ed. *The Concise Encyclopedia of Western Philosophy and Philosophers.* London: Routledge, 1960.

White, N. I. *Shelley*. 2 Volumes. New York: Knopf, 1940.

* This paper first appeared in 2008 in *Intergrams*, 8.2-9.1.

The Structural Truth
in Coleridge's Conversation Poems

In *Princeton Encyclopedia of Poetry and Poetics*, the entry of "conversation pieces" carries this information:

> The c. piece or poem is relaxed and informal, but serious. Like Horace's epistles and satires, from which it probably springs, it is a genre intermediate between poetry and prose-*propriora sermoni*, which in Coleridge's case Charles Lamb translated as "properer for a sermon. " Not uncommon in the latter part of the 18th c., the c. poem is peculiarly a favorite with Wordsworth and Coleridge, doubtless because of its unique combination of unpretentiousness and depth, attributes given it by Cowper. Wordsworth's *Expostulation and Reply* and *The Tables Turned* are c. poems, though blank verse is the genre's most appropriate medium; the *Lines Composed a Few Miles Above Tintern Abbey* might be thought of as a c. piece which got out of hand and burst its bounds. Coleridge's *Dejection: an Ode* is another such, but as a Pindaric ode it does not quite correspond to the type. Coleridge, however, is the great practitioner of the c. piece in *The Eolian Harp, This Limetree Bower My Prision, The Nightingale, To William Wordsworth,* and a number of other poems. We have nothing quite like this genre today, but W.

H. Auden and perhaps Theodore Roethke might be mentioned
as poets who have written in its spirit. (153)

This information suggests at least the following points. First, a
conversation piece is but another name for a conversation poem, and
vice versa.   This point is construed in many other books of similar
nature, although in *Merriam Webster's Encyclopedia of Literature*
it is said that a conversation piece refers to "a piece of writing (such
as a play) that depends for its effects chiefly upon the wit or
excellent quality of its dialogue," while the term "is also used to
describe a poem that has a light, informal tone despite its serious
subject" (269).

Second, the conversation piece/poem is "relaxed and informal"
in tone, just as an ordinary conversation usually is.   The tone refers,
of course, to that of the speaker in the work.   But since in a
Romantic poem like Coleridge's it is hardly necessary to distinguish
the speaker in the poem from the poet who has written the work, we
may well equate the speaker's tone with the poet's. Anyway, it is
agreed that the speaker or the poet adopts a "relaxed and informal"
tone in a conversation piece/poem, although in actual description
"light," "chatty," etc., may be used to replace "relaxed" and
"informal," and "style" may be used to replace "tone" in other
dictionaries of literary terms (e.g., see Cuddon's *Dictionary*, 157).

Third, although a conversation piece/poem is relaxed and
informal (or light and chatty) in tone, it has quite "serious" subject
matter.   That is, it often "talks" about some "important thing,"
unlike most chats or gossips (which are about trivial things). But the
question is: What is serious or important? Is the subject in a
conversation piece/poem really "properer for a sermon"?   Or is it
actually not sermon in the modern homiletic sense but rather

"discourse" or "conversation" with an addressee and some element of serious satire as in Horace's works? (Harmon & Holman 118)

Fourth, the conversation piece/poem takes its origin probably in the Roman Period from such works as Horace's epistles and satires. But the genre did not flourish until the Romantic Period with such successful practitioners as Wordsworth and Coleridge.   Today, very few poets have written in that tradition (Auden and Roethke are among the rare examples).   Yet, if we gather information from more sources, we will find that in the history of this genre, such poets as Pope, Cowper, Browning, and Frost have also been mentioned.

Fifth, certain poems of Wordsworth's and Coleridge's are on the list of famous conversation pieces, but no complete list has as yet been made for the two poets, and there is some doubt regarding certain poems (such as "Tintern Abbey" and "Dejection: An Ode") because they cannot be assigned to the genre without any problem.

With the above understanding, we are now in a position to discuss the structural truth in Coleridge's conversation poems.   We know Coleridge himself used the term "conversation poem" to call one of his poems only: namely, "The Nightingale," which appeared in the 1798 *Lyrical Ballads*.   In actuality, however, scholars have agreed that seven or eight other poems of his can take the same label. According to Donald A. Stauffer, for instance, the list of Coleridge's conversation poems includes these eight poems: "The Eolian Harp," "Reflections on Having Left a Place of Retirement," "This Lime-Tree Bower My Prison," "Frost at Midnight," "Fears in Solitude," "The Nightingale," "Lines Written in the Album at Elbingerode, in the Hartz Forest," and "To William Wordsworth." And according to George McLean Harper, "Dejection: An Ode" can be added to the list because it is "an ode in form only; in contents it is a conversation," as it is "not an address to Dejection, but to William Wordsworth" (198).

One may ask, "What do these poems have in common, besides relaxed and informal tone, serious subject matter, and conversational style?"   One thing we can easily notice is: although they are called conversation poems, they are actually monologues, not dialogues. To be sure, in each of the poems the poet (the speaker) is seemingly talking to someone.   But the someone is actually only apostrophized in the poem.   He or she never responds directly in speech or action. "The Eolian Harp," for instance, begins with the apostrophe "My pensive Sara!"   And the same addressee (Sara Fricker) is subsequently apostrophized four more times: "my love!" (34), "O beloved woman!" (50), "Meek daughter in the family of Christ!" (53), and "heart-honored Maid!" (65).   Nevertheless, despite the fact that there is some description of the addressee's response—"thy more serious eye a mild reproof/Darts ... nor such thoughts/Dim and unhallowed dost thou not reject,/And biddest me walk humbly with my   God" (49-52), and "Well   hast   thou   said   and   holily dispraised/Those shapings of the unregenerate mind" (54-55)—we do not, indeed, see the person react directly, nor hear her speak directly.   All the lines are but the poet-speaker's descriptive and meditative soliloquies.   So we can say the conversation poems are mock-   conversations   or   pseudo-conversations   because   the apostrophized addressee (Sara Fricker, Charles Lamb, William Wordsworth, Sarah Hutchinson, Hartley Coleridge, etc.) are virtually no other than absentees.

If the conversation poems are actually not conversations, the interactions therein may not focus on person-to-person relations. As it is, we find each of Coleridge's conversation poems involves an interaction between an outer scene and an inner feeling, or to state it

simply, between outer and inner worlds.   Harper has rightly called
Coleridge's conversation pieces "Poems of Friendship" because they
are products of real friendship.   But Stauffer is also right in saying
that "the vast natural world also, with its soothing power and quiet,
Coleridge treats as a friend" (xxi).   Each conversation poem of
Coleridge's is indeed a "conversation" between nature and man as
"friends," if not one between two real persons.   Take the poem,
"This Lime-Tree Bower My Prison," for example.   In it the
poet/speaker at first feels himself deserted by his friends who in his
imagination have roamed into several natural places in gladness.
But then he feels in his solitude that he is himself also accompanied
and befriended by nature in the bower which he regarded before as
his prison:

> Nor in this bower,
> This little lime-tree bower, have I not mark'd
> Much that has sooth'd me. Pale beneath the blaze
> Hung the transparent foliage; and I watch'd
> Some broad and sunny leaf, and lov'd to see
> The shadow of the leaf and stem above
> Dappling its sunshine! And that walnut-tree
> Was richly ting'd, and a deep radiance lay
> Full on the ancient ivy, which usurps
> Those fronting elms, and now, with blackest mass
> Makes their dark branches gleam a lighter hue
> Through the late twilight: and though now the bat
> Wheels silent by, and not a swallow twitters,
> Yet still the solitary humble-bee
> Sings in the bean-flower! (45-59)

The friendship of nature to man is a Romantic theme. But nowhere else is the theme more clearly embedded in the structure of the poem than in a Coleridgean conversation piece. According to John Spencer Hill's analysis, all conversation poems share a "tripartite rondo structure," beginning with the introduction of a particular situation, going through a middle part of the speaker's meditation, and ending with a return to the original situation after the speaker has some deepened insight (19). John Colmer's analysis has come to a similar conclusion. He says: "The structure consists of three main sections: an introduction in which the poet's situation is established and the atmosphere miraculously evoked through a few simple details; a central meditative section in which the subtlest modulations of thought and emotion are exactly communicated; lastly, a return to the original situation, but with 'new acquist of true experience'" (26). Let us look at "Frost at Midnight" for example. The poem begins with the speaker's description of his own situation:

> The Frost performs its secret ministry,
> Unhelped by any wind. The owlet's cry
> Came loud-and hark, again! loud as before.
> The inmates of my cottage, all at rest,
> Have left me to that solitude, which suits
> Abstruser musings: save that at my side
> My cradled infant slumbers peacefully.
> 'Tis calm indeed! so calm, that it disturbs
> And vexes meditation with its strange
> And extreme silentness. Sea, hill, and wood,
> This populous village! Sea, and hill, and wood,
> With all the numberless goings-on of life,
> Inaudible as dreams! the thin blue flame

> Lies on my low-burnt fire, and quivers not;
> Only that film, which fluttered on the grate,
> Still flutters there, the sole unquiet thing.
> Methinks, its motion in this hush of nature
> Gives it dim sympathies with me who live,
> Making it a companionable form,
> Whose puny flaps and freaks the idling Spirit
> By its own moods interprets, everywhere
> Echo or mirror seeking of itself,
> And makes a toy of Thought. (1-23)

In this description, a calm atmosphere is rendered through such simple details as the frost performing its secret ministry unhelped by any wind, the owlet's cry coming loud, the inmates of the speaker's cottage all at rest, the cradled infant slumbering peacefully, sea, hill, and wood with the populous village inaudible as dreams, and the thin blue flame lying on the low burnt fire without quivering while the film is fluttering on the grate.   The poem then comes to the middle part of meditation (lines 23-64), in which the poet first recalls his own school days and then thinks of his dear babe at present, foreseeing the Great Universal Teacher's (i.e., Nature's) influence on the child.   With this presage, at last, the poet returns to the initial situation, but with a deepened insight:

> Therefore all seasons shall be sweet to thee,
> Whether the summer clothe the general earth
> With greenness, or the redbreast sit and sing
> Betwixt the tufts of snow on the bare branch
> Of mossy apple-tree, while the nigh thatch
> Smokes in the sun-thaw; whether the eave-drops fall

> Heard only in the trances of the blast,
> Or if the secret ministry of frost
> Shall hang them up in silent icicles,
> Quietly shining to the quiet Moon. (65-75)

The typical structure of a conversation poem as explicated above actually contains two basic acts fulfilled on the part of the speaker: describing outward scenes and making inward reflection. The description always involves nature along with man in nature. The reflection or meditation always involves the poet-speaker's feeling (lyrical outpouring) and thinking, which then lead to what Wordsworth says in "Tintern Abbey"—the moment when we "see into the life of things" (13), that is, to the sudden awareness of certain "truth." This "truth" or "insight" often has certain philosophical depth. Moreover, since it is located in the middle of the poem, hidden, as it were, between two layers of outward description, it seems to be, and surely is, the gist of the matter.   Such a sandwich structure—or call it a "tripartite rondo structure" if you like—cannot do, indeed, without the meat or kernel, so to speak, lying inside it.   That is why R. H. Fogle can say that the conversation poems "have a center and a centrality, which generally come from a central philosophical idea used as a counterpoint to the concrete psychological experience which makes the poem's wholeness and life" (106-7).

Certainly, the "truth" in a Coleridgean conversation poem is often clearly stated somewhere in the central part.   We will examine all the poems concerned.   First, "The Eolian Harp"states the one-life theme in line 26 ("O the one life within us and abroad") and in lines 44-48:

And what if all of animated nature
Be but organic harps diversely framed,
That tremble into thought, as o'er them sweeps
Plastic and vast, one intellectual breeze,
At once the Soul of each, and God of All?

The poem "This Lime-Tree Bower My Prison" has its truth stated
likewise in the middle part:

Henceforth I shall know
That Nature ne'er deserts the wise and pure;
No plot so narrow, be but Nature there,
No waste so vacant, but may well employ
Each faculty of sense, and keep the heart
Awake to Love and Beauty! (59-64)

This truth is also a typical Romantic theme: the close relationship
between nature and man.   The truth in "Reflections on Having Left
a Place of Retirement" takes the form of likening "a goodly scene" to
a divine temple, suggesting at once the one-life theme and the
relationship between nature and man:

It seem'd like Omnipresence! God, methought,
Had built him there a Temple: the whole World
Seem'd *imag'd* in its vast circumference. (38-40)

The truth in "Frost at Midnight" comes from contrasting the
poet-speaker's rearing in the great city with his son's chance of
learning "far other lore ... in far other scenes":

> So shalt thou see and hear
> The lovely shapes and sounds intelligible
> Of that eternal language, which thy God
> Utters, who from eternity doth teach
> Himself in all, and all things in himself. (58-62)

This, obviously, touches on the one-life theme again and the relationship between nature and man.   The poem "Fears in Solitude" states that a humble man would love "a quiet spirit-healing nook" (12) and could find "religious meanings in the forms of Nature" (26).   But most of the middle section of the poem is a long meditation on and accusation of human follies and vices associated with the alarm of an invasion, which culminates in the prophecy that "evil days/Are coming on us" (123-4).   Nevertheless, the relationship between nature and man is also emphasized in such lines:

> O my Mother Isle!
> How shouldst thou prove aught else but dear and holy
> To me, who from thy lakes and mountain-hills,
> Thy clouds, thy quiet dales, thy rocks and seas,
> Have drunk in all my intellectual life,
> All sweet sensations, all ennobling thoughts,
> All adoration of the God in nature,
> All lovely and all honorable things,
> Whatever makes this mortal spirit feel
> The joy and greatness of its future being? (182-92)

Finally, the poet-speaker sums up this relationship by saying that the "divine and beauteous island" has been his "sole and most magnificent temple" (193-4).

In "The Nightingale," Coleridge introduces at first the truth that "In Nature there is nothing melancholy" (15), and finally he says he deems it wise to make his dear babe Nature's play-mate (96). In "Lines Written in the Album at Elbingerode, in the Hartz Forest," the poet has found the truth that "outward forms, the loftiest, still receive/Their finer influence from the Life within" (17-18), which naturally leads to his feeling that "God is everywhere" (37). The truth in "To William Wordsworth" is: "The truly great/Have all one age, and from one visible space/Shed influence" (50-52). This truth does not touch on the relationship between nature and man, of course. But it has some connection with the one-life theme, since it claims that the truly great have all one age and shed influence from one visible space. Finally, if we take, as some critics do, "Dejection: An Ode" as a conversation poem, we will see that the pronounced truths may be in such utterances as "we receive but what we give,/And in our life alone does nature live" (47-48), and "Joy ... is the spirit and the power,/Which wedding Nature to us gives in dower" (67-68). Thus, the one-life theme as well as the relationship between nature and man is again brought into focus.

If we compare Coleridge's conversation poems with Browning's dramatic monologues, we will soon find that Coleridge's purpose is clearly to tell truths while Browning's aim is to portray characters, although both conversation poems and dramatic monologues are similarly pseudo-dialogues in which the speaker carries on his soliloquies without allowing the listener to make any direct response. If we compare Coleridge's conversation poems again with Robert Frost's poems of natural description and meditation, we may find that both poets, indeed, intend to tell truths through meditation in nature. Yet, unlike Coleridge, Frost often begins with describing scenes and ends with the truths discovered in the meditations, never returning to the described scenes to make a sandwich structure of description-meditation-description, or nature-man-nature, or outer-inner-outer, or detail-truth-detail.   From this fact we can conclude that Coleridge, as Wordsworth's best friend, is a typical "poet of nature" like Wordsworth.   They live close to nature, maintain nature's friendliness to man, and see one life among nature, man, and society.   Just like Wordsworth's "Expostulation and Reply," "The Tables Turned," "Tintern Abbey," and *The Prelude* (which is indeed a quite extended conversation piece addressed to Coleridge), Coleridge's conversation poems, as discussed above, have all contributed to the Romantic gospel of one life in the universe while stressing the beneficial influence of nature on man. But what is most significant is: such conversation poems have told their truths not only in words but also in their structure.   Such a genre is therefore probably the best example of what many critics assert in claiming that the form is the content.   Or to put it in another way, a Coleridgean conversation poem can best exemplify the slogan of "Structure is truth, truth structure" (to amend Keats's "Beauty is truth, truth beauty").

Works Consulted

Colmer, John, ed.   *Coleridge: Selected Poems*. Oxford: Oxford UP, 1965.

Cuddon, J. A.   *A Dictionary of Literary Terms*.   London: Penguin, 1976.

Fogle, R. H.   "Coleridge's Conversation Poems."   *Tulane Studies in English* 5 (1955). 103-110.

Harmon, William & C. Hugh Holman.   *A Handbook to Literature*. 7th ed. Upper Saddle River, NJ: Prentice Hall, 1996.

Harper, George McLean. "Coleridge's Conversation Poems." *English Romantic Poets: Modern Essays in Criticism.* Ed. M. H. Abrams. London: Oxford UP, 1975. 188-201.

Hill, John Spencer. *A Coleridge Companion.* London: Macmillan, 1983.

Kuiper, Kathleen, ed. *Merriam Webster's Encyclopedia of Literature.* Springfield, MS: Webster, 1995.

Preminger, Alex, ed. *Princeton Encyclopedia of Poetry and Poetics.* Princeton: Princeton UP, 1965.

Stauffer, Donald A., ed. *Selected Poetry and Prose of Coleridge.* New York: Random House, 1951.

* This paper first appears in 2001 in *Intergrams*, an e-journal of the Department of Foreign Languages and Literatures, National Chung Hsing University.

Wordsworth's Sense of Place

Recently I was asked to comment on a young scholar's paper on Wordsworth's sense of place at a literature conference.[1] The young scholar's ideas in that paper are mostly correct. However, they are far from sufficient to give a consummate configuration of Wordsworth's sense of place. Therefore, I feel it incumbent on me to proceed further here with the same subject. I hope this paper can truly do justice to this major Romantic poet's "ideology" concerning the notion of place.

I. Rural vs. Urban Places

To begin with, we must admit that for Wordsworth, as for many other Romantics, the distinction between rural and urban places is vitally significant because they represent, respectively, two different sets of life styles and values. For a typical Romantic like Wordsworth, a rural area, with its hills and vales, rivers and lakes, pastures and woods, flora and fauna, etc., is a place where natural men and women live in peace and simplicity notwithstanding its inherent perils and inconveniences. In contrast, an urban area, with its streets and buildings, institutions and monuments, markets and jails, traffic and transportation, etc., is a place where social men and women live in tumult and complexity despite its provided facilities and luxuries. This distinction has in fact led to the easy, but not always just, conclusion that a rural place is "good" while an urban place is "bad."

To exemplify this Romantic bias, one may well go to Rousseau's *Confessions*, in which the young Jean-Jacques confessed how he was drawn to the Canton of Vaud by its enchanting scenery as well as by its simple and peaceful life there while he "retained a secret dislike against residence" in Paris because he saw there "nothing but dirty and stinking little streets, ugly black houses, a general air of slovenliness and poverty, beggars, carters, menders of old clothes, criers of decoctions and old hats" (IV, 458).   One may also go to Heine, a much later Romantic, who lets his speaker in "Babylonian Sorrows" bemoan his own situation because he has to leave his wife behind in Paris, which he calls "City of Loveliness, laughter and revels, /The Hell of angels, Paradise of devils" (23-24), a place much worse than a wild wood or the perilous open sea.   Or, if one prefers English examples, one may as well read Blake's "London," in which the metropolis is depicted as a place full of "marks of weakness, marks of woe" and "mind-forged manacles" (4, 8); and read Byron's *Child Harold's Pilgrimage,* in which the melancholy narrator says, "…to me/High mountains are a feeling, but the hum/Of human cities torture" (III, 681-3).   Indeed, for a Byronic hero like Childe Harold and Manfred and for other Romantic heroes like Goethe's Faust, Chateaubriand's Rène, and Pushkin's Eugene Onegin as well, the city is to the country what anything negative is to anything positive.

In an article, James Heffernan has argued convincingly that "Wordsworth's London is Jekyll and Hyde, by turns a Babylonian monster and a city of heavenly light" (427), and that is why the city so often lured as well as repelled him.   Indeed, the sonnet "London, 1802" has a somber view of England:

...she is a fen
Of stagnant waters: altar, sword, and pen,
Fireside, the heroic wealth of hall and bower,
Have forfeited their ancient English dower
Of inward happiness.   (2-6)

But this is not Wordsworth's sole description of London.   Nor is the portrait of the St. Bartholomew Fair in *The Prelude*, with such terms as 'Parliament of Monsters" (VII, 692)[2] and "blank confusion" (VII, 696), meant to be the poet's whole view of this mighty city.   We admit that Wordsworth was in earnest when he composed another sonnet upon Westminster Bridge to recognize the beauty and calm of London.   No less do we believe that Wordsworth was sincere when in *The Prelude* he began to talk of his residence in London by asking:

...shall I, as the mood
Inclines me, here describe, for pastime's sake
Some portion of that motley imagery,
A vivid pleasure of my youth, and now
Among the lonely places that I love
A frequent day-dream for my riper mind?   (VII, 148-53)

For, in describing the "motley imagery" thereafter, Wordsworth did catalogue a number of things in London that allured him.

How shall we account for Wordsworth's apparently ambivalent attitude towards London, then?   Heffernan has mentioned Charles Lamb's influence.   As a city-bred man and one of Wordsworth's best friends, Lamb truly "loved London crowds quite as much as

Wordsworth loved rural solitude" (Heffernan 428).   In January 1801, Wordsworth invited Lamb to visit him in the Lake District. Lamb was not sure he could afford to go.   So he wrote to Wordsworth to explain his situation.   But in that letter he added a long paean to London, enumerating his "many and intense local attachments" and ridiculing Wordsworth's "rural emotions" about "dead nature" (Wordsworth, *Letters* I, 267-8).   Heffernan has also pointed out that Wordsworth had long come to the realization that he could not depend wholly on rural places for life.   So, in a letter to William Mathews, a friend he made at Cambridge, Wordsworth wrote: "I begin to wish much to be in town.   Cataracts and mountains are good occasional society, but they will not do for constant companions" (*Letters* I, 136).   Besides, as stated in the Preface to the 1802 edition of *Lyrical Ballads*, Wordsworth believed that "the poet binds together by passion and knowledge the vast empire of society, as it is spread over the whole earth, and over all time" (*Lyrical Ballads*, 259).   So he could not avoid coming to London if he intended to gather passion and knowledge of society.

The above-mentioned reasons for Wordsworth's ambivalent attitude towards London are all true, I believe.   Yet, the fact remains that Wordsworth "vastly preferred the country to the city" (Heffernan 421).   And his preference is due to his Romantic worship of nature.

II. Nature vs. Society

I have discussed elsewhere *The Prelude* as a quasi epic in which we see an imaginary battle fought between nature and society as two opposing forces for the poet's soul, that is, his imagination.   About this battle I have said, thus:

This conflict does not take the form of an open war as does that of *Iliad*, nor does it introduce an active inducement (of Satan to Eve) like that of *Paradise Lost.* It is only a poet's inner conflict resulting from the soul's travel between two mutually opposing worlds, much like the conflict existing in Faust's mind as it travels in the realms of God's creation and Mephistopheles' conjury. (Tung 1981, 13)

And regarding the two opposing forces that battle for the poet's soul, I have said, thus:

Wordsworth's nature, referring to such external things of beauty as hill and vale, stream and lake, forest and sky, flower and bird, and other things living with or in them, is God's primary creation and is said to be conducive to the growth of the poet's mind.   On the other hand, Wordsworth's society as exemplified in *The Prelude*, referring to such man-made places or institutes as city and town, school and church, and such human activities as party and fair, government and revolution, is a "Parliament of Monsters" and "blank confusion," something fearfully destructive to the poet's soul. Accordingly, it is only natural that we feel a certain tension in the poet's account of his life with man in nature and society. The tension may not rise to the pitch of an epic war or inducement affecting the entire civilization or moral future of mankind.   It, nonetheless, lends itself easily to epic treatment. (Tung 1981, 13)

In Books I and II of *The Prelude*, indeed, the poet, having related his childhood and schooltime incidents at Hawkshead, confessed that he was fostered "alike by beauty and by fear" (I, 306) which nature provided, and he retained his first creative sensibility without having his soul subdued by the regular action of the world (II, 378-81). That is, nature at this beginning period triumphed over society and built, as it were, a formidable barricade for his imagination so that in "mingling with the world" he could live always "removed/From little enmities and low desires" coming from society (II, 446-7).   In the ensuing books, then, Wordsworth related his university days at Cambridge, his return to his native vale for summer vacation, his residence in London as a vagrant dweller, his retrospect of nature in the "unfenced regions of society" (VII, 63), his turbulent life in France, and finally his return again to the Lake District to reflect upon how his imagination was impaired and restored.   In all these books, we certainly can see that nature and society act really like two combating forces, each taking turns winning battles against the other as the result of the poet's travel between these two realms.   Nature, as a positive power, has been dragging the poet to the bright side of man, teaching him to love mankind unquestioningly so that he can willingly do the holy service of writing poetry, and giving him a vision of one life in all, i.e., a synthetic power for creative imagination. On the other hand, society, as a negative power, has been pulling the poet to the dark side of man, calling upon him to indulge in trivial pleasures so that he will abandon his poetic ambition, or setting him to grope fruitlessly in the blind alley of analytical science, which is harmful to poetic imagination.

It may be redundant here to recount how Wordsworth worships nature.   Yet, we should not forget his famous pronouncements regarding the benefits of nature.   In "The Table Turned," for instance, we are asked to let nature be our teacher:

> She has a world of ready wealth,
> Our minds and hearts to bless—
> Spontaneous wisdom breathed by health,
> Truth breathed by cheerfulness.   (17-20)

In "Tintern Abbey," the poet says that "Nature never did betray/The heart that loved her,"

> ...for she can so inform
> The mind that is within us, so impress
> With quietness and beauty, and so feed
> With lofty thoughts, that neither evil tongues,
> Rash judgments, nor the sneers of selfish men,
> Nor greetings where no kindness is, nor all
> The dreary intercourse of daily life,
> Shall e'er prevail against us, or disturb
> Our cheerful faith that all which we behold
> Is full of blessings.   (126-35)

In "I Wandered Lonely as a Cloud," the daffodils he saw at Ulswater are said to be beneficial because

> ...when on my couch I lie
> In vacant or In pensive mood,
> They flash upon that inward eye
> Which is the bliss of solitude;
> And then my heart with pleasure fills,
> And dances with the daffodils.   (19-24)

And in *The Prelude*, Wordsworth gives Book VIII the heading "Retrospect—Love of Nature Leading to Love of Mankind," telling us directly his strong belief in nature.   And this belief is based on the reason as explained in *The Excursion*:

> For, the man—
> Who, in this spirit, commune with the Forms
> Of nature, who with understanding heart
> Both knows and loves such objects as excite
> No morbid passions, no disquietude,
> No vengeance, and no hatred—needs must feel
> The joy of that pure principle of love
> So deeply, that, unsatisfied with aught
> Less pure and exquisite, he cannot choose
> But seek for objects of a kindred love
> In fellow-natures and a kindred joy.
> Accordingly he by degrees perceives
> His feelings of aversion softened down;
> A holy tenderness pervades his frame.   (VI, 1207-20)

I have been of the opinion that as Wordsworth was bereaved of his parents very early in his life, psychologically nature became his foster mother and father fostering him "alike by beauty and by fear" (*Prelude* I, 306).   That is why each time he returned to nature, he felt as if he were returning home: it gave him a deep sense of joy in his heart.   To prove this, we may recall that Wordsworth begins *The Prelude* by telling us that he feels there is blessing in the gentle breeze when he is returning to the Lake District, that he is coming from a house of bondage, set free from the city's walls, and that the earth is all before him to meet his joyous heart (I, 1-16).   And we may also recall that in *Home at Grasmere*, the poet says that "here/Must be his home, this Valley be his world" (44-45):

> ...from crowded streets remote
> Far from the living and dead wilderness
> Of the thronged world, Society is here
> A true Community, a genuine frame
> Of many into one incorporate.
> That must be looked for here, paternal sway,
> One household under God for high and low,
> One family, and one mansion.   (612-9)

In contrast, to leave the Vale, the place where nature prevails, is to "hold a vacant commerce day by day/With objects wanting life, repelling love" (595-6).   For Wordsworth, therefore, truly alone is

> He by the vast Metropolis immured,
> Where pity shrinks from unremitting calls,
> Where numbers overwhelm humanity,
> And neighborhood serves rather to divide
> Than to unite.   (597-601)

And a city is where "if indifference to disgust/Yield not, to scorn, or sorrow, living men/Are ofttimes to their fellow-men no more/Than to the forest hermit are the leaves/That hang aloft in myriads" (604-8). Hence, in the story of "Michael," Luke is said to ruin himself in London after he left his pastoral homeland, because "He in the dissolute city gave himself/To evil course" (453-4).

Wordsworth's Romantic worship of nature, however, does not make him blind to the fact that behind the beauty of nature there also lurks danger of its own sort.   In "The Brothers," for instance, Wordsworth shares with us the pathos of the story which lies in Leonard's coming back only to learn about the accident of his brother James' fatal falling from the precipice.   And in the story of "Lucy Gray," we are sorry to learn that the girl going out with the lantern to light her mother through the snow has herself got lost in the snowstorm.   Besides danger, in fact, Wordsworth also sees other inadequacies in nature.   For instance, Wordsworth knows no less than we do that in the countryside where nature prevails, mankind often suffers from impoverishment and illness, especially in time of famine or plague.   It is with this knowledge that Wordsworth lets Margaret's plight be narrated pathetically in the story of "The Ruined Cottage."   Indeed, Wordsworth is all but Romantic when in *Home at Grasmere* he tells us that

> I came not dreaming of unruffled life,
> Untainted manners; born among the hills,
> Bred also there, I wanted not a scale
> To regulate my hopes.   Pleased with the good,
> I shrink not from the evil with disgust,
> Or with immoderate pain.   I looked for Man,
> The common creature of brotherhood,
> Differing but little from the Man elsewhere,
> For selfishness, and envy, revenge,
> Ill neighborhood—pity that this should be—
> Flattery and double-dealing, strife, and wrong.
>
> (347-57)

Yet, to return to Wordsworth's worship of nature, we find undoubtedly that Wordsworth envisions a certain correspondence between the outer great nature and our inner human nature.   In actuality, our human nature seems, in Wordsworth's mind, an emanation from the great nature.   In *The Prelude*, he said he contemplated nature's works "As they hold forth a genuine counterpart/And softening mirror of the moral world" (XIII, 180-1). This means the same as the statement in the Preface of 1802 to *Lyrical Ballads*: The poet "considers man and nature as essentially adapted to each other, and the mind of man as naturally the mirror of the fairest and most interesting qualities of nature" (259).   It is well known that in the same Preface Wordsworth tells the reader that his principal object in writing those poems was "to make the incidents of common life interesting by tracing in them, truly though not ostentatiously, the primary laws of our nature" (244-5).   In pursuing that object, then, he chose to write about low and rustic life in the language of simple, plain people.   And his reasons for making that choice are clearly stated:

> Low and rustic life was generally chosen because in that situation the essential passions of the heart find a better soil in which they can attain their maturity, are less under restraint, and speak a plainer and more emphatic language; because in that situation our elementary feelings exist in a state of greater simplicity and consequently may be more accurately contemplated and more forcibly communicated; because the manners of rural life germinate from those elementary feelings; and from the necessary character of rural occupations are more easily comprehended; and are more durable; and lastly, because in that situation the passions of men are incorporated with the beautiful and permanent forms of nature.   The language too of these men is adopted

(purified indeed from what appear to be its real defects, from all lasting and rational causes of dislike or disgust) because such men hourly communicate with the best objects from which the best part of language is originally derived; and because, from their rank in society and the sameness and narrow circle of their intercourse, being less under the action of social vanity they convey their feelings and notions in simple and unelaborated expressions.   (245)

From these statements we cannot but conclude that in Wordsworth's mind nature, rather than society, is considered to be more conducive to his creativity as it easily corresponds to human nature, although both nature and society, just as both rural and urban places, can stir his feelings.   That is why in his *Guide to the Lakes* Wordsworth deplored that the Lake District with its natural beauty was being destroyed by society with its civilization.

III. Spots of Time

So far we have touched on Wordsworth's common sense of place, i.e., the sense that places are either rural or urban, or either dominated by nature or by society.   And we have come to the conclusion that Wordsworth shares with all typical Romantics the bias that nature or rural places are "good" while society or urban places are "bad."   This common sense of place is surely not Wordsworth's contribution to the entire Romantic Movement.   What lifts him above other Romantics with regard to the sense of place is his particular idea embedded in what he calls "spots of time."

As we know, Wordsworth first introduces the term "spots of time" in Book XI of *The Prelude* (1805):

There are in our existence spots of time,
Which with distinct pre-eminence retain
A vivifying Virtue, whence, depressed
By false opinion and contentious thought,
Or aught of heavier and more deadly weight
In trivial occupations, and the round
Of ordinary intercourse, our minds
Are nourished and invisibly repaired,
A virtue by which pleasure is enhanced
That penetrates, enables us to mount
When high, more high, and lifts us up when fallen.
This efficacious spirit chiefly lurks
Among those passages of life in which
We have had deepest feeling that the mind
Is lord and master, and that outward sense
Is but the obedient servant of her will.
Such moments worthy of all gratitude,
Are scattered everywhere, taking their date
From our first childhood: in our childhood even
Perhaps are most conspicuous.   Life with me,
As far as memory can look back, is full
Of this beneficent influence.   (258-79)

In this context we see at least three points: First, the "spots of time" can serve as a "beneficent influence," be it called a "vivifying Virtue" or a "renovating virtue" as in the 1850 text, or a "fructifying virtue" as in the 1799 version.[4]   Anyway, they can nourish and repair our mind, can enhance our pleasures, and can elevate our souls. Second, the "spots of time" concur with "deepest feeling" when the mind lords it over the outward sense.   And third, the "spots of time" are scattered everywhere in our lifetime, especially in our childhood. Therefore, Wordsworth goes on to give as examples two childhood incidents of his: seeing the gibbet scene and waiting at a crag overlooking two roads.

Before we discuss the three points furthermore, we may note in passing that the word "spot" is a space term.   It refers to a small area or place, often a mark, stain, blot, speck, or patch distinguishable by its different color or texture.   It is obvious that when Wordsworth uses the term "spots of time," he has combined the notion of time with the notion of space.   By using that term he has compared memory to a large space made up of so many "spots of time," just as today we think of the memory of a computer as a composite of so many nodes.   Accordingly, every spot of time is just a marked place in our memory.   This particular sense of place, of turning the outer scene into the inner spot, is Wordsworth's most original and most significant contribution to our present topic.

Now, if we go on to consider what constitutes Wordsworth's various "spots of time," we will find, as does Miss Pauline Wu, that the "spots of time" actually can refer to human figures, events, objects, scenes or pictures, and even dreams— any impressive moments of experiences in the poet's life (Wu 14-57).   Yet, for anything to become a spot of time in Wordsworth's memory, it always needs a specific place where something or somebody can arouse the poet's feeling towards life.   Indeed, Wordsworth is strongly obsessed with specific places.   When he recalls places, they are not just places in nature but also places in his mind, thus "musing on them, often do I seem/Two consciousnesses, conscious of myself/And of some other being" (1850, 31-33).   This obsession, called the omphalos or spot syndrome, is crystallized in the term "spots of time."   According to Geoffrey Hartman, "spot" is subtly used in two senses "as denoting particular *places* in nature, and fixed *points* in time" (212).   In the phrase "spots of time," both "spots" and "time" can be emphasized.   "The concept is, in any case, very rich, fusing not only time and place but also stasis and continuity.   The fixity or fixation that points to an apocalyptic consciousness of self is temporalized, reintegrated in the stream of life" (Hartman 212).

In trying to answer why Wordsworth claims that the "spots of time" have a beneficial power over us, Hartman resorts to the idea of *genius loci*, or "spirit of place."   He explains, thus:

> The renovating energy flowing from the spots of time is really spirit of place reaching through time with a guardian's care. The *genius loci* was a guardian as well as indwelling spirit of his abode.   To link that kind of genius to the genius of the poet—the spirit, namely, that inspires or guards his "genial" powers—is an easy matter, and the early MSS of *The Prelude* show several at least implicit instances of it.   There are apostrophes not only to powers of the earth, beings of the hills, and spirits of the springs, but also to "genii" who form the poet by means of gentle or severer visitations.   (212)

Certainly, Wordsworth's worship of nature is often tinged with anthropomorphism, or pantheism, or mysticism.   We may or may not believe with him that each place has its benevolent spirit and "she shall lean her ear/In many a secret place/Where rivulets dance their wayward round" ("Three years she grew in sun and shower," 26-28).   But suffice it that "Wordsworth's sensitivity to spirit of place" has really often "restored him as nature's inmate" (Hartman

214).   This is the gospel brought forth in "The Daffodils," in "Tintern Abbey," in *The Prelude*, in *The Excursion*, and in many other poems of his.

Aside from Hartman's supernatural interpretation, Brooke Hopkins's psycho-analytical explication of the "spots of time" is also interesting.   Hopkins relies very much on D. W. Winnicott's doctrine that the mind has root in the need of the individual for a perfect environment.   For Hopkins, the idea of "spots of time" is Wordsworth's retrospective idealization of the mind as an entity over which one has at least the illusion of control, and which thereby constitutes a kind of "perfect environment," a place of last refuge in a world that refuses to correspond to one's wishes and dreams (19). In other words, the "spots of time" constitute an ideal place for the poet's imagination to work fruitfully in.   If we follow this belief, we then acknowledge that Wordsworth's sense of place is a sense not only of outward space but also of inward space; moreover, it is a sense in which the inward space comes from and then rises above the outward space.

In our critical world, little has as yet been said of Wordsworth's claim that the "spots of time" concur with the deepest feeling.   As I understand, this claim is closely related to Wordsworth's poetics. In Wordsworth's poetics, a poet is a man "endued with more lively sensibility, more enthusiasm and tenderness, who has ... a more comprehensive soul" than an ordinary man (Preface to *Lyrical Ballads*, 255).   As he wanders in nature and society, he is not preoccupied with any worldly business; he has the time and the mood to observe with accuracy things as they are in themselves, although he may not even have the purpose now of writing poetry out of the observation later.   Now, as the poet observes, his exquisite sensibility will enable him to perceive a wide range of things.   He may perceive, as Wordsworth himself did, a huge cliff as if "with voluntary power instinct,/Upreared its head" (*Prelude* I, 406-8); or a host of golden daffodils "Beside the lake, beneath the trees/Fluttering and dancing in the breeze" ("I wandered lonely as a cloud," 5-6); or a solitary reaper "Reaping and singing by herself" ("The Solitary Reaper," 3); or a very old man with gray hairs both like "a huge stone ..." and like "a sea-beast ..." ("Resolution and Independence," 55-63).   Perception, then, may lead the poet into a certain mood: fear, joy, melancholy, perplexity, indignation, sorrow, pity, etc.   No matter in what mood, the poet's feelings will be excited and exalted until they become a "strange fit of passion."   This fit of passion may be like "A tempest, a redundant energy/Vexing its own creation" (*Prelude* I, 46), or like a "paramount impulse not to be withstood" (*Prelude* I, 242).   At this moment, the poet may be said to be already full of poetry.   It is the moment when he feels his emotion overflows spontaneously.   It is also the moment when his spontaneous, quick and effortless thinking begins, when his "primary imagination," to use Coleridge's term, occurs, and when he feels, for instance, the huge cliff and the daffodils have life like animate things, and the solitary reaper and the leech-gatherer assume special significance in human life.   At this moment, too, the poet may feel some truth "flash upon that inward eye" ("I wandered lonely as a cloud," 21), although he may have to wait until later (when he can recollect the emotion in tranquility) to begin the composition of his poem.   In this creative process, therefore, we can clearly see that any "spot of time" is indeed the moment when the poet has the "deepest feeling" about something or somebody at a certain place.

Since memory is the composite of all spots of time and every spot of time is something deeply felt, it follows naturally that in accordance with Wordsworth's most famous poetic pronouncements, memory can be said to stem from all instances of "spontaneous overflow of powerful feelings" and it is to become "emotion [to be] recollected in tranquility."   No wonder critics have agreed that Wordsworth's poetical theory and practice are both strongly tied up with his memory.   According to C. G.. Salvesen, memory for Wordsworth is not merely "an aspect of the imagination; it represents a personal attitude to time" (45).   In other words, it is not just an associative power bound by the order of time and space; it represents a person's attitude towards what binds or makes up his memory.   Indeed, for Wordsworth memory is not just a storing power keeping impressions of one's past.   It is also a unifying power capable of bridging the past with the present, so much so that sometimes the past and the present become indistinguishably fused in memory just as one "is often perplexed, and cannot part/The shadow from the substance when one "hangs down— bending from the side/Of a slow-moving Boat" (*Prelude* IV, 247 ff.).   However, the past is especially attached to the feelings which are linked to the scenes or places:

> … by force
> Of obscure feelings representative
> Of joys that were forgotten, these same scenes
> So beauteous and majestic in themselves,
> Though yet the day was distant, did at length
> Become habitually dear, and all
> Their hues and forms were by invisible links
> Allied to the affections.   (*Prelude* I, 633-40)

And the merging of various feelings often becomes strength.   After mentioning how, in his revisiting the dreary Beacon scene of his childhood, the "spirit of pleasure and youth's golden gleam" fell in his recollections of the scene, Wordsworth remarks:

> And think ye not with radiance more divine
> From these remembrances, and from the power
> They left behind?   So feeling comes in aid
> Of feeling, and diversity of strength
> Attends us, if but once we have been strong.
>
> *(Prelude* XI. 324-8)

Here, indeed, Wordsworth has disclosed the true power of memory: "not merely to preserve, but to create emotion, to work within the spirit, and in working, to enlarge understanding and the sense of existence" (Salvesen 104).   That is why Wordsworth says: "Yet something to the memory sticks at last,/When profit may be drawn in times to come" (*Prelude* III, 667-8).   And that is also why he says that our "spots of time" retain a "vivifying" or "renovating" virtue.

So much about the function and the nature of the "spots of time."   Where in Wordsworth's poetry, then, are they to be found? Since Wordsworth himself has said that such moments are "scattered everywhere, taking their date/From our first childhood" (*Prelude* XI, 275-6), it stands to reason to infer that any emotion he recollected in tranquility and composed into lines can be regarded as one "spot of time."   Consequently, a long poem such as *The Prelude* or *The Excursion* can be thought of as containing a good number of "spots of time," while a short poem like many of the so-called "Lyrical Ballads" can be seen as containing a single "spot of time" only.   So far, many critics, such as Geoffrey Hartman, John Ogden, David Ellis, Don Johnson, and Thomas McFarland, have sought instances of the "spots of time" solely in *The prelude*, referring to such incidents or figures as the robbing of birds' nests, the stealing of a boat, the ice-skating, the nutting, the Winander boy, the Discharged Soldier, and the London beggar.[5]   There are also critics who limit the spots of time to those concealing negative entities, such as fear, guilt, and dreariness.   Yu-san Yu, for instance, confines the "spots of time" to the poet's "childhood memories in which emotions such as awe, fear and anxiety are involved, as well as passages centering on the working of the imagination, such as the 'Crossing the Alps' and the 'Ascent of Snowdon' passages" (3).   Such critics as Yu need to know that "spots" can be either bright or dark at times and so all joyful memories in the poet's writing can be regarded as spots of time as well.   Indeed, the delightful scene in "The Daffodils" is no less a spot of time than the dreary scene connected with the Penrith Beacon.   If we can take this broad view, we will find that Wordsworth's entire oeuvre, from his earliest *An Evening Walk* and *Descriptive Sketches* through the *Lyrical Ballads* and *The Prelude* to many of his latest sonnets as in the *Memorials* or *Yarrow Revisited*, is certainly composed in essence of the poet's numerous "spots of time."

IV. Place vs. Memory

In the foregoing section we have come to recognize that as the composite of all "spots of time," memory plays an essential role in Wordsworth's poetical theory and practice.   Now, we need to recognize, too, that Wordsworth's sense of memory is closely related to his sense of place.   In a dissertation I have discussed Wordsworth's poetics as a from-wanderer-to-recluse process of creating poetry.[6] In that process, the poet is at first a wanderer in nature and society. As he wanders from place to place, he may be struck by all things impressive, thus experiencing the "spontaneous overflow of powerful feelings," that is, the initial stage of forming the "spots of time" in his memory.   Later, as the poet-wanderer settles down at a certain place and becomes a recluse (or a recluse-like person), he may then have the leisure and mood to remember things past.   This is the time for him to experience the "emotion recollected in tranquility," that is, the time to call back the "spots of time" in memory for the actual process of composing poems.   From this procedure we can see that place surely plays a double role for Wordsworth.   At first it helps to beget "spots of time" in memory, and finally it helps to recall the "spots of time" from memory so that composition of poetry can begin.   Or, to use Coleridge's terms in his *Biographia Literaria*, it at first helps to arouse the poet's "primary imagination" and then it helps to arouse the poet's "secondary imagination."[7]

That in Wordsworth's poetics place at first plays the role of helping to beget "spots of time" in memory is best explicated with his "Poems on the Naming of Places."   The poems include at least six poems written to name places for or from William Wordsworth himself and such family members of his as Emma (Dorothy) and John Wordsworth, along with Mary, Sarah, and Joanna Hutchinson, the places being named Emma's Dell, Joanna's Rock, William Summit, Mary's Nook, John's Fir-Grove, and Mary's and Sarah's Rocks.[8]   Certainly, naming is an act quite similar to inscribing: it seeks to commemorate something or somebody through the act. According to John G. Dings, in these poems Wordsworth "writes not only about but on the setting, so that language and object are bodily joined" (61).   To this comment I may add that in naming the places the poet has in fact not only described the person and the place to have "language and object bodily joined," but also shown the poet's attitude towards and feeling of both place and person.   In other words, through the viewer's subjective perception, the person's characteristics together with the traits of the place are simultaneously turned into a "spot of time" to be kept and recalled later in the poet's memory—a process much like Marcel's fixing in memory a special sense or significance on a little crumb of Madeleine soaked in lime-flower tea along with his feeling and everything connected with his aunt Leone, as depicted in Proust's *Remembrance of Things Past.*

If Wordsworth needs a place to form a "spot of time" in which to keep his memory of the place together with the things and the person or persons acting in or on it, he needs even more badly a place to recollect the "spots of time" so that poetry can be composed out of it.   What sort of place is this much-needed place, then?   We know Wordsworth was born in the Lake District and he returned to the District to compose his lifelong masterpiece, *The Recluse*, after he had wandered abroad to London and to France.   And we know all of Wordsworth's important works, if not his entire oeuvre, were written in the same District.   How can we account for this fact?

In the "glad preamble" of *The Prelude*, Wordsworth describes the joy he felt of leaving a prison-like city inspired by the "creative breeze" to dedicate himself to "chosen tasks."   In my opinion, the city is an idealization, an emblem of the poet's formerly pent-up state of mind, referring to all cities Wordsworth ever knew—Paris, Bristol, Orleans, Blois, etc., as well as London and Goslar.[9]   The joy he felt was that of gaining freedom from his former bondage.   But, ironically, he newly gained this freedom only to imprison himself again in his self-chosen "hermitage," the "one sweet vale" (*Prelude* I, 115 & 82).   Both the hermitage and the one sweet vale may refer primarily to Grasmere, but they also may impy Racedown.[10]   Anyway, what was in Wordsworth's mind was just a secluded place for his poetic mission.   "Long months of peace ... Long months of ease and undisturbed delight/Are mine in prospect" (*Prelude* I, 26-29).   "For months to come/May dedicate myself to chosen tasks ... the hope/Of active days ... The holy life of music and of verse" (*Prelude* I, 33-34, 50-54).   "... assurance of some work/Of glory, there forthwith to be begun,/Perhaps, too, there performed" (*Prelude* I, 85-87).   It is true that in the Racedown and Alfoxden days the Wordsworths, William and Dorothy, had more or less settled down.   But William then was still in his 'unruly times" grappling with "some noble theme" for his intended magnum opus (v. *Prelude* I, 116-271).   It was only after the composition of *Home at Grasmere*, the first book of the first part of *The Recluse*, sometime in the spring of 1800 that Wordsworth seemed to have settled his lifelong aim: "On man on Nature and on Human life/musing in solitude ...."[11]

Wordsworth's settlement at Grasmere was significant in many ways.   He had indeed assumed the state of a poet living in retirement by this time.   He had returned to his native region, where his love for nature was first nurtured by his mother and then by his foster mother, namely, nature herself.   He had realized a roving school-boy's dream to build a home in this earthly paradise.   This would be "a termination and a last retreat" (*Home at Grasmere*, 147), where his knowledge of the ways of the world, together with his knowledge of great nature, would blend into "some philosophical Song/Of Truth" (*Prelude* I, 230-1).   Henceforth, Wordsworth might be said to have fully matured to life.   The future events might still affect his heart deeply, but nothing could keep him from his musing habit.   He never became the old man of animal tranquility, but he was on the way of turning from a wanderer in this world to a recluse for the other world, although he never quite achieved his aim.

But how come the Vale of Grasmere brought him such joy and gave him such a great hope?   The reasons given in *Home at Grasmere* are simple: it was "the calmest, fairest spot of earth" (73), it gave the sense of "majesty, and beauty, and repose" (143), and "For rest of body, perfect was the spot,/All that luxurious nature could desire,/But stirring to the spirit" (22-24).   In other words, it provided a sort of guardianship for the poet to write in peace, and it also provided a sort of inspiration for the poet to recollect the "spots of time" in tranquility.

We cannot argue with Wordsworth about his sense of the vale, of course.   But it is only natural that a Romantic should choose a beautiful and peaceful place like the Lake District for his inspiration and writing career.   This choice has in fact brought us back to the initial point of this paper: that Wordsworth has the Romantic bias of regarding a rural place with its natural environment including natural men and objects as an ideal place for living and writing while regarding an urban place with its social activities as an awful place for good life.   Therefore, our conclusion about Wordsworth's sense of place is: On one hand, he has a Romantic's common sense of preferring rural or natural places to urban or social places.   On the other hand, he has his own particular sense of regarding all places, rural or urban, as capable of forming "spots of time" in memory, but also of regarding natural places only as suitable for recollecting the "spots of time" from memory so that successful composition of poetry can be achieved.

Notes

1. Here I refer to the 7th R.O.C. British and American Literature Conference held at Tunghai University, Taichung, Taiwan on

December 4, 1999.　The young scholar is Professor Yu-san Yu. Her paper is titled〈渥滋渥斯的《家住葛拉絲湖》與地方意識〉("Wordsworth's *Home at Grasmere* and His Sense of Place").

2. Unless otherwise notified, the parenthesized book number and page number of *The Prelude* refer hereinafter to the 1805 text edited by Ernest de Selincourt.

3. In her biography of Wordsworth, Mary Moorman states that after his mother died, young Wordsworth soon "learnt to transfer to Nature the affection, the faith, the 'religious love' which he had felt for his mother" (3).

4. For an explanation of the changes of this important adjective, see note 2 on page 28 of Jonathan Wordsworth, et al. eds., *The Prelude, 1799, 1805, 1850.*

5. Pauline Wu has mentioned this in her *Wordsworth's Plaintive and Gratulant Voice*, pp. 19-22.　For details, see these critics' works as listed in the bibliography.

6. The dissertation is *From Wanderer to Recluse: A Chinese Reading of Wordsworth*. Reading, England: U of Reading, 1982.

7. For a detailed discussion of the terms, see my paper "Coleridge's Primary and Secondary Imagination."

8. A seventh poem ('A narrow girdle of rough stones and crags …') is sometimes added to the group.　But in this poem the place, called "Point Rash-Judgment," is not named for or from a person, but because of an incident.

9. De Selincourt suggests that the city refers to London while the Norton Critical Edition of *The Prelude* says, "The city … is partly London, partly Goslar."

10. De Selincourt follows Garrod to identify the "one sweet vale" with Racedown while the Norton Critical Edition of *The Prelude* says it is

Grasmere.

11. These are the last two lines of *Home at Grasmere* or the first two lines of the "Prospectus" to *The Prelude*.

Works Consulted

Abrams, M. H., et al., eds.   *The Norton Anthology of English Literature*, 4th Edition, vol. 2.   New York: Norton & Co., 1979.

Blake, William.   "London," in Abrams, 40-41.

Byron, George Gordon.   *Childe Harold's Pilgrimage*, in Abrams, 518-41.

Dings, John G.   *The Mind in Its Place*: *Wordsworth, "Michael" and the Poetry of 1800.*   Salzburg: Humanities, 1973.

Ellis, David.   *Wordsworth, Freud, and the Spots of Human Sufferings.* Cambridge: Cambridge UP, 1985.

Hartman, Geoffrey H.   *Wordsworth's Poetry 1787-1814.*   New Haven: Harvard UP, 1977.

Heffernan, James A. W. "Wordsworth's London: The Imperial Monster." *Studies in Romanticism*, 37 (Fall 1998), 421-43.

Heine, Heinrich.   "Babylonian Sorrows," in Mack, et al., 641-2.

Hopkins, Brooke.   "Wordsworth, Winnicott, and the Claims of the 'Real.'" *Studies in Romanticism*, 37 (Summer 1998), 183-216.

Johnson, Don.   "The Grief Behind the Spots of Time."   *American Image*, 45 (1998), 306.

Lamb, Charles.   *The Letters of Charles and Mary Lamb.*   3 vols. Ed. Edwin W. Marrs, Jr.   Ithaca: Cornell UP, 1975.

Mack, Maynard, et al., eds.   *The Norton Anthology of World Masterpieces*, 6th edition, vol. 2.   New York: Norton, 1992-96.

McFarland, Thomas.   *William Wordsworth: Intensity and Achievement.* Oxford: Claredon, 1992.

Moorman, Mary. *William Wordsworth: A Biography: The Early Years 1770-1803.* Oxford: Oxford UP, 1957.

Ogden, John T.   "The Structure of Imaginative Experience in Wordsworth's *Prelude.*"   *The Wordsworth Circle,* 6 (1975), 293.

Rousseau, Jean-Jacques.   *Confessions,* in Mack, et al., 452-61.

Salvesen, C. G.   *The Landscape of Memory: A Study of Wordsworth's Poetry.* London: Edward Arnold, 1965.

Tung, C. H.   "Some More Epic Analogies in Wordsworth's *The Prelude.*" *Journal of Arts and History,* Vol. XI.   Taichung, Taiwan: National Chung Hsing University, 1981.   11-26.

--------. "Coleridge's Primary and Secondary Imagination."   *Journal of Arts and History,* Vol. XXII.   Taichung, Taiwan: National Chung Hsing University, 1928. 1-6.

--------.   From *Wanderer to Recluse: A Chinese Reading of Wordsworth.* Reading, England: U of Reading, 1982.   (M.Phil. dissertation)

Wordsworth, William.   *Letters of William and Dorothy Wordsworth.* 8 vols.   2nd ed.   Ed. Ernest de Selincourt.   Rev. by C. L. Shaver, Mary Moorman & Alan Hill.   Oxford: Clarendon, 1967.

--------.   *The Prelude: The 1805 Text.*   Ed. Ernest de Selincourt. Oxford: Oxford UP, 1970.

--------.   *The Prelude, 1799, 1805, 1850.*   Ed. Jonathan Wordsworth, et al. New York: Norton, 1979.

--------.   *Guide to the Lakes.*   5th ed.   Ed. Ernest de Selincourt.   Oxford: Oxford UP, 1977.

--------.   *Home at Grasmere.   The Poetical Works of William Wordsworth.*   Ed. William Knight.   London: Macmillan, 1986. Vol. VIII, 235-57.

Wordsworth, William & Samuel Taylor Coleridge.   *Lyrical Ballads.* Ed. R. L. Brett & A. R. Jones.   London: Methuen, 1963-71.

Wu, Pauline L. H.   *Wordsworth's Plaintive and Gratulant Voice: A Study of* ThePrelude as *Confessional Literature.*   Taichung, Taiwan: National Chung Hsing University, 1998.   (M. A. thesis)

Yu, Yu-san.   *"Spots of Time" in Wordsworth's Poetry.*   Manchester: U of Manchester, 1997.   (Ph.D. dissertation)

* This paper first appeared in 2000 in National Chung Hsing University's *Journal of the College of Liberal Arts*, Vol. XXX.

Blake's Dialectical Vision

William Blake (1757-1827) is generally considered the first important figure among "the visionary company" that advanced the English Romantic Movement. His importance in this respect is largely due to the fact that as a true Romantic he upheld the value of vision and expressed his own particular vision of the universe compellingly in his works. Today, therefore, much scholarship has been devoted to the study of Blake's visionary works in connection with his notion of vision. However, have we fully realized the nature of his particular vision? Owing partly to the difficulty of his mythical system, perhaps, the majority of his readers seem to be still groping for light in the dark corner of his vision.

A vision is a particular experience in which a personage, thing, or event appears vividly or credibly to the mind, although not actually present, under the influence of a divine or other agency. Almost all Romantic writers, including Rousseau, Wordsworth, Shelly, Keats, Hugo, etc., have had visions of one sort or another. Actually, many writers, like William Langland (the hypothetical author of *Piers Plowman*), have claimed that certain works of theirs are based entirely on visions. It is said that at the age of four Blake once envisioned the face of God pressed against the window, and by the time he was eight the occurrence of visions had become habitual to him. Blake's visionary faculties, as critics may agree, naturally found expression in his art theories and practices.

Blake makes his fullest, though somewhat cryptic, remarks on vision in his essay titled "A Vision of the Last Judgment." Therein he says, "The Last Judgment is not Fable or Allegory but Vision." Then he goes on to explain:

> Fable or Allegory is a totally distinct & inferior kind of Poetry. Vision or Imagination is a Representation of what Eternally Exists, Really & Unchangeably. Fable or Allegory is Formed by the daughters of Inspiration who in the aggregate are called Jerusalem. Fable is Allegory but what Critics call The Fable is Vision itself. The Hebrew Bible & the Gospel of Jesus are not Allegory but Eternal Vision or Imagination of All that Exists. Note here that Fable or Allegory is Seldom without some Vision. Pilgrim's Progress is full of it, the Greek Poets the same; but Allegory & Vision ought to be known as Two Distinct Things & so called for the Sake of Eternal Life. (Erdman 554)[1]

Here we see three points. First, for Blake vision is no different from imagination, or, as we may infer, vision is but a special kind of imagination. Second, vision is a power to see the permanent rather than the temporary, as it represents "what Eternally Exists, Really & Unchangeably." Third, vision is prophetic or, as Harold Bloom may prefer to call it, apocalyptic because with the aid not of memory but of inspiration it is to reveal a Jerusalem of eternal life.

The three points are all pertinent to Romanticism. For all Romantics extol vision or imagination in slighting fable or allegory. All Romantic truths are supposedly permanent or eternal truths. And Romantic poets often regard themselves as seers or prophets. But the second point is particularly pertinent to our present discussion.

Emphasizing the permanency of vision, Blake says in the same essay:

> The Nature of Visionary Fancy or Imagination is very little Known & the Eternal nature & permanence of its ever Existent Images is considered as less permanent than the things of Vegetative & Generative Nature; yet the Oak dies as well as the Lettuce, but Its Eternal Image & Individuality never dies, but renews by its seed.　Just so the Imaginative Image returns by the seed of Contemplative Thought.　The Writings of the Prophets illustrate these conceptions of the Visionary Fancy by their various sublime & Divine Images as seen in the Worlds of Vision. (Erdman 555)

This argument shows that for Blake a vision is a constant image kept in the imaginative mind for good.　So his conclusion is:

> This world of Imagination is the World of Eternity; it is the Divine bosom into which we shall all go after the death of the Vegetated body.　This World of Imagination is Infinite & Eternal whereas the world of Generation or Vegetation is Finite & for a small moment Temporal.　There Exist in that Eternal World the Permanent Realities of Every Thing which we see reflected in this Vegetable Glass of Nature. (Erdman 555)

The last statement in the above quotation tells Blake's idea of the relationship between the visionary world and the physical world. Plainly the latter is for Blake a mere reflection of the former.　Thus, one question arises: How can we arrive at the visionary world if not through the corporeal eye which sees only the physical world?

Blake evades this question by simply saying: "I question not my Corporeal or Vegetative Eye any more than I would Question a Window concerning a Sight.　I look thro it & not with it" (Erdman 566).　Blake never doubts, as a phenomenologist or post-structuralist critic will do today, that the perceptive organ as a medium of perception is so "transparent" that no perception is untrustworthy.　That is why in his letter to Dr. John Trusler he maintains that

> ... to the Eyes of the Man of Imagination Nature is Imagination itself.　As a man is So he Sees.　As the Eye is formed such are its Powers.　You certainly Mistake when you say that the Visions of Fancy are not to be found in This World.　To Me This World is all One continued Vision of Fancy or Imagination & I feel Flattered when I am told so.

Since this world is to Blake "all One continued Vision of Fancy or Imagination," what, then, is his vision of this world like?　Is it a picture of something eternal and unchangeable as he seems never to have ceased to talk of what he has envisioned?　Paradoxically, the answer is both positive and negative.　For, as I will demonstrate below, Blake's vision is a dialectical vision.　In his vision the one eternal verity is: this world is unchangeably changing!

To say Blake's vision is a dialectical vision is to invite an explanation of the term "dialectic."　In Hegel's philosophical system, as we know, history is not static but contains a rational progression, a dialectical process in which a given concept (*thesis*) necessarily generates its opposite (*antithesis*) and interacts with it to reach a reconciliation (*synthesis*), which then becomes a new thesis to start a new cycle of conceptual interaction and reconciliation.　So, in Hegelian dialectic "no single concept, not even the highest, represents the whole truth; all concepts are only partial truths; truth or knowledge is constituted by the entire system of concepts, every one of which has evolved from a basal concept" (Thilly 481).

Now, is Blake's vision dialectical in the Hegelian sense?   Not exactly, of course.   Blake certainly has the habit of viewing things from two contrary angles.   Hence, "binary opposition" becomes his way of thinking, and it engenders such contrasting pairs of concepts as Innocence vs. Experience and the Prolific vs. the Devouring in his mind.   Also, Blake certainly takes the interaction of contraries as a momentum of progression.   Hence his most famous sayings: "Without contraries is no progression.   Attraction and Repulsion, Reason and Energy, Love and Hate, are necessary to human existence" (*The Marriage of Heaven and Hell*, Plate 3).   However, as some critics have already pointed out, Blake is unlike Hegel in that his contraries do not disappear in some sort of higher synthesis; nor do they change their identities in the dialectical process, as Hegel's opposites do (Nurmi 63).   When Blake talks of the Marriage of Heaven and Hell, for instance, he does not mean that either Heaven or Hell is annulled in the "marriage"; nor does the "marriage" give birth to any "offspring" much unlike the heavenly or the hellish.   While religion "seeks to end the warfare of contraries because it claims to know a reality *beyond* existence, Blake wants the warfare to continue because he seeks a reality *within* existence" (Bloom 55).

It follows, therefore, that Blake sees no mutual negation between his thesis and antithesis.   In fact, "Blake comes to see negation not as the interplay of opposites, but rather as a principle that stands *outside* of the contraries" (Damrosch 180).   And in truth he regards negation as a "false Body" that "must be put off & annihilated":

> There is a Negation, & there is Contrary
> The Negation must be destroyed to redeem the Contraries
> The Negation is the Spectre; the Reasoning Power in Man
> This is a false Body: an Incrustation over my Immortal
> Spirit; a Selfhood, which must be put off & annihilated alway.
>   (*Milton* 40: 32-37)

There is a certain contradiction, indeed, in Blake's wanting contraries without negation.   Yet, it is not hard to understand that in Blake's mind there may be different kinds of contraries, "some of which are easily reconciled, others with great difficulty if at all" (Damrosch 181).   Anyway, for Blake contraries are to be distinguished from negations.

> Negations are not Contraries: Contraries mutually Exist:
> But Negations Exist not: Exceptions & Objections & Unbeliefs
> Exist not: nor shall they ever be Organized for ever & ever.
> (*Jerusalem* 17: 33-35)

While thus distinguishing contraries from negations, Blake makes Los declare: "my Emanation, Alas! will become/My Contrary" (*Jerusalem* 17: 388-39).   So, as M. H. Abrams has observed, for Blake the severed female Emanation is the central type of the contrary to the male.   But "all contraries, in Blake, operate as opposing yet complementary male-female powers which, in their energetic love-hate relationship, are necessary to all modes of progression, organization, and creativity, or procreativity" (260).

With this understanding, then, we can see how far Blake has let his contraries go to accomplish his dialectical vision of this world. First of all, we find Blake's earliest work, *Poetical Sketches*, has already shown signs of his consciousness of the co-existence of opposing forces in the world.   In "To the Evening Star," for example, the poet asks Venus to protect the flocks because he knows that even in evenings of love and peace, "Soon, full soon…the wolf rages wide, /And the lion glares thro' the dun forest" (10-12).   The flock-wolf-lion imagery in this early poem naturally brings us to the two famous contrasting poems "The Lamb" and "The Tyger" in *Songs of Innocence and Experience.*

It is surely redundant to mention that Blake's songs of innocence and songs of experience represent "two contrary states of the human soul," as the poet himself tells us.   Still, some significant points can be made about those most widely-read poems of Blake's.   First, although in the songs of innocence the poet assumes the stance that he is writing "happy songs/Every child may joy to hear" ("Introduction" to the *Songs*, 19-20), the poems do not all depict a happy, innocent world; many of them—e.g., "The Little Black Boy" & "The Chimney Sweeper"—incorporate injustice, evil, and suffering.   This shows Blake's understanding that although we can look at our world with an innocent eye, we must acknowledge that this world is forever a composite of good and evil, joy and sorrow, peace and violence, etc., a world in which God makes both the lamb and the tiger.

In such a dualistic world, Blake does not encourage us to remain innocent, however.   In his later writings, most notably in "The Book of Thel," Blake suggests that naïve innocence must of necessity pass through and assimilate the opposite state of experience and reach the third state called "organized innocence," which comprehends but transcends the first two states, if one is to arrive at perfection.   This idea brings Blake closer to Hegel's idea of synthesis.   Besides, it shows that in Blake's dialectic there are two opposing worlds, the real world of change where innocence and experience exist together, and the ideal world of permanence where no distinction of innocence from experience is necessary as they have become an organized whole.   As a Romantic, Blake naturally hopes that mankind can all transcend the former world and enter the latter with the aid of imagination.

Blake's Romantic aspiration for eternity will become clear if we follow some critics to consider "The Book of Thel" as a debate between the Neoplatonic and the alchemical philosophies.   D. G. Gillham argues that in the poem Thel, who fears to descend into generation and lose her immortal nature, represents the Neoplatonic doctrine while the alchemical beliefs are put forward by the Lily, Cloud, and Clod of Clay, who are content to accept the transience of mortal forms and the cycle of nature (172).   In view of this, then, "The Book of Thel" contains a dialectic of two antique cosmic ideas—those of change and permanence.

The change/permanence contrast is in actuality best illustrated in Blake's mythology concerning the Universal Man and the Four Zoas.   In Blake's mythical system, as we know, man's fall is a fall not away from God but into division, in the course of which the all inclusive Universal Man in Eden is first broken up into exiled parts called the "Four Mighty Ones" or the Four Zoas, who then divide again sexually into male Spectres and female Emanations.   The Universal Man in Eden is in a permanent, unfallen state of being while the Four Zoas stay then in three successively lower states in the fallen world which Blake calls Beulah, Generation, and Ulro. For one to leave the fallen world of change and return to the unfallen world of permanent perfection is for one's divided parts of selfhood to come back to the original, undivided Universal Man, or to accomplish "his resurrection to Unity."[2]

Blake's mythology as such obviously implies that contrariety comes to our fallen world as a necessary result of our repeated division.   Before mankind falls, there is no dialectical progression at all, since the Universal Man has no opposing parts in itself to war against each other.   But after the fall, the Four Mighty Ones as well as the two sexes called Spectre and Emanation simply cannot escape dialectical progression, since they are contraries in one way or another.

It may be easy to identify the male Spectre and the female Emanation as two opposites involved in dialectical processes in this world.   But how can we account for the three fallen states and the Four Zoas in terms of dialectics?   Do the numbers three and four give us any trouble, as dialectic can only take the number two for its logic?

In fact, the three successively lower states of being in the fallen world are but two extremes plus one mean between the two extremes.   On one hand, we have the extreme of Beulah, which, typifying Blake's heaven on earth, is a pastoral condition of easy and relaxed innocence.   On the other hand, we have the extreme of Ulro, which, typifying Blake's hell on earth, is a bleak world of tyranny, negation and isolated selfhood.   Then we have the unhappy (rather than "happy") mean of Generation, which, typifying our normal life on earth, is a realm of common human experience, with both heavenly pleasure and hellish sufferings. So, when we the fallen ones move in the cycle of the three states, we are actually changing between two opposing extremes only, thus actually moving in a dialectical process.

Next, about the Zoas.   In *Jerusalem* we find these lines:

They saw their Wheels rising up poisonous against Albion
Urizen, cold & scientific: Luvah, pitying & weeping
Tharmas, indolent & sullen: Urthona, doubting & despairing
Victims to one another & dreadfully plotting against each other
To prevent Albion walking about in the Four Complexions.
                                                        (43:1-5)

And the Four Zoas are Urizen & Luvah & Tharmas & Urthona
In opposition deadly, and their Wheels in poisonous
And deadly stupor turn'd against each other loud & fierce.
                                                        (74: 4-6)

These lines tell clearly that the Four Mighty Ones are forever in conflict with each other just as the contraries in a dialectic.   Since the Four Zoas represent reason, passion, sensation and instinct, respectively (Ostriker, *Complete Poems*, 1048), they lend themselves easily to psychological interpretations.   W. P. Witcutt, for instance, regards the gods as "symbols of the inner world of man" (20), and discusses convincingly the conflicts among the Zoas as the conflicts between intuition and thought, between thought and feeling, between intuition and feeling, between intuition and sensation, between thought and sensation, and between feeling and sensation (69-91).   So, in Witcutt's study the Four Zoas are two pairs of conflicting contraries at any time or two dialectics working at once with four opposites.

Regarding the names of the Zoas, V. A. De Luca has an interesting study bearing on our present discussion.   De Luca sets the names up in a diagrammatic scheme with Luvah opposing

Tharmas on the east-west axis and Urthona opposing Urizen on the north-south axis.   Then he explains thus:

> The North-South axis, *Urthona-Urizen*, distinguishes itself from the East-west, *Luvah-Tharmas*, by the following properties: the names in the first pair each have three syllables, those of the second, two; the first pair is marked by identity of the first syllable (Ur) and differentiation in the remaining syllables, whereas *Luvah-Tharmas* match final syllables through assonantal rhyme but vary initially; the first pair begins with vowels, the second with consonants; the first pair is vocalically rich, containing in the two names all five vowels, the second pair vocalically poor, sharing only the two back vowels a and u.   To this opposition generated between the two directional axes, we must add oppositions between the poles of each axis. (131)

So, phonetically the naming of the Zoas also implies dialectical oppositions.

At this point it may behoove us to examine some significant lines in a poem Blake copied out in a letter of November 1802 to Thomas Butts.   In that poem Blake at first claims that a double vision is always with him: "With my inward Eye 'tis an old Man grey/With my outward a Thistle across my way" (28-30).   But in the end he claims that he has a fourfold vision though the vision can be threefold, too, and he hopes that we can be kept from a single vision.

> Now I a fourfold vision see
> And a fourfold vision is given to me

> Tis fourfold in my supreme delight
> And threefold in soft Beulah's night
> And twofold always.   May God us keep
> From Single vision & Newton's sleep. (83-88)

These six lines, along with the two aforequoted lines, show that Blake thinks of a poetic genius as someone possessing more than a single view of the world.   To him a poetic genius must have at least a spiritual (inward) eye in addition to his material (outward) eye. Furthermore, if the poet is imaginative enough, he may be able to see the world in four different ways at once.   The four ways are actually correlated to Blake's four states of human existence: Ulro, which is purely material (Newtonian); Generation, which is more material than spiritual; Beulah, which is more spiritual than material; and Eden, which is purely spiritual.   Thus considered, the fourfold vision actually involves a dialectic of the material and the spiritual. Again, the four ways are correlated to the Four Zoas.   For, in Blake's mythology, Urizen, Luvah, Tharmas, and Urthona respectively stand for reason (thought), passion (feeling), sensation, and instinct, which are four faculties a poet can employ to view this world.   Now, the Four Zoas or the four faculties, as we have discussed above, are two pairs of contraries for dialectical processes among themselves.

Up to now, it must be clear that for Blake or *in* Blake, the number 3 or 4 is, in the final analysis, not originally three or four; it is actually derived or developed from 2, the basic number denoting the constitution of any dialectic.   If we bear this in mind, we may then be able to realize Blake's dialectical vision even more comprehensively.

Take the flower trilogy for example.   It is often noted that the concurrence of "My Pretty Rose Tree," "Ah! Sun-flower," and "The Lily" on the same page of *Songs of Experience* (Plate xxiii) is not simply to fill up a page with brief poems about flowers.   Yet, critics simply cannot agree as to what this flower trilogy signifies.   For instance, John E. Grant holds that "the poems evidently present a threefold definition of love" (333), but he cannot accept Joseph H. Wicksteed's symbolic interpretations either to identify the flowers with "earthly love, poetic love, and Human Love" or to associate the three poems with "Innocence, Vision, and Experience," although he thinks it plausible to connect the trilogy with Dante's three states of the afterlife—"transgression and pain," "holy and purifying aspiration," and "beatitude" (333).   I think both Grant and Wicksteed have been led away by the number "three."   For me Blake's three flower poems actually contain two dialectical sets: one is a dialectic between "My Pretty Rose Tree" and "The Lily," and the other is a dialectic between "Ah! Sun-flower" and the other two poems.   In the first set, the rose symbolizes impure human love or love with pains: "But my Rose turned away with jealousy: /And her thorns were my only delight" (7-8).   In contrast, the lily symbolizes pure human love or love without pains since "Nor a thorn nor a threat stain her beauty bright" (4).   On the next level, then, the sun-flower is in contrast with both the rose and the lily because it yearns for neither pure nor impure human love, and it seems to have passed the transient world of sufferings, "where the youth pined away with desire, /And the pale Virgin shrouded in snow" (5-6).   In other words, as it is "weary of time" (1), the sun-flower is beyond human love, not in love like the rose or the lily.   So, it is obvious that Blake has meant to portray the contrary states of human love through the three flowers in two dialectics.

In interpreting the flower symbolism as such, I am aware that I risk suggesting that the three "states" of human love are each stable and static.   In fact, that is not Blake's vision.   We must remind ourselves that Blake's vision is a dialectical one, in which the contrary states are each changing all the time.   One is never purely innocence or experience itself.   Rather, one's innocence or experience is increasing or decreasing in every phase of life.   Likewise, human love is never purely delight or pain.   Rather, it is sometimes more delightful than painful or vice versa.   That is to say, it is always a combination of what the rose and the lily stand for.   To escape this dialectic of delight and pain is to leave this world.   The sun-flower is trying to do that, but it may not know that its aspiration actually involves another dialectic with "time" and "eternity" or "human love" and "divine love" as its two opposites.

Blake's notion of dialectical change is best exemplified by "The Mental Traveller," which, according to Abrams et al., is related to Blake's assertion that "Man passes on but States remain forever" (74, note 1).   The poem, as we know, is a travelogue of a visitor, the Mental Traveller, who comes from the eternal realm of imagination to our fallen, temporal world.   The travelogue shows that the visitor discovers in our existence a double revolving cycle.   On one hand, there is what scholars call "the Orc cycle," in which the spontaneous, all-demanding, rebellious infant Orc ages inevitably into the rigid, materialistic and isolated old man, Urizen, who then reverts to infancy and so begins the cycle anew.   On the other hand, complementary and opposite to the male cycle, there is "the female cycle," which moves "from an old, cruel, oppressive mother figure (or wicked stepmother), through the form of mistress and prolific wife, to that of female infant, and on to oppressive crone again (Abrams, et al., 74, note 1).   These revolving cycles impressively demonstrate the three changing phases seen in Beulah, Generation, and Ulro.   The three phases or states certainly remain forever.   Yet, in a human individual or in mankind's entire culture, the dialectical opposites (male vs. female, youth vs. age) cannot refrain from showing changes in phases.

Dialectical contraries coupled with cyclical change in phases seem to be a mode of thinking habitual to Blake all his life. Therefore, the circle is an important image in Blake's world.   It is noted that in *Jerusalem* he uses the symbol of the wheel ambiguously with two sets of associations:

> One association is with the vehicular form "of imaginative mechanism, the furnace-chariot belonging to Los and Luvah; the other is with the spinning wheel and loom belonging to Enitharmon and Vala; and the meaning of the symbol may relate either to the power of civilization which invented the wheel or to the sense of an inscrutable fate, depending on whether Los and Enitharmon, or Luvah and Vala, are in charge of it. (Frye 380-1)

In point of fact, the ambiguity here denotes a dialectical contrast between the furnace-chariot and the spinning wheel.   And the four figures that are in charge of the two things also form dialectical contrasts among themselves.

Blake's cyclical and dialectical thinking manifests itself not only in his well-known works but also in his rarely-studied works. In a manuscript fragment called *An Island in the Moon*, for example, Brenda Webster finds Blake illustrating the formation of a vicious psychological cycle.   In this work, a mother refuses to let her infant suck presumably because of his biting.   This refusal is then followed by even greater aggression and creates a sadistic cycle continuing through the generations.   One important fact in this cycle is: "each member is victim and aggressor in turn, and the mode of aggression of each recapitulates the others as the surgeon's cutting is the adult enactment of the infant's biting" (Webster 15).   This story of parent-child conflict is, moreover, indicated in "juxtaposing pure lyric and gargantuan smut," which, though confusing to readers, can be taken as "characteristically Blakean effort to resolve recurrent internal conflicts" (Webster 9)[3].   So, the dialectical content of parent-child conflicts is intensified by the dialectical form of juxtaposing two contrasting styles.

In many facets, indeed, has Blake managed to make his dialectical thinking felt. Take *Milton* for example.   Susan Fox observes:

> The central structural and thematic issue of *Milton* is the progressive contrariety of equal but opposite forces.   That contrariety is represented principally in two pairs of characters, the brothers Rintrah and Palamabron and the conjugal couple Milton and Ololon.   The action of the poem is the reconciliation of contraries which have been severed by the perpetuation of the original error of the fall and the vehicle of that reconciliation is the union of Milton and Ololon, which consolidates a complex of unions gathering throughout the poem. (83)

Fox then goes on to assert that the union of Milton and Ololon is "an affirmation of the necessary mutuality of contraries" (83).   And then she discusses the "Redeemed" Palamabron in comparison with the "Reprobate" Rintrah.

While Fox sees dialectical contrariety in the characterization of *Milton*, Kay and Roger Easson see it in the two-book structure of the work.   They believe Blake structured *Milton* in two books (with Book I being the male journey and Book II, the female journey) in order to redeem John Milton's dualism:

> The two-book structure of *Milton* represents the contrary states Blake saw as necessary for spiritual progression and energetic existence.   The contraries oppose the notion of duality, an either/or relationship between opposites, which inevitably results in the tyranny of one over the other, a situation, of course, pervading Natural Religion.   In dualism there is no progression; there is merely fluctuation between opposite poles.   The eternal Milton's journey in Book I and Ololon's journey in Book II parallel each other and create the union of the contraries of male and female, creator and emanation, human and divine. (160)

Besides finding dialectical contrariety in the two-book structure of Milton, the Eassons also find that "Blake also stresses the contrary states in the narrative's three-part thematic pattern":

> The three divisions (more or less equal in length, depending upon which Copy of *Milton* is read) have overlapping implications.   These divisions depict the three stages of a spiritual journey, the three thematic divisions of *Paradise Lost*, and Milton's three classes of men in *Paradise Lost*. Milton called his three classes of men the Elect, the Reprobate, and the Redeemed.   In these labels Blake felt Milton concealed the forms of Satan, Sin, and Death.   Blake

has the three divisions reflect his three classes of men which he, like Milton, calls the Elect, the Reprobate, and the Redeemed.   Unlike Milton, Blake's three classes are not judgmental or dualistic: they are the two contrary states (the Redeemed and the Reprobate) and the negation (the Elect). (163)

Here we may note in passing that as already mentioned above, negation and contrariety are different to Blake: the two notions actually can form another pair of dialectical opposites.

We may pursue Blake's dialectical vision even further in his "composite art." As we all know, Blake did three kinds of artistic work: writing, painting, and engraving.   They were all "available ways of externalizing or objectifying his inner life" or of "recounting his vision" (Punter 3).   But basically, we may say, Blake's works are the composite art of text (the result of writing) and design (the result of painting and engraving).   Between text and design, then, there is a visual-verbal dialectic.   For it is clear that "by the engraving stage text and design had often become so intricately related that neither could be fully interpreted without reference to the other" (Lindsay 12).   According to W. J. T. Michell, "To open one of Blake's books is to be confronted with two equally compelling art forms, each clamouring for primary attention … but that in general Blake moves toward a balance of pictorial and poetic elements" (13). There may be the independence of design from text in the presence of illustrations which do not illustrate (e.g., the frontispiece to *Songs of Experience*).   Nevertheless, "other, subtler kinds of visual-verbal independence and interplay occur—as, for instance, when Blake plays text and design off against one another, an effect rather like counterpoint in music, or, more precisely, like the interaction of image and sound in cinema" (9).   An example Michell gives of this is in Plate 8 of *America* [6], where the text begins with the words "The terror answered: I am Orc, wreath'd round the accursed tree: printed on a cloud bank which hangs over the sea."   But seated on this cloud bank, we find not the youthful Orc but the aged Urizen, his political equivalent (9).   From this example and others we can see all of Blake's pictures "are in some way related to texts" (18). And for Blake, "poetry and painting were to be *multiplied by* one another to give a product larger than the sum of the parts, a reality which might include, but not be limited by, the world of space and time" (31).

In truth, even Blake's entire poetic career can be viewed in the light of dialectics.   We know Blake wrote three genres: lyrics, short prophetic poems, and major Prophetic Books.   But, to be sure, "an overview of Blake's works shows us two contrasting ambitions: the ambition which leads to the highly compressed forms of the lyric, and the other ambition which moves towards the completion of an English epic" (Punter 14).   This fact means that Blake's imagination is both lyrical and epical, although one may assume that in his earlier career he was more lyrical than epical and in his later life he became more and more epical than lyrical.   In other words, the lyrical and the epical in him undergo a dialectical change in his whole career.

Viewed from another angle, Blake can also be said to have written the genres of verse and prose.   Regarding this, Alicia Ostriker says: "in Blake's work there is a vicious wrestling between verse and prose, in which bones are broken and muscles horribly twisted, but neither side ever wins" (*Vision and Verse*, 209). Ostriker's metaphor here may be justified in its own right. However, my opinion is: like the blending of the lyrical and the epical, the blending of verse and prose in Blake is an indication of his dialectical synthesis, which, negating neither, only strengthens the bond.

Viewed from still another angle, Blake's work can also be said to belong to the two special genres: pastoral and satire.   As Blake refers us to the two states of innocence and experience, so he addresses us in both the mild tone of pastoral and the severe tone of satire.   And just as the two states imply each other, so the two tones complement each other throughout his writing career, if only one tone may dominate over the other at times.

Finally, as Michael Ferber suggests, Blake's whole life seems to be a struggle to reconcile the Hebraic ear-oriented temporal sense and the Hellenic eye-oriented spatial sense (182-3).   Indeed, we can hardly say that Blake has any religion.   Yet, he does anticipate an eternal kingdom like any religious man.   In his aspiring for that kingdom, however, we find even his eternity is a dynamic one (Ferber 180).   His Eden is "the reverse of Christianity's static and aristocratic heaven" (Fuller 223).   In his perpetually dynamic republic, dialectics are the rule.   That is why throughout his poetry "there is a profound sense of oppositions: between different faculties in the human psyche, between different approaches to life, between different interpretations of history" (Punter 14-15).   The opposites—be they Reason & Energy, Soul & Body, Restraint &Desire, Angel & Devil, Devourer & Producer, Innocence & Experience, the Neoplatonic & the Alchemical, Heaven & Hell, Temporality & Permanence, Youth & Age, Text and Design, Lyric & Epic, Poetry & Prose, Pastoral & Satire, the Hellenic & the Hebraic, etc.—are all like our two sexes.   They can be synthesized or "married"; they can struggle against or conflict with each other; they can give birth to their composites or "children"; but they can never negate or cancel one another.   Their co-existence is a must, although as time goes on one contrary in a pair may be more dominant than the other in the same pair. This ever-changing binary opposition is a Romantic irony. And this is Blake's dialectical vision in particular.

Notes

1. In this paper hereafter proper punctuation marks are added where Erdman leaves the text unpunctuated.
2. This mythical system is clearly explained in M. H. Abrams, et al., p.23.
3. Webster discusses more parent-child conflicts found in such other works of Blake's as *Tiriel, Visions of the Daughters of Albion,* and *America.*

Works Consulted

Abrams, M. H. *Natural Supernaturalism: Tradition and Resolution in Romantic Literature.* New York: Norton, 1971.

Abrams, M. H., et al., eds. *The Norton Anthology of English Literature.* 5th Ed. Vol. 2. New York: Norton, 1986.

Bloom, Harold. *The Visionary Company: A Reading of English Romantic Poetry.* Ithaca & London: Cornell UP, 1971.

----, ed. *William Blake's The Marriage of Heaven and Hell.* Modern Critical Interpretations. New York: Chelsea House, 1987.

Damrosch, Leopold, Jr. *Symbol and Truth in Blake's Myth.* Princeton, NJ: Princeton UP, 1980.

De Luca, V. A. "Proper Names in the Structural Design of Blake's Myth-Making." *Blake Studies* 8 (1978): 5-22; rpt. in Hilton, 130-42.

Erdman, David V., ed.   *The Complete Poetry and Prose of William Blake*.   Newly Rev. Ed.   New York: Doubleday, 1988.

Fox, Susan.   "The Female as Metaphor in William Blake's Poetry."   *Critical Inquiry*, 3 (spring 1977), 507-519; rpt. in Hilton, 75-90.

Frye, Northrop.   *Fearful Symmetry: A Study of William Blake*.   Princeton, NJ: Princeton UP, 1974.

Fuller, David.   *Blake's Heroic Argument*.   London: Croom Helm, 1988.

Gillham, D. G..   *William Blake*.   Cambridge: At the UP, 1973.

Grant, John E.   "Two Flowers in the Garden of Experience."   *William Blake: Essays for S. Forster Damon*.   Ed.   Alvin H. Rosenfeld.   Providence: Brown UP, 1969.   333-67.

Hilton, Nelson, ed.   *Essential Articles for the Study of William Blake 1970-1984*.   Hamden, CT: Shoe string Press, 1986

Linsay, David W.   *Blake: Songs of Innocence and Experience*.   London: MacMillan, 1989.

Michell, W. J. T.   *Blake's Composite Art: A Study of the Illuminated Poetry*.   Princeton, NJ: Princeton UP, 1978.

Nurmi, Martin K.   "Polar Being."   *William Blake's The Marriage of Heaven and Hell*.   Ed.   Harold Bloom.   59-70.

Ostriker, Alicia.   *Vision and Verse in William Blake*.   Madison & Milwaukee: U of Wisconsin P, 1965.

-----, ed.   *William Blake: The Complete Poems*.   Hamondsworth, Eng.: Penguin Books, 1981.

Punter, David.   *William Blake: Selected Poetry and Prose*.   London & New York: Routledge, 1988.

Thilly, Frank.   *A History of Philosophy*.   *Rev*. Ledger Wood.   New York: Henry Holt, 1951.

Webster, Brenda S.   *Blake's Prophetic Psychology*.   Athens: The U of Georgia P, 1983.

Witcutt, W. P.   *Blake: A Psychological Study.*   London: Hollis & Carter, 1946.

* This paper first appeared in 1997 in National Chung Hsing University's *Journal of the College of Liberal Arts*, Vol. XXVII.

The Notion of Two Wordsworths

Many people have the notion of two Wordsworths—reviewers or critics, biographers or philosophers, the poet's contemporaries or our modern men. The notion is accompanied by problems of various nature—the growth or decline of the poet's mind, the constancy or fickleness of his character, the splitting or fusion of his style, etc. And the notion arises from a great variety of situations—difference in editorial policy, personal taste, or critical bias. All the same. Later studies of Wordsworth are often benefited by the notion, as it helps to promote the idea of trying to approach totality through different partialities. Today, when the poststructuralist concept of plurality reigns over the intellectual world, it certainly behooves us to reconsider the notion.

The notion of two Wordsworths is most clearly spoken out by Herbert Read:

> There are two Wordsworths. There were two Wordsworths even during his life—a real Wordsworth and a legendary Wordsworth. It is the legendary Wordsworth that has persisted in the imagination of the public. In the obvious sense there was the Wordsworth who lived for another forty-three years, forty-three long years devoid of poetic vitality, but filled with another activity which is that of the mind seeking compensations for its defunct emotions. (15-16)

These two Wordsworths are the "early Wordsworth" and the "later Wordsworth" often seen from the poet's biographies and they are connected with the poet's private career and public life, indeed.

But the most impressive suggestion of the notion of two Wordsworths is made by Robert Browning in his poem "The Lost Leader." There the young poet suggests lamentingly that he and other admirers of the poetic leader have ceased to find the ardent, liberal Wordsworth they loved, followed and honored; they now find instead a conservative Wordsworth, who for "a handful of silver" and "a riband to stick in his coat" betrays them, "breaks from the van and the freemen" and "sinks to the rear and the slaves" (ll. 1, 2, 15 & 16).

The notion that the older Wordsworth betrayed his youthful, radical self to become a prosy Tory bore has been very popular, indeed, since Browning's day. But recently Stephen Gill in his new biography of the poet has tried to modify this common notion. For him, once Wordsworth had returned to the Lake District, determined to live dedicated to poetry at whatever cost, his life took on a unity and purpose it had previously lacked. However, this new biographer also sees two Wordsworths:

> Like Blake, Wordsworth was a visionary poet. Unlike Blake, Wordsworth became increasingly determined that people should know it and that his voice should be heard. He cared about his publications, about reviews, about his audience and his public image. Excellent books have been written about Wordsworth the solitary visionary, communing, as Hazlitt put it, only with himself and the universe. Too little attention has been paid to the imperious, self-willed Wordsworth, who wanted to be recognized as an intellectual power. (Gill, vii)

In fact, judging not from his biographical data but from his poetic works, different or even opposing views of Wordsworth have also often been held. Francis Jeffrey, for instance, is known to have proclaimed Wordsworth a mannerist belonging to a school of poets whose poetry is characterized by "vulgarity, affectation and silliness," whose "perverseness and bad taste" make them cling to their "peculiarities of diction," and whose compositions are tinged with the "air of parody, or ludicrous and affected singularity" (McMaster, 92-96). At the same time, however, John Wilson claims that Wordsworth is

> the first man who impregnated all his descriptions of external nature with sentiment or passion... the first man that vindicated the native dignity of human nature... the first man that stripped thought and passion of all vain or foolish disguises... the first man who in poetry knew the real province of language... indisputably the most ORIGINAL POET OF THE AGE. (Ferrier, 401-2)

Jeffrey's and Wilson's opposing views are, of course, strongly colored by their respective editorial policies. A little knowledge of *The Edinburgh Review* and *Blackwood's Edinburgh Magazine* is enough to explain why one indulged in invective against Wordsworth while the other constantly championed him. When we come to Leslie Stephen and Matthew Arnold, however, the controversy is much less explainable. It involves no element of policy. It is linked, I think, more to personal taste, which, as we know, is a very hard matter for fair judgment. Stephen has every right to emphasize the philosopher role played by Wordsworth just as Arnold has to emphasize the lyricist one when in fact Wordsworth plays both.

We cannot deny that Wordsworth is "not merely a melodious writer, or a powerful utterer of deep emotion, but a true philosopher... He is a prophet and a moralist, as well as a mere singer," although it may be doubted that his ethical system is "as distinctive and capable of systematic exposition as that of Butler" (Stephen, 206).   Nor can we deny that "the Wordsworthians are apt to praise him for the wrong things, and to lay far too much stress upon what they call his philosophy," although it may be an over-statement to say "his poetry is the reality, his philosophy... the illusion" (Arnold, xviii-xix).

The Stephen-Arnold controversy seems to have persisted into modern times. John Dover Wilson, for instance, claimed in 1939 that "a consistent body of ideas is certainly discoverable 'by the attentive reader' in Wordsworth's poetry" (42).   Instead of emphasizing Wordsworth's joy as Arnold does, he follows Stephen to emphasize the element of pain and affliction as the source of moral strength.

In fact, the controversy has long been replaced by another set of contrasting views.   In the beginning of the 20th century, A. C. Bradley said that "Wordsworth's morality is of one piece with his optimism and with his determination to seize and exhibit in everything the element of good" (123).   In saying so, Bradley seemed to reconcile Stephen with Arnold.   But he went on to say:

> If we review the subjects of many of Wordsworth's famous poems on human life... we find ourselves in the presence of poverty, crime, insanity, ruined innocence, torturing hopes doomed to extinction, solitary anguish, even despair.   Ignore the manner in which Wordsworth treated his subjects, and you will have to say that his world, so far as humanity is concerned, is a dark world—at least as dark as that of Byron. (123-4)

This view of Wordsworth is quite different from what Arnold sees.

In fact, the Wordsworth of Arnold's view and the Wordsworth of Bradley's are two mutually complementary views of the same person: the former represents Wordsworth "as primarily the simple, affirmative poet of elementary feelings, essential humanity, and vital joy" while the latter represents him "as primarily the complex poet of strangeness, paradox, equivocality, and dark sublimities" (Abrams, 2). M. H. Abrams asserts that the diverse views have been adumbrated by Wordsworth himself in his Preface to the *Lyrical Ballads* and "Essay, Supplementary to the Preface" of his *Poems* of 1815 (1-2). The assertion is roughly true. By the same token we can assert that the diverse views are manifest in the two Wordsworths of his biographers: the "early Wordsworth" of, say, Emile Legouis' *La Jeunesse de William Wordsworth—1770-1798*, and the "later Wordsworth" of, say, Christopher Wordsworth's *Memoirs of William Wordsworth*. Or we can assert that the diverse views are those expressed respectively in the *Lyrical Ballads* and *The Excursion*.

In effect, Wordsworth's life, his poetic theory and his poetry constitute a complete whole. Any debate based on partial readings of the poet can present at most partial truths. Nevertheless, it has one advantage. It can spur people to make further and better studies. The aforesaid Jeffrey-Wilson controversy and Stephen-Arnold debate are useful in this sense. Modern scholars have hopefully followed both voices of, or roads to, Wordsworth as indicated by Arnold and Bradley, and have brought forth a number of studies which are significant in that they no longer tend to restrict themselves to one aspect or one pole of the poet. They tend, instead, to see the poet as a complete personality growing naturally from one stage to another. For example, in biography Mary

Moorman has written a standard complete life; in criticism W. J. B. Owen has given a close account of how Wordsworth's poetics grows from a mimetic to an expressive theory (Jordan, 111).   And in poetry we have numerous studies on the growth of the poet's mind in relation to nature.

The studies on the growth of the poet's mind are not without limitations of their own; they often set their themes within some extrinsic frames of reference, for instance.   However, insofar as the development of their themes is plausible, the studies are often valuable.   Today many recognize the importance of Arthur Beatty's *William Wordsworth: His Doctrine and Art in their Historical Relations*.   One may complain that Beatty "bound Wordsworth rather too tightly to the English Associationist tradition," but one cannot but admit "the strong influence of David Hartley's associationist psychology upon Wordsworth's work" (Jordan, 96). If the theory that Beatty first made popular concerning Wordsworth's belief in the three ages of man—that is, the age of sensation for childhood or boyhood, the age of feeling for youth, and the age of thought for maturity—is not much more than a commonplace,[1] it is nonetheless useful in interpreting the development of the poet's soul. Certainly, the three-stage scheme of division is as mechanic as any other schemes,[2] and thus cannot fit in nicely with the organic nature of the poet's growth in mind.   But as convenient indicators, the stages do bring about analytical clarity at no cost of general truth.

The weakest point about Beatty's work is its implication that Wordsworth believed in the mind's being merely passive.   Later scholars have tried to prove against it by pointing to the transcendental or mystic element in Wordsworth's work. In his *Wordsworth: A Philosophical Approach*, Melvin M. Rader concludes that Wordsworth became more of a transcendentalist as he grew older, and in his

Strange Seas of Thoughts, Newton P. Stallknecht has a chapter on "Hartley Transcendentalised by Coleridge" and considers Wordsworth primarily as a mystic (Jordan, 87). Both Rader and Stallknecht's emphasis on the transcendental or mystic is well grounded. However, the resemblance they see between Wordsworth's ideas and those of Shaftesbury, Rousseau, Spinoza, Kant, Plato, Jakob Boehme, etc., is the resemblance, as it were, felt by the blind man between the elephant and a column, a wall, etc. I do not deny the validity of their findings. But their findings are no better than Beatty's, for they are as local in view of Wordsworth's complete work and as transitory in view of Wordsworth's whole history.

It is a trend of studies after Beatty to see more and more analogies between Wordsworth and other poets, philosophers, or artists of any time and any kind, native and abroad. This is indeed Wordsworth's honor. It shows how comprehensive a soul his is. But however inclusive Wordsworth's mind is, we should not forget that it is an organic growth. And a good study of this growth is one that can present the case clearly with the support of concrete examples from the poet's life and works themselves. In his *The Landscape of Memory*, C. Salvesen holds that "The essentially retrospective nature of Wordsworth's thinking is individual and temporal, grounded in self and in poetry, not in any study of psychology" (45). He then traces the development of Wordsworth's literary awareness of memory in three stages:

> from a more or less Picturesque, or visual, attitude… towards the deeply personal and often sensuous emotions involved in the act of remembering and of describing… to a third, more general, almost mystical feeling for the relation between time passing and human awareness of it by way of memory. (44)

Like Rader and Stallknecht, Salvesen also sees a mystic tendency in Wordsworth.   And like Beatty, he also sees a three-stage development in Wordsworth's mind.   However, in tracing the tendency or development, he relies much less on extrinsic studies of the poet.

Whether or not Wordsworth follows faithfully the Hartleian psychology is yet to be debated.   Before that problem is solved, however, another related, and more puzzling, problem arises—that is, the problem of Wordsworth's "decline."   We may all agree that Wordsworth's mind shows an organic growth from stage to stage, but we simply cannot agree as to where lies the cause of the poet's *seemingly* sudden loss of his poetic power a long way before his closing day.   Various conjectures have been made: "his premature aging, his break with Coleridge, his change of political affiliation, his affair with Annette Vallon, and his intimidation by Francis Jeffrey"—explanations which Willard Sperry thinks are simplistic and insufficient (122).   Sperry himself believes that Wordsworth was doomed to decline before this time as soon as he set up and tried to follow rigidly his poetic theory that stemmed from his conversations with Coleridge.   For, as Sperry also believes, Wordsworth's "supply of past experiences was limited"; after they had been used up, the poet could not but suffer from "a dearth of the necessary subject-matter" (123).

Sperry's own explanation is, of course, no more adequate. Besides, it is questionable whether or not Wordsworth customarily wrote verses "to bear out a preconceived theory about the content of poetry and the manner of its composition" (124).   In my opinion, Wordsworth's Preface to the *Lyrical Ballads* was written to defend or explain his poetry, rather than that his poetry was written to accord with his Preface.   I admit that his theory may to some extent influence his practice.   But his practice, I believe, is mostly conditioned by his emotional and intellectual circumstances which in turn have much to do with experience of not only his past but also his present. To say the poet was led along by his theory is to be led along oneself by Coleridge's account of how the plan of the *Lyrical Ballads* originated and to overlook an important comment of Coleridge's on the Preface and the poems:

> Had Mr. Wordsworth's poems been the silly, the childish things which they were for a long time described as being; had they been really distinguished from the compositions of other poets merely by meanness of language and inanity of thought; had they indeed contained nothing more than what is found in the parodies and pretended imitations of them; they must have sunk at once, a dead weight, into the slough of oblivion, and have dragged the preface along with them. ... With many parts of this preface, in the sense attributed to them and which the words undoubtedly seem to authorize, I never concurred; but, on the contrary objected to them as erroneous in principle, and as contradictory (in appearance at least) both to other parts of the same preface and to the author's own practice in the greater number of the poems themselves. (Watson, 170)

If Sperry has not said the final word about Wordsworth's anti-climax, then what can be the real cause?   Surely the death of Wordsworth's brother had some direct effect, but it is again insufficient as a cause.   In want of good reasons, people seem to begin to wonder if a poetic decline really occurred in Wordsworth. There are scholars who believe that in certain aspects, Wordsworth

never showed any sign of falling off throughout his life.   F. M.
Todd, for instance, maintains that "The story of Wordsworth's
political development is one of growth, but not one of decline or
apostasy; and through it all runs the theme of humanitarian
sympathy" (215).   Miss Edith C. Batho also finds no decline in
Wordsworth's later years in his enthusiasm for liberty and humanity.
She complains:

> Too much stress has usually been laid on his Toryism, except
> in his early days, when it is overlooked, and too little on the
> revolutionary elements in that Toryism.   Moreover, few of
> his critics have realized the close connection between certain
> kinds of Toryism and more than one kind of Radicalism,
> particularly in the later years of Wordsworth's life. (226)

And she concludes that Wordsworth's political development "was a
consistent development, not a swing to the left followed by a swing
to the right" (233).   In this respect, Miss Batho has said pretty much
the same thing as A. V. Dicey, whose remarks on Wordsworth's
political position are: "He was in reality, in regard at any rate to
foreign policy, neither a Whig nor a Tory"; and "Royalist and
conservative as he appeared, he never really ceased... to be in the
deepest and most literal sense a republican" (85).

As in politics, so in religious ideas do scholars tend to see no
inconsistency in Wordsworth. While Miss Batho affirms that Wordsworth's
religious development "was equally consistent" compared with his
political development (233), recently E. Brantley contends that

> in his theory and practice, as they relate to his generally
> religious cast of mind and his specifically spiritual shape of

character, Wordsworth held views consistent with, and even partially indebted to, the well-formulated natural theology of the Evangelical Movement. (141-2)

Brantley even claims that in endeavoring "to remythologize his Christian heritage," Wordsworth "participated, as did the Evangelicals, in the revival and not the secularization or rejection of Christian myth and morality" (2).

This last remark of Brantley's seems to have been made as a challenge to M. H. Abrams' *Natural Supernaturalism*, which uses Wordsworth's "Prospectus" to *The Recluse* as a starting point to discuss the tradition and revolution in romantic literature, the primary trait of which is, as he sees, "to naturalize the supernatural and to humanize the divine" (68).   In fact, Abrams' book is full of well-illustrated points, as far as Wordsworth's religion is concerned. But leaving aside the question of whether or not Wordsworth's is a secularized version of religion, we can at least agree that Wordsworth grew more and more formally religious in his later years. It can be interpreted as a sign of either spiritual growth or spiritual decline, depending on how the term *spirit* is to be conceived—as moral power or as esthetic power.   Morally, to grow formally religious may be to grow better in character.   But, esthetically, it may be to grow worse for creativity.

The question of growth or decline is difficult for studies of Wordsworth's ideas, philosophical, political or religious.   It is even more difficult for studies of Wordsworth's poetry and poetics.   For even when one can see two different Wordsworths in his poetry or poetics, it is very hard to say whether one grows or declines into the other Wordsworth.   R. H. Hutton, for example, says Wordsworth has two styles:

> The earlier style is marked by a pronounced use of objective
> fact, elasticity and buoyancy, and a reserved emotion that is
> suggested rather than expressed.   The later style employs
> less objective fact, with more symbol or bald morality in its
> place.   There is less buoyancy, but the emotion is more
> freely conveyed and accompanied by a richness of effect
> quite foreign to the earlier style.[3]

Granting that this is all truth, what then is the relationship between
the two styles?   A growth or a decline?   Instead of answering this
difficult question, esthetic studies of Wordsworth often choose to
stress the blending of the two Wordsworths.   F. W. Bateson, for
instance, observes "Two Voices" in Wordsworth:

> (i) an essentially objective poetry, evincing a strong sense of
> social responsibility, but crude, naïve and often bathetic (the
> Augustan manner), (ii) an essentially subjective poetry,
> egocentric, sentimental and escapist, but often charming
> because of its spontaneity (the Romantic manner). (14)

The two voices are, of course, comparable with Hutton's two styles.
And Bateson is convinced that the great poems of Wordsworth such
as the best passages in *The Prelude*, in the Lucy series, in "Michael,"
in "Resolution and Independence," and in a considerable number of
other poems are those which combine the two voices "in a new
inclusive whole" (14-5).   Similarly, in Florence Marsh's study of
Wordsworth's imagery, she observes:

> In the great decade the landscape is predominantly one of
> light and life and love; before and after appears the darkness.
> Yet the greatness of the great decade results from Wordsworth's
> seeing the darkness and the light together. (28)

The stressing of the blending effect brings us to Wordsworth's
most puzzling term *Imagination*.   A large number of Wordsworth
studies are concerned with the meaning and application of that term.
Yet we are still often at a loss when facing it.   Is it merely the power
of fusing, synthesizing, or harmonizing, or is it, as Geoffrey H.
Hartman says, "consciousness of self raised to apocalyptic pitch"
(17)?   To what extent is it the same term as Coleridge defines in his
Biographia Literaria?   Is it clearly distinguished from *Fancy*?
When does that power occur?   How can it be impaired and restored?
How can it be "baptized" as John Jones suggests?   A never-ending
series of questions can be raised.

So far I have touched upon the problems of two Wordsworths
accompanied by problems of growth, decline, constancy, fusion, etc.
These problems, together with many others which I have not
mentioned—for instance, textual problems and problems of the poet's
originality, dramatic technique, diction, syntax, etc.—have begot a
great number of studies.   Yet, very few of them, if any, can be said
to have been "solved."   If Wordsworth's works will stand forever
like his lakes, from problems arising therefrom we shall derive an
unending succession of "studying rivers, streams, or rivulets," which
cannot replace the "lakes," but are sure to explain their power, their
beauty and their nature to a more understandable degree.

With this understanding, I say I also see two Wordsworths.
But my two Wordsworths are not exactly the two seen by Jeffrey and
Wilson, nor are they exactly the two seen by Stephen and Arnold (or

Arnold and Bradley), nor are they exactly the two seen by Hutton or Bateson—though mine are, like theirs, indicators of two faces or voices of, or two roads to, the same poet. Again, although my two Wordsworths can be differentiated in time, they are not exactly the two seen from the poet's biographies: the "early Wordsworth" and the "later Wordsworth."

    I call my two Wordsworths the Wanderer Wordsworth and the Recluse Wordsworth. But before I compare them with others' two Wordsworths, let me first explain my meanings. In the *N.E.D.*, a wanderer is defined as "A person or thing that is wandering, or that has long wandered (in various senses of the verb)." And to wander is:

> To move hither and thither without fixed course or certain aim; to be (in motion) without control or direction; to roam, ramble, go idly or restlessly about: to have no fixed abode or station.

In the same dictionary, a recluse is defined as:

> a. A person shut up from the world for the purpose of religious meditation; a monk, hermit, anchorite or anchoress, *spec.* one who remains perpetually shut up in a cell under a vow of strict seclusion. b. One who lives a retired life, one who mixes little with society.

In using "wanderer" and "recluse" as two epithets to designate my two Wordsworths, I follow the dictionary meanings closely. But I take the broadest sense of the words, that is, I intend the words to bear all their possible dictionary meanings. My reasons for doing so are: first, it can give convenience to my discussion; second, it can cover more material for discussion; third and above all, Wordsworth himself also adopts the broadest sense in his poetry. To illustrate the last point, let us consider, for instance, the line "I too have been a wanderer…" in *The Prelude*, VI. It is a line Wordsworth addressed to Coleridge after regretting the departure of the latter for the Mediterranean in search of better health, ("Far art thou *wandered* now in search of health, /And milder breezes…"), and before the description of Wordsworth's own *"wanderings…/*Towards the distant Alps." This shows that in Wordsworth's mind, a tour in search of health or natural beauty could be called a wandering. To be sure, when he said he had been a wanderer, he must have had in mind his childhood "night-wanderings," his "five miles/of pleasant wandering" round the little lake during one vacation time, the "wanderings" in which he had been "busy with the toil of verse" in youth, "those sundry wanderings" with Dorothy in the summer of 1787, his wanderings through Salisbury Plain in 1793, and numerous other walks and tours (*Prel.*, I, 325; II, 315; IV, 101-2; & I, 115).

Besides employing the two epithets in their broadest senses, I also emphasize the contrasting meanings they bear to each other. The contrasting meanings are as follows:

First, as to wander is "to move hither and thither," the Wanderer is one constantly in motion, unlike the Recluse who "remains perpetually shut up in a cell." If the Wanderer can stand for motion or mobility, the Recluse can stand for stasis or stillness.

Second, as to wander is "to move hither and thither without fixed course or certain aim" or "to be (in motion) without control or direction," the Wanderer is characterized by uncertainty, indetermination, aimlessness, changeability, waywardness, etc., contrary to the Recluse's fixity in place and purpose.

Third, as the Recluse is "shut up from the world," he is characterized by unworldliness while the Wanderer can hardly be associated with that attribute because in wandering he normally has some contact, at least, with society.

Fourth, when the Wanderer goes "idly or restlessly about," he is fully exposed to the external world which may stir up his passion or emotion from time to time. In contrast, the recluse, as he pens himself up in his cell, turns always inwards for meditation; he is more distinguished by thoughts than by passions or emotions.

Fifth, the Recluse often involves "a vow" while the Wanderer usually does not.

From the above contrasts, it is clear that in the broadest sense, the Wanderer and the Recluse are two opposing terms; they represent two opposing sets of character traits. Therefore, when I attach them as epithets to Wordsworth, I am pointing out two contrasting types of persons in the same personality. In this sense, I seem to treat Wordsworth as a case of split personality. But it is not so. For, as I conceive, the Wanderer and the Recluse in Wordsworth never occur like Dr. Jekyll and Mr. Hyde, who, as we know, appear in a mutually exclusive manner. In Wordsworth's real life and in his poetry, the two types, as I see, always occur simultaneously. It is only that at some time or other, one type may dominate over the other.

As two opposing sets of character traits, the Wanderer and the Recluse are somewhat similar to the two faces or roads or voices others have found in Wordsworth. For others' two Wordsworths also represent two radically different sets of values found in the same poet. What makes my two Wordsworths different from others' is only the detail of emphasis. By opposing the Wanderer Wordsworth to the Recluse Wordsworth, I stress the contrasts between tendencies towards motion and stasis, uncertainty and fixity, worldiness and unworldiness, feeling (or emotion or heart) and thought (or meditation or head), etc.   But Stephen and Arnold stress the philosophical and the lyrical, or the melancholy and the joyful; Arnold and Bradley stress the simple and the complicated; and both Hutton and Bateson stress the objective and the subjective, aspects or tendencies in Wordsworth.   Yet, of course, even in the detail of emphasis, my two Wordsworths still have something overlapping others'.   For, somehow or other, the Wanderer Wordsworth can be associated with the lyrical, the joyful, the simple and the objective Wordsworth while the Recluse Wordsworth is nearer to the philosophical, the melancholy, the complicated and the subjective Wordsworth.

Again, my two Wordsworths are somewhat like the two Wordsworths of his biographies.   In terms of time, the wanderer did dominate over the recluse in Wordsworth's early life and *vice versa* in his later years.   But strictly speaking, the two terms I use are not indicators of time relationship.   Moreover, as I shall discuss later, the Wanderer and the Recluse are two important types of characters in Wordsworth's poetry.   They may be masks of the poet, but they are far from the real poet.   In his *Wordsworth*, Herbert Read says that his two Wordsworths "were Man and Mask—not Youth and Age, not Energy and Decay, but rather Reality and Myth" (17).   Here I might say my two Wordsworths are all of them and none of them, depending on how the terms are to be conceived.

What interests me, however, is not the relationship between my two Wordsworths and others', but the relationship between the two Wordsworths themselves that I have seen.   To discuss the relationship naturally leads to the problems of growth or decline, constancy or inconstancy, fusion or split.   I have, doubtless, conceived the Wanderer and the Recluse as two opposing types.

But it is precisely these two types, I believe, that constitute the poet Wordsworth.   And it is my contention that in Wordsworth's life, poetry and poetics, there exists a consistent pattern of going from the Wanderer to the Recluse.   As already said, it is the Wanderer that dominates Wordsworth's early life while the Recluse dominates the later years.   But even in the earliest stage the Recluse in Wordsworth is in many ways perceivable, just as the Wanderer in him is still perceivable in his last days.   Biographically, the pattern of "from Wanderer to Recluse" is a matter of degree: the Recluse grows as the Wanderer declines in distinction.   Wordsworth's poetry also betrays the same pattern.   As a whole, his earlier works are works more of Wanderer than Recluse in both quantity and quality while his later works are the reverse.   Besides, as I shall discuss in detail later on, throughout Wordsworth's poetry the Wanderer and the Recluse are the chief embodiments of two recurrent motifs (namely, motion and stasis), by which the poet exposes a great, common human problem (that is, how to achieve mental peace in life) with three solutions (Nature, Art and God). And both the nature of the problem and the validity of its solutions are findings of the poet after a long experience of life in nature and society; they reflect his life process of going from Wanderer to Recluse.   Even in Wordsworth's poetic theory, I see the same from-wanderer-to-recluse pattern is evinced.   But here I do not mean his earlier theoretic essays are more of the Wanderer type and his later essays more of the Recluse type.   What I mean is: his poetic theory is based on the psychology of "from Wanderer to Recluse."   For instance, his famous theoretic pronouncement that "Poetry is the spontaneous overflow of powerful feelings: it takes its origin from emotion recollected in tranquility," is for me a statement involving a number of powers (Observation, Sensibility,

Imagination or Fancy, Memory, Description, Invention, Judgment, etc.), some of which are exercised first by the poet in wandering and others of which are exercised later by the same poet in a reclusive state.

From the pole of the Wanderer to that of the Recluse covers a distance, of course, capable of being divided into stages.   But any way of division is necessarily arbitrary:

> Hard task to analyse a soul, in which,
> Not only general habits and desires,
> But each most obvious and particular thought,
> Not in a mystical and idle sense,
> But in the words of reason deeply weigh'd
> Hath no beginning. (*Prel.*, II, 232-8)

Beatty's tripartite division may still be helpful to my own analysis: His "Age of Sensation" and "Age of Feeling" are roughly correspondent to my "Wanderer-dominated" stage while his "Age of Thought" is roughly the equivalent of my "Recluse-dominated" stage. Rader's five-stage system also helps in its own way.   His stages of "Sensation," "Emotion" and "Fancy" are my "Age of the Wanderer" while his stages of "Reason as an Analytical Faculty" and of "Imagination and synthetic Reason" belong to my "Age of the Recluse."   However, I feel Beatty's last age too general and Rader's last two stages impractical in view of the poet's whole life and works. I feel Beatty's last age should be subdivided into two ages other than Rader's last two stages, which in fact can only apply to the interpretation of *The Prelude*.   And I suggest that the two ages after the subdivision be called the "Age of Poetic Thought" and the "Age of Ordinary Thought."

My idea stems from the distinction of two modes of thought recognized by psychologists. In his *Leviathan*, Hobbes says the train of thoughts or mental discourse is of two sorts:

> The first is *Unguided, without Designe*, and inconstant; Wherein there is no Passionate Thought, to govern and direct those that follow, to it self, as the end and scope of some desire, or other passion: In which case the thoughts are said to wander, and seem impertinent one to another, as in a Dream. Such are commonly the thoughts of men, that are not only without company, but also without care of any thing; though even then their Thoughts are as busie as at other times, but without harmony; as the sound which a Lute out of tune would yield to any man; or in tune, to one that could not play...

> The second is more constant; as being *regulated* by some desire, and designe. For the impression made by such things as we desire, or fear, is strong, permanent, or, (if it cease for a time,) of quick return: so strong it is sometimes, as to hinder and break our sleep. (Macpherson, 95)

The two modes of thought have been variously discussed by later psychologists. But the distinction remains clear: one is associative, fantastic, imaginative, concrete or poetic while the other is voluntary, reasoning, analytical, abstract or ordinary.[4]

Adopting the two modes of thought to describe Wordsworth's age of maturity has at least two advantages. First, in describing the stages leading from the Wanderer to the Recluse, a neat pattern can be achieved by ascribing the "Age of Sensation" and the "Age of

Feeling" to the Wanderer-dominated stage while the "Age of Poetic Thought" and the "Age of Ordinary Thought" are ascribed to the Recluse-dominated stage.   Second, it clarifies the mental development of the poet's mature age and, I think, bears more truth about it than either Beatty's or Rader's system.

My way of division, however, has one drawback common to others'.   That is, it also has a mechanic air about it.   Within the framework of the relationship between the poet's mind and the external world, my system cannot explicitly point out the transcendental or mystic stage that Rader, Stallknecht, Salvesen and others have found, although it can be assigned to the "Age of Poetic Thought."

Meanwhile, my four-stage scheme of Wordsworth's development from Wanderer to Recluse implies the existence of Wordsworth's decline of poetic power sometime in his mature age—an implication seemingly contradictory in a way to my own observation above that the pattern of "from Wanderer to Recluse" is a matter of degree: the Recluse grows as the Wanderer declines in distinction—which plainly says it is only the Wanderer Wordsworth that declines if there is any decline at all.   But there is no contradiction in point of fact. For, as we can all clearly see, the best poetry of Wordsworth occurs when the Wanderer Wordsworth and the Recluse Wordsworth are equally or almost equally combined into one.   In other words, Wordsworth's poetic power is best felt in the two middle ages of my four-stage system when neither the Wanderer nor the Recluse is suppressed to the point of obscurity.

It follows then that I see the cause of Wordsworth's "decline" in his failure to blend or balance two sets of his character traits.   But why should he fail in that respect?   Among other reasons are: "his premature old age, his break with Coleridge, his defection from republicanism, his profession of Toryism and Anglicanism, his affair with Annette Vallon, and the hostile criticism for which Francis Jeffrey was the spokesman" (Sperry, vi).   But I agree with Sperry that these reasons are inadequate.   For me the ultimate important cause can be traced to Wordsworth's retirement to the Lake District. For to retire there is to lose the vigor of the Wanderer Wordsworth that makes the passionate, hence lively, component of his poetry.

Turning from the problem of decline to that of constancy, I believe that Hazlitt, with his usual acumen, was not carrying on a blind attack when in his "Table Talk" series of the *London Magazine* he abused Wordsworth on the ground of his inconsistency of opinion. Indeed, Wordsworth's inconsistency of opinion (of turning from republicanism towards Toryism in politics and from nature worship towards Anglicanism in religion) was as apparent in his later years as that he had turned from a lonely wanderer to a family-bound recluse. Nevertheless, I also agree with Todd, Miss Batho, Dicey, Brantley and others that despite the apparent inconsistency in his later years, Wordsworth remained spiritually the same person engrossed in the ideals of liberty, equality and fraternity.   Spiritually, the family-bound recluse did not exclude the lonely wanderer but coexisted with him.

In fact, what we as well as Hazlitt deplore most in the later Wordsworth is not his seeming inconstancy but his apparent loss of poetic power which the poet himself felt:

> Whither is fled the visionary gleam?
> Where is it now, the glory and the dream?[5]

I have suggested that the loss might be due to the failure of fusion, that is, the failure coming from unbalanced fusion of the two mutually complementary Wordsworths I have seen.   Or, to state it simply, it is due to the over-domination of the Recluse over the Wanderer in Wordsworth's later years.   This, in the terms of Hutton, Bateson, Miss Marsh and others, would be the failure to blend two styles or two voices or two types of imagery.   And, in Abrams' terms, it would be the over-domination of mind over nature.[6]   But no matter in what terms we speak of the same phenomenon, we have actually stepped into the labyrinth of Wordsworth's Imagination, from which this study, together with many others, tries to find a clear way out.

Notes

1. R. D. Havens says that Beatty's three-age division is "a division that would naturally occur to anybody and one often made in tracing the development of painters and writers."   See his *The Mind of a Poet*, p. 463.

2. Melvin M. Rader, for instance, argues for a five-stage system.   See his *Wordsworth: A Philosophical Approach*, Ch. III.

3. James V. Logan's summary, in his *Wordsworthian Criticism*, p. 72, based on Hutton's paper read to the Wordsworth Society in May 1882.   For Hutton's original text, see *Wordsworthiana*, ed., William Knight, pp. 66-7.

4. For the detail, see Frederick Clarke Prescott, *The Poetic Mind*, pp. 36-53.

5. "Intimations of Immortality," ll. 56-7.

6. Abrams asserts that Wordsworth used mind and nature as the "only two generative and operative terms" in describing his spiritual development.   See his *Natural Supernaturalism*, p. 90.

Works Consulted

Abrams, M. H. ed.   *Twentieth Century Views of Wordsworth.*
  Englewood Cliffs, N. J.: Prentice Hall, Inc., 1972.

------ *Natural Supernaturalism.*   New York & London: Norton, 1973.

Arnold, Matthew.   *Poems of Wordsworth.*   London: Chaineys, 1879.

Bateson, F. W.   *Wordsworth: A Re-interpretation.*   London:
  Longmans, 1990.

Batho, Edith C.   *The Later Wordsworth.*   Cambridge: Cambridge UP,
  1933.

Beatty, A.   *William Wordsworth: His Doctrine and Art in Their
  Historical Relations.*   Madison: U of Wisconsin Studies in
  Language and Literature, 1922.

Bradley, A. C.   *Oxford Lectures on Poetry.*   London & New York:
  Oxford U.P., 1965.

Brantley, Richard E.   *Wordsworth's Natural Methodism.*   London &
  New Haven: Yale UP, 1975.

Dicey, A. V.   *The Statesmanship of Wordsworth.*   Oxford: The
  Clarendon Press, 1917.

Ferrier, J. F. ed.   *The Works of Professor Wilson*, Vol. V.   Edinburgh:
  Blackwood, 1965-67.

  Gill, Stephen.   *William Wordsworth: A Life.*   Oxford: Clarendon
Press, 1989.

Hartman, Geoffrey.   *Wordsworth's Poetry 1987-1814.*   New Haven &
  London: Yale UP, 1965.

Havens, R. D.   *The Mind of a Poet.*   Baltimore: Johns Hopkins UP,
  1941.

Jordan, Frank, Jr., ed.   *The English Romantic Poets.*   New York:
  MLA, 1972.

Logan, James V.   *Wordsworthian Criticism.*   Columbus: Ohio State

UP., 1961.

Macpherson, C. B., ed. *Leviathan.* by Hobbes. London: Viking, 1968.

McMaster, Graham, ed. *William Wordsworth.* Penguin Critical Anthologies. Harmondsworth, England: Penguin, 1972.

Marsh, Florence. *Wordsworth's Imagery.* New Haven: Yale UP, 1952.

Prescott, Frederick Clarke. *The Poetic Mind.* Ithaca, NY: Cornell UP, 1992.

Rader, Melvin M. *Wordsworth: A Philosophical Approach.* Oxford: Clarendon, 1967.

Read, Herbert. *Wordsworth.* London: MLN, 1930.

Salvesen, C. G. *The Landscape of Memory.* London: Arnold, 1965.

Sperry, Willard. *Wordsworth's Anti-climax.* Cambridge, MS: Harvard UP., 1935.

Stallknecht, N. P. *Strange Seas of Thought.* Bloomington: Indiana UP., 1962.

Stephen, Leslie. "Wordsworth's Ethics." *Cornhill Magazine* XXXIV (1876).

Todd, F. M. *Politics and the Poet.* London: Methuen, 1957.

Watson, George, ed. *Biographia Literaria.* By S. T. Coleridge. Everyman's Library. London: Dent, 1975.

Wilson, John Dover. *Two Critics of Wordsworth.* Cambridge: Cambridge UP, 1939.

* This paper first appeared in 1994 in National Chung Hsing University's *Journal of Arts and History*, Vol. XXIV.

From Delight to Wisdom:
Frost's Poetic Theory or Poetic Structure?

It is well known that Robert Frost, in a foreword to his *Collected Poems* (1939), wrote: a poem "begins in delight and ends in wisdom."[1] But what does this terse statement mean? Does it imply a pragmatic or expressive theory of poetry? Or does it refer to a structural principle demonstrable by his poems?

The terms *delight* and *wisdom* lead us automatically to think of Horace's statement that the aim of the poet is "either to benefic, or to make his words at once please and give lessons of life" (73). And, judging from his poetic theory and practice, Frost does have his pragmatic considerations of poetry. His emphasizing the importance of form—which refers to a composite of such things as "stanzaic pattern; rhythm and rhyme relationships; balance and equilibrium of structure; controlled unbalance; relation of emotion to emotion, thought to thought, image to metaphor, specific to general, trivial to significant, transient to permanent" (Isaacs 73); and other heterogeneous elements capable of blending into a single autonomous unit—and his defining poetry as "a clarification of reality" (Isaacs 64) show that Frost strives both to delight and instruct by his poetry. That is why he says, "In making a poem, one has no right to think of anything but subject matter, and after making it, no right to boast of anything but form."[2]

The fact that Frost will not sacrifice form for content or vice versa is again testified in his aiming to make a new sort of "music" in his poetry which he ambiguously calls "the sound of sense" (a term necessarily reminds one of Pope's line: "The sound must seem an echo to the sense."). According to William H. Pritchard, the phrase "the sound of sense" has two meanings:

> The phrase may accommodate either an underlining of "sound" or of "sense," thereby setting up a playful shuttling between the poem as communicating something, some grain of wisdom or truth about the world (the sound of *sense*) and the poem as wholly embodying that truth through its particular music, so that one is mainly aware of something heard (the *sound* of sense). (77)

These two meanings, in fact, go to affirm that Frost does claim for poetry a double function: the Horatian idea of delighting and teaching at the same time.

However, if we probe deeper into Frost's statement that "A poem begins in delight and ends in wisdom," we find the assertion is more an expressive than a pragmatic theory of poetry. It is, to be sure, a description of his concept of the creative process. As Lawrance Thompson has pointed out, Frost has said again and again that there is a striking analogy between the course of a true poem and of a true love. Each begins as an impulse, a disturbing excitement, and each ends as an understanding:

> No one can really hold that the ecstasy should be static and stand still in one place. It begins in delight, it inclines to the impulse, it assumes direction with the first line laid down, it

runs a course of lucky events, and ends in a clarification of life—not necessarily a great clarification, such as sects and cults are founded on, but in a momentary stay against confusion.   It has denouement.   It has an outcome that though unforeseen was predestined from the first image of the original mood. (quoted in Thompson 21)

But why should this poetic beginning be a sort of delight rather than pain?   Frost once said this, too: "A poem begins with a lump in the throat; a home-sickness or a love-sickness.   It is a reaching-out toward expression; an effort to find fulfillment.   A complete poem is one where an emotion has found its thought and the thought has found the words."[3]   So, it is clear that the delight stems from the moment of finding the thought for the emotion or finding the words for the thought.   The pleasure of finding a thought is implied in this other famous statement of Frost's: "For me the initial delight is in the surprise of remembering something I didn't know I knew."[4]   And the pleasure of finding the words should be extended to cover the poet's pleasure in discovering images, metaphors, and other technical matters constitutive of "form."   Based on this expressive theory, Thompson asserts that Frost's creative process involves two kinds of recognition: "The first may occur when some experience in the present inspires an emotional recognition that is more a matter of sense impression than of clear mental perception" (22).   (Is this indeed the stage correspondent to Wordsworth's "spontaneous overflow of powerful feelings"?)   "The second occurs when the emotional pleasure is derived from the sudden mental perception of a thought which comes into sharp focus through the discovery and recognition of a particularly apt correspondence or analogy" (24).   Thus, Thompson sees two basic approaches of creating poetry in Frost:

The first begins as an emotional response which gradually finds its resolution in a thought metaphorically expressed; the second begins with the perception of the metaphor, and the rational focus is so pleasurable in its sudden discovery that it produces an emotional afterglow.   The first leads the poet to venture into the writing of the poem as an act of faith, without foreseeing the outcome; the second leads the poet to give shape and weight to a rational correspondence which has been perceived clearly before he begins the writing of the poem. (24)

It follows, then, that "A poem begins in delight and ends in wisdom" is indeed no more descriptive of a poet's pragmatic concern with the functions of poetry than of his creative process.   Now, when we examine Frost's poems, can we find traces of this process hidden behind the products?

Interestingly enough, a good number of Frost's best poems seem to demonstrate this from-delight-to-wisdom pattern.   Take his most famous poem "Stopping by Woods on a Snowy Evening" for example.   It begins with the meditative speaker's description of a little dramatic scene which has prompted him into deep thought, and it ends with his symbolic understanding that

The woods are lovely, dark, and deep,
But I have promises to keep,
And miles to go before I sleep,
And miles to go before I sleep.

To be sure, the three stanzas prior to the last concluding stanza do not in any obvious manner manifest the speaker's being delighted in the presence of the scene.   If there is any delight, it is the author's and the reader's.   The author is delighted to have found some symbolic meaning in the common scene, and he is delighted to be able to put his finding in words pleasurable to the reader.   On the other hand, the reader is first pleased with the beauty that goes with the verse form and its presented details, and then pleased with the suggestive ending stanza which represents a sort of insight into life.

Philip L. Gerber points out that for Frost the essential poem arrives in a homogeneous trinity of three parts: the point or idea, the details, and the technique (92).   The poet is delighted to get the point or idea, and he is equally delighted to find the details and the technique to present the point or idea.   So the ultimate end of poetry is wisdom rather than delight.   Frost simply agrees with Emerson that "it is not meters, but a meter-making argument that makes a poem," and that "the thought and the form are equal in the order of time, but in the order of genesis the thought is prior to the form" (33). It is only that in writing many of his best poems Frost is evidently choosing to so arrange his details and so use his technique that the point or idea is not revealed until the end of the poem.   "The Road Not Taken"—another famous poem of his—for instance, gains its significant weight also in the last lines:

> Two roads diverged in a wood, and I—
> I took the one less traveled by,
> And that has made all the difference.

In Robert E. Spiller and others' *Literary History of the United States*, Frost is said to be "a metaphysical poet in the tradition of

Emerson and Emily Dickinson, with all that term implies of the poet's desire to go beyond the seen to the unseen, but his imagery is less involved than that of the older metaphysicals" (1191).   And it is further explained thus: "Most of his poems fix on the mysterious moment when the two planes cross.   Hasty readers, noting only the quiet beginning in what appears to be a simple anecdote about a person, event, or object commonly enough observed, fail to see how the commonness gradually disappears or, better, how it becomes transfigured" (1191).   Therefore, it is concluded that "The most dramatic moment in a Frost poem is the kind of anagnorisis or denouement when the mundane fact achieves its full metaphysical significance" (1191).   The "quiet beginning" is really insipid rather than delightful for the "hasty readers" at times.   But for the poet it is the necessary preparation for the delightful moment of anagnorisis. In truth, it is often a vicarious description, using the speaker (or, rather, meditator) as the poet's mouthpiece, of how the joy of finding the "full metaphysical significance" in the "mundane fact" is achieved.   In the light of this, a Frost poem seems to be a psychological record of how a "truth" is revealed to the poet.

It is generally understood that Frost has been greatly influenced by Wordsworth although he would not claim himself, nor would we claim him, to be simply the great English Romantic's heir, given their mutual attraction to nature, pastoral, and ballad.   In an essay Sydney Lea has detected the tendency that Wordsworth's pastoral "sublime" has dropped down to Frost's common "rigmarole" in comparing the two poets.[5]   I grant that Frost's language is at times more prosaic and hence more like a rigmarole.   But I must hold that Frost is no less sublime than Wordsworth in trying to elevate the vulgar ego into the high realm of truth from the routine everyday life. Just read this poem:

A head thrusts in as for the view,
But where it is it thrusts in from
Or what it is it thrusts into
By that Cyb'laean avenue,
And what can of its coming come,
And whither it will be withdrawn,
And what take hence or leave behind,
These things the mind has pondered on
A moment and still asking gone.
Strange apparition of the mind!
But the impervious geode
Was entered, and its inner crust
Of crystals with a ray cathode
At every point and facet glowed
In answer to the mental thrust.

Eyes seeking the response of eyes
Bring out the stars, bring out the flowers,
Thus concentrating earth and skies
So none need be afraid of size.
All revelation has been ours.

Yes, all revelation has been ours.   But Wordsworth's phrasing is: "how exquisitely the external world is fitted to the mind."[6]   Both poets' real concern is with our mental power.

For me Frost differs from Wordsworth not in their aim, but in their method.   They both aim to present "truth."   But while Wordsworth employs the form of "lyrical ballad," Frost adopts largely the technique of the so-called "conversation piece," which

Coleridge is better at than his poet-friend.   The "conversation poems," as exemplified by Coleridge's "Frost at Midnight," "The Nightingale," "This Lime-Tree Bower My Prison," etc., are poems in which the poet pretends to be talking to someone familiar to him (his son, friend, etc.).   Such poems have a typical structure.   According to John Colmer:

> The structure consists of three main sections: an introduction in which the poet's situation is established and the atmosphere miraculously evoked through a few simple details; a central meditative section in which the subtlest modulations of thought and emotion are exactly communicated; lastly, a return to the original situation, but with "new acquist of true experience."   And in such a poem, although the diction is conversational, "the effect is not that of direct address but rather of overhearing a quiet soliloquy." (26-27)

Now, a Frost poem like "Birches" or "The Wood-Pile" is, of course, not conversational in the sense that Coleridge's "The Eolian Harp" or "Frost at Midnight" is.   Frost's poems are not directly addressed to any particular individual, but Coleridge's are (to Sara Fricker and Hartley respectively in the two poems we have just mentioned above).   But in reading "Birches" or "The Wood-Pile," we feel the speaker therein seems to be talking to someone, too. Anyway, the tone and the speech style of both Coleridge's and Frost's poems are really conversational although the effect is indeed that of an overheard quiet soliloquy.

Again, each of Coleridge's two examples of "conversation poems" does consist of the three main sections as Colmer has pointed out.   "The Eolian Harp" begins and ends with a description of the situation Sara is in (the cot, etc.); "Frost at Midnight" begins and ends with mentioning the frost.   And in the central section the emotionally aroused speaker (or poet) carries on an insightful meditation based on the scene observed and comes up with a sudden realization of truth: that "The lovely shapes and sounds intelligible" are God's "eternal language" with which he "doth teach Himself in all, and all things in himself"; and that there is "the one Life within us and abroad": "all of animated nature be but organic Harps diversely framed."   In comparison, we find Frost's "Birches" and "The Wood-Pile" do not begin and end with the same described or mentioned scene.   But each does begin with a scene description which then gives rise to the insightful meditation.   It is only that in Frost's poem the speaker seldom gives lyrical outcries and the truth arrived at is seldom uttered clearly but hinted at by understatement: "One could do worse than be a swinger of birches"; the wood-pile is left "far from a useful fireplace to warm the frozen swamp as best it could with the slow smokeless burning of decay."   So, we see that Frost is basically following the aim of a "conversation piece," which is to reveal truth through describing an observed scene.   But while he keeps the conversational tone and style, he never adopts the structure of a typical "conversation poem."

Mention may be made here of the dramatic monologue, a poetic genre sometimes not easily distinguished from the "conversation piece."   As we know, a dramatic monologue is a poem in which there is one imaginary speaker addressing an imaginary audience. Consequently, the speech therein is conversational, too.   But while the chief purpose of a conversation piece is to reveal general truth about our world or life, the main target of a dramatic monologue is to reveal, in dramatic irony, things about the imaginary speaker and/or the people spoken to or of: the former is oriented towards theme, the latter towards character.   Thus, after reading Coleridge's "This Lime-Tree Bower My Prison," we gain chiefly the lesson that "Nature ne'er deserts the wise and pure" or "No sound is dissonant which tells of life," whereas after reading Browning's "My Last Duchess," we mainly learn a lot about the Duke's boastful, arrogant, cruel and narrow-minded character and also the characters of the innocent and tender-hearted Duchess and the obedient emissary.

Another thing sets off a dramatic monologue in contrast to a conversation piece.   In a dramatic monologue like Browning's, the imaginary speaker is always identifiable as somebody other than the poet (Duke of Ferrara, a monk in the Spanish Cloister, etc.).   But in a conversation poem like Coleridge's, the speaker is often presumably the poet himself.   However, in both types of poetry the person addressed can be identified, although in the former type the addressee (e.g., the emissary in "My Last Duchess") is often not a named intimate person while in the latter type the addressee (e.g., Sara in "The Eolian Harp") is often a named close friend.

Now, it occurs to me that Frost's conversational verse seems to be a third type developed out of the "conversation piece" and the dramatic monologue.   It has the truth-revealing purpose of a conversation piece.   Yet, the speaker in it cannot be identified with the poet but must be someone else, who experiences something as he describes in the poem.   And this third person is speaking to an unidentified audience, who may therefore be easily taken to be the reader of the poem.   Nevertheless, the tone of the speech is indeed conversational.   And one may feel that the speech style is not so elevated as that of Coleridge's conversation poems; it tends more to the vulgar and yet realistic speech of Browning's dramatic monologues.

Take the poem "After Apple-Picking" for example.   The entire poem goes thus:

> My long two-pointed ladder's sticking through a tree
> Toward heaven still,
> And there's a barrel that I didn't fill
> Beside it, and there may be two or three
> Apples I didn't pick upon some bough.
> But I am done with apple-picking now.
> Essence of winter sleep is on the night,
> The scent of apples: I am drowsing off.
> I cannot rub the strangeness from my sight
> I got from looking through a pane of glass
> I skimmed this morning from the drinking trough
> And held against the world of hoary grass.
> It melted, and I let it fall and break.
> But I was well
> Upon my way to sleep before it fell,
> And I could tell
> What from my dreaming was about to take.
> Magnified apples appear and disappear,
> Stem end and blossom end,
> And every fleck of russet showing clear.
> My instep arch not only keeps the ache,
> It keeps the pressure of a ladder-round.
> I feel the ladder sway as the boughs bend.
> And I keep hearing from the cellar bin
> The rumbling sound
> Of load on load of apples coming in.
> For I have had too much

Of apple-picking: I am overtired
Of the great harvest I myself desired.
There were ten thousand fruit to touch,
Cherish in hand, lift down, and not let fall.
For all
That struck the earth,
No matter if not bruised or spiked with stubble,
Went surely to the cider-apple heap
As of no worth.
One can see what will trouble
This sleep of mine, whatever sleep it is.
Were he not gone,
The woodchuck could say whether it's like his
Long sleep, as I describe its coming on,
Or just some human sleep.

Here indeed is a conscientious apple-picker's inner voice.   But this voice is so verbalized that it reads as if the apple-picker is talking to an unspecified person about his task of apple-picking and his concern about his after-task rest and sleep.   The entire poem with its details goes to suggest, of course, that the "human sleep" is not like a woodchuck's "long sleep" in that it may be "troubled" in the form of a dream (in which one's conscience emerges) over the pre-sleep task. So the center of this "conversational monologue," so to speak, is this sleep theme.   Although this apple-picker's conscientious character is also revealed in his speech, it is obviously not the poet's concern, nor the reader's focus of attention.

After an examination of Frost's *Complete Poems*, Elizabeth Isaacs says, "he has used mainly three genres: lyric, dramatic narrative, and satire (a term which is used here to include fable, parable, epigram, poetic essay, sermon, and oration)" (83).   In reality, all the three main genres of Frost's are tinged more or less with the characteristics of what I may call "conversational monologue."   The following poem ("Desert Places") is assigned to the category of "lyric."   But is it purely lyrical?

> Snow falling and night falling fast, oh, fast
> In a field I looked into going past,
> And the ground almost covered smooth in snow,
> But a few weeds and stubble showing last.
>
> The woods around it have it—it is theirs.
> All animals are smothered in their lairs.
> I am too absent-spirited to count;
> The loneliness includes me unawares.
>
> And lonely as it is that loneliness
> Will be more lonely ere it will be less—
> A blanker whiteness of benighted snow
> With no expression, nothing to express.
>
> They cannot scare me with their empty spaces
> Between stars—on stars where no human race is.
> I have it in me so much nearer home
> To scare myself with my own desert places.

I would say the tone is more meditative than lyrical, and the meditation with its quiet beginning of scene description just goes to end in the revelatory truth that there are desert places in one's own mind as well as in the outer space.   This revelation-centered structure is the structure of a "conversation piece," and the poem does sound like a conversation between the meditative speaker (who is not necessarily the poet) and an unidentified person, who, just like the reader, is just listening for the time being.   But since this conversation is in actuality an interior monologue (hence lyrical), I deem it not unseemly to call it, paradoxically, a "conversational monologue."

In a dramatic narrative like "The Death of the Hired Man," to be sure, the narrator's lyrical meditation is mostly replaced by the characters' dialogues.   In the present example, for instance, the narrator functions chiefly to introduce the characters (Mary, and her husband Warren, and the hired man Silas), describe the situation they are in, and tell the sequence of events—just like a narrator in any story.   But the narrator also speaks in a plain conversational language.   See, for example, these beginning lines of the poem:

> Mary sat musing on the lamp-flame at the table
> Waiting for Warren.   When she heard his step,
> She ran on tip-toe down the darkened passage
> To meet him in the doorway with the news
> And put him on his guard.   "Silas is back."

And conversational language, of course, is used in the dialogues of the characters.   Yet, all of the language is again truth-centered. Here the truth is: "Home is the place where, when you have to go there,/They have to take you in."   The hired man's coming back to die in his former employer's house is to tell us this humanitarian definition of home.

When we come to a satire like "Departmental," we find that it also follows the basic pattern of scene description plus truth revelation, and the language is again conversational.   It begins with describing "An ant on the tablecloth/Ran into a dormant moth/Of many times his size."   Then it tells how different ants react differently to what they meet and often pass with unconcern when it is not connected with their assigned tasks.   So, finally the poem ends with the truthful comment: "It couldn't be called ungentle./But how thoroughly departmental."

I will not bother to discuss in detail all Frost poems that are capable of being analyzed in terms of "conversational monologue." Suffice it that such other frequently-read poems as "Mending Wall," "Hyla Brook," "Out, Out," "Two Look at Two," "The Need of Being Versed in Country Things," "Two Tramps in Mud Time," "Design," and "Closed for Good" are really "conversational monologues" in like manner, though their verse forms vary from one poem to another.

Some good poems of Frost's are, of course, not written in the manner of "conversational monologues."   "Tree at My Window," for instance, is a speech addressed to the tree at the speaker's window, not a talk to an unspecified listener.   "Fire and Ice" is just a simple assertion without any foregoing description of an outer scene or account of an anecdote.   And "A Missive Missile" has a scene and an anecdote, but it is something bordering on a fantasy, not a real situation.   However, all these poems have something in common with all the other poems mentioned or discussed above, that is, each of them bears a truth stated or suggested, thus in conformity with Frost's emphasis on wisdom as the essence of poetry.

Once, referring to Pound's review in *Poetry*, Frost wrote to Thomas Mosher, a Maine book collector and publisher: "You are not going to make the mistake that Pound makes of assuming that my simplicity is that of the untutored child.   I am not undesigning"

(Pritchard 69-70).   In fact, Frost exerts himself so much in designing his poems that he has really brought forth a "new free form" combining the advantages of the traditional verse forms and the modern "free verse," while avoiding the disadvantages of the modernists' experimental forms (Gerber 766ff.).   As a result, his poetry is often really fraught with the "sound of sense" for the "ear readers," if not the "shape of sense" for the "eye readers."   And that is indeed one great source of delight he can render to his readers. However, do his good poems really all follow the from-delight-to-wisdom pattern?

Regarding Frost's conversational style, Yvor Winters thus comments: "...it has helped to make him seem 'natural.'   But poetry is not conversation, and I see no reason why poetry should be called upon to imitate conversation.   Conversation is the most careless and formless of human utterance; it is spontaneous and unrevised, and its vocabulary is commonly limited" (59).   Perhaps Winters does not understand that Frost's conversational style is not wholly careless and formless like an ordinary conversation. Perhaps he cannot appreciate his technique of "conversational monologue" as explored in this paper.   But one must agree that before one comes to the meaningful revelation of insightful truth towards the end of a typical Frost poem, one is really very liable to take the "conversational monologue" for a rigmarole worth no more than one's casual attention.   On the part of the reader, indeed, a typical Frost poem does not necessarily begin in delight and end in wisdom, as far as its effect is concerned.   In the concluding paragraph of his "The Figure a Poem Makes," Frost says: "Originality and initiative are what I ask for my country.   For myself the originality need be no more than the freshness of a poem run in the way I have described: from delight to wisdom."   But the way from delight to wisdom is just Frost's genetic way of creating poetry, and perhaps his aim of writing, too.   He may wish to make it a structural principle of his poems as well.   Yet, his technique, as far as the device of "conversational monologue" is concerned, more often than not fails to achieve his aim.   One may be delighted to find wisdom in the end of his poem.   But one may not be delighted to go through a rigmarole first in order to reach a delightful truth.

Notes

1. The foreword is an essay titled "The Figure a Poem Makes." Quoted in Untermeyer, ed. *A Concise Treasury of Great Poems*, p. 440.
2. "The Poetry of Amy Lowell," *Christian Science Monitor*, (May 16, 1925), p. 31. Quoted in Isaacs, p. 65.
3. This is printed on the dust jacket of *West-running Brook* (New York: Holt, Rinehart & Winston, Inc., 1929).
4. See "The Figure a Poem Makes."   Quoted in Thompson, p. 21.
5. See his "From Sublime to Rigamarole: Relations of Frost to Wordsworth," in Bloom, pp. 85-110.
6. Prospectus to *The Recluse*, II. 66-68.

Works Consulted

Bloom, Harold, ed.   *Robert Frost: Modern Critical Views*.   New York: Chelsea House Publishers, 1986.

Colmer, John.   *Coleridge: Selected Poems*.   London: Oxford UP, 1965.

Cox, James M., ed.   *Robert Frost: Twentieth-Century Views*.   Englewood Cliffs, NJ: Prentice-hall, Inc., 1962.

Emerson, Waldo. "The Poet," in Cox 32-34.

Frost, Robert. "The Figure a Poem Makes." Preface to *Collected Poems.* New York: Henry Holt & Co., 1939.

Gerber, Philip. *Robert Frost.* Revised edition. Boston: Twayne Publishers, 1982

Horace. "The Art of Poetry." *Critical Theory Since Plato.* Ed. Hazard Adams. New York: Harcourt Brace Jovanovich, 1971. 68-75.

Isaacs, Elizabeth. *An Introduction to Robert Frost.* New York: Haskell House, 1972.

Lea, Sydney. "From Sublime to Rigamarole: Relations of Frost to Wordsworth," in Bloom, 85-110.

Pritchard, William H. *Frost: A Literary Life Reconsidered.* New York: Oxford UP, 1984.

Spiller, Robert E. et al. *Literary History of the United States.* 3rd edition. New York: The Macmillan Co., 1963.

Thompson, Lawrance. "Robert Frost's Theory of Poetry," in Cox, 20-24.

Untermeyer, Louis, ed. *A Concise Treasury of Great Poems.* New York: Pocket Books, 1975.

Winters, Yvor. "Robert Frost: or, the Spiritual Drifter as Poet," in Cox, 58-60.

* This paper first appeared in 1993 in National Chung Hsing University's *Journal of Arts and History*, Vol. XXIII.

A New Linguistic Analysis
of Arnold's "Dover Beach"

This paper claims to be a new linguistic analysis on the ground that it is indeed different from a traditional linguistic approach to literature, which, as exemplified by the case studies in Donald C. Freeman's *Linguistics and Literary Style,* is concerned with literary work as merely a text composed of such formal linguistic features as sound, sense, and structure (phonological, semantic, and syntactic components). Such an old-fashioned approach seems to treat a text as the result of a mere locutionary act, not an illocutionary or perlocutionary act, to use J. L. Austin's terms. Thus, such a linguistic analysis is just stylistics as we commonly understand the term. Freeman, for instance, divides recent work in linguistic stylistics into three types: style as deviation from the norm, style as recurrence or convergence of textual pattern, and style as a particular exploitation of a grammar of possibilities (4). These three types, as their descriptions indicate, only employ the methodology of formal linguistics and therefore are confined to the view of locutionary force only.

In recent years, as we know, formal linguistics has given way to pragmatics as the theories of discourse and speech act exert their influence on modern linguistics. In consequence, a new linguistic approach to literature has appeared. "In this approach," Roger Fowler's *Dictionary of Modern Critical Terms* explains, "language is regarded as far more than formal structure and communicated ideas: it is seen as an interpersonal practice with causes and effects in social structure, and ideological implications." This means that any form of language, including a literary text, is considered as certain discourse in certain context. So the dictionary further explains:

> Linguistic criticism on discourse premises is a historically grounded practice of analysis, seeking to interpret texts with reference to their and our cultural contexts and ideological systems. In this approach the analysis of linguistic form, and reference to context, are integrated rather than divorced as in most modern criticism. (133)

In line with this new linguistic idea, R. A. York holds, in his *The Poem as Utterance*, that all utterances are used to do things; they are, in other words, speech acts (16). For him pragmatics "is concerned with appropriacy of utterance; and poetry is a form of language in which appropriacy—appropriacy of feeling to object, of character to setting, of *signifiant* to *signifie*, and perhaps most essentially of all, of utterance to situation—becomes itself the main focus of attention for author and reader alike" (26).

York's statements as quoted above have in fact told us the method of this new linguistic analysis. In this paper, therefore, I will follow his direction to analyze Matthew Arnold's "Dover Beach." In doing so, I will try to discuss all instances of appropriacy I have found in the poem's text and context. But before I start the discussion, I must make it clear that by *context* I mean all types of context, including what Roger Fowler calls context of utterance, context of culture, and context of reference, not just the syntactic context.[1]

Now, the text of Arnold's "Dover Beach' comprises thirty-seven
lines as follows:

> The sea is calm tonight.
> The tide is full, the moon lies fair
> Upon the straits—on the French coast the light
> Gleams and is gone; the cliffs of England stand,
> Glimmering and vast, out in the tranquil bay.
> Come to the window, sweet is the night air!
> Only, from the long line of spray
> Where the sea meets the moon blanched land,
> Listen! You hear the grating roar
> Of pebbles which the waves draw back, and fling,
> At their return, up the high strand,
> Begin, and cease, and then again begin,
> With tremulous cadence slow, and bring
> The eternal note of sadness in.
>
> Sophocles long ago
> Heard it on the Aegean, and it brought
> Into his mind the turbid ebb and flow
> Of human misery; we
> Find also in the sound a thought,
> Hearing it by this distant northern sea.
>
> The sea of Faith
> Was once, too, at the full, and round earth's shore
> Lay like the folds of a bright girdle furled,
> But now I only hear
> Its melancholy, long, withdrawing roar,

Retreating, to the breath
Of the night wind, down the vast edges drear
And naked shingles of the world.

Ah, love, let us be true
To one another!   For the world, which seems
To lie before us like a land of dreams,
So various, so beautiful, so new,
Hath really neither joy, nor love, nor light,
Nor certitude, nor peace, nor help for pain;
And we are here as on a darkling plain,
Swept with confused alarms of struggle and flight,
Where ignorant armies clash by night.

These thirty-seven lines are supposedly spoken by someone staying somewhere on Dover Beach.   Although the poem does have "something of the effect of overheard musing," it is nevertheless "addressed, or half-addressed, to someone present," presumably, the speaker's sweetheart.[2]   This fact is proved by the three imperative sentences beginning with "Come," "Listen," and "let" uttered by the speaker in lines 6, 9, & 29.   In other words, the entire poem can be regarded as a dramatic monologue, which is a poetic type already popular in Arnold's time.[3]

Furthermore, from the use of the word "love" in line 29, we can assume that the speaker is a man addressing his darling, for the term "love" usually refers to someone loved, especially a woman, in contrast to the term "lover" which usually refers to a male sweetheart.[4]   (We base this assumption on the idea of "appropriateness conditions" in speech and also on the idea of "Cooperative Principle" in conversation.)[5]

If intrinsically the poem has its own speaker and listener, we cannot equate at once the speaker with the poet, nor the listener with the reader, although we can decide on the possibility of such an equation after enough evidence has been gathered.   For the time being, the best thing we can do is to suggest that extrinsically the poem was the poet Arnold's speech to the readers who he thought could respond to it, and since the poem still exists today, it is also his speech to the readers whom he never knew, while intrinsically the poem was and is a particular lover's speech to his sweetheart. Therefore, the poem involves a double speech act: one of the poet, the other of the speaker in the poem.   And the double speech act has a double time reference: the past (Arnold's times) and the all-inclusive (past, present, and future).   I believe a thorough linguistic analysis of the poem must needs consider these doublenesses of speech situation.

The speech situation in the poem can only be inferred from the words uttered by the speaker, of course.   Now, as far as the lines of "Dover Beach" imply, we can be certain that the speaker may be in a room (perhaps a hotel room) looking out through the window first far at the sea and the tide of the straits (the English Channel) towards the French coast, and then near at the cliffs of England in the tranquil bay, before he asks his sweetheart to come to the window and share the same experience with him. At this point, the speaker may be musing over the facts that the sea is calm tonight, the tide is full, the moon lies fair upon the straits, etc.   Or he may be describing the scenes audibly to his sweet-heart.   In either case, it can be inferred that the addressed woman is for some reason (she may be resting on bed, or washing herself in the toilet, etc.) not noticing the same scenes that the speaker sees.   Therefore, the speaker tries to arouse her attention by saying "Come to the window ... Listen! ..."

The long sentence beginning with "Come to the window" and having "Listen!" inserted may range from a severe command to a mild request, depending on the tone of uttering it, though judging from its context we believe the latter is more likely. Anyway, we can feel that the speaker is very eager to call his sweetheart's attention to what he is experiencing then and there: the smell of the sweet night air, the sight of the long line of spray along the moon-blanched coast, the sound of the grating roar of pebbles, etc.   Here we can also decide that the speaker is a very sensitive person while his sweetheart may not be so sensitive and therefore has to be told what to see, hear, smell, etc.

The speaker is in fact not only a person with keen senses, but also one with great intellect.   The last three strophes of the poem can be regarded as three lessons the speaker has learned from his past experience and the present situation, and he is now trying to tell the lessons to his darling.   First, on the basis of his historical knowledge and literary imagination, he tells her that the sea's note of sadness was heard long ago by Sophocles on the Aegean and it brought into his mind the turbid ebb and flow of human misery: that is, Sophocles once heard the sea as a symbol of man's tragic fate. Then, by analogy, he tells her that the sound they are hearing by this distant northern sea can also give rise to a thought: that is, the sea can be seen and heard as a symbol of man's faith, too—it was once at the full just as the tide is full now (the fullness made it lie round earth's shore like the folds of a bright girdle furled), but now the Sea of Faith is ebbing away and so the speaker only hears its melancholy, long, withdrawing roar, retreating down the vast dreary edges and naked shingles of the world.   And finally, with this sad understanding, the speaker then (perhaps turning to her) calls his sweetheart with a sigh ("Ah") and an endearing term ("love") and tells her that they should be true to one another, giving her at the same time the reason why they should be so.

From his words we may conclude that the speaker is a learned man with insight into his (and our) life situation: he knows Sophocles and he knows that the world, which seems to lie before us like a land of dreams, has really neither joy, nor love, etc. Meanwhile, we can also conclude that the words constitute a common speech act: that of instruction.   Sometimes the act of instruction may become an act of mere informing (e.g., 11. 24-28).   Sometimes it may sound more like a request or an exhortation than an instruction (e.g., the last verse paragraph).   Yet, it is all clear that the speaker, in telling his sweetheart so many heartfelt thoughts, is posing as a person superior to his listener in knowledge and imaginative intellect.   He is thus to be thought of as a great imaginative thinker with very keen senses if we consider all the thirty-seven lines in the light of his speech act.

A great imaginative thinker with very keen senses is in effect a poet.   This allows us the freedom to identify the speaker with the poet Arnold himself.   But before we can claim the speaker to be a mere persona or mouthpiece of the poet, we need to gather enough biographical evidence for that purpose.   Unfortunately, however, Arnold forbade anyone to write his biography, and consequently his life has not been known sufficiently.   Even the date of composition of this well-known poem is still unknown, although it is generally assumed to be 1851.[6]

Arnold married Frances Lucy Wightman in 1851.   If the poem was really composed in the same year, can we then conclude that Miss Wightman is the woman addressed as "love" in the poem? Judging from all the biographical sources we can get, it seems quite likely.   And the likelihood will increase if we consider the case in connection with a French girl called Marguerite.

Although Arnold's family denied it, there is some evidence that he met the French girl in Switzerland.   And it is suggested that he ascribed to Marguerite "a lightness and lack of seriousness and depth of feeling, and a lack of propriety, even of chastity," which made it impossible for them to continue as lovers.   Their separation and its heartache, then, became for Arnold "the symbol of human separateness in the modern world, which is one of the dominant themes of his verse."[7]   So, based on these biographical traces, the poem becomes not just an instructive talk but a confessional piece as well.   We might suppose that Arnold did come to Dover Beach with his wife (for a honeymoon trip?), and there looking towards the French coast he automatically thought of the French girl and in his reflecting on their past affair naturally turned to his wife and said, "Ah, love, let us be true to one another!"

No matter whether this biographical interpretation is true or not, the fact remains that the poem is primarily Arnold's discourse to his readers.   He is using a lover's (or husband's) talk to his sweetheart to convey his (the poet's) message to the world.   In this sense he is talking not only of two lovers' mutual faith but also of all people's moral and religious faith.   This textual meaning, to be sure, can hardly be grasped plainly from the verse lines themselves.   To read this meaning into the poem, one has to be familiar with Arnold's times, that is, to go beyond the text into its historical context.

As we all know, Arnold was a writer of the Victorian Age. And the Victorian Age was an era of great social change and intellectual advancement.   It witnessed, among other things, the growth of democracy, the rise of the middle class, the general accessibility of elementary education, the astonishing development of the practical arts, applied science, and machine-production, and the epoch-making advances in geological and biological studies (e.g.,

Darwin's theory of evolution).   As a result of all these, materialism and the doctrine of *laissez faire* were firmly implanted in common people's minds while many intellectuals tended towards skepticism if not pessimism about matters of the soul.

Arnold's father, Thomas Arnold (or the famous Dr. Arnold, headmaster of Rugby school), was already alarmed by the "want of Christian principle in the literature of the day" (Strachey 426).   He therefore repeatedly told his pupils, "What we must look for here is, first, religious and moral principle; secondly, gentlemanly conduct; thirdly, intellectual ability" (Strachey 428). Now, the headmaster's son felt no less of the same thing.   In actuality, the literary son has fully expressed what his father and many other sensitive souls of their day have felt.

In a history book, it is said that Arnold may be described as a poet of transition. "Carlyle, Browning, Tennyson, and Newman," the same book says, "were, each in his way, already building anew the structures of spiritual faith and hope; but to Arnold, as to many others, the ebbing of the old wave was far more clearly felt than the rising of the new one" (Moody & Lovett 319).   By the same token, Lionel Trilling says, "Arnold's poetry in its most characteristic mood is elegiac—it mourns a loss, celebrates the lost thing, and tries to come to terms with the deprivation." "For Arnold," he goes on, "as for so many intellectuals of his time, the essential element of this sense of loss was the diminution of the intensity of religious faith" (319).

With this contextual understanding, then, I think we have enough reason to believe that in "Dover Beach" the problem of faith is not merely that between lovers but also that among people and that between God and man.   To explain it in Fowler's terms, the meaning of the word *faith* in this poem is to be decided not just on the basis of its context of utterance, but also on the basis of its context of culture and context of reference.

But the poem is much more than its topic or subject-matter. To appreciate the poem is to see how successfully its theme (or topic or subject-matter) is treated. In this respect we must look more into its textual details. But before we do that, I want to point out some motifs which constitute or surround the poem's theme.

The first dominant motif is that of appearance-reality contrast. This motif is necessarily linked to the theme of faith because faith is a spiritual matter, not a material object. Although what appears materially may sometimes be an emblem of the spiritual, it is more often than not a cheat, a mask to conceal the reality. So, by properly handling the appearance-reality contrast, one can suggest the presence or absence of faith.

A second dominant motif is that of constancy-change contrast. This motif is, again, necessarily linked to the theme of faith because any kind of faith is a subjective entity; it can exist only as long as people are conscious of it. In a period of transition in faith, the constancy-change motif naturally makes its appearance.

A third dominant motif is that of order-chaos contrast. It is only logical that people's unification in moral or religious faith will result in social order while the lack of that faith will bring about chaos.

The final concomitant motif of the faith theme I want to discuss here is that of loneliness. If people have all lost faith in God and his fellow beings, then everyone must of necessity feel lonely in this environment even if he is among crowds of people.

Now these four motifs, as I shall demonstrate shortly, appear time and again explicitly or implicitly, along with the theme of faith and the imageries of sea, land, etc, to form in "Dover Beach" quite a meaningful pattern, which, linguistically speaking, has coherence on the semantic, syntactic, phonological, and even graphological levels.

First, let us talk about the appearance-reality motif. The poem, as we see, begins with the speaker's description of the sea. But the description of the sea only appears to be the speaker's or the poet's aim. As we read on, the literal sea of the first strophe has changed into the metaphorical or symbolic sea of the remaining strophes. And the "Sea of Faith" in line 21 has declared itself openly to be the real theme of the speaker's or the poet's discourse.

Within the first strophe, "The sea is calm tonight. The tide is full, the moon lies fair/Upon the straits"—these beginning lines are a real description of the sea. But if the sea is to be understood as the symbol of faith, such a real description only exposes a bogus truth: for the speaker and the poet as well, the sea of faith now only appears to be calm; the tide only appears to be full; the moon only appears to lie fair upon the straits. The nearer description to the truth is what follows: "on the French coast the light/Gleams and is gone; the cliffs of England stand/Glimmering and vast, out in the tranquil bay." The light imagery here is a truer emblem of people's faith: the light of faith on the French coast gleams and is gone while on the coast of England it only glimmers on the vast cliffs in the tranquil bay.

In the sixth line, "sweet is the night air" is again a good appearance only. The real thing is "the grating roar/Of pebbles which ...bring/The eternal note of sadness in" (11. 9-14). In line 8, we meet, as the sea meets, "the moon-blanched land." How can a land be blanched by the moon? It is only an appearance, too. It in fact only suggests the blankness or hollowness of reality then and there.

With this sense of blankness or hollowness of reality, we as well as the speaker or the poet move into the second strophe, where we begin to assert that the sea is not the sea; appearance is not reality. Hence, whatever is the sea is to be seen otherwise. Hence, Sophocles was right to hear "the turbid ebb and flow/of human misery" (11. 17-18) on the Aegean; and we will also be right to find a thought in the sound by this distant northern sea (11. 19-20).

As soon as we see the sea in the eye of faith, the past and present reality emerges clearly: in the past the sea of faith was "at the full," but now it is "retreating down the vast edges drear/And naked shingles of the world" (11. 22-28).   Facing this reality, one cannot but be skeptical and come to the conclusion that "the world, which seems/To lie before us like a land of dreams,/So various, so beautiful, so new,/Hath really neither joy, nor love, nor light,/Nor certitude, nor peace, nor help for pain" and that "we are here as on a darkling plain/Swept with confused alarms of struggle and flight,/Where ignorant armies clash by night" (11. 30-37).

The appearance-reality motif even manifests itself in the verse form of the poem.   At first glance, the poem looks like a traditional poem with four different numbers of lines (14, 6, 8, & 9 lines, respectively) and four different rhyme schemes. Within each paragraph, the line length as well as the meter also varies considerably: a line can be as short as four syllables only (l. 21), and as long as eleven syllables (l. 36) while the basic iambic meter is occasionally substituted by other meters.   This apparent irregularity, however, suggests in truth the "cadence" (1. 13) of the sea, and perhaps the real cadence of faith. (For me the sound of ll. 9-14 echoes the sense especially nicely as we read them. For James Dickey, the poem's greatest technical virtue is its employment of sound-imagery, particularly in the deep, sustained vowels of lines like "Its melancholy, long, withdrawing roar."   And the lines also seem to him to break beautifully: "...on the French coast, the light/Gleams, and is gone.")[8]

This verse form lies in fact between the traditional stanzaic form and the modern free verse form.   Its transitional status echoes perfectly Arnold's one constant theme: "Wandering between two worlds, one dead,/The other powerless to be born."[9]   And the theme echoes the next motif we are to discuss: namely, the constancy-change motif.

In his discussion of "Dover Beach," James Dickey has said that the poem "is modern not so much in diction and technique—for its phrasing and its Miltonic inversions are obvious carry-overs from a much older poetry—but in psychological orientation" (750).   And he explains thus:

> Behind the troubled man standing at the lover's conventional moon-filled window looking on the sea, we sense—more powerfully because our hindsight confirms what Arnold only began to intuit—the shift in the human viewpoint from the Christian tradition to the impersonal world of Darwin and the nineteenth century scientists.... Things themselves—the sea, stars, darkness, wind—have not changed; it is the perplexed anxiety and helplessness of the newly dispossessed human being that now come forth from his mind and transmute the sea, the night air, the French coast, and charge them with the sinister implications of the entirely alien.   What begins as a rather conventional—but very good—description of scenery turns slowly into quite another thing: a recognition of where the beholder stands in relation to these things; where he *really* stands. (750-1)

This critical insight has indeed touched on the constancy-change motif.   But we have more to say about it.

Actually, "the shift in the human viewpoint" as described above is countered by the poem's progress from the literal sea in the first strophe to the metaphorical or symbolic sea in the subsequent strophes.   This fact suggests not only the changeability of human viewpoint in contrast to the seeming changelessness of things themselves, but also man's (especially a cultural man like Arnold's) constant pursuit of spiritual values in the flux of material happenings. Now, the spiritual value the speaker or the poem seeks is faith.   Yet, faith itself, be it moral faith or religious faith, is understood as something changeable, too.   The only thing that never changes seems to be "the eternal note of sadness" that one hears in the sea's "tremulous cadence slow" (ll. 17-18).

Indeed, everything else in the poem is perceived as liable to change—the calm sea, the full tide, the fair moon, the light on the French coast and the cliffs of England, the tranquil bay, the sweet night air, etc.—although the description of them does not state the fact directly.   For in our experiential world we know only too well that such natural phenomena, as phenomena, are actually changing all the time.   The epithets attached to the substantives (or adjectives used to modify the nouns, if you prefer grammatical terms), therefore, are variable ("calm" can become "rough," for instance).

Changeability has been a topic of philosophers, and man's mutability has been the despair of romantic poets.   What concerned Arnold was the loss of past moral and religious faith, which was in fact changing into a faith in material success or power which "the ignorant armies" struggled for.[10]   But Arnold chose not to express his concern directly.   Instead, he suggests it obliquely by a lover's concern about constancy of devotion in the poem.

When the speaker in the poem says, "Ah, love, let us be true to one another" (11. 29-30), there is an "implicature," to use Grice's term, in this pleading. It implicates that they can be untrue to each other. And the theme of untrue love is obliquely foreshadowed in the image of "the folds of bright girdle furled" (1. 23). When a woman has the folds of her bright girdle furled, she naturally looks tidy and chaste. When she has the folds unfurled, however, her garment is sure to loosen. In case her faith ebbs like the tide, her clothes may likewise "retreat, to the breath of the night wind, down the vast edges drear and naked shingles of the world" (11. 26-28). In that case, the lover will have reason to complain that "the world...hath really neither joy, nor love..." (ll. 30-34).

The loosening of a woman's garment may be the beginning sign of her inconstancy, her violating the order of love. If the whole world has become loose morally and religiously, then chaos is certain to come. In a chaotic world, we may easily hear "the grating roar" (l. 9), and often see "human misery" (1. 15) or "confused alarms of struggle and flight" (1. 36). In such a faithlessly chaotic world, what is one's most characteristic feeling?

It is often suggested that the key note of the poem is that of sadness, the key word in line 14. Truly, we can feel that the speaker is a melancholy lover just as a Romantic hero often is. But the poem is not pessimistic for that. For behind "the eternal note of sadness" or "the melancholy, long, withdrawing roar" the law of change implicates that the sea will again be calm some day, the tide will again be full, and there is still hope to regain people's lost faith. What is most insufferable for the present speaker is in fact the feeling of loneliness.

A lonely person is not necessarily one without companions at hand, but one lacking others' sympathy. When one suffers "crowded solitude," therefore, one will seek opportunities to talk with others.   In the poem, when the speaker asks his sweetheart to come to the window and listen to the sea, he is in effect asking for her sympathy.   When he tells her the metaphorical or symbolic meaning of the sea, he is also asking for her sympathy.   When he suggests that they be true to one another, he is of course asking for her sympathy as well.

It is often noted that a Romantic hero often turns to great nature for sympathy or consolation when in melancholy solitude, for "Nature never did betray the heart that loved her."[11]   The speaker in "Dover Beach" has likewise come to nature for consolation, perhaps. But does the sea extend sympathy to him?   In view of its rendering "the still, sad music of humanity,"[12] it does seem to have touched the speaker's soul.   But that sympathy is, after all, only the speaker's subjective projection of his own sentiment onto the appearance of nature—that is, he is committing "pathetic fallacy" of some sort. At the end, the speaker has to return to the true reality—the darkling plain where ignorant armies clash by night.   And as a knowing man he is aware that for sympathy he can only appeal to the sweetheart by his side.

So far I have analyzed the poem in the light of its four dominant motifs as related to the theme of faith.   Now to return to the doubleness of the poem as a speech act, I must assert that the speaker in the poem is obviously Arnold's persona.   It is only that Arnold is appealing to us readers for sympathy, not to his sweetheart, when he concretizes his ideas in the poem.   We need not believe naively that a lover has really spoken such poetic lines to his sweetheart.   Love is not so eloquent with verse; a poem is but a "fictitious" utterance (or speech or discourse).   But by composing the poem the poet has performed a speech act worthy of our discussion so far.

Now, to recapitulate the discussed points: The poem "Dover Beach" involves a double speech act—it was the poet Arnold's discourse to his (implied) readers at his time and place; it was also the discourse of the speaker in the poem at certain time on the Beach. But since the poem as either discourse is still heard or overheard today by the (real) readers wherever the poem is available, the time and place reference must also involve the present-day world.   But regardless of the time and place reference, the poem as either discourse is an act of instruction on the whole: it instructs in faith—moral and religious faith in general, or lovers' mutual faith in particular.   The poem's double speech act can be illustrated by the chart below:

	DOVER BEACH	
	Speech Act I	Speech Act II
addresser	Arnold	Speaker in the poem
addressee	his implied readers	his sweetheart
	real readers (hear)	real readers (overhear)
time	since the date of composition	1851? a particular day
		also today
place	England	Dover Beach
	the world	the world
type	instructive	instructive
message	faith in general	faith in particular

Although the two speech acts are performed by two different persons, we have tried to identify the one with the other.   We suggest that Arnold is quite like the speaker in the poem.   They are both male, both sensitive, intellectual, and preachy, and both lonely enough to crave sympathetic understanding from others.   The evidence for the suggestion is drawn from both the poem's text and its context, which demonstrate in fact that the poem has a central theme, faith, surrounded by four dominant motifs (appearance-reality contrast, change-constancy contrast, order-chaos contrast, and loneliness), which in turn blend into the poem's imageries, verse form, and tone of speech.   This complicated relationship can be shown by the following diagram:

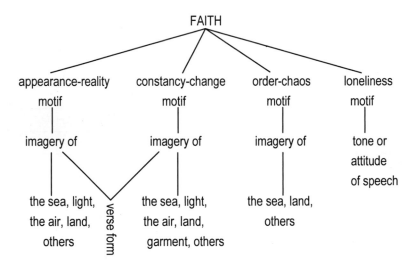

* The sea imagery includes images of the straits, the tide, the waves, etc., with their sights and sounds.
* Land imagery includes images of coast, cliffs, strand, plain, etc., with their sights and sounds.
* The air imagery, with its wind and breath, is both auditory and olfactory..

And this diagram testifies the coherent pattern of the poem as a linguistic discourse placed in its historical context.

Notes

1. In his *Linguistic Criticism,* pp. 86-89, Fowler defines context of utterance as "the situation within which discourse is conducted": context of culture as "the whole network of social and economic conventions and institutions constituting the culture at large," and context of reference as "the topic or subject-matter of a text."

2. See, for this point, James Dickey's criticism in Oscar Williams, ed., *Master Poems of the English Language,* p.75.

3. Robert Browning is of course the best-known poet of this poetic type. Alfred Lord Tennyson also succeeds in it.

4. For the different usage of the two terms, see the entry "love" in A. S. Hornby et al., eds., *The Advanced Learner's Dictionary of Current English* (London: Oxford Univ. Press, 1963), p. 584.

5. "Appropriateness conditions" is now a popular linguistic term; philosophers usually call them "felicity conditions." For its meaning, see Austin's *How to Do Things with Words* (1962). The term "Cooperative Principle" was first introduced in H. Paul Grice, "Logic and Conversation," in *Syntax and Semantics* III, eds., Cole and Morgan.

6. See, for this point, M. H. Abrams, et al., eds., *The Norton Anthology of English Literature,* 4th edition, p. 1379, note 5.

7. See Lionel Trilling's Introduction to Matthew Arnold in G. B. Harrison, ed., *A Reader's Guide to Major British Writers,* Vol. II, p. 584.

8. See Oscar Williams, ed., *Master Poems,* p. 751.

9. See Arnold's "The Grande Chartreuse," 11. 85-86.

10. It is often suggested that the "ignorant armies" refers to the revolution of 1848 or to the siege of Rome by the French in 1849.

But the phrase can also refer more generally to any parties of people
who struggle for benefits of any sort.

11. See William Wordsworth's "Tintern Abbey," 11. 122-3.

12. *Ibid.*, 1. 91.

Works Consulted

Abrams, M. H., et al., eds., *The Norton Anthology of English Literature.*
4th edition, 2B.   New York & London: Norton & co., 1979

Austin,   *How to Do Things with Words.*   Cambridge, MS: Harvard
UP, 1962.

Fowler, Roger.   *A Dictionary of Modern Critical Terms.*   Revised
Edition.   London & New York: Routledge & Kegan Paul, 1987.

--------.   *Linguistic Criticism.*   Oxford & New York: Oxford UP,
1986.

Freeman, Donald C.   *Linguistics and Literary Style.*   New York: Holt,
Rinehart & Winston, Inc., 1970.

Grice, H. Paul.   "Logic and Conversation."   *Syntax and Semantics.*
III,   Ed.   Cole and Morgan.

Harrison, G. B., ed.   *A Reader's Guide to Major British Writers.* Vol.
II. New Work: Harcourt, Brace & World, Inc., 1959.

Moody, William Vaughn & Robert Morss Lovett.   *A History of English
Literature.* 7th edition. 1902.

Strachey, Lytton, "Dr. Arnold," in W. Somerset Maugham's
Introduction to *Modern English and American Literature.* Garden
City, N. Y: Garden City Books, 1952. 426 & 428.

Trilling, Lionel.   Introduction to Matthew Arnold in G. B. Harrison, ed.,
A Reader's Guide to Major British Writers, Vol. II,   p. 584.

Williams, Oscar, ed.   *Master Poems of the English Language.*   New
York: Trident Press, 1966.

York, R. A. *The Poem as Utterance.*   London & New York: Methuen & Co., 1986.

* This paper first appeared in *Studies in English Literature and Linguistics*, National Taiwan Normal University, No.18 (May 1992).

Hemingway's Existential Ending

In December 1944, Ernest Hemingway met Jean-Paul Sartre for once in Paris, and in August 1949 he met the existentialist again. "When Sartre appeared for a meal," it is reported, "the two writers talked like businessmen of royalties" (Meyers 429). But what on earth did they talk about? Were they trying to influence each other's ideas of writing?

On Hemingway's part, very few biographers, if ever, trace his ideas to the influence of the Frenchman. For most critics, Hemingway only played apprentice to such Anglo-American writers as Ezra Pound, Gertrude Stein, Ford Madox Ford, James Joyce, T. S. Eliot, and F. Scott Fitzgerald (Elliot 876). It seems that Sartre has not talked his existentialist ideas into Hemingway's mind.

Hemingway was Sartre's senior by six years. When they talked "like businessman of royalties," it might be Sartre, not Hemingway, that was trying to "profit" from the "business." And we know that before that talk Sartre had become known "for a series of articles on contemporary literature which did much to popularize in France the works of American novelists such as Faulkner, Hemingway, Dos Passos, and Steinback" (Benet 898).

But was Hemingway ever influenced by any other existentialist? The still younger Albert Camus, for instance, who was in Sartre's circle? Or Kierkegaard, Nietzsche, Unamuno, etc., who were at least one or two generations older than Hemingway?

In his *Hemingway and the Dead Gods*, John Killinger has an extensive discussion of Hemingway in connection with all those existential thinkers.   But he does not say Hemingway was ever directly influenced by any existentialist in person or in book.   Thus, we may infer that if Hemingway had any existential thought, it might be chiefly, if not completely, the result of his own personal experience.

This understanding is important.   For, as we know, the time of Hemingway was a time of the "lost generation," a time when irrational feelings and destructive actions made most conscientious souls escape to "separate peace," a time, that is, when sensible men were unavoidably nurtured in the existential Void.   We, therefore, are not surprised that a writer like Hemingway should have his life and works tinged with the color of existentialism.

But Hemingway is no existentialist, nor is he a philosopher in an academic sense.   He is indeed no more a philosopher than Byron is.[1]   Nevertheless, no one, I presume, can finish reading half of Hemingway's work without feeling an existential vein in it.   In fact, as I shall demonstrate below, many of his chief novels and short stories have ended in an existential manner just as his life has, if we know what an existential ending is.

Existentialism is, of course, a difficult philosophy.   Its difficulty stems not only from its numerous originators but also from its various expounders.   But all originators and expounders agree on the basic premise that "existence precedes essence."   From this premise different corollaries have been drawn.   One book, for instance, takes it to mean "the total relativism of all sensation, experience, and morality."   And the book thus explains:

Most of what we ordinarily consider absolute principles are purely subjective in nature; they have been created synthetically by the human brain, and therefore may be altered or suspended at will.   Human nature is one of these principles; Sartre holds that human nature is fixed only in the sense that men have agreed to recognize certain attributes of human nature; this nature may be changed if men merely agree on different attributes, or even if one man courageously acts in contradiction to the principles as ordinarily accepted. Thus Sartrian Existentialism is by nature (a) atheistic, since God is one of the subjective and synthetic concepts which men have contrived for their own convenience; (b) pessimistic, since man cannot hope for any surcease or aid outside himself; and (c) humanistic and progressive, since the possibilities of altering society and human nature for the better are unlimited. (Heiney 394)

Another book reduces all varieties of existentialism to three simple facts: First, the basic attempt of all existentialism has been to establish the separate identity of the individual.   Second, every man faces the choice of being a genuine individual or being just part of the crowd.   And third, in this world, where a man can thus choose to be himself or to remain anonymous, good and evil become mere qualities of the way of life which the individual chooses (Killinger 6-11).

Although the two books seem to have quite different interpretations, they do agree that existentialism is a philosophy of freedom, one that recognizes man's active role in establishing his own "essence."   "It's what one does, and nothing else, that shows the stuff one's made of," Inez in Sartre's *No Exit* tells Garcin, adding,

"You are—your life, and nothing else."   Inez is here Sartre's mouthpiece, of course.

An existential hero is indeed an individual who actively exercises his personal freedom to construct his authentic self.   It is only that he knows only too well he is placed in an absurd world, a world in which no definite meaning or purpose of life can be indubitably affirmed, just as in mathematics an irrational root (surd) can never be expressed by a definite number.   Facing the absurd world, the existential hero often feels the threat of nihilism and sees mere Nothingness or Void in everything.   Consequently he always lives under the tension of anguish (Heidegger's *das Angst*), a state not exactly of anxiety nor of fear, but of agonizing dread about something indefinite and uncanny.

One characteristic of the absurd which makes most of the anguish is repetition—meaningless repetition, or repetition of insensible "beginning again from zero."[2] It is because the existential hero cannot bear the repetition that he wants to build his new identity by actively doing something extraordinary. He despises, accordingly, the way of all flesh for that repetition, and he cannot even allow himself that repetition, for repetition is by definition a restraint of freedom, a cutting off of one's chance to set up his individuality anew.

It follows, therefore, that an existential work often has the absurd repetition exposed for comic ridicule or for serious consideration.   Camus's *The Myth of Sisyphus*, for instance, has touched on this theme most poignantly.   Sisyphus, as we know, was accused of levity towards the gods and of purloining their secrets. He was therefore put in Hades to the task of repeatedly rolling a huge stone up a hill, from whence it always rolled down again. One day Pluto permitted him to return to earth to chastise his unloving wife.   When he went home, however, he enjoyed it so much that he refused to go back to the underworld until Mercury was sent to fetch him.   Sisyphus is indeed the "absurd hero" par excellence.   But he just cannot bear that futile repetition of life.

Now, to return to Hemingway, I emphasize that Hemingway's work is not so existential as Camus's or Sartre's is.   However, Hemingway and his heroes, we feel, are often so anguished with their purposelessly repetitious lives that they really react to them time and again quite like absurd heroes.   In truth, many of Hemingway's chief novels and short stories end with a sense of disgust with or even protest against the absurd repetition.

To begin with, *The Sun Also Rises*, as we know, widely established Hemingway's reputation for depicting "the lost generation" and the disillusionment that followed World War I. This fact, however, should not make us forget that it is a novel most obviously devoted to the treatment of the repetition theme.   We know the title of the novel is adapted from *Ecclesiastes*, and a passage of this Old Testament book with the words for that title is printed in the novel's front page.   The passage thus goes:

> One generation passeth away, and another generation cometh; but the earth abideth forever...The sun also ariseth, and then the sun goeth down, and the hasteth to the place where he arose...the wind goeth toward the south, and turneth about unto the north; it whirleth about continually, and the wind returneth again according to his circuits. ...All the rivers run into the sea; yet the sea is not full; unto the place from whence the rivers come, thither they return again.

Isn't this a pointed observation of the repetitious phenomena?   If we bear this passage in mind when we read the novel, we shall be able to understand that the novel is not only the story of a set of expatriates in Paris who make a hectic trip over the Pyrenees to Pamplona for the bull-fights.   Nor is the life of the "lost generation" depicted merely as a record of the post-war situation. Rather, it is the description, too, of many a generation to come. At least for Hemingway there will be more Bills, Jakes, Mikes, Cohns, Bretts, etc., coming to abide in this absurd world and live similarly absurd lives.

At the end of *The Sun Also Rises*, we find Jake and Brett in Madrid.   As usual, they drink and eat and talk in the bar and in the hotel.   Finally they take a taxi ride to see the city.   In the taxi, Jake puts his arm around Brett and she rests against him comfortably. Then Brett says, "Oh, Jake, we could have had such a damned good time together."   And Jake answers, "Yes, isn't it pretty to think so?"

Here Jake's answer is ironic.   It implies that their life can be "pretty" only in supposition.   We as readers know, of course, that their life is as purposeless as the war-wrecked world in which they live; their ride now is as aimless as the drifting generation to which they belong.   And we can suppose with justification that later on Brett may do and say pretty much the same thing to the next man coming her way.   In fact, not only Jake and Brett but also all the characters in the novel may repeat pretty much the same meaningless café-bar-and-street life and claim it "a damned good time together" again and again.   This absurd repetition, we may assume, is not beyond the awareness of Jake, who as the novel's narrator represents at least part of Hemingway's awareness.

If all characters in *The Sun Also Rises*, including Jake, are still immersed in their absurd life (thus, no one of them can be called a hero), the hero and the heroine in *A Farewell to Arms* have at least tried to escape from the war's repetitious injuries to "separate peace." In fact, the couple's heroic escape has raised the novel to a tragic dimension, and created a tragic atmosphere well linked to the novel's symbolic touches.

Besides the symbolic contrast between the plain and the mountain, a much discussed symbol in *A Farewell to Arms* is the rain. Malcolm Cowley asserts that in the novel, "the rain becomes a conscious symbol of disaster" (16). And he shows convincingly how the rain recurs in the novel with the disastrous associations. At the end of the novel, for instance, rain is still falling when Catherine dies in childbirth. After Frederick leaves her in the hospital, he says he walks back to the hotel in the rain.

Regarding the rain symbol, John Killinger has a different interpretation. He says:

> Several critics have noted the recurrence of rain (or other forms of precipitation) in Hemingway's fiction, especially in *A Farewell to Arms*, as a harbinger of disaster. Since it *is* connected with death, they generally agree that this function is diametrically opposite that of the precipitation symbol in the wasteland world of T. S. Eliot. But I believe that the rain is a symbol of fertility in Hemingway, too, though in a slightly different sense than in Eliot. To Hemingway death means rebirth for the existentialist hero in its presence, and therefore the rain, as an omen of death, at the same time predicts rebirth. (48)

I think that no matter whether it is a symbol of death or birth, the recurrence of rain in the novel is just like the recurrence of disaster (plague, war, etc.) and welfare (love, success, etc.) in the fictional as well as real world.   When finally Frederick steps into the rain, he must realize that things always come to nothing and one always has to start again from zero, just as the rain always comes on and leaves off in time.

"A Farewell to Arms" is in fact an ambiguous title.   "Arms" can mean "weapon" and this refer to fighting or war.   It can also refer to lovers' arms and thus suggest amorous affection.   At the end of the novel, Frederic does bid his farewell to both war and love.   Since war is the result of hate, of lack of love, he in truth bids farewell to the roots of all human passions.   Thus, he may be said to have stepped into the existential Void.   In order to find a purpose in life again, he has to start again from the "pre-essence" state of existence.

Whereas the repetition theme in *A Farewell to Arms* is strengthened by the rain symbol, the same theme is suggested by the recurrence of snow in *For Whom the Bell Tolls*.   But this later novel is often noted for another theme.   Owing to its title, the novel is automatically connected with John Donne's idea of "No man is an island."   Hence the story of a young American devoted to the Loyalist cause in the Spanish Civil War has become a story of his noble feeling that "any man's death diminishes me, because I am involved in Mankind."

Indeed, when the book ends, Robert Jordon is insisting nobly, despite his fatal wound, on remaining with a machine-gun in a spot where he can ambush and mow down the pursuing Rebel column before he is killed.   He thinks he is covering the retreat of his friends and doing the last heroic act.

But is that really a heroic deed?   Robert Penn Warren has noticed a sort of irony in the novel.   He says the irony runs counter to the ostensible surface direction of the story.   And he explains:

As surface, we have a conflict between the forces of light and the forces of darkness, freedom versus fascism, etc. Hero and heroine are clearly and completely and romantically aligned on the side of light. We are prepared to see the Fascist atrocities and the general human kindness of the Loyalists. It happens to work out the other way. The scene of horror is the massacre by the Loyalists, not by the Fascist. Again, in the attack on El Sordo's hill by the Fascists, we are introduced to a young Fascist lieutenant, whose bosom friend is killed in the attack. We are suddenly given this little human glimpse—against the grain of the surface. But this incident, we discover later, is preparation for the very end of the novel. We leave the hero lying wounded, preparing to cover the retreat of his friends. The man who is over the sights of the machine gun as the book ends is the Fascist lieutenant, whom we have been made to know as a man, not as a monster. This general ironical conditioning of the overt story line is reflected also in the attitude of Anselmo, who kills but cannot believe in killing. In other words, the irony here is much more functional, and more complicated, than that of *To Have and Have Not*; the irony affirms that the human values may transcend the party lines. (52-53)

The idea that life is more important than parties is in effect better suggested in an anecdote which relates how Maria's father, before his execution at Rebel hands, shouted, "Viva la Republica!" while his wife cried, "Viva my husband who was the Mayor of this village!"

Anyway, if we consider the end of the novel in the light of Hemingway's concern about human life and human values, we instantly recognize the absurdity of Robert Jordan's idealistic decision. We know then his life purpose is actually not so noble as he imagines it to be.   He is in truth but another "crazy fellow" involved in the endless, nonsensical process of killing and being killed.

This endless, nonsensical process, I find, is subtly suggested by two touches at the end of the novel.   First, Hemingway writes the following words in italics, indicating they are the hero's thought: "And if you wait and hold them up even a little while or just get the officer that may make all the difference. One thing well done can make—"   These are, grammatically speaking, incomplete sentences. Their incompleteness naturally suggests the unending process. Besides, one thing well done can make what?   Really make all the difference to the world?   We know as well as Hemingway that whatever Jordon may do, war—absurd war—will in fact go on forever all the same.

The other subtle touch is the last paragraph of the novel.   It goes thus:

> Lieutenant Berrendo, watching the trail, came riding up, his thin face serious and grave.   His sub-machine gun lay across his saddle in the crook of his left arm.   Robert Jordon lay behind the tree, holding on to himself very carefully and delicately to keep his hands steady.   He was waiting until the officer reached the sunlit place where the first trees of the pine forest joined the green slope of the meadow.   He could feel his heart beating against the pine needle floor of the forest.

This ending is actually no ending.   We can infer from it, of course, that Jordon might really kill Berrando at last.   But it is just a logical inference.   In an irrational world like Jordon's, will the inference surely come true?   Perhaps we may as well imagine that Jordon would just remain waiting there until he died from his former wound, or he might be found and killed before he had a chance to carry out his plan.   Anyway, we know the result of this encounter will not change war into peace.   It is at best a mere repetition of the typical, absurd warfare: somebody kills someone.

Still, Robert Jordon can be regarded as an existential hero trying to establish his individual identity by persisting in his idealistic struggle.   Yet a better example of persistent struggle is that of Santiago, the old man in *The Old Man and the Sea*.   We know he has gone out to the sea for eighty-four days without catching a single fish before he hooks the biggest marlin ever seen.   When finally he catches the fish after a long struggle with it, he has to fight against the sharks that come to slash with raking teeth at the dead marlin.   During the course, he does fight like an undefeated hero.

But a more manifest element of existentialism in the novelette is the nihilistic ending.   We know Santiago returns at last with nothing but the stripped skeleton of his great catch.   If he goes out to the sea again (and we are sure he will), he will in a sense be starting from zero again.   The last paragraph of this "long story" goes thus:

> Up the road, in his shack, the old man was sleeping again. He was still sleeping on his face and the boy was sitting by him.   The old man was dreaming about the lions.

Here the old man is repeating two activities of his wonted life: sleeping and dreaming about the lions.   Sleeping is of course a common routine.   But dreaming about the lions is something unusual.   It symbolically indicates the old man's longing for great heroic achievement.   Hence the story becomes an allegory of the existential hero's constant, idealistic struggle to set up his identity in the meaningless routines of life.

The nihilistic ending of *The Old Man and the Sea* can be easily connected with the theme of the "Winner Take Nothing" which is in fact the title of Hemingway's another book published almost twenty years earlier.   In *Winner Take Nothing*, we have the famous short story "A Clean, Well-Lighted Place."   In the story, nihilism is strongly expressed by the word *nada* through the old waiter's meditation on the old man's preferring to stay in the clean, well-lighted café:

> What did he fear?   It was not fear or dread.   It was a nothing that he knew too well.   It was all a nothing and a man was nothing too.   It was only that and light was all it needed and a certain cleanness and order.   Some lived in it and never felt it but he knew it all was nada y pues nada y nada y pues nada.   Our nada who art in nada, nada be thy name thy kingdom nada thy will be nada in nada as it is in nada.   Give us this nada our daily nada and nada us our nada as we nada our nadas and nada us not into nada but deliver us from nada; pues nada.   Hail nothing full of nothing, nothing is with thee.

This passage obviously suggests that the older waiter (Hemingway's intellectual ego) represents the type of man who knows perfectly the existential Void in which a few people like the old man (who walks "unsteadily but with dignity") will keep "a certain cleanness and order" in his lighted corner, while most common people like the younger waiter will just repeat their daily life without any concern about others.

In his discussion of the tale, Steven K. Hoffman agrees with William Barrett that "the *nada*-shadowed realm of 'A Clean, Well-Lighted Place' is no less than a microcosm of the existential universe as defined by Martin Heidegger and the existential philosophers who came before and after him, principally Kierkegaard and Sartre."   And he further suggests that

> Obviously, *nada* is to connote a series of significant absences: the lack of a viable transcendent source of power and authority; a correlative lack of external physical or spiritual sustenance; the total lack of moral justification for action (in the broadest perspective, the essential meaninglessness of *any* action); and finally, the impossibility of deliverance from the situation.   (175)

And he adds that the impact of *nada* extends beyond its theological implications:

> Rather, in the Heideggerian sense ("das Nicht"), it is an umbrella term that subsumes all the irrational, unforeseeable, existential forces that tend to infringe upon the human life, to make a "nothing."   It is the absolute power of chance and circumstance to negate individual free will and the entropic tendency toward ontological disorder that perpetually looms over man's tenuous personal sense of order.   But the most fearsome face of *nada*, and clear proof of man's radical

contingency, is death—present here in the old man's wife's death and his own attempted suicide. Understandably, the old waiter's emotional response to this composite threat is mixed. It "was not fear or dread," which would imply a specific object to be feared, but a pervasive uneasiness, an existential anxiety that, according to Heidegger, arises when one becomes fully aware of the precarious status of his very being. (175)

Indeed, the shadow of *nada* looms behind very much of Hemingway's fiction. Hemingway's characters are either repeating their meaningless lives unconscious of it or struggling very tragically to defy it. It is only that his heroes have thereby come to different tragic ends for different interpretations.

Harry in "The Snow of Kilimanjaro," for instance, is a man "getting bored with dying as with everything else." When his wife asks him what a bore is, he answers, "Anything you do too bloody long." He is actually tired of repeating his extravagant life with his rich wife because he knows it is "all a nothing." When he comes to Kilimanjaro, he is doing something extravagant just like the legendary leopard mentioned in the story's epigraph. Although it is said that "No one has explained what the leopard was seeking at that altitude," we know for certain that Harry is seeking an ideal place, a "clean, well-lighted place," where he can turn himself into a true writer. But the irony is: a mere scratch in the leg has ended his life there—an absurd ending it is!

Another absurd ending is felt by Nick Adam (Hemingway's young ego) in "The Killers." For me, the killers are merely symbolic figures. They are anything that will come to take a person's life at any time. Ole Andreson in this interpretation is a man who "knows what it's all about."   He knows he can do nothing but wait for death—he knows, indeed, we are all of us waiting for death whatever we do.   For young Adam, however, it is absurd to remain inactive all the time: "I can't stand to think about him waiting in the room and knowing he's going to get it. It's too damned awful."

Unlike Ole Andreson, Francis Macomber does not remain inactive all the time, nor does he know "he's going to get it."   He is at first a spineless character much despised by his wife.   Yet, later in hunting a buffalo, he suddenly finds his courage in the excitement of the chase.   In the course of a half-hour (his "short happy life") he develops his manhood to such an extent that his wife Margot, fearing she will no longer be able to control him, kills him from behind with a gunshot while he is bravely firing at the wounded but charging animal in an underbrush.   This ending is ironically absurd. Macomber dies (becomes nothing) right on the point of proving himself to be something.

But the buffalo also dies.   In truth, Macomber can be identified with the buffalo.   Like the buffalo, he has to struggle for life.   But the struggle is of no avail in terms of physical life.   Corporeal life is but a repetition of death.   It is only that the way of struggle can prove one's "essence" in terms of existentialism.

This truth Hemingway knows only too well.   In fact he has a great sympathy for the bull that dies in the bullfight.   In his *Death in the Afternoon*, he says:

> The bullfight is not a sport in the Anglo-Saxon sense of the word, that is, it is not an equal contest or an attempt at an equal contest between a bull and a man.   Rather it is a tragedy; the death of the bull, which is played, more or less

well, by the bull and the man involved and in which there is danger for the man but certain death for the animal.[3]

If we imagine mankind being the bulls in the ring, then the meaning of the existential ending will become very clear.   Like the bulls, human beings are forever put to fight with an unequal opponent (the natural environment).   And like the bulls, human beings must die eventually.   However, when death is repeated each time, man as well as the bull can prove his guts, the stuff or "essence" he is made of.

It is observed that Hemingway finds a sort of mystical experience, a quasi-metaphysical quality, in pain, violence, and death (Heiney 75).   The tragic elements of pain, violence, and death are actually the necessary elements of the existential world.   These elements exist like the rules of games or principles of rituals.   In Hemingway's world, people are forever repeating their games or rituals—war, sex, bull fight, hunting, fishing, etc.—the absurd endings of which only breed more cause for pain, violence, and death.   An existential hero is one intensely aware of this situation and yet determined to make something out of this repetitious nothing.

In his *Against the American Grain,* Dwight MacDonald says that Hemingway was "hopelessly sincere"; his life, his writing, his public personalities and his private thoughts were "all of a piece." And he thinks that it was Hemingway's own "lack of private interests" that caused him to kill himself "when his professional career had lost its meaning" (76-77).   I agree that Hemingway's life and works are of a piece and that he killed himself when his professional career had lost its meaning.   But I am not sure whether he had any private interests or not.   I believe, instead, that

Hemingway killed himself *because* he knew his professional career had lost its meaning.   And he knew that because, as everybody could see, he was just repeating himself in his later years.   And mere repetition, we have suggested, is absurd, is not allowed by an existential hero.

In his later years, Hemingway repeated not only his former themes and subject matter, but also his former style.   In actuality, his "simple style"—with simple words in simple sentences connected with coordinate conjunctions—is a style with intrinsically intensive repetitions.   To write a lifetime in such a style is really absurd. Hemingway must have been aware of this absurdity of his. In order to get rid of this absurdity, to establish his new identity, he naturally had to break through his old self.   But how to break through?   How to build himself anew?   Alas, after immersing himself so much in the "games" or "rituals" of pain, violence, and death in the real world as well as in his own fictional world, he could only find a way out—committing suicide!

It is pointed out that Hemingway has great respect for the lion as an animal that meets death with dignity (remember the old man in *The Old Man and the Sea* is always dreaming of lions), while he has only contempt for the hyena because it dies eating its own intestines with relish (Killinger 76-77).   Hence, it is also pointed out that Hemingway does not approve of any cowardly suicide and has thus alluded with shame to his father's suicide in *For Whom the Bell Tolls.*[4]   Why, then, should Hemingway kill himself?   Isn't it a cowardly act, too?

In *The Myth of Sisyphus,* Camus observes: "There is but one truly serious philosophical problem and that is suicide.   Judging whether life is or is not worth living amounts to answering the fundamental question of philosophy."   Jeffrey Meyers says that

Hemingway once told Janet Flanner that "liberty could be as important in the act of dying as in the act of living." Meyers also reports that Hemingway agreed with Nietzsche's belief: "Die at the right time" (558). And about Hemingway's suicide he concludes: "It had elements of self-pity and revenge, but was not inspired by desperation and derangement. It was a careful and courageous act" (559).

Mayers is right, of course. But I must add: Hemingway's suicide is still an absurd repetition of his father's. He is himself an existential hero with an existential ending. I say "ending" instead of "end" because there is no end to the "essence" of "existence" for an existentialist. In order to "ex-sist," to stand out as true *daseins*, as authentic human beings, all existential heroes, including Frederic, Jordon, Santiago, Harry, Macomber, and a host of other Hemingway characters as well as Hemingway himself, must struggle constantly and choose all the time not only the proper way to live but also the proper way to die. For, they know, to die is not the end of all, but the ending of something at most. To die is, rather, to live in another way; ending is just a new beginning.

Notes

1. Dwight MacDonald deems it a foolish statement to call Hemingway "essentially a philosophical writer," and thinks he is less a philosopher than Byron.
2. In Camus's *La Peste* (*The Plague*,1947), Tarrou is his existentialist spokesman. Throughout the novel Tarrou argues for "beginning again from zero," i.e., the ethic that in a time of catastrophe each individual must recommence his life from the

point where he stands instead of brooding over "what might have been."   See Heiney, p. 400.

3. This is the beginning of this work's Chapter 2.

4. In the novel, Jordon's father had shot himself with a gun, which Jordon took later to the lake above Red Lodge and threw down into eight hundred feet of water.

Works Consulted

Benet, William Rose, ed.   *The Reader's Encyclopedia.*   2nd edition. New York: Harper & Row, 1965.

Bloom, Harold, ed.   *Ernest Hemingway: Modern Critical Views.* New York: Chelsea House Publishers, 1985.

Brooks, Cleanth, et al., eds.   *An Approach to Literature.*   4th edition.   New York: Meredith Publishing Co., 1964.

Cowley, Malcolm.   "Introduction" to *The Portable Hemingway.* New York: The Viking Press, 1944.

Elliot, Emory et al., eds.   *Columbia Literary History of The United States.*   New York: Columbia UP, 1988.

Heiney, Donald W.   *Essentials of Contemporary Literature.*   Great Neck, NY: Barron's Educational Series, Inc., 1954.

Hoffmann, Steven K.   " 'Nada' and the Clean, Well-Lighted Place: The Unity of Hemingway's Short Fiction."   *Essays in Literature* 6, No. 1 (Spring 1979); rpt. in Bloom, 174-177.

Killinger, John.   *Hemingway and The Dead Gods: A Study in Existentialism.*   Lexington: U of Kentucky P, 1960.

MacDonald, Dwight.   "Ernest Hemingway," rpt. in Brooks, 533-535.

Meyers, Jeffrey.   *Hemingway: A Biography.*   New York: Harper & Row, 1995.

Warren, Robert Penn.   "Earnest Hemingway," rpt. in Bloom, 50-55.

* This paper first appeared in 1991 in National Chung Hsing University's *Journal of Arts and History*, Vol. XXI.

Who Transcends What and How?:
A Re-reading of Emerson

Ralph Waldo Emerson has been generally acknowledged to be the chief spokesman of American transcendentalism and his transcendental thought (or, rather, thinking) has indeed had a tremendous impact on American culture since his days. However, there have been readers who would agree that "transcendentalism in the United States was never a coherent philosophy, even within the works of Emerson" (Frye 468). Therefore, this important term, which represents the first American intellectual movement, remains as hard to define as an enigmatic, shapeless giant, just as Nathanial Hawthorne conceived it to be.

Any careful reading of Emerson, I admit, is sure to detect a great number of contradictory statements in his works and therefore one is entitled to doubt the thinker's conceptual consistency. Facing this undeniable fact, a loyal advocate of Emerson may seek various favorable reasons to account for it. For instance, one may assert that neither Emerson nor his fellows ever wanted to have a clearly-defined, unchangeable tenet because they favored a rhetoric of oracular pronouncements and, as prophets of change, they were "non-conformists" even to their own belief (Elliot 364). Or one may gather facts to assert that his contradictions are due to his adopting various systems of thought——a natural outcome of the melting-pot culture of his country and its democratic spirit.[1]

I am not an Emersonian.   Yet as I read and re-read Emerson, I find one of his own ideas can indeed be used to explain away his inconsistency in making his oracular pronouncements.   I refer to his idea of "Unity in Variety," which he shares with such English Romantics as Coleridge and Wordsworth.[2]   And I mean his essays, poems, lectures, journals, letters—all his words spoken and written are to be taken as the Variety which must needs manifest different and even mutually opposing aspects in the light of its converging to a single Unity.   For his works are parts of an organic whole and as such have to grow in different ways to form a large integrity with a vital life, just as a tree must have such different things as its roots, branches, leaves, flowers and other parts growing in different directions to make up its unified life.   In other words, everything is a unity in variety; Emerson's thought or thinking is no exception.

A reader is a viewer.   A viewer can always look at something from the angle of sameness or from that of difference and come up with different views.   In the case of Emerson's transcendentalism, we can also view its different ideas or its same principles, depending on our different interests.   In the light of difference, for instance, we can contrast his ideas in "Experience" with those in his earlier essays and come to the conclusion that he contradicts himself now that he stresses the disconnection rather than the unity of the world:

> There will be the same gulf between every me and thee, as between the original and the picture.   The universe is the bride of the soul.   All private sympathy is partial.   Two human beings are like globes, which can touch only in a point, and, whilst they remain in contact, all other points of each of the spheres are inert. (CW, III, 77)[3]

But for a reader who persists in looking for consistency, Emerson is here still seeing the possibility of unity in separation; the transcendentalist is only to tell us a new discovery of his about the ultimate unity: "the longer a particular union lasts, the more energy of appetency the parts not in union acquire" (CW, III, 77).

In fact, no one can say anything characteristic of Emerson's transcendentalism without being a viewer of sameness.   If his mind as expressed in his works has been an amorphous anarchy not amenable to any synthetic understanding at all, we would have no cause to compare it with, say, Unitarianism or liberal rationalism or visionary mysticism, as many critics have done.   The moment we start talking about his mind on a comparative basis, we have presupposed the existence of some shared unchanging principles in it. It is only that different viewers will start from different grounds of sameness.   Robert E. Spillers and others, for instance, believe Emerson's essays have their unity and it "lies in the 'First Philosophy' expressed, not in its expression" (376).

For me, Emerson is indeed a great transcendentalist.   No matter how different or contradictory his expressions are concerning that mental bent, he never really deviates from his typical mode of thinking.   If he is sometimes vexingly vague at some points, he is in my view forever clear about his basic points, which never "transcend" his transcendentalism.   What, then, is his typical mode of thinking and what are his basic points?

Any comfortable understanding of Emersonian transcendentalism, I think, must begin with an investigation into the origin and meaning of the critical term.   In its Latin roots, the word *transcendentalism*, as we must agree, conveys essentially a sense of "passing over" or "climbing beyond."   Now, the idea of passing over or climbing beyond necessarily presupposes the existence of two realms, over one of which to pass or beyond one of which to climb, to the other. Therefore, all transcendental thoughts are fundamentally dualistic thoughts.

We are told in *Encyclopedia Britannica* that the term "transcendental" was not created by Kant.   It in fact goes back to the scholastic philosophy, and it is synonymous with "transcendent." Transcendental or transcendent concepts, the *Encyclopedia* goes on to say, are

> such as transcend the realm of finite, conditioned being, and lead on to the Infinite and Unconditioned.   Only by such a transcendence is metaphysical and religious cognition possible.   It is necessary to go beyond the variability of finite things and the limits of empirical self-consciousness, if a true knowledge of God is to be reached.[4]

This scholastic sense of transcendentalism, with its two-world view, is obviously fundamental to Emerson's thinking.

Indeed, Emerson may aim at One only, but he can never cease thinking in terms of Two.   In his Introduction to *Nature* he says, as we all know, "the universe is composed of Nature and the Soul" (CW, I, 4), and that dichotomy is followed by further dichotomies. Parallel to that basic dichotomy, in fact, are many other binary ideas of his which characterize his transcendental mode of thinking.   This mode of thinking, I think, is best summarized by Emerson Grant Sutcliffe.   He speaks of Emerson thus:

> Departing from Locke and agreeing with Kant, asserting that there are intuitive truths as well as those perceived by the senses, the transcendentalist of New England is a man of two

worlds. He has an abiding faith that there is a sphere of sense and a sphere of spiritual perception; that two views of things are possible, the material and the ideal, and the ideal is paramount. For him some things seem, others are; some are apparent, others real; some finite, others infinite; some relative, others absolute. He is aware of the facts of consciousness, but he knows of truths above consciousness. And far more than the worldly facts he esteems the spiritual truths. (11)

Here I will not bother to locate all Emerson's relevant contrasting terms and count their frequency of occurrence. But all readers of Emerson, I believe, will agree that the following list of contrasting terms, besides those already mentioned above, often, occur in his works, serving to indicate his dualistic way of thinking:

Many (diversity)	One (unity)
Each (part)	All (whole)
particular	universal
fragmentarity	integrity
man	God (deity, divinity, etc.)
external	internal
transcient	permanent
temporary (timely)	eternal (timeless)
means	end (purpose)
visible	invisible
body (nature, matter)	spirit (supernature, mind)
illusion	truth (being, essence)
sensation	intuition
understanding	reason

The two columns of terms represent, of course, the two opposing worlds: the world of Nature vs. the world of the Soul. Although Emerson often varies his terms of reference on various occasions, the two worlds he refers to are basically the same. In his "The Transcendentalist," for instance, he says: "As thinkers, mankind have ever divided into two sects, Materialists and Idealists." Then he goes on to explain that

> the first class founding on experience, the second on consciousness; the first class beginning to think from the data of the senses, the second class perceive that the senses are not final, and say, "The senses give us representations of things, but what are the things themselves, they cannot tell." The materialist insists on facts, on history, on the force of circumstances and the animal wants of man; the idealist on the power of Thought and of Will, on inspiration, on miracle, on individual culture. (CW, I, 322-30)

This explanation is sufficient to show that the Materialists' world is, for Emerson, the world of nature, and the Idealists' world is the world of the Soul. These two worlds are in his mind forever clearly defined and mutually opposed. But is mutual opposition the only relationship between these two worlds?

Again in his "The Transcendentalist," Emerson says that "Every materialist will be an idealist; but an idealist can never go backward to be a materialist" (CW, I, 330). So it is obvious that for Emerson the world of nature is to be transcended whereas the world of the soul is a realm to be entered upon transcendence. In actuality, Emerson sticked so stubbornly to his fixed order of transcendence that he would not allow any reversal of the order, theoretically or practically.   And that is why in his "Divinity School Address" he holds, to the chagrin of the School authorities, that Jesus Christ was not a divine person becoming human, but a human person becoming divine—an idea quite reverse to the old Christian concept.[5]   For he obviously regarded Christ as a man who has transcended our mundane existence, not as a divinity who has descended from the Kingdom of God.

This fixed order of transcendence, indeed, makes Emerson's transcendentalism similar to Idealism.   Emerson himself says, "What is popularly called Transcendentalism among us, is Idealism; Idealism as it appears in 1842" (CW, I, 329).   Like an idealist, he thinks that "Mind is the only reality, of which men and all other natures are better or worse reflectors" (CW, I, 333), and he thinks that "his way of thinking is in higher nature" (CW, I, 330). Therefore, to transcend is, for him, to ascend, not to descend. Transcendentalism is in his imagination "ascendentalism."   If he has the idea of the "the great chain of being,"[6] we can be certain that to transcend is, for him, to mount from the status of man to the status of God—an order reverse to that suggested in Pope's *Essay on Man* (Epistle I, 237-41).

To think lowly of the sensual reality and highly of the spiritual and thus to think of going from the one to the other realm as a mounting act is, of course, a traditional, moralistic way of thinking which can date as far back as to Plato.   That way of thinking, in fact, has no objective ground to stand on.   One may, therefore, think just the other way round, claiming the process from sensual to spiritual to be a descension, if one likes.   But Emerson, inheriting the American Puritanic (and therefore highly moralistic) tradition, simply could not think otherwise in this regard, despite his professed non-conformism.

While he adopts Kant's term, he is still thinking like an austere New Englander.   He himself never transcends his environment.

In truth, if we judge from the terms Emerson uses to represent the two realms involved in his transcendentalism, we can easily see that his transcending process is, more correctly speaking, an abstracting process.   For "Spirit is matter reduced to an extreme thinness" (CW, III, 53).   To reduce many to one or to generalize the particular is to abstract, and so is to idealize by turning the external into the internal, the visible into the invisible, or the finite into the infinite.   When any transcendentalist sees any "truth," we dare say, that truth is always something very highly abstract: the Over-Soul, or Supreme Cause or ineffable being or God.   If one reaches that higher level of abstraction, one has indeed passed over our physical world.   If we prefer an aesthetic term, we may say he has stepped into the Sublime after crossing the Sensible.   But if we do not mind being prosaic, we may just say he has gone from the world of something to that of nothing.   Anyway, a transcendentalist's practice is really a discipline of climbing the ladder of abstraction.[7]

Climbing the ladder of abstraction is actually a common phenomenon of verbal communication. So if we want to understand Emerson's transcendentalism, we can just examine his style of discourse.   In his study of Emerson's machinery of transcendence, Kenneth Burke points out that the eight chapters of *Nature* contain two sets of terms making a form of dialectical transcendence: the first four chapters (on "Nature," "Commodity," "Beauty," and "Language") constituting the "*Hic et Nuc,*" the last three chapters (on "Idealism," "Spirit," and "Prospects") constituting the "Beyond," and the middle fifth chapter (on "Discipline") serving as a bridge between the two sets.   I think this finding is true and very significant.   The structure as Burke sees in the chapter organization actually implies the process of transcendence and is typical, indeed, of Emerson's style and discourse as well: under the influence of his own transcendental ideas, Emerson is always inclined to proceed with his discourse by beginning with "the NOT ME" (the outward nature) and ending with "the ME" (our inward nature).[8]   Notice, for example, that "The American Scholar" also talks about the influence of nature first, then about that of the Past (i.e., books, etc.), and then about men's discipline as "practical men" or "speculative men" before they can become real scholars inspired by the Divine Soul. This Emersonian style of discourse is in fact seen in his poems, too. David Porter says, for instance, he sees "facts transformed to principle" in such poems as "The Snow Storm," "Humble Bee," "Each and All," and "Rhodora" (80).

It is often suggested that in his "Experience," Emerson has replaced his transcendental optimism with a sort of skepticism which borders on pessimism.[9]   The mention therein of "power and form" (rather than "form and power") as the two elements of human life which, as he says, is "a bubble and a skepticism, and a sleep within a sleep" (CW, III, 65) does in a way reverse Emerson's usual from-form-to-power process of transcendence and betray his uncertainty regarding his optimistic faith in man's ability to finally transcend form and ascend to power.   But generally surveyed, this mature essay, I maintain, still holds on to its author's basic faith. For me, the topics of Illusion, Temperament, Succession, Surface, Reality, and Subjectiveness discussed therein also manifest a from-sensation-to-soul process.   At least we can say these topics are important questions related to a transcendentalist's self-discipline in life.   Experience, Emerson seems to tell us by this essay, is a necessary step towards transcendence, though it may be painful at times to go from phenomenal illusion to subjective reality.   If we like to go into detail, we may well quote the following:

> We wake and find ourselves on a stair; there are stairs below us, which we seem to have ascended; there are stairs above us, many a one, which go upward and out of sight. (CW, III, 45)
> Grief too will make us idealistic. (48)
> We animate what we can, and we see only what we animate. Nature and books belong to the eyes that see them. (50)
> Divinity is behind our failures and follies also. (57)

The most skeptical statements in "Experience" may be these:

> We have learned that we do not see directly, but mediately, and that we have no means of correcting these colored and distorting lenses which we are, or of computing the amount of their errors.   Perhaps these subject-lenses have a creative power; perhaps there are no objects...Nature, art, persons, letters, religions, —objects, successively tumble in, and God is but one of its ideas.   Nature and Literature are subjective phenomena, every evil and every good thing is a shadow which we cast. ...People forget that it is the eye which makes the horizon, and the rounding mind's eye which make this or that man a type of representative of humanity with the name of hero or saint. (CW, III, 75-6)

But these statements in fact avers emphatically, like a Romantic gospel, that in our contact with nature or life, it is our mind, our subjective consciousness, that makes meaning, creates sense, and soars into the Sublime.   In order words, to transcend is to exercise our mental power.   But our mental power can only be exercised in our experience, that is, through our contact with nature or life. Thus, experience, no matter whether it is painful or not, is in a full sense but our discipline, our preparatory practice for ultimate transcendence.

Talking of discipline, Emerson's belief in self-reliance immediately comes to our minds.   For him, self-reliance is not just to feel confidence in oneself, not just a nonconformist gesture to "go alone, to refuse the good models, even those most sacred in the imagination of men and dare to love God without mediator or veil" (CW, I, 145), but a necessary measure for anyone, who cares to transcend this world, to learn "to detect and watch that gleam of light which flashes across his mind from within, more than the lustre of the firmament of bards and the sages" (CW, II, 45).   Since transcendence is a matter of one's personal mind only, one naturally has no use for social compliance or collective action.   That is why Emerson lacked interest in the Brook Farm enterprise, and that is why he maintains in his "New England Reformers" that "Union must be inward...Union must be ideal in actual individualism."[10]   This belief in fact also explains why his transcendentalism is tinged with Oriental thought, especially with such early Indian Buddhism (Theravăda or Hínayăna) as emphasizes personal salvation.[11]

As we know, Buddhists believe in the "Eight-fold Path" to nirvana: namely, right faith, right judgement, right language, right purpose, right practice, right obedience, right memory, and right meditation.   Such a Path involves in effect a course of self-discipline chiefly for the purpose of uniting one's individual soul with the universal divine spirit which he calls "The Over-Soul."   So Emerson's transcendentalism is in one sense not really a "stepping over" from one realm to another, but a confluent return of individual men back to their original integrity—an idea not unlike Blake's mythical premise of "Resurrection to Unity" after "The Universal man" fell into division through "Selfhood."

In his "The Over-Rated 'Over-Soul'" Robert Detweiler suggests that Emerson insists on a "panentheistic" view of deity, which "understands God as both transcendent and immanent, as inhabiting—in fact, constituting—the universe yet also existing (nonspatially) 'outside' it" (92). And he points out that this view makes the term *Over-Soul* possess three distinct connotations: first, in the sense of "over-the-soul," as the soul quantitatively greater than the individual soul; second, in the sense of "super-soul," as the soul qualitatively greater than the individual soul for its being unaffected by the material qualities of mortality; third, in the sense of "general soul," as the all-pervading soul, the principle of divine immanence in man and the world (92). Examining the essay "The Over-Soul" and other related writings of Emerson, we find Detweiler is quite right in his points. So, to transcend is, for Emerson, to magnify and sublimate our individual souls on one hand, and to identify them with, and return them to, the One Universal Soul on the other. In the process of transcendence, what is transcended is only the time-and-space-bounded corporeal self, which contains or encases the soul.

But this is where Emerson's difficulties arise. How can one get rid of his corporeal self in any practical sense without annulling his soul at the same time, since the latter must of necessity co-exist with the former? And how can an individual soul become as large and superior as "the Over-Soul" if the latter is forever greater than the former in quantity and quality? Emerson tells us that the soul's advances "are not made by gradation, such as can be represented by motion in a straight line; but rather by ascension of state, such as can be represented by metamorphosis,—from the egg to the worm, from the worm to the fly" (CW, II, 274).   We admit "the ascension of state" or metamorphosis can bring about a transformation.   But can it undo "the incarnation of the spirit in a form" (CW, II, 276) so that what is formed becomes formless "power" only?   When Emerson asserts that a man is capable of abolishing time and space, he is only asserting, theoretically, man's power of imagination as a Romantic does: "The spirit sports with time—'Can crowd eternity into an hour, /Or stretch an hour to eternity'" (CW, II, 272).[12]   He is far from testifying the possibility of man's ever transcending his physical self.

It is well-known that Emerson distinguishes between the logical and the intuitive roads to truth through the influence of Coleridge, who in turn owes his ideas to German transcendental philosophy.   Whatever its source, Emerson's idea of intuition is for him the only valid way to the perception or revelation of the ultimate truth.   And to attain the truth through the soul's intuition is for him to grasp "the Supreme Mind," to perceive "the absolute law," or to effect "the influx of the Divine mind into our mind" (CW, II, 281).   But how can one intuit anything when one is wrapped up in his empirical understanding?   To explicate that possibility, Emerson, as we know, has to distinguish Reason from Understanding and consign the former faculty to the realm of absolute truth.[13]   But is this distinction a reality?   Is it not a mere convenient invention of the transcendental thinker himself?   Here, indeed, we have entered the territory of mysticism.   Therefore, we can neither deny nor verify the validity of the Emersonian intuition or Reason.   Perhaps we can only repeat these empty-sounding remarks by Emerson:

> ...the soul's scale is one; the scale of the senses and the
> understanding is another.   Before the great revelations of the
> soul, time, Space and Nature shrink away. (CW, II, 273)
> Of this pure nature every man is at some time sensible.
> Language cannot paint it with his colors.   It is too subtle.   It
> is indefinable, unmeasurable, but we know that it pervades
> and contains us. (CW, II, 271)

Emerson has never clearly stated that the faculty of Reason with its intuitive power can be cultivated or developed, although he never ceases to preach that it is a faculty innate to every individual. However, his idea of self-reliance and his discussion of discipline, which occupy a large part of his writings, both suggest unambiguously that each man can foster that faculty and increase that power.   It is only that he seems to have never shown us the practical way of advancing our innate power, either, except that his strongly idealistic tendency and his strong emphasis on the importance of "the moral sentiment" seem undoubtedly to suggest that the way to foster our intuitive power of Reason is to form the habit of abstracting, spiritualizing, or internalizing anything within our reach.   Aside from this suggestion, Emerson seems to believe, like a Wordsworthian, that such a high power will come automatically to the one who feels the existence of harmony between oneself and the external world.   Emerson himself had such an experience.   "Crossing a bare common," he said once, "in snow puddles, at twilight, under a clouded sky, without having in my thoughts any occurrence of special good fortune, I have enjoyed a perfect exhilaration" (CW, I, 9).   Then he went on to speak of the woods: "In the woods, too, a man casts off his years, as the snake his slough ...In the woods, we return to reason and faith" (9-10).

Finally he said: "Standing on the bare groud,—my head bathed by the blithe air and uplifted into infinite space,—all mean egotism vanishes.   I become a transparent eyeball; I am nothing; I see all; the currents of the Universal Being circulate through me; I am part of or parcel of God" (10).   This mystic or pseudo-mystic experience[14] shows that one's "moral sentiment" can be cultivated in one's close contact with outward nature.

Yet, can cultivating "the moral sentiment" (in any way one thinks fit) guarantee one's transcendence?   We know Thoreau is a practitioner of Emerson's transcendentalism.   But has he transcended even his surroundings?   We grant that he has a strong "moral sentiment" and his discipline at Walden may have helped him in advancing that sentiment.   Nevertheless, there is no evidence whatever that he did become a pure soul shed off his carnal case except after his death.

Emerson knows, of course, that it is important for a man to really transcend his world.   In his essay "The Transcendentalist," he says very plainly,"…there is no such thing as a transcendental *party*; that there is no pure transcendentalist; that we know of none but prophets and heralds of such a philosophy; that all who by strong bias of nature have leaned to the spiritual side in doctrine, have stopped short of their goal" (CW, I, 338).   So, transcendentalism is merely "the Saturnalia or excess of faith" (CW, I, 338).   There can be many transcendentalists, but no actual "transcenders."

Notwithstanding that there can be no actual "transcenders," there are for Emerson some "representative men" who, owing to their approximating "the central man," the creative source of all vitality, can be said to be only next to real "transcenders."   Socrates, Shakespeare, Raffaelle, Michel Angelo, Dante, and Jesus are all such figures.[15]   In fact, a philosopher like Plato, a mystic like

Swedenborg, a skeptic like Montaigne, a "man of the world" like Napoleon, and a writer like Goethe are all "incarnations in mortal form of that godhead whose distribution into individuals Emerson had marveled over as long ago as 'The American Scholar'" (Elliot 393).   Such "representative men" may not have really transcended their empirical world even in the end.   Yet, as they each embodied one attribute of that central divinity Emerson saw as the birthright of every man, they must have each achieved that transcendence sometime or other in their life, that is, the time when their "moral sentiment" so overcame their sensual life that a revelation of Truth or Beauty or Goodness was all left of them.

In actuality, the Poet, not any particular poet, is perhaps for Emerson the most likely type of man for transcendence, because, as he puts it, the poet is "the sayer, the namer, and represents beauty"; the poet is "a sovereign, and stands on the center" (CW, III, 7); and the poet is he who "sees and handles that which others dream of, traverses the whole scale of experience, and its representative of man, in virtue of being the largest power to receive and to impart" (CW, III, 6).   Merlin, Emerson's ideal poet or, as he calls him, "The kingly bard," is to "mount to paradise/By the stairway of surprise."[16] As we see, the entire essay of "The Poet" is full of extolments aimed to exalt the poet to the highest position possible: "The Poets are thus liberating gods" (CW, III, 32).

In what sense can we call the poets liberating gods?   Here is Emerson's own explanation:

> They are free, and they make free.   An imaginative book renders us much more service at first, by stimulating us through its tropes, than afterward, when we arrive at the precise sense of the author.   I think nothing is of any value in

> books, excepting the transcendental and extraordinary. (CW, III, 32)

> If the imagination intoxicates the poet, it is not inactive in other men. The metamorphosis excites in the beholder an emotion of joy. The use of symbols has a certain power of emancipation and exhilaration for all men. We seem to be touched by a wand, which makes us dance and run about happily, like children. (30)

In other words, imagination is, for author and reader alike, something to delight us by helping us transcend our present sensual occupation.

In his *The Liberating Gods,* John Q. Anderson points out that Emerson set forth four key points about the poet in 1844 in the essay "The Poet" and thenceforth those points were amplified in other essays and in journey entries and sometimes illustrated in his poems. The four points are: the poet is a representative man, he is endowed with superior intellectual perception, he is a seer and prophet, and he is the "Namer" and "Language-maker" (15). But in the same book Anderson also tells us that "beyond, always above the reach of such a superior mortal, stands the pristine ideal—the stark, supreme *idea—* poet" (57). After discussing Emerson's essay "Poetry and Imagination," Anderson says, "...the poet differs from ordinary men in degree, not in kind. Similarly, the poet differs from the ideal poet in the same manner" (58). Then he gives us a summary of the characteristics and functions of the ideal poet seen in Emerson's essay:

> He is a man speaking to man...

He has developed more completely than other men his innate powers as a divine being.

He depends on Reason to ascertain truth, although he does not ignore Understanding.

He incorporates all phases of native genius.

He is the seer whose perceptions not only penetrate to final meanings but comprehend immediately their full import.

He is the prophet whose knowledge of universal law permits the foreseeing of events and actions in the light of that law.

He is the Sayer whose ability to express truth in words of divine fire exceeds all others.

He is a truly representative man. ...

He is the supreme artist. ...

He possesses powers of transcendency.   He transcends human limitations more frequently than other men.   He enables other men to transcend limitations through his art. (58-59)

I think the last-mentioned characteristic and function above can in fact be considered as the conclusive point.   The ideal poet is Emerson's true "transcender," besides whom even Homer or Shakespeare will appear far short of perfection.   No wonder Emerson himself once said, "I am born a poet, of a low class without doubt, yet a poet."[17]

Emerson explains that he is still a poet "in the sense of a perceiver & dear lover of the harmonies that are in the soul & in matter, & specially of the correspondences between these & those."[18] In other words, he is a poet in the sense that he is a transcendentalist, if not a "transcender."   Despite this self-proclamation, however, there are critics who would grudge him that title.   Harold Bloom, for instance, opens his introduction to an edition of critical views on Emerson by deciding that "Emerson is an experiential critic and essayist, and not a transcendental philosopher" (1). We can, of course, understand Bloom's intention. He wants to direct us towards Emerson the writer and veer us from Emerson the thinker. But can he succeed?

I find myself still consenting to these remarks: "If nothing else, Emerson is a cerebral writer. (Too cerebral, many feel.) Ideas are his central concern, and it is precisely his ideas that get in the way of many twentieth-century readers" (Duncan xi). Bloom has his own right to assert his point, indeed. But for me Emerson is really a transcendentalist though not a "transcender." His value lies mainly in his transcendental ideas, which, though not always expressed with clarity without apparent contradictions, are at least consistent in trying to tell us indubitably who transcends what and how. And so far this paper has clarified, I hope, this value of his as well as his basic transcendental ideas regarding the *wh-* questions.

Notes

1. This is the argument made in Quinn, p.291.
2. For the term "Unity in Variety," see *Nature*, Chapter IV. In his *On the Principles of Genial Criticism*, Coleridge uses the term "multeity in unity" instead.
3. All quotations of Emerson hereinafter are from the Centenary Edition of *The Complete Works of Ralph Waldo Emerson*, CW being the abbreviation of this edition.
4. See *Encyclopaedia Britannica* (1948), vol.22, p.405.

5. This point is discussed by George Edward Woodberry in his *Ralph Waldo Emerson*, rpt. in Thomas J. Rountree, ed., *Critics on Emerson*, p.84.

6. I think Emerson does have such an idea.   Evidence can be found in such lines as: "Striving to be man, the worm/Mounts through all the spires of form." (Epigraph to *Nature*, 1847).

7. I owe this idea of abstraction ladder to S. I. Hayakawa. See his *Language in Thought and Action* (1952), Chapter 10.

8. Spiller et al. say that Emerson developed his characteristic method for lecture and essay—namely, starting on the level on common or material experience and rising to that of spiritual realization—from two assumptions: the centrality of man, and the exact correspondence between the planes of material and spiritual law.   See their *Literary History of the United States*, p.371.

9. In her "Skepticism and Dialectic in Emerson's 'Experience,'" Elizabeth Tebeaux argues that Emerson's skepticism in this work is "philosophical skepticism" rather than ordinary skepticism and as such it is not to deny his faith but to present a dialectic process to the certainty of his faith.   I think this view is true, but the "haunting overtones" of "Experience" really cannot but induce a suggestion of ordinary skepticism felt by such critics as David Browers, Joel Porte, and David W. Hill.

10. This point is noted with emphasis in Mark Van Doren, ed., *The Portable Emerson* (The Viking Press), pp. 21-22.

11. For a full study of Emerson's Oriental influence, see Carpenter's *Emerson and Asia*.

12. Emerson's two quoted lines here are obviously adapted from Blake's *Auguries of Innocence*: "To see a World in Grain of Sand/And a Heaven in a Wild Flower,/Hold infinity in the palm

of your hand/And Eternity in an hour." And these lines of Blake's are merely to extol the power of imagination.

13. In their study of Emerson's literary method as seen in the essay "Art," Walter Blair and Clarence Faust demonstrate a twice-bisected scheme in Emerson's Platonic thinking: the World first divided into the Intelligible and the Visible, which are further bisected into the realms of truths, opinions, objects and images, corresponding to four operations of the soul, namely, Reason, Understanding, Faith, and Conjecture. See Rountree's *Critics on Emerson,* p.94.

14. Henry B. Parkes uses these descriptions to prove that Emerson was a pseudo-mystic with a mythical experience based only on moments of exhilaration caused by a feeling of harmony between oneself and the external world. See his "Emerson," p. 126.

15. See, on this point, F. O. Mathiessen, "The Democratic Core of *Representative Men,*" rpt. in *Critics on Emerson*, p.101.

16. From the poem "Merlin," 11. 36-7.

17. See his Letter to Lydia Jackson, Concord, February 1, 1835.

18. See also his Letter to Lydia Jackson, Concord, February 1, 1835.

Works Consulted

Anderson, John Q. *The Liberating Gods.* Coral Gables, Florida: U of Miami P, 1971.

Bloom, Harold, ed. *Modern Critical Views: Ralph Waldo Emerson.* New York: Chelsea House Publishers, 1985.

Burke, Kenneth. "I, Eye, Ay —Emerson's Early Essay on 'Nature': Thoughts on Machinery of Transcendence." *The Sewanee Review*, 74 (Autumn 1966).

Carpenter, Frederic Ives. *Emerson and Asia.* Cambridge, MS:

Harvard UP, 1930.

Detweiler, Robert.   "The Over-Rated 'Over-Soul.'"   *American Literature.*   36 (March1964), rpt. in part in Rountree, 91-93.

Doren, Mark Van, ed.   *The Portable Emerson.*   New York: The Viking Press, 1946.

Duncan, Jeffrey L.   *The Power and Form of Emerson's Thought.*   The UP of Virgina, 1973.

Elliot, Emory, et al.   *The Columbia Literary History of the United States.*   Columbia UP, 1988.

Emerson, Waldo.   *The Complete Works of Ralph Waldo Emerson.*   The Centenary Edition.   New York: AMS Press, 1979.

Mathiessen, F. O.   "The Democratic Core of *Representative Men.*"   Rpt. in Rountree, 100-102.

Northrop Frye, et al., eds.   *The Harper Handbook to Literature.*   New York: Harper & Row, 1985.

Parkes Henry B.   "Emerson."   *Twentieth Century Views of Emerson.*   Ed. Milton Konvitz and Stephen Whicher.   Englewood Cliffs, NJ: Prentice-Hall, Inc., 1962. 125-7.

Porter, David.   "The Muse Has a Deeper Secret."   Rpt. in Bloom, 79-81.

Quinn, Arthur Hobson, ed.   *The Literature of the American People.*   New York: Meredith Corporation, 1951.

Rountree, Thomas J. ed.   *Critics on Emerson.*   Coral Gables, Florida: U of Miami P, 1979.

Spillers, Robert E, et al.   *Literary History of the United States.*   3rd ed.   New York: Macmillan Co., 1972.

Sutcliffe, Emerson Grant.   *Emerson's Theories of Literary Expressions.*   New York: Johnson Reprint Co., 1970.

Tebeaux, Elizabeth.   "Skepticism and Dialectic in Emerson's 'Experience.'"   *ESQ*, Vol, 32, 1st Quarter (1986).

Woodberry, George Edward.   *Ralph Waldo Emerson.*   New York: Macmillan, 1907.

* This paper first appeared in 1990 in National Chung Hsing University's *Journal of Arts and History*, Vol. XX.

The Contrarieties of Life in Keats' "The Eve of St. Agnes"

In his "Ode on a Grecian Urn," Keats calls our attention to an interesting fact. That is, although the pipers painted on the surface of the Grecian urn can only "Pipe to the spirit ditties of no tone" (1.14), they are, nonetheless, "For ever piping songs for ever new" (1.24). In the context these lines, of course, point to the irony of "sound in silence," or of "existence in absence," which can be associated with the recurrent motif of "life in death." However, for a modern critic these lines may as well point to the truth that a printed text, like the painted pipers, is indeed an externalization of the author's temporal impression of his object; but as soon as the text is printed, it is forever subject to the changeable interpretations of readers of all times, all places and all sorts—the text will forever render readings forever new.

It is with this understanding that I wish to proceed to give a re-interpretation of "The Eve of St. Agnes," one of the few longer poems of Keats' that have presumably the most obvious "argument" and hence the closest critical consensus. However, I do not mean to re-interpret the romance in a startlingly new way. Instead, I intend to start from the much-discussed theme of "the inextricable contrarieties of life," a theme often seen to subsist with Keats' works. What may seem unusual about my discussion herein is: after a close examination of the relevant textual detail, I will end this essay by considering the value of my adopted approach for this discussion and judging in what way this approach, together with some other available approaches, falls short of the expectation of hermeneutics. That is, I want to pose first as a critic of the poem's text, and then as a critic of my criticism itself and of some other types of criticism related to my theme.

It is well-known that Keats utters in his poems the keenest sense of the paradoxical co-existence or kinship of any two opposite attributes of life conceivable to his mind.   For instance, a tragedy like *King Lear* is for him a "bitter-sweet fruit."[1] *La Belle Dame* is regrettably, and often truly too, *sans merci*.   The melodious singing of a nightingale "in full-throated ease" will make the poet's heart ache and will pain his sense with "a drowsy numbness."[2]   For him, Melancholy "dwells with Beauty—Beauty that must die"; "Ay, in the very temple of Delight/Veiled Melancholy has her sovran shrine."[3] And for him, "Verse, fame, and beauty are intense indeed,/But death intenser—death is life's high meed."[4]

Any reader that has become familiar with this sense of life (no matter whether it is through reading the quoted poems or through other readers' information) must of necessity find the same sense exuberantly suggested in the story of Porphyro and Madeline in "The Eve of St. Agnes."   For, as William Stafford has pointed out, "every part of the [story's] scene stands out in contrast with another part, by a series of dimensioned extremes" (640).   It is easy to find in the poem such paired opposites as old-young, then-now, enemies-lovers, heavenly-earthly, outside-inside, sacred-profane, and many others.   And from these opposites we can easily construct a theme in line with the already-familiar theme of "contrarieties of life," by referring to the story's plot, characters, setting as well as the poem's images, etc.

As we know, the plot of "The Eve of St. Agnes" is based on a legend of the patron saint of virgins (i.e., a virtuous young girl will dream of her future husband on the eve of St. Agnes' Day if she performs certain rituals properly) and the Romeo and Juliet theme of young love thwarted by feuding families.   As the story begins, we see a beadsman perform his prayers and penances under an extremely cold weather while a sort of revelry is taking place in the heroine's Gothic castle.   Next we learn that Madeline, the heroine, resolves to follow the superstition of St. Agnes' Eve by retiring to her room for proper rituals while Porphyro, her beloved youth, risks his life in coming over to see her.   Then we are told that through the help of Angela, the only one in Madeline's family that is kind to the brave youth, Porphyro does succeed in seeing his sweetheart dreaming of him in bed.   And then the two lovers turn dream into reality by consummating their love then and there.   Finally the story ends with the information that the couple fled away into the storm at dawn while

> Angela the old
> Died palsy-twitch'd, with meagre face deform;
> The Beadsman, after thousand aves told,
> For aye unsought for slept among his ashes cold.
> (375-8)[5]

This story can lead us into consideration of "contrarieties of life" in at least three respects.   First, as we know, Keats ends his "Ode to a Nightingale" with two rhetorical questions: "Was it a vision, or a waking dream?/Fled is that music:—Do I wake or sleep?"   It is a characteristic of Romantic poets to feel the perplexing difficulty of telling poetic vision from actual reality.   In

"The Eve of St. Agnes," as Porphyro "melted" into Madeline's dream (1. 320), the dreamer certainly failed to see the practical intrusion of real life into appearance.   But the intrusion was there. In so depicting the scene Keats seems, doubtless, to point out the possible co-existence of two opposing aspects of life: the real and the fanciful.   And it is this possibility (against the theme of Cervantes' *Don Quixote*) that allows the spurting of love between Porphyro and Madeline.   For normally we do not expect love to develop between two feuding families.   The attachment of Porphyro to Madeline, like that of Romeo to Juliet, is ironic in practice.   But this sort of thing does happen.   It is another instance to show how two contrary things can wed with each other under certain circumstances.   But Porphyro and Madeline cannot have consummated their love without others' help.   Keats does not make clear the function of the Beadsman in the story's action.   This sacred man seems merely an ordinary priest praying as usual.   But it must seem more than a casual touch of Keats' for complicating the plot to begin and end the story with the description of this Beadsman's life and death.   We can never know for certain what the sacred man was praying on the Eve of St. Agnes.   Yet it is likely that he might, like any layman, pray for the fair to have the brave.   Therefore, we may justifiably suggest that the Beadsman and Angela represent two contrasting types of devotion: sacred vs. profane.   And it is the combination of these two that makes possible the young lovers' consummation in love.   However, the consummation is treated in terms of replacement. The old ones died significantly in the fulfillment of the young ones' will; the old ones' love is replaced by the young ones'.   And here we notice another contrariety of life: death is birth—the old ones' death is the young ones' birth of happy life.[6]

When we consider the story's setting, some more contrarieties of life can be found.   As we know, this story is in fact a poetic romance (the genre designation Keats gives to his *Endymion*) set in a medieval Gothic castle.   This setting naturally brings us far back to the mysterious times of St. Agnes, that is, the "Dark" Ages which have fascinated most Romantics and from which many Romantics draw their inspirations.[7]   This setting, aided by the implication the Spenserian stanza carries and the connotation of archaic words, can easily lead the reader to expect the permeation of miraculous (in the old sense of the word) elements in the poem.   However, this expectation is frustrated.   None of the story's events can be called miraculous in the archaic sense of the word; every happening can be logically interpreted (e.g., the hero's melting into the heroine's dream can be said to happen when Madeline is in a trance).   Furthermore, the vivid reality of the scene and the characters can strike the reader with a sense of immediacy.   Just as Stafford has said:

> The empathy for which Keats is celebrated is evident everywhere, even as he pushes his material into a distance of time and place.   The power of language to overcome distance, and in fact to use distance as inverse perspective, looms throughout the poem. (640)

The remoteness in time and place mixes into the present scene of actual life; the romantic clashes, nay, goes with the realistic; "then" becomes "now"; and time becomes eternity (a singular happening becomes an immortal tale)—and this is one of the most consoling contrarieties in life.

The sense of actuality is to be achieved by close attention to detail.   When we go into the detail of "The Eve of St. Agnes," we find a big set of contrasts: heat and cold, crimson and silver, revelry and austere penance, sensuality and chastity, hell and heaven, in addition to those mentioned above.[8] Indeed, not all these contrasts are contraries in one and the same experience.[9] But some of them, at least, can be used to demonstrate Keats' idea of "contrarieties of life." For instance, the opening stanza of the poem has been greatly praised for its unsurpassed description of "bitter chill":

> The owl, for all his feathers, was a-cold;
> The hare limp'd trembling through the frozen grass,
> And silent was the flock in woolly fold:
> Numb were the Beadsman's fingers, while he told
> His rosary, and while his frosted breath,
> Like pious incense from a censer old,
> Seem'd taking flight for heaven, without a death,
> Past the sweet Virgin's picture, while his prayer he saith.

These images of the cold naturally set a sharp contrast to the "level chambers" which are "glowing to receive a thousand guests" (ll. 32-33). But this contrast is only superficial. The truly significant contrast is to be seen between the cold outside of the world and the warm inside of the lover's heart:

> Meantime, across the moors,
> Had come young Porphyro, with heart on fire
> For Madeline. (ll.74-76)

It is indeed frantic to cross the moors in such a bitter weather. But is it not true that neither the cold weather nor the cold manners of men can chill a true lover's impetuous fire? In matters of love, heat really often grows where coldness is most keenly felt.

The inclemency of the weather makes another contrariety of life in the story. In stanza 39, we have these two lines supposedly spoken by Porphyro to Madeline: "Hark! 'tis an elfin storm from faery land,/Of haggard seeming, but a boon indeed." Truly, to the inclement weather the lovers owe, partly at least, their safe stay in the castle and their safe escape from it. This proves the ironic truth of one of our proverbs: Where there seems to be more danger, there is more safety.

So far I have discussed Keats' "The Eve of St. Agnes" exclusively in the light of its suggested "contrarieties of life," and my points have been supported with evidence and good reasoning. But does this sort of discussion have any value at all?

The answer can be in the affirmative if we are concerned with the poet's thought only. For my interpretation so far has been theme-oriented; my approach is thematological. And we know that more often than not the theme of a work can reflect its author's thought. As the present case indicates, through a thematic study of "The Eve of St. Agnes" we can surely affirm that for Keats life is indeed something full of inextricable contrarieties.

But there is some danger in this approach. That is, one may forget the poem as soon as one arrives at this thematic conclusion. Or to speak figuratively, one may take a plum in a pie for the whole pie.[10] And we know this is a great mistake. The theme of a poem is no more representative of the poem than a particular tree is of the forest in which it grows. And that is why thematic interpretations are often disparaged by modern critics.

Yet, my interpretation above of "The Eve of St. Agnes" need not be seen as wholly thematological. The idea of contrariety in life contains an element associable with the idea of irony, or of paradox, or of tension—that is, with the three key terms which New Criticism often adopts in judging literary works.   For instance, the contrariety we see in the wedding of lovers from feuding families is also ironic; the recognition that cold often begets heat is the recognition of a paradox, and one can detect without fail the existence of tension between the poem's medieval setting and its realistic detail.   So, if we are not content with our message-hunting in perceiving the contrarieties in Keats' poem, we can proceed to judge the work with any of the three terms of New Criticism, using the instances of contrariety to round off any necessary argument.

To discuss the contrarieties in terms of irony, paradox or tension is to employ a textual approach to the work.   It may satisfy a believer in these terms.   But to one who doubts the validity of such terms in judging a work, the contrarieties that constitute the irony, or paradox, or tension of the poem remain only part of the whole; to use a new label for the old material cannot save one from the danger of mistaking partial reading for full interpretation.

In fact, the poem with its full set of contrasts lends itself most easily to a structuralistic study.   For, as Jonathan Culler has said, "the relations that are most important in structural analysis are the simplest: binary oppositions" (14).   Now, the aforesaid pairs of opposites which arouse Keats' (as well as the readers') sense of contrariety in life can serve as the basic constituents for a whole system of structural analysis; they are the discovered functional *significants* and *signifies* in the "discovery procedure" which is indispensable to the analysis of *la langue* (that is, the poem as a Saussurean structure).

On this ground a clear-cut analysis of the poem's structure may really be built.   However, the question remains: is it the sum total of the poem? "No, of course not," one may answer quickly. For, as far as the structure of this poem is concerned, the binary oppositions are not the only elements that can be used to draw a structural diagram. If we are not afraid to use old-fashioned terms, for instance, we can trace the story's plot in chronological order from "exposition" through "complication" or "development" to "denouement," and end up by defining quite a different structure based on happenings, instead of on contrasts.

So, a structuralist study still cannot do justice to the poem. What can, then? How about mythological and archetypal approaches? Is there not a myth or archetype embedded in the contrariety of "death breeding life"? Are not Porphyro and Madeline, in a sense, the new king and queen who in due course of time replace the old ones, the Beadsman and Angela? Or are not the old ones a sort of "scapegoats"? If we want to think so deeply, we can find that a Freudian psycho-analytical approach is also possible here. The contrariety of "light in shade" or "shade in light" is the co-existence of "consciousness" with "unconsciousness"; the door in the poem that both shuts and opens is a sign of the female principle; and the contrast of revelry with austere penance is the opposition of the libidinous "Id" to "super-ego." Nevertheless, do these interpretations make sense? They do, we must allow. But again they are partial interpretations; they cannot stand for the entire poem.

It follows then that the contrarieties of life we find in Keats' "The Eve of St. Agnes" can lend themselves to various approaches of reading the poem. But the results of these approaches are at best only partial interpretations with limited validity, not to say Procrustean beds for a lively body. This leads us naturally to wonder if these new approaches can be better than the somewhat ancient and impressionistic one Leigh Hunt adopts in his exhaustive commentary on the same poem.[11]

"A thing of beauty is a joy forever," Keats thus begins his *Endymion*, which is a failure as a work in the poet's eye as well as in many critics'.   If *Endymion* is not a thing of beauty, "The Eve of St. Agnes" certainly is, for a good host of competent readers.   They can read the poem line by line as Leigh Hunt does, and find it a joy forever, without resorting to any definite approach with any invented terms signifying some pre-conceived qualities.   Although "beauty is truth," truth is not necessarily beauty in the case of literary appreciation.   Yes, "We murder to dissect."[12]   When we adopt an approach to analyze a poem, we are often murdering its beauty.   We may gain some partial truth about it; yet we do so at the risk of neglecting its totality.   "Any reading is a misreading" is a paradoxical statement aimed especially at those who are only too ready to take apprehension for comprehension at the instigation of any ready-made critical jargon.

This conclusion has obviously run in the vein of Susan Sontag's "Against Interpretation."   However, I do not mean, as does this eminent critic, to discourage hermeneutics in favor of "an erotics of art."[13]   In my opinion, no careful reader can avoid interpreting his reading and no serious critic should save the labor of analyzing his material.   Instead of disparaging all critical approaches, I am only pinpointing one of their common limitations.   In doing so, in fact, I also admit the value of any critical approach so long as it can give a convincing interpretation of the work before one's eyes.   If Keats' "The Eve of St. Agnes" were incapable of being approached in so many various ways, it might not prove so interesting to so many readers or critics.

Notes

1. "On Sitting down to Read *King Lear* Once Again," l. 8.
2. "Ode to a Nightingale," ll. 1-10.
3. "Ode on Melancholy," ll. 21-26.
4. "Why Did I Laugh Tonight? No Voice Will Tell," ll.13-14.
5. All the quoted lines of Keats' work herein are from the 1820 text reprinted in Jack Stillinger, ed., *The Poems of John Keats*.
6. Whether or not the Beadsman and Angela died on the very night when the young lovers fled away is a question of much debate among critics.   But the lack of clarity in the text does not weaken the point I am making here, as mine is only a symbolic interpretation.
7. It is for this sake that Fred Inglis thinks of the poem as "a parody, both amiable and ferocious, of the medieval courtly-love romance and its pseudo-Gothic imitations."   See his *Keats*, pp. 94-96.
8. These contrasts have been listed with others in the title note of the poem in M. H. Abrams, et al., ed., *The Norton Anthology of English Literature*, 4th edition (New York: Norton, 1979), vol. 2A, p. 808.
9. In his *Notes on Keats' Poetry and Prose*, p. 31, Deryn Chatwin has discussed the contrasts of "light and shade" and says, "The one contrary never entirely shuts out the other, though they remain separate, for Keats has not yet reached the position of finding contraries in one and the same experience...."
10. This danger is already pointed out in Laurence Perrine, ed., *Sound and Sense*, 6th ed. (New York: Harcourt Brace Jovanovich, 1982), Chapter 9.

11. The commentary was reprinted in his *Imagination and Fancy* and it first appeared in *London Journal* on 21 January 1835.   See G. M. Matthews, ed., *Keats: The Critical Heritage*, pp. 275-80.

12. Wordsworth, "The Table Turned," l. 27.

13. Susan Sontag concludes her "Against Interpretation" by saying that "In place of a hermeneutics we need an erotics of art."   This famous essay is re-printed in many anthologies of criticism: e.g., Lionel Trilling, ed., *Literary Criticism: An Introductory Reader* (New York: Holt, Rinehart & Winston, 1970), pp. 610-19; and David lodge, ed., *20th Century literary Criticism* (London & New York: Longman, 1972), pp. 652-660.

Works Consulted

Chatwin, Deryn. *Notes on Keats' Poetry and Prose.*   London: Methuen, 1978.

Culler, Jonathan. *Structuralist Poetics.*   Ithaca, NY: Cornell UP, 1975.

Inglis, Fred. *Keats.*   New York: Arco, 1969.

Matthews, G.. M., ed. *Keats: The Critical Heritage.*   London: Routledge & Kegan Paul, 1971.

Stafford, William. "The Eve of St. Agnes."   *Master Poems of the English Language.*   Ed. Oscar Williams.   Trident Press, 1966. 639-42.

Stillinger, Jack, ed. *The Poems of John Keats.*   London: Heinemann, 1978.

* This paper first appeared in 1985 in National Chung Hsing University's *Journal of Arts and History*, Vol. XV.

Coleridge's Primary
and Secondary Imagination

Imagination is the most important term for romantic poets. But their use of the term is far from consistent. Wordsworth's Imagination, for instance, is admittedly a very elusive term. Renè Wellek observes that in many pronouncements of Wordsworth, Imagination is "substantially the eighteen-century faculty of arbitrary recall and willful combination of images," and in others it is "the neo-Platonic intellectual vision." "The neo-Platonic metaphysical conception," he adds, "permeates the last books of *The Prelude* and *The Excursion*, the psychological the Preface of 1815." But in using the term, Wordsworth "disconcertingly vacillates among three epistemological conceptions."

> At times he makes imagination purely subjective, an imposition of the human mind on the real world. At other times he makes it an illumination beyond the control of the conscious mind and even beyond the individual soul. But most frequently he takes an in-between position which favors the idea of a collaboration, an ennobling interchange of action from within and from without. (144-5)

Wellek has indeed thrown much light on the meanings of Wordsworth's Imagination. But to clarify the term even more, I may add that the neo-Platonic or metaphysical imagination is a pre-composition power, the power Wordsworth felt in his wanderings (e.g., when crossing the Alps or ascending the Snowdon), the power that made Wordsworth feel the unity of all living things, the power that halted the travelers (as Hartman suggests) in Wordsworth's poems, or the power that Blake simply calls "the Divine Vision" and Coleridge confusingly calls "primary imagination."   And the subjective or psychological imagination is a composition power, the power Wordsworth employed to write his poems when he was no longer wandering but had settled down and thought long and deeply, the power that Emerson defines as "the use which the Reason makes of the material world," or the power that Coleridge calls "secondary imagination."[1]

In his *Biographia Literaria*, Coleridge thus defines the two sorts of imagination:

> The primary imagination I hold to be the living power and prime agent of all human perception, and as a repetition in the finite mind of the eternal act of creation in the infinite I AM. The secondary I consider as an echo of the former, co-existing with the conscious will, yet still as identical with the primary in the kind of its agency, and differing only in degree, and in the mode of its operation. (167)

In interpreting the definitions, Basil Willey equates "the infinite I AM" with Nature and says that by the definition of the primary imagination Coleridge "is affirming that the mind is essentially and inveterately creative" (122).   Willey may be right, but somehow he fails to explain why Coleridge calls the primary imagination "the living power and prime agent of all human perception."   For me this definition echoes Wordsworth's assertion that imagination is "the faculty which is the primum mobile in Poetry."[2]   It tells the initiative as well as the creative nature of the power.   In other words, the words *prime, primum* and *primary* are all indicators of time sequence as well as of degree in importance.   By "prime agent" or "primum mobile" is meant the power which every man is born with and keeps until he loses it (as Wordsworth suggests in his "Immortality Ode"), the power which primitive people are most familiar with and civilization has somewhat suppressed (according to some anthropologists as well as Wordsworth), or the first power that brings the poet's perceptive and creative mind into play when he is receptively in contact with nature like a new-born babe or a primitive man.   And this first power is unmistakably the Divine Vision, the power that helps the poet to "see into the life of things."[3]

If Willey has missed a point about Coleridge's definition of the primary imagination, he has, however, rightly pointed out that "it is the Secondary Imagination which is at work in the making of poetry" (122). According to Coleridge, the secondary imagination is "an echo" of the primary.   This means, of course, that both are quite like each other. When Coleridge says the secondary co-exists with "the conscious will," he is saying that it involves our active thinking, and implying that the primary imagination, unlike the secondary, may co-exist with the *unconscious* mind.[4]   When Coleridge says that the secondary is "identical with the primary in the kind of its agency, and differing only in degree, and in the mode of its operation," he may be saying that both sorts of imagination have the same mind for their agency, and that when they operate, one may seem stronger than the other although they operate in different ways.   These words certainly do not make it clear that the secondary imagination is what I call a composition power.   But some further considerations will make it clear.

First, for both Coleridge and Wordsworth, imagination is closely associated with feelings or emotion.   If we read Coleridge's definitions of the two sorts of imagination together with Wordsworth's famous passage beginning with "Poetry is the spontaneous overflow...," it may strike us that Coleridge's definitions and Wordsworth's passage seem to be echoing or illustrating each other.   Wordsworth's "spontaneous overflow of powerful feelings" or the emotion to be " recollected in tranquility" is equivalent, as it were, to Coleridge's primary imagination, while Wordsworth's "emotion-copy," which is produced after tranquil contemplation, seems parallel to Coleridge's secondary imagination. Just as Coleridge says the secondary imagination is "an echo" to the primary, so Wordsworth says the emotion-copy is "similar" to the original.   Wordsworth's emotion-copy involves contemplation (that is, the "conscious will") just like Coleridge's secondary imagination, while "the *spontaneous* overflow of powerful feelings" is *unconscious* like the primary.   Besides, since the overflow of feelings is "powerful," it may be stronger than the emotion-copy, thus explaining Coleridge's idea of "differing only in degree," whereas the conscious and the unconscious minds explain his idea of difference "in the mode of its operation."

Second, for both Coleridge and Wordsworth, imagination is also an image-forming faculty.   This faculty can be employed in "the voluntary as well as in the merely associative" thought (Prescott 144).   When one sits at one's desk thinking for images to put in a poem, one is using not the freely associative thought but the voluntary thought.   But when a poetic vision with vivid images comes to one's mind, one feels it is really like "Aeolian visitations" to the harp—the operation is "spontaneous, quick, and effortless" (Prescott 52).

Third, after saying that the secondary imagination operates in a different mode, Coleridge goes on to say:

> It dissolves, diffuses, dissipates, in order to re-create; or where this process is rendered impossible, yet still, at all events, it struggles to idealize and to unify. (167)

This is indeed to explain the voluntary mode of the secondary imagination engaged in composing poetry, in contrast with the involuntary mode of the primary that comes to the poet spontaneously. To dissolve, diffuse and dissipate is the function of analytical reason, akin to that of Wordsworth's Judgment. To idealize and unify, on the contrary, is the function of synthetic reason, somewhat similar to that of Wordsworth's Invention. But, of course, the secondary imagination is not pure reason, which is too "cool" to be life-like. As both an analyzing and a synthesizing power employed in composting poetry, the secondary imagination is still like the primary in that it involves a strong fit of passion and therefore seems to be a living faculty, capable of changing others and changing itself. This is the reason why Coleridge adds that the secondary imagination "is essentially *vital*, even as all objects (as objects) are essentially fixed and dead" (167).

There seem to be a number of people who agree with R. D. Havens that the primary imagination is "just a unifying and interpreting power, which all persons possess" and the secondary imagination is "the higher gift" (possessed by the poet alone).[5] This may be true for Wordsworth in the sense that every man is for him a born-poet, has his first "creative sensibility" or "poetic spirit" until death if not "abated or suppressed" in after years.[6] But it will be untrue if we think of the primary imagination as a pre-composition power, as the first cause of the spontaneous overflow of powerful emotion which is to be recollected later in tranquility as the "raw material" of poetry.   For, in that case, the primary imagination will be equal to poetic vision which not all men can have at all times. In my opinion, contrary to Havens and others' opinion, the secondary imagination is easier to get since it involves our conscious will.   In other words, we can all become thinkers of images and shapers of forms, creative in the sense of artifice, but we cannot all become real poets with second sight, divinely connected with the Muses, creative in the sense of nature.   Thus, the primary imagination is a higher gift than the secondary imagination.

In fact, Wordsworth never explicitly or implicitly judges which of the two modes of imagination is "higher."   But he does seem to hold that Imagination is a superior power to Fancy.   In the Preface to the 1815 Edition of his works, Wordsworth objects to Coleridge's calling Fancy "the aggregative and associative power."[7]   His reason is: "The definition is too general. To aggregate and to associate, to evoke and to combine, belong as well to the Imagination as to the Fancy" (See Owen 184).   He prefers to have a distinguishable definition although his own exposition regarding these two terms is likewise far from distinctive.   His distinction seems to culminate in the statement that "Fancy is given to quicken and to beguile the temporal part of our nature, Imagination to incite and to support the eternal" (See Owen 185).   This suggests that Fancy is more capricious and less serious than Imagination.

Notes

1. See Hartman, *Wordsworth's Poetry 1787-1814*, Ch. I; Blake, *Annotations to Wordsworth's Poems*; Coleridge, *Biographia Literaria*, Ch. XIII; and Emerson, *Nature*, VI.
2. See his letter to Henry Reed of 27 September 1845.
3. See Wordsworth's "Tintern Abbey," 1. 49. F. C. Prescott says that the poetic thought (i.e., the visionary thought) is "older" than the ordinary thought; therefore, it is primary. See his *The Poetic Mind*, p. 53.
4. J. Shawcross says, "In the first case our exercise of the power is unconscious: in the second the will directs, though it does not determine, the activity of the imagination." See the Introduction to his edition of *Biographia Literaria*, p. 1xvii.
5. See his *The Mind of a Poet*, p. 207. Cf. Willey's article and Shawcross's Introduction to *Biographia Literaria*.
6. See Wordsworth's *The Prelude*, II, 379 & 276-80.
7. This definition appears in Southey's *Omniana* (1812).

Works Consulted

Coleridge, S. T. *Biographia Literaria.* Ed., George Watson. London: Dent, 1965.

Hartman, Jeffrey. *Wordsworth's Poetry 1787-1814.* New Haven: Yale UP, 1964.

Havens, R. D. *The Mind of a Poet.* Baltimore: Johns Hopkins UP, 1941.

Hill, John Spencer, ed. *The Romantic Imagination.* London: MacMillan, 1977.

Owen, W. J. B., ed.   *Wordsworth's Literary Criticism.*   London:
    Routledge, 1974.

Prescott, F. C.   *The Poetic Mind.*   Ithaca, NY: MacMillan, 1922.

Shawcross, J., ed.   *Biographia Literaria.*   Oxford: Oxford UP,
    1973.

Wellek, Renè.   *A History of Modern Criticism, 1750-1950.*   New
    Haven & London: Yale UP, 1955.

Willy, Basil.   "Imagination and Fancy."   *Nineteenth Century
    Studies* (1949); rpt. in Hill, 120-5.

Wordsworth, William.   *The Prelude.*   Ed., Ernest de Selincourt.
    Oxford: Oxford UP, 1970.

* This paper first appeared in 1982 in National Chung Hsing
    University's *Journal of Arts and History*, Vol. XII.

Some More Epic Analogies
in Wordsworth's *The Prelude*

An originally unnamed work later published posthumously, Wordsworth's *The Prelude* has been a subject of much controversy for not only its genetic complexity (What a complicated textual history it has!) but also its generic mystery (What kind of work is it after all?). It is doubtless a poem, a long poem. But is that all? It can be a "regular versified autobiography" (De Quincey 548) or "subjective autobiography" (Bateson 165), as it talks so much about the poet himself. It is, of course, "a verse-epistle to Coleridge" (Hartman 1971, 257). And we cannot deny that it "achieves philosophical poetry," as in it the poet really "grapples with philosophical problems" (Gallie 164). Then what else? A combination of the *Bildungsroman* and the *Kunstlerroman* (Abrams 586)? A psychological (Hartleian) treatise? A doctrine of education or politics? An extended lyric? A "prophetic Lay more than historic"?[1] The fact is, it is all of these and none of these. It is a literary chameleon that always changes its appearance. If one wants to be free from mistakes, one had better call it, to borrow the poet's phrase, "a thing unprecedented in literary history"[2] or, as Herbert Lindenberger points out, "a composite of several genres" (13).

With this understanding, I would not maintain that the work should be labeled an epic, although it is my intention to discuss in

this paper how it is like a poem of that genre.   But before the
discussion begins, we may note in passing that although to write an
epic had been Wordsworth's ambition, he did not consider *The
Prelude* an epic at the time he finished this masterpiece of his; he
thought humbly, instead, that he was not yet equal to an epic task.
This is clear in the two statements he made in his two letters of 1805
to Sir George Beaumont:

> It is not self-conceit, as you will know well, that has induced
> [me] to do this, but real humility: I began the work because I
> was unprepared to treat any more arduous subject, and
> diffident of my own powers.[3]

> This work may be considered as a sort of portico to the
> Recluse, part of the same building, which I hope to be able
> erelong to begin with, in earnest; and if I am permitted to
> bring it to conclusion, and to write, further, a narrative Poem
> of the Epic kind, I shall consider the *task* of my life as over.[4]

Despite the fact that Wordsworth did not consider *The Prelude*
an epic, his readers have been finding epic analogies in the work.
Superficially, a poem of 8,584 lines[5] does have "epic length"
(Hartman 1971, 208); the opening address to the breeze is really like
an epic invocation; examples of epic simile and digression can also
be found indeed.   And one can even argue that the narrative begins
in *medias res*. (Hartman 1962, 607).   But such superficial and local
similarities are not the most important facts to establish the work as
an epic.   Then, one may point out that it has "high seriousness,
sustained exercise of the will, and even amplitude and breadth"
(Lindenberger 13) in its theme (or tone), hero and setting.   But the

use of such abstract terms without the support of more concrete justifications will seem too impressionistic and subjective to be convincing. Again, one may discover in the poem's structure a Beatrice-Dante-Virgil relationship (Hartman 1962, 613) or an Odyssean journey for home (Abrams 592); in the poem's language (or style) so many traces of Miltonic rhetoric.[6] But conclusions of comparative nature as such are not drawn without the danger of arbitrariness and oversimplification.

It seems, therefore, that the epic analogies already explored in the poem are as valid and vain as so many other studies of the poem. And one wonders whether one can discover more striking resemblance for the "ape" to bear to "man." I dare not claim I can do the miraculous job. However, I believe I can eke out the analogy-hunting interest by looking again from ape to man, and this time with equal attention to the local and the overall features of the body, with due analytical zest (to the chagrin of the poet), and with some imagination (to the great joy of the same person).

As we all know, an epic like *Iliad* or *Paradise Lost* often involves two sides in plain conflict for the sake of something: the confederated Greeks against the men of Troy and their allies for the sake of Helen (or, honor), or God and good angels against Satan and his subordinate devils for the sake of man's soul. Now in *The Prelude* we see a similar conflict between nature and society for the sake of the poet's soul, that is, imagination. This conflict does not take the form of an open war as does that of *Iliad*, nor does it introduce an active inducement (of Satan to Eve) like that of *Paradise Lost*. It is only a poet's inner conflict resulting from the soul's travel between two mutually opposing worlds, much like the conflict existing in Faust's mind as it travels in the realms of God's creation and Mephistopheles' conjury. Wordsworth's nature, referring to such external things of beauty as hill and vale, stream and lake, forest and sky, flower and bird, and other things living with or in them, is God's primary creation and is said to be conducive to the growth of the poet's mind.   On the other hand, Wordsworth's society as exemplified in *The Prelude*, referring to such man-made places or institutes as city and town, school and church, and such human activities as party and fair, government and revolution, is a "Parliament of Monsters" (VII 692) and "blank confusion" (VII 696), something fearfully destructive to the poet's soul.   Accordingly, it is only natural that we feel a certain tension in the poet's account of his life with man in nature and society.   The tension may not rise to the pitch of an epic war or inducement affecting the entire civilization or moral future of mankind.   It, nonetheless, lends itself easily to epic treatment.[7]

Much depends on the idea of imagination.   If imagination is not just a particular romantic poet's soul but "the faculty which is the primum mobile in [all] Poetry," [8] then a narrative of the genesis, growth, impairment and restoration of a poet's imagination under the opposing influences of nature and society should be more than a personal history.   If "we are hard put to think of *The Prelude*... as a spokesman for its age" (Lindenberger 13), we can justifiably think of it as a spokesman for poets of all ages.   So, let's examine whether or not imagination is Wordsworth's soul only.

For Wordsworth, love is the originator of poetic imagination. In *The Prelude*, II 238 ff., he explains how an infant babe "gathers passion from his mother's eye," and how as his senses are quickened and his mind possesses a synthetic power, "the first/Poetic spirit of our human life" comes into the child.   For Wordsworth, love is also an indispensable element of poetic imagination.   In Book XIII, he says:

Imagination having been our theme,
So also hath that intellectual love,
For they are each in each, and cannot stand
Dividually. (178-81)

Of course, Wordsworth has, directly or indirectly, said much more about imagination in all his works: for instance, its relation to fancy, to memory, to intuition, to sense and mind, to the moods of joy, pain, fear and solitude, or to mystic, animistic or pantheistic experiences. But whatever else he has said or implied, it remains true that as he takes love for the originator and indispensable element of poetic imagination, the history of his poetic imagination is a history of love; and as he regards imagination as his creative soul, by equation love is his creative soul, too. Now isn't love the soul of all other great poets too (if one prefers not to use the mystic term "imagination")?

The question cannot be easily answered because it will involve the hard job of investigating the great poets' lives first. But it is interesting to note that almost all the great epic writers we can think of are interested in love of one form or another: love for a beauty or honor in *Iliad,* love for home in *Odyssey,* love for national glory in *Aeneid,* love for divine virtue in *Divine Comedy* and love for God in *Paradise Lost.* Now when we come to Wordsworth's *The Prelude,* we find it shows the poet's interest in love for nature and man. And the story in it is a story of how this kind of love (sometimes "nicknamed" *imagination* or *creative mind* or *undersoul* or other fancy terms) grows or is stunted in the interaction of nature and society. This is as interesting a story as that of any epic mentioned above, if we can review it step by step as follows:

In Books I and II of *The Prelude*, the poet tells mainly about his childhood and schooltime (roughly from five to seventeen years old) at Hawkshead.   The incidents related include: playing with the Derwent as a playmate, snaring woodcocks and stealing others' prey, plundering birds' nests, rowing a stolen boat, skating in games, fishing and kite-flying, pursuing home amusements, boat race, riding a horse to Farness Abbey, outing to the White Lion, morning walks with a friend, etc.   In these incidents, the poet, no matter whether he was single or in others' company, was strongly exposed to the influence of nature.   At first, he might only hold "unconscious intercourse/With the eternal Beauty" (I 589-90).   Yet, he confessed he was fostered "alike by beauty and by fear" (I 306) which nature provided.   At first, he might only indulge in "those fits of vulgar joy" (I 609); the beauteous forms of nature might only be "collaterally attached" (II 52) to his sports.   Yet, he finally came to seek nature "for her own sake" (II 208).   He summed up this period by saying:

> … I still retain'd
> My first creative sensibility,
> That by the regular action of the world
> My soul was unsubdu'd…. (II 378-81)

This manifestly tells that society then did not seriously, if ever, damage the imagination that nature had fostered in him.   In fact, by feeding his "lofty speculations" (II 462) and giving him a "never-failing principle of joy,/And purest passion" (II 465-66), nature had built, as it were, a formidable barricade for his imagination so that in "mingling with the world" he could live always "remov'd/From little enmities and low desires" (II 446-47)—the products of society.

In Book III, the setting is moved to the poet's earlier university days at Cambridge.   There the "battle" for the poet's soul between nature and society became apparent.   At first, the poet's sight was "dazzled by the novel show" of university environments and activities: society, as it were, dealt its first mighty blow.   But soon his mind "returned/Into its former self" (III 96-7) and became "busier in itself than heretofore" (III 104).   He "more directly recognized [his] powers and habits" (III 106).   Through contact with man and nature in that recognition, he seemed to have reached "an eminence" (III 169) of his creative power.   However, as his heart "Was social, and lov'd idleness and joy" (III 236), he then "slipp'd into the weekday works of youth" (III 244)—society won him over by its attraction.   It was a time when his "Imagination slept" (III 260), when the "deeper passions... were by me/Unshared" (III 532-36), when "Hush'd.../Was the undersoul, lock'd up in such a calm,/That not a leaf of the great nature stirred" (III 539-41). Society had temporarily triumphed over nature in the poet's heart.

Book IV brings the poet back to his native vale for summer vacation.   There he resumes constant contact with nature and feels "a human-heartedness about my love/For objects hitherto the gladsome air/Of my own private being, and no more" (IV 225-27). He begins to observe his villagers as well as his old Dame and his dog with interest.   When he first made another circuit of their little lake, he found "restoration came" (IV 146).   He also found "A freshness ... /In human Life" (IV 181-2).   Nevertheless, the newly restored imagination soon gave way to society again:

> ... a swarm
> Of heady thoughts jostling each other, gawds,
> And feast, and dance, and public revelry,

> And sports and games... these did now
> Seduce me from the firm habitual quest
> Of feeding pleasures, from that eager zeal,
> Those yearnings which had every day been mine,
>   ... (IV 272-80)

Although he might know "That vague heartless chace/Of trivial pleasures was a poor exchange/For books and Nature at that early age" (IV 304-06), it was not until that magnificent morning when he came late from a party and became, under the influence of the natural beauty then, "A dedicated Spirit" (IV 344) that he could be said to have restored his imagination again.   However, after his dedication, he experienced in himself "Conformity as just as that of old/To the end and written spirit of God's works,/Whether held forth in Nature or in Man" (IV 357-9).   His love for nature and man had led him to rescue the Discharged Soldier in distress.[9]

Thus, we are told in Book VI that his return to the University witnessed in him a change for the better:

> ... now the bonds
> Of indolent and vague society
> Relaxing in their hold, I lived henceforth
> More to myself, read more, reflected more,
> Felt more, and settled daily into habits
> More promising.   (VI 20-25)

And he felt "The Poet's soul was with me at that time" (VI 55).   His imagination led him to see an ash tree in human terms and to find a guide in living nature (v. VI 119).   His intensified love for nature made him rove among distant nooks in summer (v. VI 208) and carried him to the Alps.   He stated two motivations for going to the Alps: to see the mighty forms of nature and to witness the result of the French Revolution (*v.* VI 346-54).   But as his description shows, this trip owed its impressiveness more to the natural powers than to social activities.   It was when he and his friend were left alone to cross the Alps that he realized the great power of imagination. Hence his conclusion for this trip:

> A Stripling, scarcely of the household then
> Of social life, I look'd upon these things
> As from a distance, heard, and saw, and felt,
> Was touch'd, but with no intimate concern. (VI 693-6)

Society had not gathered enough forces to drag him from nature.

In Book VII, the poet describes himself as a vagrant dweller among the "unfenced regions of society" (VII 63).   In London now he fully experienced the life of a metropolis.   His response to it had three stages:

> No otherwise had I at first been mov'd
> With such a swell of feeling, follow'd soon
> By a blank sense of greatness pass'd away
> And afterwards continued to be mov'd
> In presence of that Metropolis... (VIII 742-6)

The three stages constitute a similar pattern of mind as occurred in his Cambridge period.   At first, society dazzled him by its novel show, then he knew he was trifling (*v.* VIII 707), and then he returned to himself.   The only significant difference is: at Cambridge he had chances to go directly back to great nature for the restoration of his poetic mind; in London he only depended on his memory of the past for preventing himself from falling into the trap of "that vast receptacle" (VII 735):

> Attention comes,
> And comprehensiveness and memory,
> From early converse with the works of God
> Among all regions; chiefly where appear
> Most obviously simplicity and power. (VII 717-21)

The great strength of nature was here testified. The immediate society with its "parliament of monster" failed to repulse the remote influence of nature on him. His imagination remained—he was able to see "the parts/As parts, but with a feeling of the whole" (VII 712-3)—because "The Spirit of Nature was upon me here" (VII 736).

If during the London period society still could not gain ground, it at least made the poet love his fellow beings more (v. VIII 860 ff.) and made him prepared ironically for his mental breakdown in the later France period. In France he was at first attracted to the novelties of the country (v. IX 82-5), and then spent a short time of loitering life in society (v. IX 114-22), much like his first experience at Cambridge or in London. But, after that, instead of being claimed back by nature, he "gradually withdrew/Into a noisier world" and soon became "a Patriot," his heart all given "to the people" (IX 123-6). He got acquainted with some military officers, among whom was the meeker and more benign Beaupuy, whose revolutionary zeal threw him into complete sympathy. When he came back to England, a number of events pushed him to his mental crisis—in England, the baffled contention against the traffickers in Negro blood (v. X 204-6) and Britain's declaration of war against the new Republic of France (*v.* X 229 ff.); in France, Robespierre's reign of terror (*v.* X 110-1 & 329) and the Frenchmen's changing a war of self-defense for one of conquest (*v.* X 792-3).   In each case he tried to reason himself into accepting the *status quo*.   However, as his analytical reasoning failed to answer satisfactorily his perplexed mind or simply proved false, he finally lost all feeling of conviction and "yielded up moral questions in despair" (X 900).   So, society at last won a victory over nature by first involving the poet in the most passionate form of mass behavior, namely revolution, and then confusing him with the maze of intellectual reasoning.   If nature had taught him to love mankind intuitively before, he had forgotten it by then.[10]   For the restoration of his poetic power, he had to go back again to nature.

So far we have clearly seen that the conflict between nature and society in *The Prelude* is developed as a result of the poet's travel between these two realms.   Nature, as a positive power, has been dragging the poet to the bright side of man, teaching him to love mankind unquestioningly so that he can willingly do the holy service of writing poetry, and giving him a vision of one life in all, a synthetic power which is the power of imagination.   On the other hand, society, as a negative power, has been pulling the poet to the dark side of man, calling upon him to indulge in trivial pleasures so that he will abandon his poetic ambition, or setting him to grope fruitlessly in the blind alley of analytical science, which is harmful to poetic imagination.   So, as far as the plot of conflict is concerned, nature and society in *The Prelude* are really like the two opposing forces often found in an epic.   Now from this we can push the matter even further and find more epic analogies in the poem.

We know there are usually supernatural forces—gods, angels and demons—intervening in the action of an epic.   Now we find that in *The Prelude* men seem to take the role of supernatural forces. On one side, we have poets, wanderers, hermits, shepherds, all those who love nature or live in nature; they are like good angels sent by nature to call or take the poet to its side.   On the other side, we have lawyers, preachers, politicians, revolutionists, all those who love society or live in society; they are like bad angels sent by society to counteract the effects of nature.

The division of men into these two kinds is obvious from the favorable and unfavorable terms used to describe them respectively. And the clearest examples of their intervention in the action are the comings of Dorothy, Mary, Coleridge and the poet's other friends to accompany the poet in nature or take him back to nature whenever he is in danger of losing his soul as at certain times in his Cambridge, London and France periods.   Meanwhile, we may think of not only Robespierre and the Royalist officers but also Beaupuy as particular figures sent by society to tempt the poet's soul and damage his imagination, directly or indirectly.

If in *The Prelude* men are the equivalent of supernatural forces in an epic, then books are the equivalent of epic figures' arms or weapons.   In Book V the poet makes it clear that books are also of two kinds: books of poetry, fairy tales, romances, etc. (products of passion and imagination, Works of Bard, or the Semi-Quixote's shell) in contrast with books of mathematics, philosophy, logic, politics, etc. (products of reason and knowledge, Works of Sage, or the Semi-Quixote's stone).   Both kinds of books are "ever to be hallowed" because they are both "only less.../Than Nature's self" (V 220-2).   However, in *The Prelude* the former is always a strengthening power for the poet's imagination while the latter except books of geometry is a weakening power.   In Book V, the poet tells how fairy tales and romances helped him to have "no vulgar fear" (V 474) of dead men's ghastly faces, how he was fond of reading the Arabian Tales, how such imaginative works are friends of "yoke-fellows" (V 544), and how reading poetry provided his young heart with pleasure from "images, and sentiments, and words" (V 603). In Book VI, he tells how he also gathered pleasure from geometry by meditating "Upon the alliance of those simple, pure/Proportions and relations with the frame/And laws of Nature" (V 144-6). And we know the poet seldom cared to read books of different nature, but when "wild theories were afloat" (X 774), he must have been more or less influenced by them. It makes no difference whether he ever read Godwin's *Enquiry Concerning Political Justice* or not. What counts is, ideas from books extolling pure reason for human affairs must have helped to undermine his poetic soul.

> ... even so did I unsoul
> As readily by syllogistic words
> Some charm of Logic, ever within reach,
> Those mysteries of passion... (XI 81-4)[11]

Therefore, we can say books of analytical nature and logical reasoning were like the weapons society used to battle against nature, whose arms to protect the poet's soul seemed to be books of imaginative (synthetic) nature and passionate feeling.

So far I have pointed out some more epic analogies in *The Prelude* in view of its theme, plot, characters, etc. They may not strike the reader as obviously plausible, as they require the reader to imagine nature and society as two combatant bodies, men as supernatural forces, and books as arms or weapons. However, if they are far-fetched, they are never absurd, for we can deduce from them a work quite like another version of Milton's *Paradise Lost* and *Paradise Regained* combined.

In *Paradise Lost*, God created the first man and woman to live happily in the Garden.   But Adam and Eve were tempted by Satan. Notwithstanding that God had sent angels to keep the couple in obedience to Him, Eve's intellectual pride lent to Satan's temptation, and her false reasoning ("Good unknown, sure is not had, or had/ And yet unknown, is as not had at all"[12]) plus the visual deception of the serpent brought about man's fall and the knowledge of evil while Adam agreed to fall with Eve out of love for her.   The disobedient pair was led out of the Garden in despair.   Now the first ten books of *The Prelude* tell much the same thing, only in an obscure manner and in different terms.   In substitution for God and Adam and Eve, we now have nature and the poet only.   Nature "created" the poet's soul and gave him an Eden (his Vale), too.   The poet is equal to Adam and Eve in combination, or Adam and eve are in effect two mutually complementary elements of mankind, not just man and woman but "the two natures,/The one that feels, the other that observes" (XIII 323-4) or simply feeling (heart) and sense (eye). Now society, like Satan, came to tempt the poet.   Nature sent angels (Dorothy, Mary, Robert Jones, etc.) to guard him, too.   But since he could not "welcome what was given, and craved no more" (XI 207), the serpent (the French Revolution) came with its visual deception. He took the outward facts for truth—"the eye was master of the heart" (XI 173)—and plunged into false reasoning (Godwinian rationalism) much like Eve.   And the result was: his loving heart (Adam) fell with his reasoning head (Eve) into knowledge of evil and his paradise was lost.   Coleridge and Dorothy (Milton's Michael and Raphael) came to lead him out of the befouled Garden (society).   He was launched in despair until the paradise was regained.

The last three books of *The Prelude* are in some sense the equivalent of Milton's *Paradise Regained*.[13] In *Paradise Regained*, we have Jesus, the all-knowing savior of mankind, resisting all Satan's temptations by adhering to His Father's admonitions. In the last three books of *The Prelude*, we have the enlightened poet getting rid of society (the embodiment of temptations) by thinking back over the past lessons given him by nature (his spiritual father). It is noteworthy that when the poet speaks of "spots of time" as a "vivifying Virtue" to nourish and invisibly repair our minds (*v.* XI 258 ff.), the examples given are his seeing a woman in wind-vexed garments surrounded by visionary dreariness, and his waiting impatiently with his brothers for two horses to bear them home on a stormy day up a lonely crag. By these two incidents, nature seems to suggest to the poet two messages: a "missioner" (one with pitcher on head)[14] is sure to suffer from adversities; one should wait patiently for God's arrangement. These two messages are what Jesus uses to carry out his mission of regaining man's lost paradise; they are also what Wordsworth needs to carry out his mission of creating great poetry.[15] If this interpretation should sound too personal to be convincing, suffice it that Wordsworth's memory, which is celebrated throughout his work for its restoring and elevating power, is almost always connected with nature, and as such it is virtually like God's word if Wordsworth's nature can be equated with God in certain context. So, if for Wordsworth memory is a virtue which "enables us to mount/When high, more high, and lifts us up when fallen" (XI 267-8), it is like Christ's memory of God's word.

Of course, it was not memory alone that helped to restore the poet's impaired imagination. His sister's "sweet influence" (XIII 209) and Coleridge's "gentle Spirit" (XIII 245) had the same effect, and so had his direct contact with nature again, e.g., his going to the top of Snowdon to see the sun rise.   All these elements, among others, naturally find no explicit parallels in *Paradise Regained*. However, it may be worth thinking too that whereas in the end of *The Prelude* a friend accompanied the poet to a mountain top to find later in a "blue chasm" "the Soul, the Imagination of the whole" (XIII 55 ff.), in the end of *Paradise Regained*, Satan took Jesus to the highest pinnacle of a glorious temple to be transferred later by angels to a "green bank" for refreshing and repairing his body.   Is Wordsworth here making an unintentional parody?

As the last example shows, the similarities between Wordsworth's work and others' are often so subtle and obscure that one wonders if he ever had a mind to imitate others.[16]   Nevertheless, whether intentional or not, so long as the similarities can be felt, they may add interest to our reading.   I dare not claim that *The Prelude* is an epic of the usual kind or that it is a complete imitation of Milton's epics.   But I believe that to view the work as an epic and to explore some more epic analogies in it can at least bring into focus an interesting, if not very valuable, facet of it.

In his *On Wordsworth's Prelude*, Herbert Lindenberger quotes III 171-83 and says that Wordsworth "claims to find heroic argument in man's personal history" (12).   It is all very true.   But it is not only the "heroic argument" that makes an epic.   To equate *The Prelude* to an epic requires consideration of many other things. And I hope that so far this paper has significantly touched upon some of the many other things and can, by arguing and "imagining" for the epic stature of the work, set the poet's soul at rest since he had so much wanted to write an epic before his life was over.

Notes

1. See Samuel Taylor Coleridge, "Lines to William Wordsworth," rpt. in Jonathan Wordsworth, M. H. Abrams & Stephen Gill, ed. *The Prelude: 1799, 1805, 1850*, A Norton Critical Edition (New York & London: W. W. Norton & Co., 1979), p. 542. The critical edition is hereinafter referred to as Norton.
2. See Wordsworth's Letter of 1 May 1805 to Sir George Beaumont, rpt. in part in Norton, p. 534.
3. Letter of 1 May, rpt. in part in Norton, p. 534.
4. Letter of 3 June, rpt. in part in Norton, p. 534.
5. According to Ernest De Selincourt's edition of *Wordsworth: The Prelude*, Text of 1805 (Oxford UP, 1970). All book and page numbers in this paper refer to this text.
6. Lindenberger, among others, refers to this in his book, p. 10.
7. In his Introduction to the 1805 text, Ernest De Selincourt says: "Wordsworth was in evident agreement with Milton on the true nature of the epic subject. Both of them repudiated military exploits, 'hitherto the only argument heroic deemed,' in the desire to bring within its confines a more spiritual conflict. Only the pedant will dissent from their conception; and those who regard the mind of Wordsworth as both great in itself and essentially representative of the highest, the imaginative type of mind, will recognize its adventures as a fit theme for epic treatment."
8. See Wordsworth's letter to Henry Reed of 27 Sept. 1845. Quoted in Raymond Dexter Havens, *The Mind of a Poet* (Baltimore: The Johns Hopkins Press, 1941), p. 206.

9. The statement is valid in that the poet met and saved the soldier when he was taking a walk "along the public way," as was his "favorite pleasure."

10. In XI 199-257, the poet told how he was then unlike Mary Hutchinson (the "maid"), who could love whatever she saw unquestioningly.

11. Cf. also XI 123-8.

12. *Paradise Lost*, Bk. IX 756-7.

13. Cf. Hartman's remark: "... *The Excursion* continues *Paradise Regained* in the same way as the *Prelude* dovetails *Paradise Lost*."

14. I think the woman can stand for a missioner because she must have been carrying out the mission of fetching water with the pitcher from the pool or something like that.

15. Notice that the idea of writing poetry as a holy mission is stated in the beginning of *The Prelude*.   See I 60-3.

16. But, of course, Wordsworth is certainly influenced by Milton.

Works Consulted

Abrams, M. H.   "The Design of *The Prelude*: Wordsworth's Long Journey Home." Rpt. in Jonathan Wordsworth et al., 585-98.

Bateson, F. W.   W*ordsworth: A Re-Interpretation*.   London: Longman Group Ltd., 1971.

De Quincey, Thomas, "William Wordsworth."   *Tait's Edinburgh Magazine* (VI, 1839).   Rpt. in part in Jonathan Wordsworth et al., 545-7.

De Selincourt, Ernest, ed.   *Wordsworth: The Prelude*.   Oxford: Oxford UP, 1970.

Gallie, W. B.   "Is *The Prelude* a Philosophical Poem?"   Rpt. in

Jonathan Wordsworth et al., 663-78.

Hartman, Geoffrey H.   *Wordsworth's Poetry 1787-1814.*   New Haven & London: Yale UP, 1971.

--------.   "A Poet's Progress: Wordsworth and the *Via Naturaliter Negativa.*"   *Modern Philology*, LIX (1962).   Rpt. in Jonathan Wordsworth et al., 598-613.

Havens, Raymond Dexter.   *The Mind of a Poet.*   Baltimore: The Johns Hopkins Press, 1941.

Lindenberger, Herbert.   *On Wordsworth's Prelude.*   Princeton, NJ: Princeton UP, 1963.

Wordsworth, Jonathan, et al, eds.   *The Prelude: 1799, 1805, 1850.* A Norton Critical Edition.   New York & London: Norton & Co., 1979.

* This paper first appeared in 1981 in National Chung Hsing University's *Journal of Arts and History*, Vol. XI.

A Note on the Scansion of Keats's "La Bella Dame Sans Merci"

Here I want ot give a note on the scansion of Keats's "La Bella Dame Sans Merci." But before we enter into the discussion, let us read the poem again first.

> O what can ail thee, knight-at-arms!
> Alone and palely loitering!
> The sedge has withered from the lake,
> And no birds sing.
>
> O what can ail thee, knight-at-arms!
> So haggard and so woe-begone?
> The squirrel's granary is full,
> And the harvest's done.
>
> I see a lily on thy brow
> With anguish moist and fever dew,
> And on thy cheeks a fading rose,
> Fast withereth too.
>
> "I met a lady in the meads,
> Full beautiful—a faery's child,
> Her hair was long, her foot was light,

And her eyes were wild.

"I made a garland for her head,
And bracelets too, and fragrant zone,
She looked at me as she did love,
And made sweet moan.

"I set her on my pacing steed,
And nothing else saw all day long.
For sidelong would she bend, and sing
A faery's song.

"She found me roots of relish sweet,
And honey wild and manna-dew;
And sure in language strange she said,
'I love thee true.'

"She took me to her elfin grot,
And there she wept and sighed full sore;
And there I shut her wild, wild eyes
With kisses four.

"And there she lulled me asleep,
And there I dreamed—ah! woe betide!—
The latest dream I ever dreamed
On the cold hillside.

"I saw pale kings, and princess too,
Pale warriors, death-pale were they all:
They cried—'La belle dame sans merci

Hath thee in thrall!'

"I saw their starved lips in the gloam
With horrid warning gaped wide,
And I woke, and found me here
On the cold hillside.

"And this is why I sojourn here
Alone and palely loitering,
Though the sedge is withered from the lake,
And no birds sing."[1]

Four-line stanza rhyming abcb, dialogue form, stock-descriptive phrase, refrain, the theme of love- - yes, the above poem is a ballad. But does it have the common metrical pattern of a ballad?   Scanners of this poem seem to differ even on this apparently simple question. There are people, for instance, who insist on scanning the last line of each stanza as a trimeter line, seeing that it is often the case with most other ballads.   Accordingly, the line "And no birds sing" is said to have two instances of "metrical silence" distributed before the words *birds* and *sing*, the meter being iambic:

And no (   ) birds (   ) sing. [2]

In the meantime, however, there are also people who maintain that the line should be scanned as a dimeter line with only one instance of metrical silence before the word *sing* while the word *no* is unstressed:

And no birds (   ) sing.

Now, which version of scanning the line is more justifiable?   I think the latter is. And my reasons are:

First, not all the final lines of all the stanzas can be scanned as trimeter lines while they can all be conveniently scanned as dimeter ones.   For instance, it would be very awkward, if not absolutely impossible, to read the line "A faery's song" or "With kisses four" with three heavy stresses whereas it obviously contains two iambs. We admit that many of the lines have rendered our analysis difficult because some words can receive either more or less stress, depending on our way of scansion.   Nevertheless, I believe the metrical complexity of all the final lines does not make it impossible for us to analyze them as dimeter lines.   In fact, if we accept the ideas of "metrical silence" and "metrical substitution," then the analysis will be far from awkward.   For example, some lines can be said to contain an anapest plus an iamb: "And the harvest's done," "And her eyes were wild," "On the cold hillside." All the others can be said to contain two iambs except the line "And no birds sing," which, as already said, contains an anapest ("And no birds") plus a metrical silence which, together with the following stressed word *sing,* constitutes an iamb.

Second, it seems that Keats has no intention whatever to keep the standard metrical pattern of a ballad stanza in writing this poem. As we know, a ballad stanza usually has four lines, the first and the third of which are tetrameter lines while the second and the fourth of which are trimeter ones.   Now, as we examine the poem, we find at once that the second lines of all the stanzas are all tetrameter lines instead of trimeter ones.   That is, they have each of them one extra foot added to the normally trimeter lines.   As a result, the first three lines of each stanza are metrically of the same length.   This variation can help us to conclude that Keats may also have intended to break away from the norm of a ballad stanza by changing the number of metrical feet in the final line of each stanza.   In effect, it seems that for each stanza Keats has removed a foot from the fourth line and grafted it onto the second.

Third, I believe Keats has purposely made use of the metrical variation to suggest something although this "something" is open to various conjectures.   Indeed, much effect is added to the ballad through "the poignant and richly suggestive suspension achieved by shortening to two stresses the final line of each stanza."[3]   But doesn't the lengthening of the second line to four stresses also give contribution to poem's effect?   I think both instances of metrical variation work together to give the reader a shock or at least a feeling of puzzlement, just as the first speaker in the poem is shocked or puzzled to find the knight-at-arms "alone and palely loitering on the cold hillside."   But why?   How come the reader will feel shocked or puzzled through the metrical variation?   Because, you know, after reading three tetrameter lines, one may expect the next line to be a tetrameter line, too.   But since that is not the case, one cannot but be shocked or puzzled to find that the next line is only a dimeter one.   Somehow, he feels it is too short; he feels it ends all too abruptly.

"Yes, it is too short.   It ends all too abruptly."   Not only will the reader say so, but also the knight-at-arms though he refers to his love affair with the "faery's child" instead of to the poetic line that ends each stanza.   Thus, we see the metrical variation also serves to reflect the knight's state of mind.   The three tetrameter lines build up our expectation for as long a line next, just as the knight's stay with the elf builds up his longing for more happy days.   But our expectation fails just as the knight's hope perishes abruptly.

Yet, does the metrical variation only suggest that?   No. Another plausible consideration is: Since a dimeter line is literally half the length of a tetrameter line, might it not be used to suggest the now single state of the knight or the imperfection of the knight's elfin lover?   In each stanza of the poem, the last line is a dimeter one, that is, half the length of its foregoing line.   Does this not suggest that at last only half (that is, one) of the two lovers is left? Meanwhile, does it not suggest that at last the lady proves only half perfect for being without pity although she is beautiful (just as the literal translation of the poem's title means)?

If we want to push the matter to an extreme, we can even use the analyzed metrical variation to account for the much-discussed question of why Keats at first writes "With kisses four" for the thirty-second line.   In a letter Keats himself told his brother that he wrote the number four because he "was obliged to choose an even number that both eyes might have fair play."[4]   This explanation is not satisfactory.   For we may ask, "Why, then, not two or six?"   Is the number four really, as he also said, a "sufficient" number to show the knight's love on one hand and to "restrain the headlong impetuosity of [his] Muse"[5] on the other?   As a matter of fact, the direct and plain reason is: the word *four* rhymes naturally with the word *sore* in the thirtieth line.[6]   If we can give a far-fetched explanation as Keats seems to have done, I might say: "The number four is well-chosen here because four is the 'normal' number for the poem.   It is composed of four-line stanzas.   In each stanza all the lines except the last one have four feet each.   As the knight finds nothing abnormal in the elfin lady at first, it is normal for him to give her four kisses."

Surely I myself may have gone too far now.   But it remains that for a better effect the scansion of "La Belle Dame Sans Merci" demands our special attention to the unusual numbers of metrical feet which occur in the second and the final lines of each stanza.   If we scan the final line of each stanza as a dimeter one and consider it in connection with its three foregoing tetrameter lines, then we will be in a better position to make the sound echo the sense, as the above discussion shows.   And, perhaps, we can then fully see the artistic achievement in the art ballad.

Notes

1. From George B. Woods, et al., *The Literature of England* (N. P.: Scott, Foresman & Co., 1985), II, 282.
2. This is precisely what is suggested in Marlies K. Danziger & W. Stacy Johnson, *An Introduction to Literary Criticism* (New York.: D. C. Heath and Co., 1961), p.52
3. See Note 1 in M. H. Abrams, et al., eds.   *The Norton Anthology of English Literature,* revised, (New York: Norton, 1968), II, 526.
4. Quoted in Cleanth Brooks & Robert Penn Warren, *Understanding Poetry*, 3rd ed. (New York: Holt, Rinehart & Winston Inc., 1960, p. 69.
5. *Ibid.*
6. But Keats himself does not grant that this is the reason.

* This paper first appeared in 1979 in National Chung Hsing University's *Journal of Arts and History*, Vol. IX.

The Persistent Superior: Symbolism in Graham Greene's *A Burn-Out Case*

Today it is all but amusing to see Dickens undiscerningly attack those Victorian British people who, like Mrs. Jellyby in *Bleak House*, were overzealous in philanthropic schemes for the benefit of such "backward" people as the African Borrioboola-Gha natives. For, with the publication of Conrad's *Heart of Darkness*, we have become fully aware of the aggressive implications lurking behind the white men's zeal in Africa; we have come to believe that most of the Europeans who went to the great wilderness of Africa only pretended to bring good to the aborigines while they themselves were ever-aggravatingly corrupted there like Kurtz in the "heart of darkness." Indeed, Conrad's story, with its symbolic locale and symbolic action, has made Africa a land more horrible and mysterious than where Faulkner's bear looms big or Melville's whale appears white.

But has Conrad struck the final note and said the final word about the "invaders" of Africa? No. Some sixty years after the publication of *Heart of Darkness,*[1] Graham Greene in his *A Burnt-Out Case* has—not unconsciously, I believe—taken over Conrad's setting, the Belgian Congo, and told quite a different story. Instead of sending an innocent Marlow on an enlightening voyage to find a demoralized Kurtz, Greene has sent a certain heart-already-darkened Querry—"a successful man who has come to the end of success...the victim of a terrible attack of indifference...a sensualist for whom pleasure has gone stale, an artist for whom art has lost his meaning" (Wyndham 26) — to that part of the Congo where "the boat goes no further" (16),[2] where he regains his feeling for people and things though he ironically gets killed thereafter.   So, basically, one might assert, Greene's novel can be a parody of Conrad's: the one has made Africa a moral asylum while the other has made it an infectious area.

Aside from the basic difference, Greene also differs from Conrad in manipulating symbols in his novel.   Whereas Conrad mainly makes use of the setting and action of his story for symbolism, Greene mainly contrives to develop the theme of his story by symbolic characters.   It is true that in *Heart of Darkness* we also find such symbolic characters as the three Fate-like women in the office of the steamship company and Kurtz's "barbarous and superb"[3] women in the dark jungle.   Yet, such characters tend "not to be well rounded nor to carry on long conversations," but each of them "tends rather to be a character seen briefly and significantly— more an inanimate portrait than a person" (Kennedy 131).   In other words, Conrad's symbolic characters are common ones, more easily recognized and more easily interpreted than Greene's.   In *A Burnt-Out Case*, there surely is an evident symbolic character— namely, Querry's servant Deo Gratias, a leper in whom the disease has run its course, having eroded in this instance all the fingers and toes.   For, as many critics have pointed out, his physical handicap matches Querry's spiritual mutilation; they are two burn-out cases in different senses.   And, as A. A. DeVitis further suggests, Querry comes to Congo in search of "a return to usefulness and integrity," and this search for usefulness and integrity "is symbolized by Pendèlè, a place of contentment that Deo Gratias remembers from childhood" (123).

However, other symbolic characters in *A Burnt-Out Case* are not so distinct and understandable though they can be symbols. The reason is: unlike Conrad's Fate-like women, they are portrayed more like real persons, hence as often as not evading the reader's symbol-hunting eyes. For instance, the preposterous and snobbish Rycker, the cynical and sensational Parkinson, and the insensitive and self-seeking Father Thomas have been each of them a different looking-glass which returns such a straight image of Querry's past self as makes him afraid.[4] They are like Deo Gratias in that they hint at Querry's life. But they do not so clearly indicate their function.

In his study of Graham Greene, David Lodge calls our attention to the novelist's words in the Dedication: "This is not a *roman à clef*, but an attempt to give dramatic expression to various types of belief, half-belief and non-belief" (Lodge 40). Indeed, all other characters in *A Burnt-Out Case*, including the above-mentioned three, stand for the "various types of belief, half belief and non-belief," while Querry may be said to have gone through all the three stages of faith and have ceased to exist in our world exactly when he comes back from non-belief to belief. And if "Colin is easily the most sympathetic nonbeliever in Greene's work" (Lodge 41), the Superior, I believe, is easily the most sympathetic believer. In the meantime, I believe he is another success of Greene's in creating symbolic characters.

As the only character without a personal name in *A Burnt-Out Case*, the Superior, however, assumes quite a personal character throughout the novel. And this personal character of his is best defined, though indirectly and with some inevitable ambiguity, by his "close friend" (17), Doctor Collin, as "persistent" (247). He is persistent in smoking the cheroot, and he is persistent in many other things. And, as will be discussed below, all his persistent characteristics have their functions in the novel as a whole.

As head of the leprosy-treating center, for one thing, the Superior first of all impressed us with his hospitality towards Querry, the visitor.   He asked Querry if he wanted anything, told him the brown water was quite clean, and "lifted the lid of a soap dish to assure himself that the soap had not been forgotten" (11).   Later, he also applied the same hospitality to other visitors or new-comers. For example, he offered to give Mme. Rycker a cup of coffee or a glass of beer, and asked Father Thomas if his chair was uncomfortable and if he slept well.   Indeed, he was always very kind towards visitors and new-comers.   And this kind of hospitality at least made sure Querry's stay in the leprosarium.

But his kindness was not confined to that towards visitors and new-comers.   He was so kind to everybody that a small child dared to go unasked to his desk and "pulled out a sweet" (84) from the drawer.   He could even "be happy to work with an atheist [Dr. Colin] for a colleague" (99).   Indeed, he was so kind that he always managed to "do his best for everybody" (99).   He argued for Querry that he was not a leprophil, and in turn argued for the leprophil nun that she was only "anxious to do good, to be of use" (20).   He tried to keep Querry's word and "defended him to the last ditch" (87) from Mme. Rycker's visit, but yielded to her tears and sadness.   He defended Marie Akimbu, and consoled Father Thomas.   To make the latter have a "more favorable view of the [African] mission" (166), he appointed him as the acting Superior, even though he had been there the shortest time, compared with the other fathers, and he had "the least notion of bookkeeping" (162).   Surely, he had an amiable disposition which tended to "help, never condemn" (103). It is no wonder then that everybody wished him to be present when Rycker came with a gun.   For he might have been really able to soften Rycker's temper with his pleasing kindness and words.   In fact, when the novel's author chooses to let the killing happen in his absence, he (the author) is skillfully taking away the peacemaking character to make the novel more convincing.

Yet, he was, as a kind man often is, not a very intelligent man. "Multiplication with him was an elaborate form of addition and a series of subtractions would take the place of long division" (82). His knowledge was so narrow that he had mistaken a bidet for a new kind of foot bath, and "had never learned that whisky was too strong for the midday sun" (85).   His reasoning power was limited, too. So he was inclined to "make superficial judgments" (21).   For example, the reasons for his believing that Mme. Rycker loved her husband were, "He's her husband," and "They're both Catholics" (89).   And part of his sermon goes thus:

> ...because Yezu made for you, he is in you.   When you love, it is Yezu who loves, when you are merciful it is Yezu who is merciful.   But when you hate or envy it is not Yezu, ... (97).

However, this simple mind, so to speak, of his is a good contrast to the intelligent mind of Querry or Doctor Colin.   By imparting this simple mind to the Superior, the novelist has successfully made clear the challenging assertion concerning faith that Querry made in Doctor Colin's face: "it's possible for an intelligent man to make his life without a God" (99).

But simple-minded as he is, he is not without insight into things. In effect, he is unintelligent only when compared with Querry or Colin, and only in the sense that he is too much preoccupied with some *a priori* ideas.   To do him justice, he is intelligent and wise so long as the *a priori* ideas stand favorable.   For instance, there certainly are cases to prove that "it's safer to make superficial judgments" (21).   And although his refutation against the idea that "Klistians are all big thieves" (96) left us as well as Doctor Colin enough room to question and appeared to be a hateful simplification to Querry, it was after all a good sermon for the Africans, and the idea of "crypto-Christian" (99) should not be debased anyhow. Furthermore, we do feel that in some cases the Superior's remarks smack of profound philosophy: "Suffering is something which will always be provided when it is required" (12); "When a man has nothing else to be proud of, he is proud of his spiritual problems" (18); "We most of us make our own complications" (90).   Above all, he was profound enough to see the death of Querry as a happy ending.

In fact, his "*a priori* intelligence" serves to explain the reason why he has the persistent characteristics mentioned above.   With the idea that "we are here to help, not condemn" (103) in mind, it is only natural that he would act kindly toward others, especially visitors and new-comers.   And if he is simple in mind, it is because his attention is too much focused on his precepts, and thus seldom gives way to free thought and trifles.   Under such circumstances, he naturally becomes a fast-holder of his beliefs, a persistent "Christian claimer" who "never lets anyone go" (247), a father who "tries too hard to make a pattern" (247).

And this pattern-making persistency is symbolized by his smoking of the cheroot.   The cheroot is said to be something which he "was never without" (17).   To be sure, a mere glimpse of the novel will strike any reader with the constant mention of his cheroot. Thus, it should be more than an attendant description of his habit. In fact, there are certain contexts which can justify the claim that it has its symbolic meaning.   For example, when he was leaving the leprosarium and had no cheroot, he accepted a cigarette from Querry, but he wore it as awkwardly as he would have worn a suit of lay clothes. (159) [And he] took the cigarette out of his mouth and looked at it as though he wondered how it had come there. (161)

This not only shows the trouble he had in breaking his habit, but also symbolizes the fact that he felt ill at ease for the loss of the pattern he had been making.   When he went to visit the cemetery with Doctor Colin after Querry's death, he felt no cheroot in the pocket of his soutane.   This further implies that he had lost the pattern he would claim his own.   But he still fancied the pattern was there.   Hence his reply to Doctor Colin, "But if the pattern's there...You haven't a cheroot, have you?" (247).   This latter part of the reply may even mean that Doctor Colin, being an atheist, does not make any pattern as he does.   So, if this novel poses any question of faith at all, it is the Superior's cheroot that symbolizes the pattern of Christian value. And the Superior himself, with his persistent characteristics in thought and action (namely: hospitality, kindness, simple-mindedness, fast-held precepts, and cheroot-smoking), is a good representative of priests, a good contrast to place beside the atheistic Querry and Doctor Colin or the "faithful" Rycker, and, above all, a good symbol of the eternal positive value of Christianity.

So far, I have shown how significant a role the Superior, as a symbolic character, plays in the novel when we consider the novel in terms of religion.   But, as we all know, the novel, as a symbolic novel usually is, is capable of other interpretations. Then comes the question: does the role the Superior plays remain significant in view of different readings?   If so, then my argument is strengthened; otherwise, it might be misleading.   For a good symbol is usually open to various interpretations.

To clarify this point, let us consider the most popular view that the novel is "a study of indifference" (Turnell37), that it shows "the artist's lust for suffering" (Kermode 132).   Indeed, there is ample evidence to show that Greene believes in the life-giving power of suffering, and the unfeeling Querry is the character he has been in search of in Africa.[5]   For instance, before the novel opens, he quotes Dante's line: "I did not die, yet nothing of life remained," which presumably refers to Querry's indifferent state of mind.   And as soon as the novel opens, we see Querry thus parody Descartes's famous saying in his diary: "I feel discomfort, therefore I am alive." But one may ask: how come Querry feels so insipid about life as to long for pain?

Psychologically speaking, it may be true that worldly success may cloy one's appetite for life just as too much rich food leads one to give no thought to eating, especially when one knows, as does Querry, that his success only exists in others' eyes.   Querry, the successful   architect,   is   certainly   benumbed   by   his   former "successful" life with regard to fame and women, and his escape to Africa is certainly a sign of his hope for some cure of his sick heart. But the irony is: wherever he goes, there are still people like Rycker, Parkinson and Father Tomas to remind him of his sham past through their misinterpretations of him.   Fortunately, however, his leper servant leads him away from the tawdry, secular, adult world to Pendèlè, the "mysterious land of childhood...where in his dreams he wishes to go after death" (Scott 241).   His present seems to be full of zest again.   Meanwhile, his love for life develops to the extent that he is willing to design a new hospital for the mission and innocently spends the night with Rycker's wife telling her the story of his life, which brings about his death.   Towards the end of the novel, Colin says that Querry has already found "a reason for living"

(247) while the Superior thinks that Querry is "beginning to find his faith again" (247).

Now, we can plainly see that Querry has passed from Rycker, Parkinson and Father Thomas's insipid world into Deo Gratias's charming Pendélè through love. This is a spiritual changing process. Colin can never tell what Querry's "reason for living" is, for such an atheistic doctor as he can only detect physical symptoms of leprosy and cure it physically. To cure a moral leper, one needs a real spiritual physician like the Superior. This does not imply that the Superior has any right to claim Querry for his own after his simple sermons. Nevertheless, it should be plain that the values the Superior stands for are here claimed to be the remedy for any spiritual impasse. If such a term as "faith" sounds too religious, suffice it to say that Querry has turned more like the Superior at length.

In comparing Greene with Malraux and Conrad, John K. Simon opines that *A Burnt-Out Case* fails because Greene "allows society to re-enter his abstract world and permits direct contact with his hero" (166), whereas Malraux's *La Voie Royale* and Conrad's *Heart of Darkness* succeed because in their novels "a doubling of the hero permits the reader to accede to this solitary figure only by way of an intermediary, thus preventing full knowledge about him and safeguarding a necessary authenticity concerning his spiritual adventure" (166). I cannot refute Simon's position, but somehow I think Simon fails to see that the various characters circling Querry in Greene's novel function as symbolic characters, with Deo Gratias indicating Querry's present situation while the Superior and the other characters hint at his future and past life. If Greene fails to "pigeonhole his characters and show them as limited and recognizable types" (Magill 101), he never curtails the character's symbolic values. If *A Burnt-Out Case* is not an allegory like *Pilgrim's Progress*, it is a symbolic novel like *Moby Dick*. If Conrad's hero is himself a mysterious symbol, Greene's hero has got his mystery symbolized by all the other characters surrounding him.

Notes

1. Conrad's *Heart of Darkness* was first published in 1902 and Greene's *A Burnt-Out Case* in 1961.
2. The parenthesized page number of the work hereinafter refers to Graham Greene, *A Burnt-Out Case* (New York: The Viking Press, 1961).
3. See Conrad's *Heart of Darkness*, p.69.
4. See, on this point, Philip's *Faith and Fiction,* p. 329.
5. Greene published two journals entitled *In Search of a Character* before and when he went to Africa to find material for *A Burnt-Out Case.*

Works Consulted

Allot, K. & Farris, M.   *The Art of Graham Greene.*   New York: Russell & Russell, Inc., 1963.

Conrad, Joseph.   *Heart of Darkness.*   New York: Norton & Co., 1963.

DeVitis, A. A.   *Graham Greene.*   New York: Twayne Publishers, Inc., 1964.

Evans, Robert O.   *Graham Greene: Some Critical Considerations.*   U of Kentucky P, 1963.

Greene, Graham.   *A Burn-Out Case.*   New York: The Viking Press, 1961.

Hynes, Samuel, ed. *Graham Greene: A Collection of Critical Essays*. Englewood Cliffs, NJ: Prentice-Hall, Inc., 1973

Jones, David Pryce. *Graham Greene*. Edinburgh & London: Oliver & Boyd, 1963.

Kennedy, X. J. *An Introduction to Fiction*. Canada: Little, Brown & Co., 1976.

Lodge, David. *Graham Greene*. New York & London: Columbia UP, 1966.

Magill, Frank N., ed. *Masterpieces of World Literature in Digest From*. 4th Series. 1969.

Simon, John K. "Off the Voie Royale: The Failure of Greene's *Burn-Out Case.*" *Symposium* (summer 1964). 165-7.

Stratford, Philip. *Faith and Fiction: Creative Process in Greene and Mauriac*. U of Notre Dame P, 1964.

Turnell, Martin. *Graham Greene: A Critical Essay*. New York: Wm. B. Eardmane Publishing Co., 1967.

Wyndham, Francis. *Graham Greene*. London: Longmans, Greene & Co., 1962.

* This paper first appeared in 1978 in National Chung Hsing University's *Journal of Arts and History*, Vol. VIII.

From Ape to Man: An Impressionistic Reading of Eugene O'Neill's *The Hairy Ape*

Readers of literary masterpieces are often of the opinion that the title must be suggestive of the work, and indeed writers normally will not fail their readers in this regard. But the thing is: not all readers are content to leave the title alone there as merely a signboard by which they are ushered into the body of the work. In fact, the title has more often than not become the reader's first impression of the work, and as the first impression lasts throughout his reading, the title has practically become a leading guide that the reader has to follow step by step up to the end of the work. Thus, the title is often the first cause of reading a literary masterpiece impressionistically.

Take Europe O'Neill's *The Hairy Ape for* example. In reading that play for the first time, the writer of this paper had, from the beginning till finishing it, been expecting to see a hairy ape in the "real life" of the drama, had been trying to identify as far as possible the beastly Yank with an imagined hairy ape after learning that the title explicitly refers to the main character of the play, and finally had been thinking of the play in terms of the image the title elicits. Likewise, there are readers who, perhaps finding the main title not suggestive enough, go further to seek help or hint in the subtitle so as to come up with a better interpretation of the play.[1] In fact, as will be seen below, this paper also draws on its subtitle for interpreting the play.

Of course, a title-guided reading as such may easily bring about erroneous interpretations.   However, so long as a writer entitles his work with adequate care and exactitude, an impressionistic reading based on the title may witness less danger of misinterpretation than many other approaches to the same work.   After all, we readers are like so many blindfolded men feeling the same elephant.   By knowing first what we are feeling now is called an elephant, we can prevent ourselves from associating our impressions with anything totally non-elephantine though no one has as yet any full clear sight of the huge animal before our eyes.   It is with this belief that the author of this paper will proceed to discuss O'Neill's *The Hairy Ape* as follows.

To begin with, in an age when Darwin's theory of evolution still holds its influence, it is only natural for a reader of O'Neill's *The Hairy Ape* to think of the hypothesis that man might originate from the ape, and to presuppose that the title of the play might have something to do with the hypothesis.   Next, when the reader sees the subtitle of the play—"A Comedy of Ancient and Modern Life," his presupposition may somewhat be strengthened.   And finally as he carefully reads over the play,[2] the ape image together with the ideas embedded in Darwin's great works (for instance, the modification of species by environment, survival of the fittest, etc.) may constantly exercise influence on his reading.   To be sure, this is precisely what has happened to the writer of this paper.   And the upshot is: I find the theme of evolution is no less conspicuous in the play and no less convincing to the readers, compared with other critics' different thematic discussions of the same play.   To prove this, we shall consider some critics' arguments first.

Arthur and Barbara Gelb in their biographical study of the play have quoted O'Neill's own words to show that the play actually germinates from the playwright's search for an explanation of why Driscoll, O'Neill's sailing companion at sea, committed suicide despite the fact that Driscoll was so proud of his animal superiority and in harmony with his limited conception of the universe (268). They in fact hold with many other critics that the play shows the playwright's revived interest in the theme of "not belonging," treating Yank as well as Driscoll as a frustrated robust personality deprived of his self-respect for his own tremendous vigor and strength.

It is true that Yank, the "most highly developed individual" (Scene 1)[3] of the stokers, may serve as some reminiscence of Driscoll, a real person with ample individuality of his own. Yet, somehow we feel that Yank is not a mere individual. He is, in E. M. Forster's terms, a very "flat" character. He does not have Hamlet's complexity. "An ape-like man" will be an all sufficient epithet for him. Hence, he is only a type like one of Ben Johnson's characters of humors. As a type, he naturally represents not only his personal identity but also some dominant trait of mankind. That is the reason why John Gassner says he is "Worker as well as Man" (325).

If Yank does represent man in some respect, then his pet locution of "belonging" should be more than an indication of his own personal problem. Surely, it has become a cue of Everyman's problem. In a letter to *The New York Herald Tribune,* O'Neill is reported to have said that the play is to show how man, unable to feel the harmony with nature that as an animal he once knew, has not been able to establish a new harmony through sympathy with his kind (Leech 41). And it is also said that, in an interview O'Neill gave in 1922, he said that "Yank is really yourself, and myself" (Leech 41). Of course, the playwright's words are not necessarily the final words about his plays. Nevertheless, here O'Neill has, as will be proved below, not misconstrued but pinpointed the real function of Yank in the play which has become ever so controversial a question since the play was first presented.

To claim Yank as a symbol of man in some respect instead of simply a particular individual, we can also gain some support from the play proper.   For instance, at the beginning of Scene 1, O'Neill gives the following description:

> … The men themselves should resemble those pictures in which the appearance of Neanderthal Man is guessed at.   All are hairy-chested, with long arms of tremendous power, and low, receding brows above their small, fierce, resentful eyes. All the civilized white races are represented, but except for the slight differentiation in color of hair, skin, eyes, all these men are alike.

The men are the firemen working in the forecastle of an ocean liner, and Yank is one of them.   He is basically the same as his fellow workers though he "seems broader, fiercer …" (Scene 1).   So he is actually their best representative.   And since the men speak a medley of dialects (of Irish brogue, Cockney, Swedish, American lower class, Scots, etc.), the "melting-pot" idea is suggested (Raleigh 219).   And, therefore, Yank as their representative must of necessity assume the role of Everyman.

Yank is, of course, not an entire Everyman.   He is Everyman only in that he stands for man's prototypal self, the incarnation of bestial strength as seen in a picture of Neanderthal Man.   That is why he is described as a fierce, truculent, powerful and ugly ape. Now, as Darwin's theory of evolution goes, the ape is gradually becoming more and more human while its environment is becoming more and more civilized. And the present-day result of that process is seen in Mildred Douglas, the heroine, so to speak, of the play.

Mildred is in every way the contrast to Yank except that she is as full of disdainful superiority as he. She is "slender, delicate, with a pretty face ... fretful, nervous and discontented, bored by her own anemia" (Scene II). She and her aunt are two "incongruous, artificial figures, inert and disharmonious ... looking as if the vitality of her stock had been snapped before she was conceived, so that she is the expression not of its life energy but merely of the artificialities that energy had won for itself in the spending" (Scene II).

Here it is clear that Mildred is as flat a character as Yank. She is also a type symbolic of some human trait. If Yank is masculine beyond measure, she is feminine in the extreme. If Yank belongs to a rough, primitive, hellish world, she belongs to a heavenly fine world of culture. Indeed, they are two opposing extremes of mankind, two pictures of man in his ancient and modern forms.

Now, what has O'Neill got to say with such two types of characters? In his "Eugene O'Neill as Social Critic," Doris Alexander asserts that the play "presents an extremely negative view of the state, of mechanized America, where the worker best adjusted to the system is a 'hairy ape,' and where the 'Capitalist class' is even more terribly dehumanized, for it has lost all connection with life, is simply 'a procession of gaudy marionettes'" (390). This assertion implies that in this play man, dichotomized into worker or capitalist, is dehumanized as a result of the new economical system in the modern mechanical age. Certainly we can see this in Yank's being tauntingly reduced to an ape by Mildred and, in turn, in the latter's being tauntingly reduced, too, to a ghost by the former. Still, such is too superficial and too narrow a view of the play.

In actuality, we may also see this play as a peculiar or fantastic treatment of split personality just like Stevenson's *Dr. Jekyll and Mr. Hyde*.   But the target of study here is man with his ancient self embodied in Yank and modern self embodied in Mildred.   Instead of representing the proletarian and aristocratic (or working and leisure) classes respectively, Yank and Mildred actually stand for our primitive wild nature and civilized tame feature.   And the conflict of the play lies not in the incompatibility of the two social classes but in man's inability to get his two selves reconciled in our modern world.   In a plain word, there is something wrong with our evolution from ape to man now.   To prove this, let us go back to the plot of the play.

We know when Mildred is going down to the stokehold, she says she wants to discover "how the other half lives" (Scene II). This other half, as we know, refers to the firemen in particular, of whom Yank is the best representative.   What is left of this other half is of course the one half that Mildred herself represents.   If we take the two halves not as two social classes but as two embodiments or components of man (like male and female sexes), then we can easily interpret the climax of the play, that is, Yank and Mildred's being mutually astounded on seeing each other.   We know that in real life upper-class people and lower-class people are not so unfamiliar to each other as to be mutually shocked when they are first put together. But when a refined man becomes suddenly aware that he is originally as brutish as Yank or a vigorous man becomes suddenly aware that he has turned as emasculate as Mildred, a great shock is sure to be there.   The shock is indeed that of ape and man facing each other.   The climax is doubtless that of man's ancient and modern selves meeting each other.

What is the aftermath of the climax, then?   We know Yank has thenceforth become a revenge-seeker and, by misusing his force has gone step by step to his self-destruction at last.   Here an interpretation based on a social viewpoint may claim Yank as an unhappy individual "thwarted in his groping after social significance" (Goldberg 242), or as the hero of a "tragedy of the proletarian's exile from all the charms of culture" (Bab 351). However, if we accept Yank and Mildred as two extremes of man, we may come closer to an understanding of why O'Neill gave the play the subtitle: "A Comedy of Ancient and Modern Life."

Yank, the ape-like, all masculine half of man, has to die because the brutal force which he stands for is, like the dynamite he suggests using for blowing up Douglas's steel works, more dangerous and destructive than useful in a civilized world although in man's primitive state of life it really is the most important and even now it can be "de start," "de ting in coal dat makes it boin," "de muscles in steel, de punch behind it!"—as Yank claims himself to be in Scene 1. Indeed, we can sympathize with Yank and think of him as "a sort of modern Caliban, produced by our industrial society, disowned by it, and rebellious" (Woodbridge 315).   For he is, like the caged gorilla, forever imprisoned in the civilized world.[4]   And his death in the "murderous hug" (Scene VIII) of the gorilla is in reality an instance of suicide which often occurs in the end of a tragedy since the gorilla is Yank's like in every respect.   Nevertheless, as he is so blind to the real value of animal strength in a civilized world, we really can also think of him as a "blind cyclopean Demos that cannot build but only destroy; malformed, powerful—when he stirs fair cities topple—thick-witted, dangerous, ugly" (Long 82).   Consequently, his death can be considered as a happy ending for mankind.

In fact, Yank's death is not an entire death.   We know Yank releases the gorilla from the cage and then he himself dies in it. Since Yank can be identified with the gorilla, the gorilla's coming out of the cage and into the outside world may symbolize the idea that Yank's animal self—that is, man's primitive vigor and strength—still exists in our world.   What has died is only Yank's illusion of self-respect, his blind conviction in the use of brutal force. In this connection, Yank's death is justifiably a mere symbol of man's doing away with his bestial whims.   With his bestial whims removed, man naturally can become fitter to live in the civilized world.   This, I think, is the reason why O'Neill makes the comment before the curtain falls that "perhaps, the Hairy Ape at last belongs," and the reason why O'Neill labels the play as a comedy.

So, in the perspective of its action, the play is seen to manifest itself as a comment on the use of force in the course of man's progress from ancient to modern times.   It seems that O'Neill has clearly seen the direction in which mankind has been undeviatingly advancing, that is, from the strength-governed primitivism towards the wisdom-governed civilization, or simply from ape to man.   This advancement is inevitable.   Any nostalgic reflection upon the bygone things is of little use just as Paddy's looking back upon the old days of sailing ships is.   And any attempt to radically change the *status quo* is doomed to fail just as Yank's threat to revenge himself by force never works (See Alexander 396).   The thing is, the *status quo* has its own course of movement.   After a long period of time, man may be shocked to see his primeval archetype just as Mildred is at the sight of Yank.   Or man may be dumbfounded, just as Yank is on seeing Mildred, by the long distance he has gone from his original self.   But evolution is forever under way.   We can always see with Darwin or O'Neill our original ape-self moving towards our ideal man-self and, at the same time, wondering where to "belong" in our ever-new world.

Now, is the from-ape-to-man evolution good? Obviously, O'Neill does not regard it as wholly good. On the one hand, he does disapprove of anything that "would tear down society, put the lowest scum in the seats of the mighty, turn Almighty God's revealed plan for the world topsy-turvy, and make of our sweet and lovely civilization a shambles, a desolation where man, God's masterpiece, would soon degenerate back to the ape!" (Scene VI). On the other hand, however, he also fears that the civilization-oriented evolution of man may ultimately result in "the relentless horror of Frankensteins in their detached, mechanical unawareness" (Scene V), may finally make man, to quote Mildred's words, "inherit the acquired trait of the by-product [in the Bessemer process], wealth, but none of the energy, none of the strength of the steel that made it "(Scene II). It follows then that O'Neill seems to uphold man's inextricable cause of evolution but at the same time tries to remind us not to forsake our primordial vitality. Civilization is not to make "posers" (Scene II). Without Yank's natural power, man is what Mildred's aunt calls her—a mere "ghoul."

So far, the author of this paper has been taking his hint from the title and subtitle of the play in interpreting O'Neill's *The Hairy Ape*. All arguments raised or advocated concerning the play have been the product of reading it with its title and subtitle always in mind. Therefore, this paper may be called a title-guided impressionistic reading of the play. If impressionistic criticism is "the adventures of a sensitive soul among masterpieces,"[5] what counts at last is of course the question: how far have the adventures carried the "sensitive soul"? From ape to man?

Notes

1. E.g., Clifford Leech argues that the play is "more truly a comedy" by referring to its subtitle: "A Comedy of Ancient and Modern Life." See his *O'Neill*, pp. 40-1.
2. It is to be borne in mind that the play, as a play usually is, is written to be acted rather than read. All discussions in this paper are the result of reading it, however.
3. Hereinafter each parenthesized number of the scene refers to the text of O'Neill's *The Hairy Ape*.
4. Yank is first figuratively imprisoned in the abysmal stokehole, then in the cell of the prison on Blackwell's island, and finally, after his death, in the gorilla's cage.
5. Anatole France's words, quoted in Hugh Holman, *A Handbook to Literature,* (rpt. Taipei: Tun Huang, 1968), p. 238.

Works Consulted

Alexander, Doris. "Eugene O'Neill as Social Critic." Rpt. in Cargill et al., 395-7.

Bab, Julius. "As Europe Sees America's Foremost Playwright." *The Theatre Guild Magazine.* Nov. 1931. Rpt. in Cargill et al., 350-2.

Cargill, Oscar, N. B. Fagin & W. J. Fisher, eds. *O'Neill and His Plays.* New York: New York UP, 1961.

Carpenter, Frederic 1. *Eugene O'Neill.* New York: Twayne Publishers, Inc., 1964.

Coolidge, Olivia. *Eugene O'Neill.* New York: Charles Scribner's Sons, 1966.

Gassner, John. "Homage to O'Neill." *Theatre Time,* Summer

1951.   Rpt. in Cargill et al., 324-8.

Gelb, Arthur & Barbara Gelb.   *O'Neil.*   New York: Dell, 1965.

Goldberg, Isaac.   "At the Beginning of a Career."   *The Drama of Transition.*   Rpt. in Cargill et al., 240-4.

Griffin, G. Ernest, ed.   *Eugene O'Neill.*   New York: McGraw-Hill Book Co., 1976.

Harper, B., & Clark, ed.   *Eugene O'Neill : The Man and His Plays.* New York: Dover Publications, 1947.

Leech, Clifford.   *O'Neill.*   Edinburgh & London: Oliver & Boyd, 1963.

Long, Chester Clayton.   *The Role of Nemesis in the Structure of Selected Plays by Eugene O'Neill.*   The Hague & Paris: Mouton & Co., 1968.

Raleigh, John Henry.   *Eugene O'Neill: The Man and His Works.* Toronto: Forum House, 1969.

Woodbridge, Homer E.   "Beyond Melodrama."   *Theatre Time,* Summer 1951.   Rpt. in Cargill et al., 313-6.

* This paper first appeared in 1977 in National Chung Hsing University's *Journal of Arts and History*, Vol. VII.

The Psychological Unity
in Milton's "Lycidas"

Since Dr. Johnson's charge of insincerity, critics of Milton's "Lycidas" have gone one step further to cast their stones at its unity. In consequence, many readers nowadays will conclude easily with G. W. Knight that "Lycidas" is simply "an accumulation of magnificent fragments" (70). Of course, conclusions like this are not drawn without reason; they can be justified in their own right. However, insofar as we are concerned with the unity of a work, especially with the crucial question of whether there is unity or not existing in such a famous work as Milton's "Licidas," it may behoove us to keep "exploring" the work (as a scientist does his planet) before we make our final declaration. As we know, a work can be unified "by any means which can so integrate and organize its elements that they have a necessary relationship to each other" (Holman 500). Where the surface structure of a work fails to show any unifying agent, there may be some underlying element which, upon our close examination, may prove to be a powerful means to glue all the pieces together. When we read a stream-of-consciousness novel, for instance, we may easily be struck with its seemingly chaotic sequence of narratives. Not infrequently, however, we can sense lurking behind the surface structure of that work a psychological thread which does serve to string its seemingly non-correlated parts together. Thus, what is fragmental at first glance may prove quite integral at last.

Returning to our discussion of Milton's "Lycidas," we find the poem is just like a stream-of-consciousness novel in this sense: it manifests no smooth and continuous movement unless we probe into its inner psychological structure.   Perhaps the greatest difference in this connection is: whereas what flows in a stream-of-consciousness novel is the stream of a certain character's consciousness (Stephen Dedalus's or Mrs. Dalloway's), what flows in "Lycidas" is, as will soon be discussed below, the stream of the poet Milton's consciousness.   And, therefore, to fully appreciate the work—especially to see it as a coherent whole instead of disparate segments—some knowledge of the poet, especially of his psychological background, becomes necessary.[1]

We all know that the death of Edward King, Milton's "learned Friend," is the occasion of the poem.   But it is to be noted that before he was drowned, King was prepared to qualify himself for the ministry and was considered a poet, too.   Besides, at the time of King's death Milton had been at home for five years, "engaged mainly in laying a foundation in humane knowledge and thought for his *unknown future*" (Hughes 545).   Under such circumstances, the news of King's sudden death naturally would lead Milton to reflect upon his own past intentions of entering the ministry and his hopes of writing a great poem.[2]   Graves's comment upon the situation is a little too frankly bitter, but none the less to the point:

> Milton was obsessed by thoughts of his own fame. His strongest reaction to the news of Lycidas's drowning was: "Heavens, it might have been myself!   Cut down before my prime, cheated of immortal fame!"[3]

Indeed, it is by no means an oversimplification to say that King is only "a surrogate for Milton himself" (Hamford 1949, 69).   In no other English elegies (e.g., Shelly's "Adonais" or Tennyson's *In Memoriam*) do we find so much pain felt for the mourner as well as for the mourned.   In reading the elegy, one might feel that Milton was really insincere in "bewailing" his learned friend.   Yet, one would definitely never feel that Milton was insincere in mourning for himself.   That is why we find, with the exception of a few lines (ll.23-36), little mention or description of King's life or personality in the poem, but instead we find Milton laboriously emitting therein a succession of willful passions (some of which are even totally irrelevant, e.g., the digression from l. 110 to l. 131) by the use of both pagan and Christian allusions as well as pastoral images, which reveal and represent merely the poet's great learning and thought.   Woodhouse is right in saying that "the principal source of the poem's extra-aesthetic emotion is not grief for the loss of Edward King, but an awareness of the hazards of life and of Milton's own situation."[4]   And we would be equally right in postulating that more than most other English works the poem is built on the basis of the poet's own psychology.

If the psychology in this poem is Milton's, we should then read the poem with Milton always in mind.   First, we should know that Milton is an erudite scholar fully familiar with classical works and therefore spellbound by their conventions.   So, when he chooses to write the "Monody" (virtually a pastoral elegy), to ask him not to use multitudinous allusions and pastoral images is "to ask the painter not to dip in the colours of the rainbow, if he could."[5]   With this understanding, we should then disregard Dr. Johnson's ingenious remark that "where there is leisure for fiction there is little grief" (see Elledge 229), and take instead Thomas Newton's that "grief is eloquent" (see Elledge 227).

Next, we should know that Milton is a serious Christian.   So, although he is deeply imbued with classical humanism, he does not forget its limitations within the terms of the Christian vision.[6] Hence we should not be surprised to find St. Peter and Christ introduced into the elegy, nor should we deem it merely intrusive, and therefore nonsensical, verbosity for Milton to "foretell the ruin of our corrupted clergy then in their height" in the elegy.[7]   Indeed, it is likely that "Lycidas" is Milton's first attempt to "assert eternal Providence and justify the ways of God to men" (Allen 84).   For as we read carefully on, we can really find, to quote Sands's words, that throughout the work, "there appear overtones of profound spiritual struggle, as well as a strong doubt, barely resolved at the end, concerning the possible uselessness and vanity of the hard consecrated life" (13).

In fact, these two basic facts about Milton himself (his being a classical scholar and his being a serious Christian) serve to explain why "Lycidas" is an "architectural and willed" work (Belloc 118). A scholar naturally will make his work artistic, hence "architectural"; a Christian naturally will make his work preachy, hence "willed." In "Lycidas" we find the architecture is based on the conventions of pastoral elegy: a history of past friendship, a questioning of destiny, a procession of mourners, a laying-on of flowers, a consolation, etc., presented through the mouth of the poet as a shepherd.   And the will is based on the Christian beliefs that fame exists in Heaven, the "two-handed engine at the door/Stands ready to smite once, and smite no more," (ll. 130-31), a good man will not be "sunk low, but [will be] mounted high" (l. 172) by death, etc.   These conventions and beliefs, when molded into a single work, naturally will seem heterogeneous outwardly.   But inwardly if we inspect their links, they will only appear to be a homogeneous whole.

For example, we all agree that there are three major movements in this poem. And, as Wayne Shumaker believes, the most consummate analysis of them is Arthur Barker's:

> The first movement laments the poet-shepherd; its problem, the possible frustration of disciplined poetic ambition by death, is resolved by the assurance, "Of so much fame in heaven expect thy meed." The second laments Lycidas as priest- shepherd; its problem, the frustration of a sincere shepherd in a corrupt church, is resolved by St. Peter's reference to the "two-handed engine" of divine retribution. The third concludes with the apotheosis, a convention introduced by Virgil in Eclogue V but significantly handled by Milton. He uses the poet-priest-shepherd worshipping the Lamb with those saints "in solemn troops" who sing the "unexpressive nuptial song" of the fourteenth chapter of Revelation. The apotheosis thus not only provides the final reassurance but unites the themes of the preceding movements in the ultimate reward of the true poet-priest. (94-95)

Certainly the final movement of the apotheosis "unites the themes of the preceding movements in the ultimate reward of the true poet-priest." But the way it unites them— "the ultimate reward of the true poet-priest"—is characteristic of Milton's concept, of his religious faith. In his mind every human frustration or despair can be swept away by religious faith; so long as there is faith, there is hope. This is his inner psychology. And it finds an outlet not only in this work, but in many others. For example, the last part of his greatest work *Paradise Lost* also has the same idea. When Adam and

Eve are in utter despair, Christ comes to assure them that paradise can be regained through their faith in God.   So, we can say Apollo's words and St. Peter's words, as well as the apotheosis, are but different expressions of Milton's same religious faith.   Accordingly, the three movements have but one theme.   And it is as Grierson puts it: "the personal resolve, the life-long aspiration, with its attendant fluctuation of hopes and fears, expressed by Milton in the seventh prolusion, in the sixth elegy, in the sonnet on his twenty-third birthday, and now most recently in the letter to Diodati" (69).   Or to state it simply, it is the transition from human despair to hope through religious faith.

In effect, the transition from the mood of despair to that of hope is best expressed in the language of the poem, especially in its imagery and diction.   For instance, at first we see the vegetation imagery is completely tinged with the color of melancholy and disorder, thus suggesting despair (as when Eden is lost): the myrtles are brown; the berries harsh and crude; the thyme wild; the vine gadding and overgrown; most flowers are damaged by the frost while the "sanguine flower inscrib'd with woe," and the rose killed by the canker; and the willows and the hazel copses are not green any more.   Likewise, at first the water imagery suggests a stagnant and lifeless quality: Mincius slides smoothly; the brine is level; Camus goes "footing slow," and "inwrought with figures dim."   Other images, too, firstly only express their despairing aspects: Lycidas has to "welter to the parching wind"; the "top of Mona high" is shaggy; "the weanling herds that graze" are subject to the killing of the taint-worm.   And together with these images and other descriptions are the dismal adjectives used to reinforce the despairing impression: *sere, bitter, sad, sable, heavy, desert, remorseless, hideous, gory, felon, hard ,rugged, beaked, fatal, perfidious, dark,* etc.

But after the reassurance of Apollo and St. Peter, hopeful images and diction gradually blend into the description. A catalogue of flowers with "a thousand hues" is brought forth to "interpose a little ease." The seas are "sounding" with life; the brooks "gushing"; the tide "whelming." And words with good connotations begin to appear: *quaint enamell'd, honied, vernal, rathe, glowing, well-attir'd, newspangled, pure, nuptial, meek, dear, joy, love, sweet, glory, fresh, new,* etc. Indeed, "all is color and motion as the brooding melancholy of the poet is swept away" (Belloc 68). Despair has been changed into hope.

So, echoing the theme, the imagery and the diction also suggest a consistent pattern of moods which are no longer variously "pathos, indignation, [and] reassurance" (Grace 143), but are simply "one mood, one overriding tension, transcending and reconciling opposites" (Grace 144) composed of despair and hope which are the "faithful Herdman" Milton's own inner psychological responses to the stimulus of King's sudden death.

In his *The Shadow of Heaven*, Jon S. Lawry wittingly observes that the mood of "Lycidas" "is to be agonically thoughtful, thought is to be its subject, and mood and subject will be conveyed in language simple, sensuous, and passionate" (97). It is true that the mood of "Lycidas" is, as an elegy often is, agonically thoughtful. But the agony is felt as much for Milton himself as for King; and the thought is centered more on the former than on the latter. Consequently, the mood and the subject can be directly drawn from Milton's own psychology. As discussed so far, the subject is Milton's usual subject: the mutation of human despair into hope through religious faith. Following that subject, the mood is that of his struggling between despair and hope. And in turn following that mood, the language—especially the imagery and diction—also shows his transition from despair to hope, be it "simple," or "sensuous," or "passionate."　So we see the work manifests a perfect unity in its content and expression when viewed in the perspective of Milton's own psychology.

It follows then that the work should not be censured for "lack of unity." And if unity is a necessary and laudable element for a work, one should not trace it merely in the surface structure of the work For, as already said, a work may be unified by any means. As in the case of Milton's "Lycidas," we find the poem is somewhat like a stream-of-consciousness novel: its unifier lies not in its surface structure but in somebody's consciousness (and here in the poet Milton's consciousness).　So, some knowledge of the author's inner psychology becomes necessary to fully appreciate the work. And G.. W. Knight, I think, is one of those who have neglected the importance of Milton's psychology in understanding "Lycidas."

Notes

1. Hereby I would like to emphasize in passing that although supporters of the so-called New Criticism are right in stressing the intrinsic worth of literature, there are cases (and "Lycidas" is one) when we have to admit with Dr. Johnson that without knowing the author one would be unable to appreciate the work.
2. See, on this point, Grierson's *Milton and Wordsworth,* p. 92.
3. See Elledge's *Milton's "Lycidas,"* p. 248.
4. See Hughes,, Vol. 2, p.593.
5. William Hazlitt's remark.　See *Elledge,* p. 232.
6. See, on this point, Grace, p. 141.

7. It is said that Milton was induced to add the second sentence "And by occasion foretells ... height" to the originally one-sentence epigraph by the attack on episcopacy, which began with the meeting of the Long Parliament in 1640. But the fact remains that Milton was a serious Christian and so he could be induced to do so. See Hughes, p. 637.

Works Consulted

Allen. Don Caneron. *The Harmonious Vision: Studies in Milton's Poetry.* Baltimore: Johns Hopkins UP, 1954.

Belloc, Hilaire. *Milton.* Philadelphia: J. B. Lippincott Co., 1935.

Elledge, Scott, ed. *Milton's "Lycidas."* New York: Harper & Row, 1966.

Grace, William J. *Ideas in Milton.* London: U of Notre Dame P, 1968.

Grierson, J. C. *Milton and Wordsworth.* London: Chatto & Windus, 1963.

Hamford, James Holly. *John Milton, Englishman.* New York: Crown Publishers, 1949.

----------. *A Milton Handbook.* 4th ed. New York: F. S. Crofts & Co., 1946.

Holman, C. Hugh. *A Handbook of Literature.* New York: The Odyssey Press, 1968.

Hughes, Merritt Y., ed. *A Variorum Commentary on the Poems of John Milton.* Vol. II. New York: Columbia UP, 1972.

Knight, G.. W. *The Burning Oracle.* London: Methuen, 1939.

Lawry, Jon S. *The Shadow of Heaven: Matter and Stance in Milton's Poetry.* Ithaca, NY: Connell UP, 1968.

Rudrum, Alan, ed.   *Milton: Modern Judgments.*   London: Macmillan & Co., 1968.

Sands, Maurice.   *An Outline of Milton.*   New York: Students Outline Company, 1956.

* This paper first appeared in 1976 in National Chung Hsing University's *Journal of Arts and History*, Vol. VI.

語言文學類　AG0108

Critical Inquiry: Some Winds on Works

作　　者 / 董崇選
發 行 人 / 宋政坤
執行編輯 / 詹靚秋
圖文排版 / 陳湘陵
封面設計 / 蕭玉蘋
數位轉譯 / 徐真玉　沈裕閔
圖書銷售 / 林怡君
法律顧問 / 毛國樑　律師
出版印製 / 秀威資訊科技股份有限公司
　　　　　台北市內湖區瑞光路 583 巷 25 號 1 樓
　　　　　電話：02-2657-9211　　　傳真：02-2657-9106
　　　　　E-mail：service@showwe.com.tw
經 銷 商 / 紅螞蟻圖書有限公司
　　　　　台北市內湖區舊宗路二段 121 巷 28、32 號 4 樓
　　　　　電話：02-2795-3656　　　傳真：02-2795-4100
　　　　　http://www.e-redant.com

2009 年 3 月 BOD 一版
定價：360 元

讀　者　回　函　卡

感謝您購買本書，為提升服務品質，煩請填寫以下問卷，收到您的寶貴意見後，我們會仔細收藏記錄並回贈紀念品，謝謝！

1.您購買的書名：＿＿＿＿＿＿＿＿＿＿＿＿＿＿＿＿＿

2.您從何得知本書的消息？

　□網路書店　□部落格　□資料庫搜尋　□書訊　□電子報　□書店

　□平面媒體　□ 朋友推薦　□網站推薦　□其他＿＿＿＿＿

3.您對本書的評價：(請填代號　1.非常滿意 2.滿意 3.尚可 4.再改進)

　封面設計＿＿＿　版面編排＿＿＿　內容＿＿＿　文/譯筆＿＿＿　價格＿＿＿

4.讀完書後您覺得：

　□很有收獲　□有收獲　□收獲不多　□沒收獲

5.您會推薦本書給朋友嗎？

　□會　□不會，為什麼？＿＿＿＿＿＿＿＿＿＿＿＿＿＿＿＿＿＿＿

6.其他寶貴的意見：＿＿＿＿＿＿＿＿＿＿＿＿＿＿＿＿＿＿＿＿＿

＿＿＿＿＿＿＿＿＿＿＿＿＿＿＿＿＿＿＿＿＿＿＿＿＿＿＿＿＿＿

＿＿＿＿＿＿＿＿＿＿＿＿＿＿＿＿＿＿＿＿＿＿＿＿＿＿＿＿＿＿

＿＿＿＿＿＿＿＿＿＿＿＿＿＿＿＿＿＿＿＿＿＿＿＿＿＿＿＿＿＿

讀者基本資料

姓名：＿＿＿＿＿＿＿＿＿＿　年齡：＿＿＿＿　性別：□女 □男

聯絡電話：＿＿＿＿＿＿＿＿　E-mail：＿＿＿＿＿＿＿＿＿＿＿

地址：＿＿＿＿＿＿＿＿＿＿＿＿＿＿＿＿＿＿＿＿＿＿＿＿＿

學歷：□高中(含)以下　　□高中　□專科學校　□大學

　　　□研究所(含)以上 □其他＿＿＿＿＿＿＿

職業：□製造業 □金融業 □資訊業 □軍警 □傳播業 □自由業

　　　□服務業 □公務員 □教職　□學生 □其他＿＿＿＿＿

(請沿線對摺寄回,謝謝!)

秀威與 BOD

BOD（Books On Demand）是數位出版的大趨勢，秀威資訊率先運用 POD 數位印刷設備來生產書籍，並提供作者全程數位出版服務，致使書籍產銷零庫存，知識傳承不絕版，目前已開闢以下書系：

一、BOD 學術著作—專業論述的閱讀延伸
二、BOD 個人著作—分享生命的心路歷程
三、BOD 旅遊著作—個人深度旅遊文學創作
四、BOD 大陸學者—大陸專業學者學術出版
五、POD 獨家經銷—數位產製的代發行書籍

BOD 秀威網路書店：www.showwe.com.tw
政府出版品網路書店：www.govbooks.com.tw

　　永不絕版的故事・自己寫・永不休止的音符・自己唱